THE SPECTRAL BOOK OF
HORROR STORIES

Edited by
MARK MORRIS

Spectral

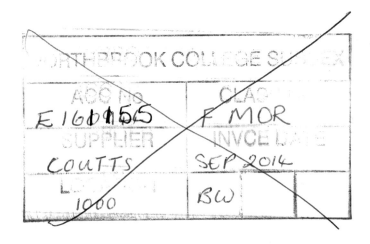
The Spectral Book of Horror Stories
A SPECTRAL PRESS PUBLICATION

ISBN: 978-0-9573927-8-6

First edition, September 2014

Editor: Mark Morris

Publisher: Simon Marshall-Jones

Layout by www.johnoakeydesign.co.uk

Cover art by Vincent Chong © 2014

Printed and bound in the UK by Lightning Source, Milton Keynes

Spectral Press, 13 Montgomery Crescent, Bolbeck Park, Milton Keynes, Bucks, MK14 6HA

Website: spectralpress.wordpress.com

Email: spectralpress@gmail.com

CONTENTS

ACKNOWLEDGEMENTS

My heartfelt thanks to Simon Marshall-Jones at Spectral Press for having the vision, enthusiasm and sheer guts to give this project the green light. Thanks to all the writers who responded with enthusiasm to the idea of a new annual non-themed horror anthology, especially those who backed the project further by sending me stories. Thanks too to all those editors who have gone before me, and in particular to those whose anthologies have inspired me over the years: Herbert Van Thal, Mary Danby, Robert Aickman, Rosemary Timperley, Christine Bernard, R. Chetwynd-Hayes, August Derleth, Peter Haining, Richard Davis, John Burke, Ramsey Campbell, Karl Edward Wagner, Charles L. Grant, Kirby McCauley, Dennis Etchison, Peter Crowther, Stephen Jones, David Sutton and Ellen Datlow. A special mention must go to Johnny Mains, who for the past decade or so has tirelessly campaigned to keep *The Pan Book of Horror Stories* in the public eye, and who is now the proud editor of the (hopefully long-running) *Best British Horror* at Salt Publishing.

DEDICATION

This book is dedicated to the memory of Joel Lane (1963-2013) and Lucius Shepard (1943-2014). Both consummate storytellers, both on my original list of potential contributors to this volume, and both very much missed by their families, friends and fans.

INTRODUCTION
Mark Morris

I'm pretty sure that the first horror anthology I read—possibly even the first one I saw—was *The 7th Fontana Book of Great Horror Stories*, edited by Mary Danby, in late 1972. I was nine years old, and I was back in England for the first time since 1968, having spent the previous three and a half years living in Hong Kong with my parents and younger sister.

The Fontana anthology belonged to my cousin, and I remember being as fascinated by it, and as drawn to it, as I had been by copies of the magazine *Famous Monsters of Filmland* and by the Gold Key title *Boris Karloff Tales of Mystery*, both of which occasionally appeared on the magazine rack in the mini supermarket we frequented in Kowloon Tong. Now and again I had even been allowed to buy one or other of these magazines with my pocket money, and to this day can still recall the dry-mouthed dread I experienced as I slowly and carefully turned each page of *Famous Monsters*, fearful of encountering an image so terrifying that it might worm its way irretrievably into my mind and haunt my nightmares.

I don't know what it was that drew me to the dark and scary stuff as a kid, but drawn I certainly was. As soon as my eyes alighted on *The 7th Fontana Book of Horror Stories* I knew I had to have it—or at least, I had to borrow it from my cousin, and read it.

As I write this introduction, I have a copy of the very edition of the book on my desk, and—as with *The Eleventh Pan Book of Horror Stories*, which frightened me so much that it gave me my first genuinely sleepless night on New Year's Eve 1975—the cover still provokes in me a delicious *frisson* of shivery fear. With hindsight the bubbly and cartoonish 'Horror Stories' logo is somewhat less than sinister, and yet I love it because I associate it with (almost certainly erroneous) memories of being curled up in bed on many a cold and rainy winter's night, reading by torchlight until well past the point at which I should have gone to sleep, and frightening myself silly with stories of cannibals and living mannequins and man-eating plants.

Below the 'Horror Stories' logo the photographic cover image is washed with a sickly yellowish-green hue, and depicts a rat skulking between glass bottles on a laboratory bench, its beady black eyes fixed on the reader. It's not a particularly inspiring or well-designed cover, to be honest, and yet, for me, nostalgia lends it a power and an elegance that far transcends the sum of its rather lacklustre parts.

The same is true of many of the anthologies I owned – and indeed, still own. Back in the 1960s and '70s the cover art for mass market genre anthologies was often shabby, the paper the books were printed on cheap, the print itself eye-strainingly small—and yet in the four years or so between 1972-1976 I devoured dozens and dozens of such anthologies, and developed a love for them which endures to this day. During that time I worked my way voraciously through a great many of the Pan and Fontana Books of Horror and Ghost Stories, most of the Armada Books of Ghost, Monster and SF Stories, and through numerous stand-alone anthologies, many of whose titles are now lost in the mists of time, which I borrowed on a regular basis from the local library. By the time I read my first 'proper' horror novel, which (if you don't include *Jaws* by Peter Benchley) was probably James Herbert's *The Fog* round about 1976, I had read hundreds, perhaps thousands, of short horror and ghost stories, many of them by established masters of the form such as M.R. James, Algernon Blackwood, Sir Arthur Conan Doyle, Robert Bloch, Ray Bradbury, Robert Aickman, Roald Dahl, Elizabeth Bowen, Ambrose Bierce, Joan Aiken and L.P. Hartley.

I have often maintained that short fiction is the lifeblood of the horror genre, and as such it will probably come as no surprise to learn that I have harboured an ambition to edit my own non-themed anthology of horror and/or ghost stories ever since my career began over twenty-five years ago. Now, with *The Spectral Book of Horror Stories*, I have finally fulfilled my ambition, and my hope is that there is enough of an interest among readers for *The Spectral Book of Horror Stories* to become not only an annual fixture in the horror calendar, but to continue to prosper and grow in the years ahead.

My ambition, in fact, is for *The Spectral Book of Horror Stories* to become a watchword for genre excellence. I hope that each year's new volume will provide a showcase for the very best short fiction that this wonderful genre has to offer.

With this in mind, I was determined to make as much of an impact with this first volume as possible, and so contacted all the writers I could think of working within the field whose short fiction I particularly admired. I explained my vision for the book and invited each of them to submit a story for consideration. I had no idea what sort of feedback I would get, and so was extremely heartened not only by the enthusiastic response I received, but by the amount and sheer excellence of the stories that immediately began to fill my inbox. Such was the quality of the stories, in fact, that I found myself quickly faced with the onerous task of having to turn down good stories by established writers—even, in some instances, having to say no to personal friends. In the end, though, it was worth it, because I'm delighted not only with the line-up for volume one, but with the quality and range of fiction that the contributors have produced.

You'll find supernatural and non-supernatural stories within these pages; you'll find stories of madness, of dread, of warped longing and twisted love. You'll find humour juxtaposed with gore; you'll find forbidden rites and ancient forces, and moments of surreal terror. Most of all, you'll find that the horror genre has very wide parameters – and very sharp teeth.

The journey begins. Tread carefully.

– 15th July 2014

ON THE TOUR
Ramsey Campbell

As soon as Stu looked into Yesterday's he saw Jaz sitting near the bar. "They've remembered me," Stu told him. "They've got me on the bus."

The smallest man at Jaz's table took a mouthful of bitter and wiped his wry lips with the back of his fist. "Which one's that, pops?"

"The tour bus. The Beatles tour that goes past my house."

"Are we supposed to know who you are?"

"He used to be with Scotty and the Scousers," Jaz said. "He was the drummer."

"Ever meet the Beatles?"

"We were on with them," Stu declared. "Ringo bought us a drink, only John pinched mine and made out it was a joke. Scotty said he should buy me another but John wanted to settle it outside, and then Paul said it wasn't worth it and George got me one instead. We always thought John knew the others wouldn't let him fight and that's why he was safe to start it."

"That's your claim to fame, is it? That's what they'll be saying about you on the tour."

Jaz made to intervene until Stu said "I don't know what they're saying yet. I'm off home to hear."

"Sounds like you're taking after your friend Lennon, not getting us a round."

"I never said he was a friend. He didn't like us being bigger on the bill than they were."

The man was opening his mouth when Jaz said "Stu's right. I've seen his poster."

Just the same, as Stu made for the street he heard the man laugh. The fellow seemed determined to stay unimpressed, and Stu called to Jaz "You know about the band. You tell him."

Early partygoers were already heading for the clubs. All the girls were dressed for a hot night, though it was April. On Church Street, where a police van was the solitary vehicle exempted from the ban on traffic, a musician was picking coins out of his guitar case. Everybody waiting at the bus station appeared to be on their own, and the line Stu joined was as silent as a photograph. At least the homeward bus arrived before the wind through the glass shelter could start his knees clapping together. The downtown hotels gave way to tall Victorian houses that had fissured into apartments, and then the buildings set about shrinking almost as small as his house.

The bus left him at the end of the road next to his. The house where he'd grown up was just his now, and looked as dilapidated as he felt when he let himself. The tree outside the gap-toothed wooden fence smeared the dusty brownish bricks with twilit shadow, which sprawled on the dead leaves strewn across the untended token garden and had settled in both front rooms. Like its neighbours, the house was boxed in by the pair that flanked it, from one of which came the mumble of a television. Stu twisted the key in the rusty lock and barely paused to slam the door on the way to tramping up the variously resonant stairs to his bedroom. He shoved the sash of the window high and dragged the sheet over the corner of the mattress before pulling the quilt up to the pillow as a preamble to throwing clothes off the chair onto the bed. He brought the chair hobbling to the window and propped his elbows on the sill.

At first he wasn't sure that he was hearing the tour guide, especially since he couldn't see the bus. Was the blurred voice coming from the television next door? When the small white single-decker coach appeared at the end of the road Stu succeeded in making out some words, and rubbed his bruised stomach as he sat down from craning over the sill. One of the quirkiest Liverpool bands of the sixties… Their only album was a collector's item… People used to say the drummer was the star. Once Ringo had said he was the better musician, and here was his house.

Stu waved to the passengers who were gazing up at him. Some of those on the far side of the vehicle leaned into the aisle to see him, and several people waved at him as the tree on the pavement set about blocking his view. He didn't shut the window until the bus had coasted out of sight. As an afterthought he said "Catch us next time"— the invitation the band shouted at the end of every gig.

After dinner from Wong's Pizza round the corner he listened to the album. He'd had his copy made into a computer file, which preserved fifty years' worth of clicks and pops. He didn't mind them; in fact, they meant he didn't regret selling his vinyl quite so much. He sang along with *Annie from Anfield*, matching the falsettos from half a century ago, and *Sally the Scally* and *All the Big Ships*, where the band had used Liverpool street songs they'd overdubbed and he'd performed the riff Ringo had admired. "You could be better on the skins than me, man," he remembered Ringo telling him.

He slept more soundly than he had for weeks. He mightn't have wakened in time for work if his bladder hadn't sent him a message and then a reminder. A bus twice the size of the tour coach and crammed with passengers took him downtown. He had breakfast at the Calorie Counter near both the Philharmonics—the concert hall, which had never booked the Scousers, and the pub—and then marched downhill to Vin's Vintage Vinyl.

Though the shop wasn't due to open for ten minutes, Vin was already staring out between the nostalgic posters on the window. Several turns of a red rubber band secured his greying ponytail and seemed to tug his lined forehead higher, his long glum face thinner. "How's your diddle, Stew?" he said.

"How's yours?"

"Hanging right last time I looked." Whenever Vin made what was presumably a joke his face grew yet more lugubrious. It stayed that way while he said "Get your coat off, then. Let them see where you belong."

Stu could tell he'd only just switched on the heater, which creaked as it lent the shop the smell of burning dust. He thought he saw his own breath as he hung his padded jacket in the mouldering back room that barely had space for a toilet and a sink. Like Vin, he wore a T-shirt printed with an image of a vinyl record that said VIN'S on the label. "Look proud of my twelve-inch," Vin said.

This joke and variations on it were so familiar that his face stayed routinely morose as he opened the shop and looked for an album to attract customers. Stu didn't recall ever having seen the chosen band; he'd never shared a gig with them. Once the first side of the album—cover versions sung with basic sixties harmonies, standard twangs on two guitars and a bass, doggedly dull drumming—had failed to entice the public, Stu said "Can't we have mine on?"

He didn't need Vin's look to tell him he sounded childish. "Me and the Scousers," he insisted.

"Is that what you're calling it now?" Vin's expression didn't relent as he said "Go on, give it a spin."

Though he could always go straight to an album if it was in stock, they weren't in any order. Stu had a sense where some of them were, but by the time he found the Scousers he was struggling not to ask Vin to find the album for him. He peered at his own youthful face—angular features concentrating on a grin to match the rest of the square of faces, cropped hair bristling with a hint of rebelliousness—and then he picked the arm off the rival album halfway through a track. "Watch it," Vin protested. "What's your rush?"

After just a couple of jittery attempts Stu succeeded in locating the spindle on the turntable with the hole in the middle of the record. As he propped the sleeve against the till he noticed the dog-eared price tag. "Maybe it's worth more now I'm on the tour."

The ageing bell gave a clang or at any rate a clunk before Vin could answer, and a couple wandered into the shop. Stu thought the music was responsible, especially when the man raised his eyes from browsing in the racks to glance towards the till. "That's me," Stu said as he heard himself brushing the cymbal in the fadeout of *Fly Away, Liver Bird*. "That was my band."

"You reckon," the man said while the girl looked no less bored than she did with the shop in general.

"He's saying he was on the drums," Vin said. "That's our era, us."

"You just heard there's more to it than that." When nobody seemed to understand or find the effort worth making, Stu said "They talk about it on the Beatles tour."

"About Ringo," the man told his partner. "Remember, they did."

"Him as well," Stu said and had to raise his voice to be heard over his own drumming. "There's me again. Stu Stewart with the Scousers. That's why they've got me on the tour."

"Don't remember you," the man told him, and the girl took a moment to shake her head.

"Maybe I haven't been there long. I only realised just this week."

Vin was working on a hint of a smirk. "What's he been saying about you on the bus?"

"She," Stu informed him. "They can be, you know."

He might have expected the girl to appreciate that, but he knew how frustratingly unpredictable they were. "You're not saying what they're saying," Vin said.

"How good I was."

"How good was that?" the girl hardly seemed to want to know.

Stu nearly demanded what was wrong with her if she wasn't able to hear. He already resented having been provoked to sound as though he was boasting. "I'll find out," he told Vin. "I'll tell you when I've heard it all."

"Bet you can't wait," the girl said.

"We'll let you carry on," the man said as he hurried her out of the shop.

Stu could have thought the bell had rendered Vin more combative. "Never mind scaring off the customers," Vin said.

"I never. He took her out for being rude. Anyway, I brought them in."

"Not so I noticed."

"Me and the band did. You saw how he wanted to know who we were. You ought to play us more often. Come to think, why don't we make copies to sell?"

"That's not my style and you've been around long enough to know it." Before Stu could decide if this referred to copyright or the vintage image of the shop, Vin said "You don't want to go on about selling. You didn't sell him your disc or any bastard else."

"You didn't either," Stu blurted, not immediately grasping how much he'd antagonised his employer. "I will another time," he promised. "You know I'll do anything I can for the shop."

"Like what, Stew?"

"Anything at all." In some desperation Stu said "Maybe I can get her on the bus to tell everyone I work here."

"That'd be a smash."

Stu couldn't tell from Vin's doleful face how skeptical this was. Perhaps Stu shouldn't have undertaken quite so much, but surely the tour would like to know. He only wished he'd taken time to hear precisely what she was saying about him before he mentioned her, and now he was anxious to listen. Did she vary her commentary? How often would the tour pass his house while he was at the shop?

Vin changed the record as soon as the first side was over, but Stu held back from objecting. He jammed the kettle under the tap in the sink and plugged it in behind the counter, where it hissed at the first tracks on *Rubber Soul*. "That's what the public want," Vin said, though Stu thought fewer people were lingering outside than while the Scousers had been audible. He confined himself to making coffee in the Vigorous Vinyl mugs Vin had ordered before changing the name of the shop. "Fair enough, you're good for something," Vin said as he took his mug.

Stu only just stopped short of retorting that he was good for a lot better. He'd been hired because Vin had seen him with the Scousers, after all. When the next prospects ventured into VVV he asked if he could help and loitered near them to enthuse about whichever album either of them took out of the racks, though he had to commute between them once they moved to opposite ends of the shop. Eventually one man bought a Pacemakers album. "Let's hope we never need one," Stu said, and thanked him and his partner for supporting the shop and urged them to come back.

"Don't get in a stew about it," Vin said with additional moroseness once they were alone. "Give the buggers room to breathe."

Stu tried keeping his distance from a customer and made no sale. He might as well have been at home to listen for the tour guide. He was acutely aware how Vin was observing him while packaging albums the shop had sold online. Vin was at the post office when Stu succeeded in selling three Rolling Stones albums to a man who'd brought just one to the counter. "I got rid of a bunch of Stones," he told Vin as soon as he plodded into the shop.

"Hope you didn't need an operation," Vin said, lengthening his face.

After that the shop felt like an obstacle to going home, the way too many of the last hours of a school day used to feel. Stu jogged and then rather less than jogged uphill to catch the bus home. The first one sailed past without stopping, and the next one had standing room only, like a Scousers' concert—he couldn't recall which. He lurched about whenever the bus stopped or started or changed speed, and lurched worse as it turned along a road not on the route. "Where are we going?" he cried.

The driver gave him less than a second in the mirror. "Police."

The road the bus ought to have used was cordoned off as a crime scene, and the mass of diverted traffic wouldn't have been able to overtake a funeral. By the time the bus reached Stu's stop he was nearly half an hour later than he'd meant to be home. He ran and trotted and trudged panting to his house, where his hands shook so much that he had to use both of them to aim the key at the lock. He clutched the banister and hauled himself upstairs to fumble the bedroom window open and drag the chair across the room.

Suppose he couldn't hear the guide even if the tour hadn't already passed by? The harder he strained his ears, the more they filled up with the pounding of his heart. He'd fallen onto the chair, but as soon as he was able to stagger to his feet he craned out of the window. He could hear no sound beyond the thuds like the action of a pile-driver that felt capable of shaking his skull. He was gripping the sill with both hands so as to lean out another few inches by the time he heard the guide.

As he struggled to distinguish words—the effort felt like striving to focus his entire body—he only seemed to squeeze the voice smaller. Once the bus came into sight he did his utmost to relax, and a few words reached him. The guide was saying someone was a legend and a genius, but Stu couldn't yield to believing whom she had in mind until she described him as Ringo's favourite drummer.

Was that going a little too far? Perhaps not if the audience accepted it, and as the bus coasted alongside his house Stu saw them begin to smile up at him. When he stuck his fists out of the window and flourished his thumbs, some of his audience returned the gesture. "Visit me at Vin's Vintage Vinyl," he called after the bus, and didn't sink onto the chair until his stomach began to throb.

He only wished he'd heard all the guide's comments about him. Might there be a later tour on Fridays? Enough of last night's pizza was left that he didn't need to go out to fetch dinner, and he hurried back to the bedroom window, where he held the chilly carton on his lap. All the voices he heard were on the street or in the houses, and they could hardly be talking about him. When he started to jerk awake from nodding towards the remains of the last slice of pizza, he sent himself to bed.

The voice that kept wakening him couldn't be the guide's. If it wasn't in Stu's head, it certainly couldn't be on the bus, even once the dawn set about seeping into the room. How early was the first tour? Did he have time to listen to it before he left for work? He waited as long as he dared, finishing off the pizza for breakfast, and then had to dash for the bus into town. At least he had news for Vin, though for a while he wondered if he would ever regain enough breath to tell him.

Vin had made himself coffee, and Stu wasn't sure how to take the departure from the protocol. "Kettle's been on." Vin seemed to think he needed to be told.

As Stu stirred in the contents of one of the cartons of milk Vin pocketed from fast food restaurants – barely enough to turn the coffee even slightly paler—he said "I didn't get the chance to hear everything they say about me yet, but—"

"I wasn't asking," Vin said and raised all the noise he could find in the bare floorboards as he went to open the door.

He put *Abbey Road* on the turntable and gave Stu a warning look that Stu found unnecessary if not worse. By the time the album ended, having abandoned the drummer and the rest of the band, not a single customer had visited the shop. Saturday ought to be the busiest day, and Stu watched Vin growing glummer. Halfway through the first side of the mystery tour Vin said "We need to bring more people in or I may as well trade from home."

"How are you going to do that? Bring them in, I mean."

"Maybe it wants somebody that can."

"Well, there is." When this earned him a stare that scarcely even hinted at a question, Stu said "There's me."

Vin was silent long enough to have thought of quite a few words before saying "I meant a girl."

"We don't need them. You saw that one yesterday. They aren't on our wavelength."

"My wife is." Almost as ominously Vin said "Not much to look at any more, that's her trouble. No use to my shop."

"Well then there's still me. I don't need to look like anything except who I am. I started to tell you, I did hear some of the things they're saying about me. Don't think I'm boasting, will you, but they've got me down as a legend and a genius and Ringo's fave."

"That's what you think, is it, Stew?"

Stu didn't want to be trapped into making the claims for himself. "What I think, I've thought of a slogan for us."

"Then maybe you're some use."

"Visit him at Vin's Vintage Vinyl." When Stu didn't see even a glimmer of recognition he said "That's me."

He thought the weary clang of the bell that announced the day's first customer had robbed him of a response until Vin muttered "Just leave it, Stew."

Could Vin doubt him, or did he think Stu's inclusion on the tour wouldn't help the shop? He wasn't going to undermine Stu's rediscovered confidence. Stu kept close to any customers in case they wanted his advice, but managed to hold back from pointing out the Scousers' album and drawing attention to the drummer. Less than half an hour before the shop was due to close he said "Do you mind if I leave a bit early as long as we're so quiet?"

"Going on your tour, are you?"

"That'd wow them, wouldn't it? They wouldn't be expecting that." When Vin gave him a look that seemed determined to fend off his enthusiasm Stu said "I want to go and hear. Not just for me, not even mostly."

"Been telling yourself that, have you, Stew?"

"That's not my name," Stu said with a fierceness that, in all the years since his second wife had left him, he'd forgotten he possessed. "I'm not a pan of Scouse."

"Sounds more like that's all you think you are, a bit of one." Before Stu's rage could find another word Vin said "Go on, go home and sort your head out. That's what the weekend's for."

Stu had a better use for it, and he'd be bringing the proof to the shop. He reached the homeward stop less than a minute ahead of a bus. The police had restored its usual route, and he was home so early that he only just missed the penultimate tour of the day, which left him feeling prickly with frustration. At least he had time to make sure he heard everything about him on the final tour.

He mustn't risk being unable to hear. He dodged out of the house to stand behind the tree outside the front garden, and wondered how much he resembled a drunk overtaken by a need. Sometimes he'd been like that – both his wives had lectured him about it more than once – but he couldn't afford to be now, financially or otherwise. In any case, his neighbours oughtn't to be watching him; they would have a better reason when they heard the guide. Here was the tour at the end of the road at last, and as the bus turned towards him he put the tree between them.

Suppose it prevented him from hearing? Should he just stroll along the road? It might look as if he was loitering in search of praise – as if he needed that to lend him confidence. He'd begun to tear strips of bark off the tree by the time he heard his name. The bus was on the far side of the tree, and he kept it there by sidling around the trunk. As soon as it was well past he sprinted to the next tree, and thought he glimpsed passengers turning away from gazing at his house. He followed the tour to the end of the road, where he had to let it go, having run out of cover. Whether since the trees were in the way or because his exertions had amplified his heart, he'd failed to hear another word.

When his pulse had finished shaking his body he let go of the last tree and limped back to the house. "What have you been up to now?" he could hear his wife demanding—either of his wives. They'd accused him of making too much of all his Scousers posters, as if both of them weren't doing that themselves. He'd argued all night with the first one after she'd torn a poster on the wall by the stairs—only dusting, she'd said. He'd waited for her replacement to carry on the damage, and she was gone too once she had. Being unmarried had let him have the posters framed under glass, although that left them feeling less alive to him. Now that the tour was bringing it all back to life he shouldn't need them so much.

The light from the street glared out of the frames, and the contents went dark as he shut the door. Might there be another tour today? Even if that was only a hope, a couple of pieces of toast would keep him going while he waited. He kept stopping after just one bite for fear that the crunching that resounded through his head might deafen him to the approach of the bus. When at last it grew too dark and cold for him to imagine there would be one, he brushed the crumbs off his lap and out of the window, then leaned on the sash to haul it down. He drew the curtains before switching on the light, and then he got ready for bed. He wanted to be awake well in time for the first Sunday tour.

His name wakened him, but he couldn't tell how high the voice had been. He thought it might have been falsetto, the way the Scousers sang—and then he realised what it must be, and lurched out of bed. His feet were tangled in the quilt, so that he almost fell headlong as he floundered to the window. The rumble of the sash blotted out the guide's next words, which surely couldn't be responsible for the behaviour of her customers. While Stu couldn't see many people on the bus, as it passed his house they were pointing and laughing at him.

The tour was almost out of sight before he managed to laugh in response. He supposed he might have reacted like them if he'd seen himself standing naked at the window, blinking dozily at the world. He didn't mind being a Scouse joke for once, especially since the wall under the windowsill had preserved his decency. He used the bathroom as speedily as he was able and dressed on his way back to the window. As he fumbled to fasten the strap of his wristwatch he was disconcerted to find it was nearly noon. He'd been roused hours later than he'd planned to sleep.

He still didn't feel awake. Surely he had time to make himself a coffee before the next tour, but he left the front door open so that he would hear the guide while he was in the kitchen. The mug spattered his hand with drops that felt like embers as he tramped down the slippery path to his gate. There was no sign of the tour, but might he have failed to hear it by straining too hard? His shaky hand was smarting in half a dozen spots by the time he succeeded in carrying the mug to the chair at the bedroom window. He didn't know how many bitter sips he'd swallowed when he saw the bus sneaking up the road.

He hadn't been hearing his pulse, but now he did. Could it have deafened him to the commentary, or was the guide waiting until her passengers saw his house? She didn't speak as the bus nosed past the gate, but she must already have mentioned him, since the scattered passengers were gazing up at him. Although their faces didn't change when he waved and stuck his thumbs up, he was overtaken by the notion that they were trying not to laugh.

He had to be mixing them up with the earlier tour, and he just needed to be more awake. He took gulps of coffee that felt as if they were skinning his mouth. His head was throbbing with caffeine, not to mention his attempts to hear the guide, before the tour reappeared. As he watched the bus cruise towards his house she didn't utter a single word, and he was suddenly convinced that she'd been talking about him while he couldn't hear. Was the bus slowing to give the passengers a better look at him? Faces turned up to him, and as his arms shivered with his struggles not to gesture he was sure he saw lips writhing in an effort to suppress mirth.

He heard laughter as trees hid the bus. What had she said about him? He dropped the mug, splashing his ankles, and stalked downstairs, grabbing the banister at every step. She must think he was stupid if she imagined she could prevent him from hearing her remarks. He marched to the end of the road to watch for the next tour.

When it showed up on the main road he withdrew behind the first tree, but he must have taken too long over making sure it was her bus. The tree wasn't quite broad enough to hide him, and as the bus turned the corner a passenger craned to watch him. Stu dodged around the tree, but more people twisted in their seats to spy him. As the bus sped towards his house he heard it trailing laughter. He was unable to catch up with it, not that he knew what he would have done if he had, and so he retreated into the house.

He oughtn't to have let the guide realise he could hear. On the next tour she kept her comments well out of earshot, but he wasn't fooled. Even if the passengers didn't point and laugh, he could see how their faces were hiding whatever she'd said about him. Each reappearance of the bus enraged him further, and when he started breaking splinters off the windowsill he stormed down to stand at the gate. Staring fiercely at one consignment of passengers didn't daunt them; some of them didn't even bother withholding their amusement until they were out of sight, while the guide pretended she was too busy driving to notice him. His drumming on the gate failed to impress the next group, though the performance scattered bits of wood across the pavement, and his vocals fell short of restoring his image, however high he strained his voice. It left his throat raw, and he'd had enough of trying to counteract her mockery. He snatched out his phone—for once he was grateful to his last wife, who'd nagged him to buy the mobile so that she would be able to locate him—and found the number for the Beatles tour.

He might have known the office would be shut on Sundays. He needn't think they were refusing to answer, having recognised his number. The chilly twilight sent him into the house, but he wasn't about to close the window. How many tours did he still have to watch? It seemed there was just one, and perhaps ending her day made the guide careless of whether Stu heard, unless she wanted to provoke him to put on more of a show. As the bus entered the road she grew loud enough for his neighbours to hear. Scotty and the Scousers had become a cult band, she was saying, partly thanks to the Beatles. John Lennon had told their drummer he was Ringo's favourite as a joke. People in the know packed the Scousers' gigs out because the drummer was the best in the business – the best laugh. He'd earned the nickname Chicken Drumsticks because he played as if he was using them.

"I never heard that," Stu told her passengers. "I never heard any of it. It's not true, none of it. What's wrong with you?" He scarcely knew whom he was addressing, let alone how high his voice had risen; his wives would have been covering their ears by now and telling him not to screech. They'd managed to incite him to put on the wrong kind of show—the guide had. She wouldn't think it was so funny when he told her employer.

The tour was out of sight by now, but who else had it started talking about him? How many of his neighbours might be? Even with the window open as wide as his shoulder could heave the sash, he was unable to decide if the muffled voices were on television. They seemed to be repeating one another's words, but was he the subject they were agreeing about? He shivered whenever he craned out of the window, to be met by another faceful of frosty air. Eventually the dawn became daylight that was just about as grey, and he began phoning Vin's Vintage Vinyl.

If Vin was there he wasn't owning up to it, and the tour firm didn't answer. Stu had been trying both of them for most of an hour by the time Vin made his weariness audible. "What's up now, Stew?"

"It's Stu." Having established this, Stu said "It looks as if I'll have to be late."

"What's keeping you? Don't say your tour."

Stu wasn't going to admit that until he'd dealt with it, and so he said "I think I'm a bit sick."

"You're not telling me anything. Anyway, don't go rushing back. I'm working on a girl like I said."

She wouldn't replace him, Stu promised himself. Nobody could. He cut Vin off without replying and tried the tour firm once again. He was answered so immediately that he almost forgot he didn't want to be identified—not yet, at any rate. He did his best to elevate his voice even higher than the woman's that had greeted him. "Can I ask about someone you've got on your tour?"

"Someone who works for us, do you mean?"

"Not her, no." In some haste Stu added "Somebody you talk about. Stu Stewart."

"Who's that, sorry?"

"Me," Stu was almost provoked by her tone to blurt. "The drummer with Scotty and the Scousers," he said aloud.

"He isn't part of our tour."

"You can't tell me that. You've always gone along my, gone along his road and now you're talking about him."

"Which road is that, sir?"

Her last word nearly robbed him of speech. When he named his road and then told her where it was, hiking his voice higher still, she said "We've never used that route. We don't come within a mile of it."

She'd recognised him, of course. By calling him sir she'd betrayed that she had. He didn't need to hear her start to laugh as he cut her off. How much of an idiot did she take him for? Did she really believe she could trick him into doubting the evidence of his own senses? She and the other one would have even less of a chance when he took the tour. He would have to go downtown to catch it from the terminus, and he hurried to the bus stop on the main road. A bus was approaching, and Stu hadn't finished fumbling for his travel pass when the doors opened to him. "You're all right," the driver said. "We'll let you on."

For an instant he thought she meant because he was Stu Stewart, and then he recognised her voice. Her accomplice must have been in touch with her, and now they were trying to convince him that he'd caught an ordinary bus. He didn't need to scrutinise the passengers to see they knew better. "That's kind of you," he said through his teeth, and sat behind her as the bus swung into his road.

She wasn't going to deliver her commentary. That was obvious as soon as he met her eyes in the mirror. Perhaps she had already ridiculed him; in fact, when he twisted around to peer at the passengers he was sure she had. The knowledge brought him to his feet, and he grabbed a seat on each side of the aisle as he faced his audience. "Now you're on my part of the tour," he declared. "Stu Stewart, as if you didn't know."

They needn't try to look as though they didn't. The guide who was posing as merely a driver demolished all the pretence by saying "Can you sit down, sir."

Could he have spoken to her on the phone? It hardly mattered; they were all the same. "Ringo's favourite drummer and don't let anyone tell you different," he said louder and higher. "People came to see me right enough, but it wasn't for a laugh."

"Sir, if you don't sit down—"

"What'll you do? Tell your lies about me, like you haven't already?" His pitch was rising out of his control, and more than one passenger had covered their ears, though he wondered if they had because they didn't want to hear the truth. The bus was slowing, and he let go of the seats to demonstrate a few riffs on them. "That's just a taste. You know what, I think Ringo learned from me," he said and felt bound to explain the falsetto he couldn't bring down. "And this is how we used to have to sing."

He faltered, because his was no longer the only voice. The other one was repeating the tale about John Lennon's joke at Stu's expense. As the bus stopped outside his gate Stu lurched at the guide, but her lips appeared to be pinched shut. Was she devious enough to be throwing her voice? "Here's what you've all been waiting to see," Stu announced, "my house," but he could still hear the commentary underlying his own. "I'll find you," he cried. "I know you're there. You aren't hiding from me."

As he stalked along the aisle he began to recognise the passengers—the man at Jaz's table in Yesterday's, the girl who'd been brought into Vin's shop. He couldn't see his wives, however many faces he caught hold of. He was well on the way to prying a face wide to grasp the source of the relentless voice before its owner struggled free, having bitten Stu's fingers, and fled like the rest of them. Several were emitting sounds higher than Stu was making. The guide was the last to flee, and shut him on the bus. He didn't mind being left when he still had his audience, more of whom were joining them on the pavement. It was completely his tour now, and he took the guide's seat, but he hadn't discovered how to start the bus by the time several men drove up to help him.

THE DOG'S HOME
Alison Littlewood

Sometimes, the cruellest thing a creature can give you is love. I get up and Sandy the retriever is there. He comes running when I go downstairs and tries to lick my face. I feel sad, or irritated, depending on my mood, and then I go out and the last thing I see is his head tilted to one side, surprised to see me leaving him all over again. I get back and he's there, tail wagging – I can hear it, beating the radiator by the door – and it begins again. There's no end to his love. It's capacious; it's infinite. It was the first thing I was told about him, and it was true, and every day I'm surprised to see that it's true. You'd think both of us would have got used to it by now, but we haven't. I suppose, in that, I'm more like him than I realise.

"You wouldn't stand a chance if it wasn't for the dog," my mother had said when she raised the question of visiting Aunt Rose. At first I didn't know what she meant, though I remembered my aunt from when I was small; she'd come on a duty visit. I was about five years old. She'd loomed over me in the hall and dropped her bag next to her feet, which were clad in brown brogues that I could see my snotty little nose in. She'd leaned down, her scrawny hands reaching for me, and she'd touched both my cheeks. Her hands were cold, I remember that too, and then she leaned in closer, pursing her lips. I'd waited for the touch of her tight mouth on my cheek, but it never came. Instead she'd whispered, her voice dry and fierce but her breath surprisingly warm against my skin, "Wash your face before you greet your elders and betters."

I'm not sure my mum even heard; certainly, I never saw her react. And that was how I remembered Aunt Rose, crone-like, tall, thin, claws for hands and a death rattle voice. I filed her away in a mental box with *Do not open* on the lid, and left her there. Or so I thought.

"It'll go to the dogs' home," my mother said.

She had no love of my aunt. She had no love for my dad, either.

27

He'd left the two of us a long time ago and I thought we'd managed all right, got along without too many problems; until she'd said that about the dogs' home.

Aunt Rose had 'married rich', Mum always said, and she always had a note of resentment in her voice when she said it. Better still, judging from her tone, Rose had 'married dead', the guy popping it soon after, leaving her loaded. A big inheritance with nowhere to go. No wonder Mum had pound signs in her eyes.

That was when she'd said, "Course, Andrew, you wouldn't stand a chance if it wasn't for the dog." She looked at my blank expression and snapped, "Rose doesn't like people. But that dog—that dog likes people. So Rose tolerates them. She'll visit folk just because the dog likes to see them. She'll stop and chat to people on their walks, because her dog likes *their* dog. If it wasn't for that animal—" she clicked her tongue in disapproval. "And now," she added with a note of triumph, "the dog's home all alone, isn't he? The neighbour's feeding him and that's about it. So she needs someone to go and stay. She needs *you* to go and stay."

I opened my mouth to protest. I saw the look on my mother's face and closed it again.

"Make sure that dog loves you," she said. "Make him love you and *she'll* decide she loves you too."

Sandy wasn't at all the kind of dog I'd expected. I'd thought Aunt Rose would have some sniffy little thing, a chihuahua or a peke, but when I collected her key from the neighbour and let myself in, there he was, a flurry of tail, big paws and weight behind them, all joy and enthusiasm. There was a volley of barks but not a second's hesitation before he was all over me, licking, covering my sweater in hair and drool. I couldn't reconcile the idea of Aunt Rose and this living, breathing, messy creature; it didn't seem they occupied the same universe, let alone the same house. But occupy it Sandy did. I could smell him there, a cooped-up smell that was unmistakably dog, and I sighed and set down my bag at my feet. It looked like I wouldn't just be staying in her house; I'd be cleaning it too. But first, it was time to visit Aunt Rose.

＊

The hospital's antiseptic smell, barely masking what lay beneath, was a sharp contrast to the shut-in, musty house. Rose was in a room of her own and I was thankful for that. I'd never been around illness, not really. I didn't look at the wards to either side as I went towards number seven and I found it a small, narrow box, a metal bed clearly visible through a large window. In the bed was the collection of bones and skin that Aunt Rose had become. Looking at her there, I had no idea how I could ever have thought of her as tall. She seemed barely larger than a doll, and when she let her head fall to the side, looking at me from hollowed sockets, she seemed to move like one too.

"Hello, Aunt Rose," I said, and she rolled her head back again with a little grunt. I'd intended to play it carefully, but found myself blurting, "I came to look after Sandy. Mum said you might need some help."

Some help. I knew, looking at her, how inadequate those words were. She needed more than help, would soon pass beyond the kind of help that anyone could give. But she didn't appear to think about what I said. She made a brief gesture and I recoiled from it, then realised she had indicated the plastic chair next to her bed. I slid into it. The legs scraped against the tiles and her lip twitched.

Aunt Rose stared at the ceiling. I didn't know if she was waiting for me to speak, but I tried. I told her that Mum was fine. I said she'd have come herself, but she couldn't get away from work—I almost found myself saying that Mum couldn't afford to have her wages docked, but I wasn't sure how that might sound. I thought of the slight body in the bed in front of me, hidden under a single sagging sheet, and all the money it possessed. It seemed terribly unlikely.

"Sandy's fine," I said. "He was happy to see-"

The breath was shocked out of me when she grasped my hand. I looked down. Her fingers, narrow and putty-coloured, held mine, which had turned white under their pressure. I tried to pull away but she held on, moving with me, and I had a sudden image of it being like that forever, her cadaverous hand closed on mine.

"Bring him to me," she said.

"What?"

Pardon, is what I expected her to say – the remnant of some childhood memory, perhaps—but she did not. "They won't let him in," she said, "and they won't let me out. I want to see my dog." Her eyes met mine. "It's *all* I want. You understand?"

Her eyes were pale blue and weak-looking, but a cold strength shone through them. It didn't appear natural. I looked away.

"I want to see my dog." She sank back against the pillows. Her face was blank, as if the life had already gone out of it—*already*, that was what I thought—and then a nurse came in talking about changing the sheets, smiling at me a little too brightly, in a way that told me it was time for me to go.

❊

Sandy greeted me when I got back to the house. It was as if he hadn't seen me in years. I was surprised by his love. It was capacious; it was infinite. I imagined the look on Aunt Rose's face if she could see it being bestowed upon me.

❊

"He'll understand," she said, the next time I went to see her. I tried to tell myself I didn't know what she meant, but I did.

"They'll think he'd jump all over me," she said, "but he won't. He'll know. He'll take one look at me and he'll know." Her head lolled, her gaze moving towards—but not quite meeting—my own.

"He's a smart dog. He always knew me and I knew him. He just needs to see me, so he knows—he knows I haven't—"

Abandoned him, I thought. In my pockets, my hands curled into fists. I'd spent the morning cleaning out her fridge. The smell had been indescribable. Then I'd started on the cupboards, but not before I'd walked the dog; *her* dog.

He was too joyful a creature to be her dog.

I told myself that Sandy wouldn't give two shits if he thought she had abandoned him, not now, but how could I know that was true? A dog is not a person.

A dog is not a person. I curled my fists tighter when I remembered what I'd found in the cupboard in the lounge. I scowled, just as I might have when I was five years old, but she didn't notice.

"I thought I'd have to make an awful choice for him one day," she said. Her throat was working, as if she was holding back tears. "That's the only thing that makes it bearable now. Going first, I mean. I know I won't have to do that. I'll never have to look at him while he goes to sleep. And he'll forget, won't he? After he's seen me. He can move on."

You're damned right he can, I thought. That morning I'd taken him to the park. He'd gone scurrying after all the sticks I threw.

She grasped my hand again. This time her grip was weak. "Please," she said. "If you do anything for me. Do this."

✻

That night Sandy curled up on the floor and stared up at one of the chairs. No one was sitting in the chair. I scowled at him. I went and sat in the chair. After a while, he came and sat at my side and rested his head on my knee. I whispered to him while his eyes closed and he slept like that, the breath catching noisily in his throat.

✻

How easy it is for a dog to love you. How hard it is, for a person. Sometimes people don't even love their own family. It just isn't in them. It wasn't in Rose's small, wasted body; it never had been. I knew that from the letters I found. Not hers, of course; I never saw whatever answers Rose had sent, but I know we never received anything more than words.

I always thought we'd got along all right, me and Mum. But I was a child, and children don't always know. They aren't like dogs. They can't take one look and understand. I wasn't even sure I understood after I'd read the letters I found stashed out of sight in Rose's cupboard.

He grows so fast, Mum had written. *He already needs new shoes. The trousers I got him last month are too short already. He looks a bit like Dad, have I mentioned that? You'd love him if you saw him now. I don't suppose you might be able to…*

But she never had, had she? Aunt Rose hadn't helped us. She never helped her own sister. She'd read these letters and she didn't love me. She'd seen me when I was five and she didn't love me then and here I was taking care of her house and her dog and visiting her in hospital because that was what family did, and she hadn't even noticed. Mum had been right, but she had been wrong too. The dog may have got me in, but I never had stood a chance, not really. There was only one way Aunt Rose was ever going to notice me; one way I might be able to persuade her to help.

Aunt Rose was right. She'd never actually said it, but it's true. A dog can break your heart.

"Five minutes," I said. "Five minutes, or maybe not even that if anyone finds out." The papers shook in my hand. My fingers had dug into them, claw-like, gripping too tightly. "But you have to sign first. And it has to be witnessed. We'll find a couple of nurses to do it." She stared at me. Mostly she stared at the ceiling, but this time she never took her eyes from mine. Hers were small, the pupils constricted, the pale blue almost blending with the greyish whites of her eyes. It was horrible to see, but I didn't look away. She was family, after all.

If there's any way you could help—he has to start school next week. He needs a uniform. I've been offered more hours but it means I can't be with him. I'll have to leave him with a neighbour, and he screams the place down when I'm not there…

I shook the thought away and forced myself to focus on the will. "Are you going to sign it?"

"But—"

"You don't need to worry about Sandy." I thought about how he'd been that morning, watching me leave, his head poking through a gap in the curtains, his tongue lolling in a wide doggy smile. I forced myself to stroke her hand. We both looked down at our fingers. "I'll make sure he's okay." I thought about telling her about his love, how he had enough for everyone; about how he'd be comforted. I stopped myself just in time.

"Will you sign?" I repeated.

Her head rolled away, but I could still make it out when she nodded.

✳

Back at the house, I read the letters once more. It wasn't so much the words that got to me, but their frequency. My mother had written to her sister once a week. Her hope—no, her faith—had never wavered. Family; she had believed in family, in their love.

Sandy rested his chin on my knee while I went through the letters, and occasionally I paused long enough to stroke his head. His fur there was a little shorter but softer than on his back. Long whiskers jutted from the side of his head, besides the ones that grew around his nose; others formed extra-long eyelashes. I listened to him breathing, the little catch where the air was constricted in his throat. His posture must have been uncomfortable, but he still didn't move.

Sandy was a big dog. He wasn't the kind that could be smuggled inside a handbag or under a coat. He was big and full of life and anyway, he loved me now.

But a promise is a promise.

*

The last time I visited Aunt Rose was the first time I'd seen her smile. I got there a little late, because by then the nurse at the door tended to be occupied with other visitors. I waited until she turned her back before I slipped down the corridor and into Aunt Rose's room. It was easier than I'd thought, though my heartbeat felt as if it would trigger alarms. I listened to the steady *beep—beep—beep* of my aunt's monitors, and calmed myself. Her rhythms sounded strong and steady, as they had for the last couple of days; as they had since I made my promise. *A turn for the better*, the nurses had said. *Who knows . . .?*

I pictured it, Aunt Rose back in her house, in her favourite chair, the dog gazing up at her, adoration in his eyes. It wouldn't happen. It *couldn't*.

I shook my head. A promise is a promise, especially to family. Because promises to family are mainly unspoken, aren't they? The ones about love, especially. The ones about help.

I smiled when I turned to face my aunt. She was sitting up in bed, looking brighter than she had in days. Her eyes were shining; there was joy in them. She knew I'd keep my promise—that was what families did—and now I was here.

"Where is he?" she asked.

My smile became a little wider. It took her a moment longer to see the expression in my eyes.

*

I get up and Sandy is there. I live in Aunt Rose's house now, though it isn't her house any longer. It's mine. He comes running when I go downstairs and tries to lick my face. I feel sad, or irritated, depending on my mood, and then I go out and the last thing I see is his head tilted to one side, surprised to see me leaving him all over again. I get back and he's there, tail wagging—I can hear it, beating the radiator by the door – and it begins again.

The thing I see, though, when I look at him, is Aunt Rose. Aunt Rose, little bigger than a doll, her limbs desiccated, covered by a single sagging sheet. Her eyes lolling back in their hollowed sockets, the emptiness in them. The *nothing* in them. It was the only thing left that she had really wanted, and once I gave it to her—once I opened the bag and leaned towards her and let her look inside—I guess she'd done.

It had been hard to cut. He wouldn't hold still, for one thing, and I couldn't see what I was doing because the fur on his neck was longer than that on his head. It was still golden though, and it spilled over my fingers. He licked me when I got hold of his collar. He tried to jump up at me, excited, not understanding.

It wasn't easy to cut; I think I said that, but it really wasn't.

I thought I'd have to make an awful choice for him one day, she'd said. And I remembered the relief on her face when she'd said it. I understood it. I took one look, and I understood.

I couldn't see for crying.

Make him love you, Mum had said, and I had. The awful thing was, I loved him too. I took a knife to his neck and I pushed it in. The noise he made was terrible. Pain, yes. But mostly, it was the sound of betrayal.

It didn't kill him, not at first. He bucked in my hands, and the knife slipped out. It took me a while to gather myself. He struggled. It was a while before I could do it again.

When Aunt Rose looked inside the bag, at first, she didn't do anything. She just froze, me trying to hold it steady so that she could see his eyes, not the bloody part, the matted fur, just those adoring eyes – and her own eyes swivelled and she looked at me. She looked at me for a horrified second before she opened her mouth – to form words or take a breath, I wasn't sure which – and then she started to claw at her chest.

Aunt Rose didn't get better. She didn't come home. She did get to see her dog, though, or what remained of him, before she died. I didn't want to do it, but he was a big dog. He wasn't a dog that would fit under a coat or in a bag. Not all of him, anyway.

Sandy comes to greet me whenever I get home. He wraps himself around my legs, and on some level, I can feel his touch, though the house never smells of dog any more. It doesn't smell of him because he isn't really there. I remind myself of that whenever I look into his eyes and see the adoration written in them. Sometimes the cruellest thing a creature can give you is love. I'd rather see *her*. Aunt Rose, the last look she ever gave me, her face twisted in pain and her eyes – the coldness in them. The hatred. It's what I deserve, but I tell myself; it's what she deserved too.

The dog was only caught between us.

There's no end to his love. It's capacious; it's infinite. It was the first thing I was told about him, and it was true, and every day I'm surprised to see that it's true. You'd think both of us would have got used to it by now, but we haven't. I don't think I ever will, and that's a pity, because I have the feeling we're going to be living together for a long, long time.

FUNERAL RITES
Helen Marshall

Her home university in Toronto was notoriously cheap when it came to travel budgets and, though Nora was something of an experienced traveller, she was still possessed of a certain naiveté—or, rather, disregard—when it came to subjects outside her field of expertise, a trait not entirely uncommon in her breed of scholar. That had led to bad luck in the past.

There was one time in particular, three years back, when trying to rent in London she had accidentally found herself in contact with Nigerian scam artists, with the result that the magically underpriced flat she'd purportedly rented in Bloomsbury had turned out to belong to a confused and overworked accountant who wouldn't put her up for anything. The summer being the height of the tourist season, Nora had barely managed to find herself a place in a hostel. When she had clumsily dragged her oversized suitcase up five flights of stairs into blistering humidity—heat rises, she remembered and cursed—and then hauled herself into a top bunk that, with its black privacy netting slung over the side boards, resembled a coffin for all intents and purposes, she vowed that never again would she find herself in such a place. It wasn't the closeness she hated, the small cramped space; no, it was the noise and the people, their demands, their excesses. No one whispered; music and conversation in foreign languages spilled out from the bunks, snores, such heavy breathing. A clotted tangle of black hair in every shower drain.

Because of that memory—a memory that came back to her with such grim vividness in any time of social unease, in the crush of the subway, at department parties, moments of forced camaraderie and feigned intimacy—Nora had been careful to check in advance that Mrs Moreland, the purported owner of a house on Observatory Street in Oxford, was indeed real. A friend of Nora's from her undergraduate days, now positioned as a Lecturer at Magdalen College, had stopped by to investigate on her behalf. She had reported the place to be clean, if a bit cramped, but entirely trustworthy. On the subject of Mrs Moreland herself, the friend had little of note to add.

"I don't expect you'll have any problems with her," Nora was told, "she keeps to herself. Nothing *too* fussy. By my count she's no madder than anyone else here." It was enough of a recommendation to seal the deal. Nora's needs were few, in any case, and she was used to keeping to herself. No matter how mad the old woman was, provided she had a single furnished bedroom available on the cheap, she could be handled, of course she could be handled. Or avoided entirely, if Nora kept out late enough at the Bodleian. The place would do nicely, she thought.

It was—when Nora found it, thoroughly soaked from a fresh burst of rain whipped up by gusting January winds—exactly as advertised: a narrow terraced house along a nicely maintained street in Jericho where the facades had each been brightly painted in yellows, robin's egg blues, and pinks. Hers was salmon-coloured with a dark green door. Nora took a deep breath, nervous. She hated the formality of lodging in a stranger's house, but in some ways it was easiest— strangers could be put off more easily, their questions avoided with pat answers about the nature of her work, the weather back home. Yes, strangers were easier. She could cope. She needn't stay very long at the house. The Bodleian would be open for several hours yet, and if she hurried she could still get a Reader's Card. Come back late in the evening after dinner, creep back to her room. She only had to smile politely and get the keys. Thinking this, she took a breath and knocked very gently using the brass ring.

Nothing.

She waited.

Should she try again? No. Best not to appear too eager. It might be considered crass.

She waited several more minutes. The sky opened up in a downpour. Nora gritted her teeth.

Finally, she knocked on the door furiously. It opened amidst the rain of blows with an unexpected suddenness, as if the owner had been waiting directly on the other side. The knocker was almost wrenched out of her hand.

"Nora Higgins?" asked the old lady who stood in the doorway.

Nora tried on what she expected was a rather sheepish and apologetic smile. "Sorry about the clatter. It's a bit damp, you see."

"I suppose you'd better come in."

The place had a funny feeling about it right away. Stuffy, but that could be excused. Mrs Moreland moved with a slow ungainliness, everything precise but shaky. It took her several seconds to vacate the doorway. Her eyes were red-rimmed, face pale and taut, a bruised purple over the cheekbones, lipstick once very bright but now partially blotted away.

Nora stepped inside. "Sorry about the dripping," she said. She struggled with the suitcase, afraid she might knock over the little wooden table with its framed glass photograph. She felt entirely too big for the space; it made her want to hunch over.

"This way, if you please."

Nora followed her into a little sitting room, all lumpy floral patterned cushions that hid, nestled between them, two girls the age of undergraduates, one as wan as Mrs Moreland despite her youth, the other dark-haired with a feverish look to her. They had clearly been speaking with some intensity before Nora's arrival. There was a heavy silence filled only with the ticking of a very ancient clock. They all stared at Nora.

"I've brought the deposit," Nora said uncertainly.

"Good, good," whispered Mrs Moreland.

"I'll take it," said the dark-haired one. She stood up abruptly. Almost snatched the cheque out of Nora's hand.

"It's fine, dear, let me, let me. I can still do that, can't I?"

The dark-haired one did not sit down, but her lips twisted gruesomely.

"Leave it," said the other.

"I won't."

"She wants to do it. Let her do it."

Mrs Moreland took the cheque from Nora and bent over a large-format accounts book. Her handwriting was very neat.

"A week then?"

"If that's all right." Nora was feeling nervous. "I'll be at the library most days. Not much time to spare." She laughed and regretted it instantly.

"She can't stay here. It's not right." A hushed whisper from the girls. Mrs Moreland waved her hand as if to dispel it.

"Let me show you the room."

❋

"I call my place the doll's house," Mrs Moreland said, "it's very sweet, very pretty, nothing much changed in twenty years. I manage the property myself, you know. I only take in scholars, not students. I can't abide students. You've finished your degree?"

"Yes," Nora said, "in Toronto. I teach there now."

"Good. Then I expect you'll be all right."

The room boasted a cream carpet and several framed pictures of plants labelled in Latin, with a single bed covered in a heavy wool blanket tucked against the wall. A tea service had been placed on the bedside table with an electric kettle.

"I laid this all out in the morning for you. Good thing too." Her gaze wandered.

"Shall I leave you to your visitors?" Nora asked.

"Them? They'll spend the night if they can. They don't want to leave me alone. But I've told them, you'll be in tonight, yes?"

"I suspect so."

"There you have it then. No need for them to stay."

"Auntie," said the dark-haired one from the doorway. She was holding Nora's suitcase, having dragged it thuddingly up the staircase on her own.

"You don't need to carry that," Nora said. "I can get it."

"We're absolutely staying the night."

"No, Kitty. I insist. Miss Higgins will be here. Miss, yes?"

Nora nodded.

"You see? I shan't be alone, no, I understand your concerns, but I have a lodger and I couldn't possibly put her out. There won't be enough beds for all of us. I'll sort it out with Rose," Mrs Moreland said. Nora watched her totter carefully down the stairs.

The dark-haired woman—Kitty—stayed in the hallway, clutching at the suitcase as if she wanted to strangle it. She was a slip of a thing, pretty, and moving with the unconscious arrogance of someone who knew she was pretty. Her lipstick was very red, her mascara very black. Nora knew the type, had seen countless Kitties in her classes. They were invariably lazy, fatuous, and lacking any sort of intellectual rigour.

"She's had a nasty shock," Kitty hissed. It was an ugly sound.

"Sorry?" Nora asked as politely as she could.

"We've just had word. Her son died. My cousin, Sean. A heart condition, completely unexpected, he was only twenty-three." She stared at Nora with a bird-like intensity, never blinking. There was a hectic colour to her cheeks. "Listen, I can get back the deposit for you."

"The deposit?" Nora asked.

"Of course. I don't imagine you'll want to stay, what with all this."

Nora said nothing. She remembered the heat of the hostel, the way the smell of the other travelling students—sweat and pot and perfume and sex—had overwhelmed her. Two Italians had been curled up on the bunk beneath her. She remembered staring at the intertwined shape of them. She remembered the noises they made, the bedframe shaking and pitching as they whispered love phrases to each other: *Mi fai il solletico, oooh, no, non ti fermare! Mi piace!*

"I'm sorry," said Nora again.

"It's settled then?"

"No, I'm sorry." *Allora continuo ancora per un po'!* Nora

41

remembered them panting in the dark, their mingled breath so hot she thought she could feel it through the bed. The absolute horror of it, it made her skin crawl. *Vengo! Vengo! Vengo!*

"I'll be staying." The words came out in a rush. Nora hated when she spoke like that. It made her feel stupid.

"What?" Kitty's eyes shone with malevolence.

"I am staying," Nora repeated.

"Fine," Kitty replied with a flip of her dark hair. "Fine, if that's the way you want it."

Nora decided not to chance leaving her room again for several hours until she heard the noise of departure at the foot of the stairs and finally the opening and closing of the front door. She lamented the lost time at the library, and instead set to work on proofing the footnotes of a paper she intended to submit for publication. Twice she cracked open her own door, but the thought of encountering Mrs Moreland kept her creeping back to the bed.

What if the old woman were distraught? Would she have to say something? Do something? There was silence from downstairs. No audible tears. That was good. That was very good. Nora did not like people, she did not understand them much. They made her feel uncomfortable and squeamish. The English were much better that way. Everyone kept to themselves, no one asked too much of you.

The old woman would handle her grief. Of course, she would. There was no need to be alarmed at the silence. The silence was good. The silence meant nothing was expected of her.

Unless?

What if something had happened? It had been a heart problem with the son, that's what the dark-haired girl – Kitty – had said. What if the grief was too much for her? What if there had been an accident?

Nora checked another citation. The thought niggled at her. Perhaps the silence was not a good thing. Nora found herself listening for weeping. There was none. Surely there should be weeping of some sort? Surely? It was deathly silent. She tapped at her keyboard, moved an errant comma. Revisited an extended quotation and excised it judiciously. *Take that, Evans*, she thought, gleefully shredding her rival. But still there was no noise.

Silent as death, Nora thought. Silent as the grave. And then she stopped herself, but failed to find a simile that did not send a chill down her spine.

She would have to check.

Nora opened the door a crack – nothing – but this time she drifted out further into the hallway. Light from the sitting room spilled out across the bottom of the staircase. It had gone pitch black outside and Nora could still hear the wind clattering at the shutters. The noise it made was nothing so urgent as a howl, but rather a long keening note that went on and on, inhuman in its breathlessness.

She tiptoed down the stairs, all of her muscles tensed as if she might flee back up to the safety of her room at any moment. She forced herself to breathe, gripped and released the handrail. Carefully, she carried herself into the sitting room.

At first she did not see Mrs Moreland, she was sitting so still, almost as if she had been frozen in place, her eyes fixed firmly ahead and unblinking. Then Nora did and she almost gave a little shriek: she looked like a corpse, just sitting there.

Mrs Moreland turned slowly as if there were joints unloosening in every part of her. The movement felt mechanical, awful in its lethargy, and Nora took an instinctive step away when the older woman's gaze fell on her.

"I'm sorry," Nora said, "I've interrupted."

Mrs Moreland's mouth opened, her tongue touched the top of her teeth and lingered there. Then she spoke: "No, dear, of course not. Forgive me."

"I thought," Nora started. "Perhaps I would get something to eat? Just a sandwich or something, really." Yes. That seemed plausible. "I'll just run out and fetch something."

"Don't be silly," Mrs Moreland said. "No, I've got some canned beans in the cupboard. I'll heat them up for you, shall I? It won't be any trouble."

"Oh, I couldn't ask you to do that."

"Don't be silly," she repeated. "Come with me, Miss Higgins."

✳

Nora watched Mrs Moreland open the tin with a large can opener. The kitchen was very cramped. Nora had to stand quite close, close enough that she could smell the powdery lavender of her landlady. She kept her elbows pressed against her side, afraid to touch anything.

"Sean liked beans on toast."

Nora looked up, startled. She had been watching the old woman work the can opener: a clawed affair that had the look of a medieval torture device. It was amazing the old woman could manage it at all, she had to stab away at the can, her elbow flapping wildly in the air, her frail hands clearly not up to the task.

"He hasn't been here for some time, but every morning, it was always beans on toast, just how he liked it. I bought so many cans! Too much for one woman to eat, I suppose, but it shan't go to waste with you here."

"Sean was your son?"

Mrs Moreland looked at her sharply. But after a moment the gaze wetted and softened.

"I had him late in life. He was very much wished for. A very handsome man."

Slop went the beans onto the toast.

"You don't have a husband?" Mrs Moreland asked. Nora shook her head. She had dated a man briefly in her undergraduate days, but they had never gone much beyond the stage of holding hands. He had damp, bony hands—it had been like clutching a lobster! But when she had broken the thing off with him, he had wept and wept. Nora never understood why: she had been startled to learn he had such depth of feeling inside him.

"Sean would have liked you, I think. He liked pretty girls. You're very pretty, with those blue eyes of yours."

"Thank you," Nora said. The sharp edge of a shelf bearing jars of spice pressed into her spine painfully. There was no room for retreat.

"Those were his cousins. Kitty and Rose. Bright girls, and sweet in their own way, but they all expect such a show from me. Such grief, they expect, such showers of tears! But that's how the young people are, isn't it? All hysterics, no restraint. They loved him so much, Kitty in particular. She thinks she knows best. She thinks she knows what he would have wanted."

"Family can be tricky."

"But we'll show them, won't we?" Mrs Moreland chuckled. "I won't fall apart, no, I won't fall apart, no, I won't fall apart." Nora saw her knuckles whitening around the can opener. The sight sent a strange shudder through her. She pressed herself further into the shelf, but it did no good.

"I could show you pictures of him?"

No, Nora thought, *please no*. Mrs Moreland handed her the plate. "Listen," she said, "perhaps I could take this up to my room?"

"Of course," Mrs Moreland said, "I mean, it's a bit peculiar, isn't it? But, yes, I mean I don't see why not—" and her face began to shine "-like a party then? Like a slumber party? How American! Yes, that could be quite fun!"

"I mean-" The thought was intolerable! Nora retreated from the kitchen hastily. "I'm a bit ill, you see. The flight."

Mrs Moreland's face crumpled. "Yes, I see."

"I suppose, if you wanted?"

"No, better not." She turned away from Nora and began to clean up the crumbs.

"Goodnight then, Mrs Moreland."

"Goodnight, dear."

Nora learned to move like a mouse. She crept through the house, kept her door closed, slept with a mask on, woke early and came in late. She spent her days in the Duke Humphrey Reading Room, pouring over sheaves of unprinted correspondences of the eighteenth century elite: there were so many of them, such debris of history to sort through, but she knew that amongst them would be something—something overlooked, missed by her senior colleagues, by Evans and his lot— that would surely do the trick.

Her eyes swam. Her back ached. Her fingers took in a deep chill that stiffened them to dull instruments of wood. But on she pressed. She enjoyed the work for all its physical discomforts, enjoyed the sense of camaraderie in sitting amongst the other researchers, each in their own separate carrel, never speaking, never needing to, but sharing in the same endeavour nonetheless.

Nora managed to avoid Mrs Moreland for three days. The old woman must be busy, she expected. The family had visited several times. Nora could tell by the great mass of teacups and side plates she found in the drying rack.

All was silent until the third night. All was perfect until then, not a worry, not a care, just the worrying at that pile of letters, sorting through, discarding, chasing down signatures. Nothing at all from Mrs Moreland.

But on the third night, Nora woke very suddenly. There had been a noise.

"Where are you, oh, where are you?"

The old woman was hollering on the stairs.

"Where are you, where are you?"

And then: "Miss Higgins!"

Nora got out of bed. She threw a robe around herself and pawed at the light switch until the room was bright. Mrs Moreland was on the stairs. Nora could hear her. Normally Mrs Moreland walked as if she weighed nothing at all, but today her feet were loud as elephants.

"Oh, where?"

Nora came out of the room. "Here," she said. "Here I am."

"Miss Higgins! There you are!"

Mrs Moreland's eyes were glassy and lost. Her silver hair was flung loosely over her shoulders.

"I'm sorry, Miss Higgins, you must have been sleeping."

"I was," Nora said. She clutched the robe tighter about herself. The fireplace was letting in a dreadful chill. The wind knocked against the front door.

"I'm sorry, I'm so terribly sorry. I was afraid you were dead!"

Mrs Moreland did not move from the stairs. Her fist clutched along the railing, and she took a step upward.

"But, of course, it isn't you, is it? No. It's my Sean. Please. I'm sorry. I must have startled you, but you see I had this terrible dream that you were dead. That you had died in my house. Just expired, it was terrible, you were just cold and lifeless, lying there on the bed."

"I'm quite all right. Can I—" Nora searched for the protocol "-make you some tea?"

"No, dear, no. I'll just call Kitty. She said I must call her if there was a worry. I'll do that, shall I?"

"Of course," Nora said. She watched the old woman drift off, then turned, shivering terribly, and closed herself in the bedroom.

Kitty was waiting for her outside the Bodleian. Nora recognised her immediately—that pert mouth, that scowl—she had something of Mrs Moreland's features, a faint family resemblance. She was puffing hungrily at a cigarette. The smoke came up in little clouds that hung in the gloom.

"Miss Higgins," she called. "Over here."

"Kitty, is it?"

"Look, it isn't good for Auntie," she cut in, her voice tight and furious. "I can get you space at my college. I'm sure you'd much prefer that, wouldn't you?"

Nora felt an immediate distaste for the girl. Kitty was used to getting her way; that was clear. Nora had dealt with many girls like this in her undergraduate classes, girls pretty enough that they could coast by in most of their classes, girls who when they couldn't flirt, cajoled and threatened. It made Nora angry. She had seen girls like this with her male colleagues. She had seen these simpering, sneering creatures making eyes at the men, placing their slim little hands on their thighs. It was shocking. Absolutely shocking. Not that the girls tried, who could blame them? Nora could understand calculation. Nora could understand how you might make a choice to do something distasteful – it was a choice after all. What she couldn't understand was that, with most of them, it wasn't all calculation. There wasn't *enough* calculation, not enough thought. Even in their seductions was a certain messiness, a lack of rigour.

"No," Nora said firmly.

"Be reasonable."

"Does your aunt want me to go?"

"She doesn't know her own mind. She's not well."

"So she hasn't said I ought to leave?"

"No," the dark-haired girl said through gritted teeth. "She likes you."

"Then."

Now the girl looked desperate. She sucked away furiously at the cigarette, the red tip glowing, ash flying off in great white flakes.

"Auntie is old, of course she wants someone around. But it shouldn't be you, that's what I'm saying. It shouldn't be *you*. It should be someone who cares for her and can take care of the arrangements."

"I'm sure she can take care of them herself."

"No, *listen*, it's too much for an old woman. She'll be lonely, and-" Kitty let the cigarette fall to the ground, then trampled it with her toe on the cobblestones. She seemed close to tears. Nora had seen that trick too. They always thought they could shame you into seeing them as weak, giving them what she wanted.

"What?"

"You aren't part of the family! What do you care about her? Tell me that, what do you care about her? Do you care enough, that's what I want to know? Does she even matter to you?" Kitty clutched dangerously at her arm, and Nora recoiled in shock.

"Don't you dare touch me! Don't you dare! I'll call the police!"

"No," Kitty said, wiping at her eyes, smearing her mascara. "No, I can see quite clearly how things are. She's just an old woman to you—and Sean? You didn't even know him! How could he possibly mean anything to you? But that's fine, if that's the way you want it. There's no need for such bullying. I only wanted to help."

"Help yourself then," Nora said, turning away from the girl. "I don't need it."

✻

When Nora got home, still shaking from the encounter, she felt a strange sense of rage at the presumption of the girl. The feel of her hand on the wrist, fingers tight. It was shocking behaviour, absolutely shocking! Touching as easily as that. She was like one of the disgusting girls from the hostel, ready to make love to whomever she found simply because. Because, because, because. Because it was easy, that's why! Because they could! Because they *liked* it!

Nora hated the nerve of the girl.

"Mrs Moreland!" she called, taking off her shoes. "Mrs Moreland! Oh, there you are."

The old woman had appeared at the top of the stairs.

"Of course, dear, now what's the matter?"

Nora opened her mouth to speak, but another idea came to her. She abandoned her original course of action. "I thought, perhaps-" she forced a wide smile "—you might like some company?"

"Why, yes, that would be splendid."

Mrs Moreland stepped quickly down the stairs and disappeared into the kitchen, appearing a moment later with a tray loaded with a teapot, cups and biscuits.

"I've just been tending to Sean's affairs," she said. "He left quite a lot of them. It haunts me so! He was a messy boy, you know. But I miss him, I really do. I can't bear to think about him shut up in a box underground."

"Where did he live?" Nora asked, trying to divert the subject. She smiled again, kept the smile, all curious politeness, fixed and ready.

"Oh, in America. He left to go to school there."

"Was he a good student?"

"The very best."

"That's important, you know," Nora said. "So many young people neglect their studies. Freedom doesn't suit them."

She thought of Kitty with her cigarette. Her haughty air. Her casually fashionable clothing. Her hand on Nora's wrist.

"He was very thoughtful. Just like you, Miss Higgins. You seem quite thoughtful. Very pretty. He would have liked you, I think. Here's the tea now, mind you blow on it."

"Thank you."

They sat in silence for several minutes. Nora blew on her tea. It was much too sweet.

"I wonder—" Mrs Moreland began. She clutched her cup with both hands.

"Yes?"

"I don't want to trouble you."

Nora's smile widened. She would be entirely solicitous. She would be entirely helpful. She would make this little old granny feel perfectly comfortable, perfectly comforted. That would show the girl, always trying to make trouble. She knew the type. But Nora would show her. She let Mrs Moreland take her hand. She let her clutch at it with those knobbly old fingers of hers even though it half-revolted her to do so.

"It's just, well, if perhaps you wouldn't mind coming to my room with me?"

"Of course, Mrs Moreland. Whatever you need."

The old woman creaked up the stairs. Nora followed after her, past her own room, down the hallway. She had never come this far inside the house before. She had kept to her own little corner. But perhaps that was wrong. Perhaps she should have been more sociable. Perhaps she should have made an effort. Mrs Moreland was sweet. She had clearly taken a liking to Nora. And she must be so sad, so terribly, terribly sad. Nora could imagine that sadness. She felt light-headed just thinking about it.

Positively light-headed.

Nora followed Mrs Moreland into the bedroom. It was much like Nora's, a narrow single bed, cream carpets, the whole place maintained perfectly, and there sitting in the centre of it: an enormous black coffin.

"Oh my," said Nora. It had the wet shine of an expensive car recently polished.

"Sean's come home today. They sent Sean home to me."

Nora said nothing. She stared. It looked so absurd in the tiny room, like finding a loaded gun amidst the tea cosies.

"But they've sealed him up, you see," Mrs Moreland said.

Nora took a step toward the coffin. She felt the strangest urge to touch it. To see her breath mist up the finely polished surface. To see her fingerprints like little round pebbles on the black.

When had the moving men brought him in? Had it been while she was out? And who would deliver such a thing?

"They've sealed him up so very tightly. And I must see his face."

Nora bumped up against a little wooden chair. But Mrs Moreland was behind her now, Nora could feel her very close, there was nowhere to go but in. In and in and in.

"Would you help me, Miss Higgins?"

Now Mrs Moreland was pressing something into her hand. Something cold and hard. Nora looked down and she felt like laughing, it was ridiculous, it was a can opener from the kitchen, that giant clawed beast! Nora looked closer at the coffin and she could see a thin strip of something like rubber running along the inner margin of the casket.

"My arthritis, you see," Mrs Moreland said, and Nora could see, could see where Mrs Moreland had begun the work. Where the teeth of the can opener had bit into the polish and begun to cut through the sealant. Of course the old woman hadn't been able to make much more of a mark. Nora had seen her with the can of beans. She'd barely been able to punch through a flimsy piece of tin, it was ridiculous!

"I can't help you," Nora said faintly. "I can't. Please." But Mrs Moreland was close behind her, that powdery lavender smell filling up her nostrils. She was nauseated, drowsy. A giddy numbness was climbing up her spine.

"But you understand, don't you?" Mrs Moreland said. "I knew that the moment I saw you. You know what loneliness is, don't you, Miss Higgins? You know what it means to have been alone for a very long time?"

"No," said Nora.

"You do, I can see it about you. It doesn't even matter that you aren't family. Kitty wanted to help, she was so close to him, you see, but she didn't understand properly. You're a kindred spirit, aren't you?"

"No," said Nora again.

But then she hesitated. Because she did understand, didn't she? She *did* understand—better than Kitty, better than anyone, what it was like to feel that lonely. To crave loneliness, and to hate it as well, to want to be touched, to fear to be touched. Nora felt the can opener moving in her hand, as if by accident, as if the motion was automatic. And at first it was automatic, like she had no control at all, but then she was leaning in close to the coffin. She was digging the teeth into the metal.

"I know what it's like for your type, I've housed so many of you! All of you squirreling away in your rooms, scribbling away in those dark libraries! You're all the same, as quiet as little mice!"

The can opener was moving, moving, and turning ever so slowly. And it was hard. The metal stubbornly resisted. Nora had to work at it. She had to shove her weight behind it. She was gasping, panting with the effort. Her fingers cramped and twitched. There was blood on her wrist from where the jagged metal of the coffin bit into her skin. And perhaps it took hours, it *felt* like it was hours, but she turned the screw, and she turned it again, and she turned it again until she could see the trail it left behind, the way the lips of the coffin were opening up to her like an enormous mouth.

"This is what you want, isn't it?" Mrs Moreland asked. Her voice was kind, she was really a very sweet old lady. And Nora couldn't help but find herself nodding along.

"Do you feel tired, Miss Higgins?"

"I do feel tired," she said. Her hands were heavy and bruised. Her Mount of Venus ached from the imprint of the handle. Nora stared at the coffin, stared at the reflection of herself in it. The black line cut across the surface, like it had been gnawed by teeth. Like it had been cut open by a lobster claw. And wasn't that a strange thought! Nora wanted to laugh.

"I know you feel tired, Miss Higgins. You must. But it's all right, dear. I'll take care of the rest."

"Good," Nora said. There was blood running down her wrist, dripping off her index finger. "Thank you. That's really very kind."

And the lid was lifting up very slowly. Mrs Moreland was huffing and puffing, throwing all of her tiny, fragile frame into the effort of opening that lid. Then—there, it was open! And inside it wasn't black at all, it was white, a pure white satin.

And, of course, there lay Sean, nestled cosily on the pillows. He had been a handsome boy, Mrs Moreland was right. And perhaps he looked like Kitty, but he was so much *cleaner* than Kitty was. He had a broad forehead, and such pink lips. So lifelike, even now. Like they might tremble and open.

And Nora felt tired. Her eyelids drifted. Opening them took quite a lot of work. It was a Herculean task, but she did it. And there was Sean again. Handsome Sean.

"You don't want to be alone, do you, Miss Higgins?" Mrs Moreland asked. "Not such a pretty girl as you?"

"No," she said, "please."

"Of course," Mrs Moreland said. "Of course, dear. It's very easy now."

Nora climbed up onto the chair slowly. It wobbled underneath her but held firm. Really, it was just like that hostel, wasn't it? Climbing up those rungs? But this would be nice. The air was cool, not stagnant as it had been there, in that awful place.

"In you go, dear. In you go."

And it would be quiet, wouldn't it?

And there wouldn't be all that touching. All that noise. Those damp, eager hands touching her. Those thick Italian voices, so full of passion.

It would be just as she wanted it.

She lay herself down. She could feel the cold body pressed against her—Sean, the handsome son—but she didn't mind, it didn't seem to matter so much. She was so very, very tired.

And the lid came down.

And the darkness.

She would be safe here. She would be happy here.

Her eyelids drifted shut. She let herself relax at last, her whole body slack and nerveless.

Good, she thought. *Yes. Just like that. I'll go to sleep now.*

But something was wrong. It was warm in here. It should be cold in a coffin but now it felt warm, so very warm, stiflingly so. The hot air seemed to choke her. Nora pressed against the lid but there was no give, none at all. And the heat began to rise, and there was nowhere to move, she didn't want to disturb Sean, she didn't want to writhe around in that narrow, narrow space. She wouldn't. She would stay perfectly still. She would let the warm air flush her neck, glowing on her cheeks, and she would do her very best to ignore it: the sound of someone breathing beneath her.

SLAPE
Tom Fletcher

"Them stones are slape as fuck." He gestured at the slabbed path. "Went over on them last week."

Eel was much bigger than the rest of us and could hold three full milk bottles in each hand, their necks gripped tightly between his sausage fingers. He'd been carrying six bottles in such a fashion when he'd slipped—'slape' meaning 'slippery', I realised—and he'd landed on them, on his hands. His feet had gone out from beneath him, he'd put his hands out to break his fall, and—smash. Milk and blood everywhere. The round bottle necks had driven right up into his palms. He'd shown me the wounds later, back at the yard, laughing. We'd been standing by his van, and the steering wheel and door handle were all dripping with blood. The boss had been furious, because another worker had had a similar accident the month before—really, it happened a lot, especially in spring, when paths and driveways were green with moss, and the showers were heavy—and that worker had severed several tendons. But then, he'd been returning to the van with empties. And everybody knows how milkmen carry empties—with their fingers right inside the bottles. (You can carry up to ten that way, to save time). Also, he was only twenty-one, and his hands were very soft and vulnerable. Whereas Eel was in his sixties and had worked outside all his life, so he had thick skin, literally.

The stones that Eel warned me about were slate slabs forming a narrow, uneven path through a wild thicket of brambles and nettles. It was also covered in broken glass by that point, because Eel hadn't bothered to clean up the aftermath of his accident, and neither had the owner of the property—our customer. This path, these stones slape as fuck, led us from the van to the customer's back door.

Eel was teaching me the round, because he was leaving the company. I didn't know why and I didn't much care. I didn't like the man. I was glad he was going. I just wished that it didn't mean spending two weeks in a van with him as he showed me the route.

After he'd gone, I didn't think about him except when I was delivering milk to that one particular customer; the one with the particularly slippery path. Even then, it wasn't so much that I *thought* about him; it was more as if I heard his voice. I heard him say the words 'slape as fuck' every time I stood at the first of those stones.

As I got to know the round, and memorised which customers had which milk on which days, and how much, and I learned where to park the van to minimise walking time, and I familiarised myself with a frankly bewildering variety of garden gate latches, I became quicker, which meant that I arrived at any given customer's property earlier. As summer became autumn and the days grew shorter, more and more of my round was completed in darkness. Eventually, of course, this meant tackling the slippery path before dawn. That in itself didn't bother me. But the first time the words 'slape as fuck' came to me from out of the impenetrable blackness of that wild and overgrown garden, I nearly had a seizure. For the first time, they felt real and audible; not like the memory that they were. If I wasn't sensible enough to carry the milk bottles in a crate, I probably would have dropped them all. I think that because it was so dark—because I couldn't see that he *wasn't* there—I felt as if Eel was actually present. I wondered, for the first time, if he'd died immediately upon leaving the company and his ghost was lurking around trying to scare his old co-workers.

On that occasion I delivered the milk without further incident.

I should tell you a little more about this customer. His name was Bacon. He was a widower. All those spring and summer months, I never saw him. His house had once been the parish workhouse, and it still looked like a workhouse. It was large and grey and forbidding. It was set back from the road and had a wall around it. Both inside and outside of the wall was a deep sea of brambles. Driving down the long lane towards it, you'd see the wrecks of old cars submerged in that sea. Eel told me, before he left, that every car Bacon had ever owned was in there somewhere. Whenever he bought a new car, he just parked the old one up and left it. There were at least three old Jaguars and an MG being pulled apart by those plants. And close up to the house, it was evident that he didn't care about the building much more than he did about his old cars. It was tired-looking and it smelled bad. It was overrun by cats, and in the back porch—where I left the milk—there were several bowls of meaty cat food too rotten and writhing for even animals to eat.

Sometimes, I'd find a fire burning in the lane, or even just amongst the brambles. Piles of cardboard boxes, old newspapers and magazines and even books, all just left out burning in the sun, unattended. It was as if Bacon wanted the house to get burned down. Once, a fire was burning on the slippery path itself. I had to hold my breath and jump over it, holding a crate of full milk bottles. Well, obviously, I didn't. I could've left Bacon's milk at the end of the path. But I didn't want to risk pissing him off, because he might complain, and that would mean I'd piss the boss off. And that was a far scarier prospect than setting fire to my jeans. The boss was in a terrible mood, generally, because severed-tendon man was taking a long time to finish his round these days, and we were paid by the hour. I was pretty sure that severed-tendon man would be getting the sack soon, and replaced by somebody faster. But anyway; sometimes it seemed like Bacon didn't even want his fucking milk delivered, it was so difficult to get to the actual porch.

All of which is to say that by the time I was delivering in darkness, the place was already creeping me out.

On the third dark morning, the moon and stars were intermittently obscured by clouds, and I could see very little. I ignored the 'slape as fuck', telling myself that however much it sounded real, it was obviously only a memory, a thought, something interior to me, and nothing to be afraid of. And I took the path slowly.

I crouched down to place the full milk bottles in the gloomy, stinking workhouse porch and reload my crate with empties. There were lots—Bacon got a lot of milk—and they were crusty and unwashed. I noticed light reflecting from the glass; the clouds must have shifted again, letting the moon shine through. I was glad. But then, as I stood, I noticed that the door to the house proper was slightly open, and that there was a face in that shadowed gap, peering at me. The moonlight caught on two big eyes, and on a row of big, yellow teeth, perfectly even, and shaped like a smile. They were the upper teeth. I recoiled against the porch wall. How long had he been there? Bacon, if this was he, did not speak, and neither did I. He maintained his smile. His mouth was slightly open, but I couldn't see his lower teeth. I wondered if he was wearing dentures, and if they were fitted incorrectly. He had deep creases running straight down from the corners of his wide mouth. He looked utterly delighted about something. I couldn't speak. I was frozen. I don't know how long we stood like that. Then, the clouds came back, and the door was closing, and his face—smile unchanged—was hidden from view.

I ran at full speed from that doorway then, rain splattering my face. And of course, on the very last of them slape-as-fuck stones, I slipped. I slipped hard. My feet flew backwards and my face flew forwards. For a brief, hopeful moment, I thought that I might flip right over, three hundred and sixty degrees, and land on my feet again. But I performed only half such a manoeuvre. I tried to break my fall with my hands, but my hands were holding a crate of empty milk bottles. The crate landed on top of my fingers and my face landed in the crate. One bottleneck aligned perfectly with my right eye socket. Glass, bone, skin and cartilage all broke. My knuckles broke. I lay there, shattered, and I was conscious of that face peering at me from out of the darkness once more, still grinning, and fat fingers trying to turn me over.

The boss was not going to be very happy about this, I thought, as I was being dragged away. I was going to become really very slow. And probably too expensive.

THE NIGHT DOCTOR
Steve Rasnic Tem

Elaine said the walk would be good for them both. "We don't get enough meaningful exercise these days. Besides, we might meet some of the new neighbours." Sam couldn't really argue with that, but he couldn't bring himself to agree, so he nodded, grunted. Although his arthritis was worse than ever, as if his limbs were grinding themselves into immobility, it hurt whether he moved them or not, so why not move?

He would have preferred waiting until they were more comfortable in the neighbourhood—they'd been there less than a week. Until he had seen a few friendly faces, until he could be sure of their intentions. People here kept their curtains open most of the time. He supposed that was meant to convince passersby of their trusting nature, but he didn't like it. Someday you might see something you didn't want to see. You might misinterpret something. Since they'd moved in he'd glanced into those other windows from time to time—and seen shiny spots back in the darkness, floating lights with no apparent source, oddly shaped shadows he could not quite identify and didn't want to think about. He was quite happy not knowing the worst about other people's lives. He could barely tolerate the worst about his own.

Not that he had justification for much complaint. He'd always known the worst was somewhere just out of reach, so it shouldn't have affected him. Like most people, he supposed. Human beings had a natural sense for it, the worst that was just beyond the limits of their own lives. The worst that was still to come.

What with one minor annoyance or another—finding pants that didn't make him look fat, determining what pair of shoes might hurt his feet the least, deciding on the correct degree of layering that wouldn't make him wish he'd worn something else as the day wore on—they didn't leave the new house until almost eleven. Sam worried about getting his lunch on time. If he didn't get his lunch on time his body felt off the rest of the day.

"I'll buy you some crackers at the drug store if you need them," she said. "Don't fret about it."

"Crackers? What kind of meal is that? You're always saying I should eat healthier."

"For heaven's sake, Sam, let it go. Crackers to tide you over. Wheat, something like that. A lot of small meals are better for you anyway. That's the way the cave people ate—they grazed all the time."

"Cave people," he repeated, as if reading some absurd road sign. He didn't say anything more. He didn't want to whine like Bryan, thirty-four years old and he still whined like a little boy. They'd done something terribly wrong for Bryan to be that way, but Sam still had no idea what it was. Parenting was a mystery, like diet, like exercise, like how to still keep feeling good about yourself in this world.

Sam felt uncomfortable most of the time. Physically, certainly. And as much as it annoyed him to think about it, emotionally as well. A walking mass of illogic, and that was no way to be.

After they left the house they turned onto the long lane that meandered through the neighbourhood. When he realised how long the street was, and how far away they were from the tiny mall—not so bad if you were driving, but Sam had stopped driving two years ago—he felt on the verge of tears. Just like some kind of toddler. Humiliating.

As they were starting out a large black bird landed in the street beside him. It threw its head back, shuddering, something struggling in its mouth. Sam glanced at his wife to see if she had noticed this. But her eyes were fixed forward, and he decided not to mention it. He twisted his head around to look at the bird. Still there. Was it a crow? It looked too big to be a blackbird. In fact it might be the biggest bird he'd ever seen up close. Its beak was so sharp. It could take your eyes out and there was nothing you could do about it, it would happen so quickly. Just like they were grapes.

His knees were hurting already. There were tears in his eyes, but at least they weren't yet running down his cheeks. Birds didn't cry. He should be like the birds.

He wasn't sure how it had come to this—he'd always been such an optimist. And he'd always been healthy—no, it was too late in life to exaggerate—relatively healthy. But relatively healthy still meant you could drop dead at any time. So he walked around sore much of the time, each step like a needle in his heels and a crumbling in his knees, and attempted to think about everything but death.

They passed another older couple. Elaine would have said "elderly" but Sam hated that word. Elaine smiled at them and said hello. The couple nodded and said hello back. They had already passed the couple when Sam managed to speak his delayed "nice day!" The man said "oh, yes," awkwardly turning his head to Sam in order to be polite, but staggering a little, almost falling off the curb. Sam could feel the warmth flooding his face. He'd caused that distraction, and the resulting stumble.

"We should have introduced ourselves," Elaine said a few minutes later. "They may have been neighbours." Sam hoped the couple didn't recognise him the next time they met. "Sam, did you hear me?"

"Of course I heard you, you're right here."

"Then why didn't you say something?"

"I don't know. I didn't know it needed answering, I guess."

"I don't talk just to hear myself."

"Maybe they're not neighbours. Maybe they're just passing through, taking a walk. They might live several blocks away—they look pretty healthy. They could probably walk that far."

"Uh huh," she said, her head down, walking a little faster. It hurt to try to keep up with her. *Too late*. That's what she would have said if he asked her what was wrong, so he didn't. She deserved better— he didn't understand how he'd gotten so fuzzy-headed. There was probably a pill for that, something to erase a certain percentage of your thoughts, clear out some space so you could pay better attention to the people you loved. So much for the benefits of exercise. Sam was feeling worse and worse.

By the time they reached the drug store Sam was ravenous. He sat on the padded bench and devoured two packets of crackers while Elaine got her many prescriptions. He'd already filled his last week before they moved. The lady across from him frowned. He looked around—he was spraying cracker crumbs everywhere. He didn't know what to do—he couldn't very well get down on his hands and knees right there in the store and sweep them up. He closed his eyes so he wouldn't see either the lady or the crumbs and continued to eat.

When he was small his mother would drag him all over town on her errands. She took him along even if he was sick, but that was just what you had to do when you were a single mother. The worse he felt the more clothing she put on him; he supposed it was meant as a kind of protection. Sometimes he'd get so hot his head would swim. She'd sit him down somewhere in a chair, or in the shopping cart, or even in some out-of-the-way corner of the floor and let him nap. He'd dream he was a bug in a cocoon, waiting to be someone else. That night she'd reward him with a long bath before he went to bed.

"Sleep is what you need," she'd say, stroking his forehead. "Go to sleep and let the night doctor take care of you."

Over the years he'd tried to make some sense out of it. Plentiful sleep, of course, was bound to help, to lower stress, to permit the body to bring its own healing. However it worked, he almost always felt better the next day. He didn't even have to wait until the day arrived, he could take a nap in the middle of the day, and then the night doctor could come. The night doctor didn't necessarily require night, he simply required that you be asleep so that he could properly do his business on you. All that was needed was that it be nighttime inside your head.

Had he really believed that the night doctor was an actual person? He'd never believed in magic, exactly—a person or a thing had to act, had to do something. So as a child he'd believed in Santa Claus because he was a person, sort of, this larger-than-life thing, an *agency*. He didn't believe in the Easter Bunny because he knew a kid who had a rabbit who'd smelled and bitten him once.

It had been oddly reassuring, and yet not reassuring at all. Because if Santa were a person, then he was fallible. He could be late, or if you moved he might not find your house. The same with the night doctor. And he had had proof—he'd once visited his grandparents for two weeks and he'd been sick the whole time. The night doctor obviously couldn't find him.

It had all been a great cause for anxiety. The fact that no one but his mother ever talked about the night doctor had only made it worse— he'd never even seen a picture of the man. Or woman, or whatever.

"Sam, darling? Are you ready to go?"

He blinked. Elaine was looking down at him, smiling. Had he overslept? Suddenly he felt lost, outside his body and not quite knowing the way back in.

"I fell . . ." He yawned. "I fell asleep waiting. Sorry."

"You must have needed it," she said, helping him to his feet. "I'm sorry, sweetheart. Maybe I've pushed you too hard today."

"Exercise is good for me. I don't get enough," he said, moving slowly with her arm in his as they rocked their way down the aisle, Elaine's bag full of pill bottles rattling at her hip. He willed the blood to flow; his feet were numb. By the time they got out of the store they were better, he could feel them tingling. He supposed the day would eventually come when they didn't get better, when they didn't start tingling but remained as dead as fallen logs. But not today, thank God. Not today.

It was strangely dim outside, and Sam wondered if they could have been there at the pharmacy all day. How long had he been asleep? Then he realised it was simply the clouds rolling in, and he hoped they could get home before it rained. He never liked getting rained on, not even as a child. He usually got sick afterwards. There must have been something in the rain, not just water.

They were at the highest point in the road, the remainder of the neighbourhood receding gradually below them. Had they really climbed such a hill? Maybe they were lost—they didn't know the neighbourhood well. They could wander for hours and not find their way back. Sam gazed around in a futile search for recognisable landmarks. But he had no landmarks in his memory for their new home.

From here they had a clear view of the afternoon sky. The clouds were heavy, laden—it might begin raining at any moment. The dark shapes of birds were darting in and out between the banks of clouds as if knitting them together. Sam thought of the giant bird he'd seen earlier and wondered if these were more of the same. They appeared to be rising up from the roofs of the neighbourhood where they'd been resting, rushing up to join the others as if in collusion.

Then he saw that larger dark shape depart an upstairs window of one of the houses, climbing onto the sill like a suicide, but leaping up instead of down, rising with a swirl of its long dark coat, the bag trailing from the skinny fingers of one hand, more claws than fingers, as the figure attempted to blend in with those other flying shapes.

Sam couldn't be sure, they were too far away, but that figure seemed so very familiar. As if sensing Sam's attention the head of the thing turned back an instant over its shoulder, large eyes staring, narrow face so pale and long as a blade.

Although he didn't intend to, Sam sat down on the sidewalk then, his knees giving way. Elaine yelled in alarm as he almost dragged her down with him. He heard the panic in her voice as she screamed for someone to help them. But there was nothing he could do, as he was too busy elsewhere. Sixteen years old and walking home in the dark from the movie with his friends. He'd just left them to turn in to his own front walk, the darkness denser now because of the trees that used to shade their lawn.

His mother had been ill for several weeks, keeping to her bed except to feed him his meals and prepare his lunch for school. At times like these he'd think a father would have been useful, for her if not for him, because she had to do everything, and Sam was very aware he did not appreciate her nearly enough. But a father had never been more than a story as far as he was concerned, a few photographs that might not actually have been the man. How could he know for sure?

As he was walking up the sidewalk he felt a change in the air. It wasn't a smell, although he felt it in his nose. It was more like a heaviness had entered the space around him, a pressure increasing in his ears, his nose, his skull, and a strong sense of vertigo as if he were looking down from a very high place.

He glanced up, cowering, feeling as if the sky were about to slide down on top of him. His mother's bedroom window was open, her twin pale curtains reaching outside the frame to the night beyond like a frantic signal. Something membranous and black flapped. He could hear her moaning from where he stood, or thought he could.

Sam ran into the house and up the stairs. He came to her door and stopped because he was afraid. He thought he should knock—she would be furious if he went inside without knocking, but that didn't apply in this case, did it? Even the memory made him feel ashamed, and he could hear Elaine's voice somewhere above him attempting to offer some comfort.

He eased open the door even as the figure crouched over his mother was mucking about with her bare torso, taking something from her, sliding some spidery thing that struggled and screamed soundlessly out of her side and into his leathery dark bag. Sam cried out and the night doctor turned his head slightly to look at him with those cold pale eyes, those wet globes glistening yellow from the dim light in the hall, and that oh so elongated face which made no sense, the lower bit coming down into a kind of open snout, the upper half curved into a kind of bony blade. Before Sam could say anything else the night doctor had slid off the bed and through the window into the night and wind with a flap flap flap and a drawn out sigh.

For days she seemed better, and Sam had begun to think the creature had simply removed the thing that had done her harm. And then his mother took a turn for the worse. And then she was gone.

And next he woke up an old man again, in the bedroom he shared with the wife who took care of him now, who'd been taking care of him since the first day they'd met back in college. The bed stand was covered with his pills, or hers, he couldn't really tell anymore.

He could barely remember the names of the pills. Not because he couldn't, but because he didn't want to be that interested.

"Sam, you scared me half to death."

He shifted his head around and saw Elaine's grey face there floating within the darkened chair, propped up by a pillow under the back of her head. The rest of the room was so deeply in shadow he wondered if his eyes were going, then saw the dark in the window and realised it was night. The window was open, the curtains stirring, beginning to flap. He held his breath and twisted his head, trying to examine the room. Things stirred there beyond his ability to actually see them, and he tried to blame it on the wind and his anxiety. "How long have you been sitting there?" he asked, trying not to search the room anymore.

"A few hours. You missed dinner. Do you want something?"

"I don't know." Was he hungry? He made himself sit up in bed. His right leg hurt—he recognised the feeling. He must have been asleep for a while, his right leg pinched beneath his left. "I really missed dinner?"

"It's been about six hours. I decided to let you sleep. Sam, do you remember anything? I thought you'd had a heart attack at first, the way you just collapsed, like you'd been hit on top of the head or something."

"I just . . . just had a moment I guess. What, did I black out? How did you get me home?"

"That couple came by, the one we ran into earlier? The Hernandezes. You don't remember? Apparently they live only three houses down. He ran back to their house and pulled his car around, they helped you into the seat, and after we got here he helped me get you into bed. I kept wanting to call the doctor but you insisted you were okay, that you just needed to rest, but that you didn't want to fall asleep."

Sam did remember some of this, but it was like an imperfectly recalled dream. He couldn't explain the lapse, which was disturbing. But he'd been distracted, hadn't he? It seemed he hadn't thought about his mother's death in years. "But you still let me sleep?"

"I couldn't keep you awake if I tried! You were so tired you could barely lift your head."

So he had slept. He couldn't stop himself from searching the room with his eyes again, straining himself, his chest beginning to hurt. He was being a whiny thing. He was going to make himself sick. It would be an open invitation for the doctor to slip in and meddle with his insides. He made himself stop, even though promising details were resolving out of the dark as his eyes adjusted.

"Sounds pretty embarrassing. I'm sorry, I don't know what came over me." Maybe he was better, maybe the doctor had already done his work. He could only hope it didn't cost him too dearly. "Did they, the Hernandezes, did they say anything?"

"Just how concerned they were. Janet and Felix. I told Felix you take blood pressure medication and he wondered if the dosage might be wrong. I'll call Doctor Castro tomorrow and tell him what happened."

You don't know what happened, he thought, but left it unsaid. "Of course. But this is all backwards. You should be the one resting. I'm putting all this extra stress on you." He glanced at the sea of medicines on her side of the bed. There were new bottles, he thought, the ones from today.

"I'm fine. We're not our illnesses, Sam. That's what you always say, remember? We're much more than that."

He couldn't quite interpret her tone. Had there been resentment in the way she'd quoted him? "I could use a ham sandwich, I think," he said.

"Fine." She got up and started toward the door, then stopped, smiled. "And if you're better tomorrow, I've invited them over for dinner."

"What?"

"Janet and Felix. The Hernandezes. They'll be our first dinner guests."

After she closed the door behind her he glanced at the shadowed incomprehensibility of the room and rolled over, turned his back to it. He'd allow himself to be healed or taken, and at the moment he wasn't sure he cared which. He waited a long time, but nothing occurred.

✳

He did feel better when he woke up the next day, although tired and a bit on edge. The room felt empty, however. He could hear Elaine in the next room running the vacuum cleaner. When the noise stopped he heard her singing. It had been a while since he'd heard her singing. He smelled disinfectant, furniture polish. He glanced around – all their medicine bottles were gone.

"Elaine!"

She came running, out of breath. She grabbed the footboard and leaned over. "Are you . . . okay?" She wheezed, paused, then asked more steadily, "Are you still ill?"

"No, no, I'm fine. You shouldn't have run, honey. Where are all the medicines?"

"The Hernandezes may want to see the house, and it hasn't had a really good cleaning yet."

"But the medicines?"

"I put the over the counter stuff in our respective bathroom cabinets, depending on who uses what the most. The prescriptions, and the supplements— since we don't take the same—are in a box in each bathroom closet. But I took out a week's worth of dosages and put them into two of those weekly pill organizers—his and hers. I even split the ones that needed it into quarters and halves."

"But why? Do you want them to believe we're the super healthy older couple or something?"

"No, but I don't want them to think the opposite, either. And it was just too much—I started to realise that as I tidied up. It needed to be handled—we're both lucky we didn't grab the wrong pills one day, or even overdose. It looked— I don't know—it didn't make us look like sick people so much as crazy people."

In the bathroom Sam found the pill dispenser (blue, hers was probably pink) and took his daily dose. He pulled off his T-shirt and examined his pale torso. He wasn't sure what he was looking for, some kind of markings. Cuts or worn places, incisions or maybe even bite or chew marks. There was nothing definitive, but when had he gotten so pale? He looked almost slug-like in parts.

Elaine cleaned well into the afternoon, then she started cooking. Sam didn't like the dark half-moons under her eyes. He stepped in with the cleaning, although he suspected he didn't do it well, scrubbing obsessively in some areas and neglecting others. Before dinner he did a final sweep, jammed some random flowers from the backyard into a vase, and set the table. By this point he desperately didn't want to interact with anyone new, but he understood they were fully committed now.

From the time the Hernandezes arrived the evening became a blur for him. They seemed like perfectly nice people but he didn't understand a thing they were talking about.

It seemed that Felix Hernandez had just acquired a new car, one of those boxy affairs with a small body and high ceiling. He used it to drive to the golf course, another habit newly acquired. Janet Hernandez talked endlessly about their son, an apparently always well-meaning young man who could not hold a job. Elaine commiserated and shared stories about Bryan which Sam was sure he had heard nothing about. A fall from a tree? When had that happened? Could Elaine possibly be making these things up in order to have something to share with the new neighbours?

They sat down girl-boy-girl-boy about an L-shaped portion of the dinner table, with Sam at the top of the L's stem and Elaine at the end of the L's arm. Sam wasn't sure how this had happened, but it seemed to have been Felix's idea.

Janet Hernandez was sitting next to Sam. He hadn't realised before how tall she was—at least her torso was tall. She also seemed to have an unusually large head, although that might have been an illusion because her forehead was quite high, and white hair showered down the back of the skull to float just above her shoulders. She leaned forward over her food somewhat, as if afraid it might escape the plate. And she trembled slightly. He noticed because she was sitting right beside him. The profile of her face practically vibrated.

Sam was thinking then that the Hernandezes were older than them by a few years. He looked down the table, but his view of Felix was completely blocked. He tried to catch Elaine's eye, but she was leaning over slightly, probably talking to Felix.

Suddenly Janet leaned back, her face pale, her expression puzzled. Felix seemed blurry and out of focus on the other side, but then Sam determined that something between Felix and Janet was making him difficult to see, something smearing the air, as if Sam's vision had suddenly gone greasy.

The night doctor appeared to unfold from inside that black leathery coat of his, his shoulders going up like axe blades. He turned one globular eye Sam's way. He tilted his elongated head slightly as if inviting Sam to protest. Sitting this closely Sam could see small finger-shaped bits of flesh down around the end of the doctor's snout. They stirred slightly. Some appeared corrupted by some sort of skin cancer.

Sam felt suddenly ill, his head slipping sideways. The night doctor disappeared, and Sam now had a clear view of Felix, who appeared to be in shock. Elaine was shaking the man's shoulder in concern, saying his name. Then Sam moved his head again, and the night doctor was back in focus. Sam experimented, moving his head this way and that. He could see the doctor only at certain angles, the rest of the time the figure disappearing completely.

Suddenly Felix coughed explosively and a pale chunk of chewed-up food—at first Sam was convinced it was some damaged organ— bounced off the table and onto the floor. Sam thought he heard the cat scramble for it, then remembered they hadn't had a cat in years.

Felix was laughing, tears rolling down his cheeks. Elaine was laughing as well, but Sam recognised it as the laugh she made when she was under great stress. Any minute now she would sob. Janet was pushing something around her plate with her fork. Sam saw that it was another piece of what had just come out of Felix's mouth.

A sidelong glance brought the night doctor into focus again. He sat still and erect, as if listening, or at least sensing, things Sam couldn't even begin to imagine. The night doctor's skin was soft and translucent, slightly yellow. Sam thought he could see the sharp skeleton underneath, like a gathering of blades fashioned from bone and then covered in this somewhat transparent epidermal goop.

They all sat that way an uncomfortable period of time. Felix quietly shared his recent health issues with Elaine. Elaine shared things back, but with less detail. Janet continued to move things about her plate with her fork, but ate nothing. Sam watched them all. He wondered if he was the only one aware of the fifth presence at the dinner table – he was pretty sure he was.

Periodically the night doctor stroked the leather bag he wore hanging from his shoulder. It squirmed in various directions, as if containing more than one captive.

Felix was taken to the hospital a few days later. Sam and Elaine watched as Janet rode off with a young man Sam assumed was their son. They never saw any of them again.

For several weeks Elaine became increasingly frenetic. She cleaned the house constantly, and reorganised the medicine cabinets more than a few times. Sometimes Sam would wake up in the middle of the night and find the bed empty. He'd go downstairs and discover her at the table quietly drinking coffee or taking down notes. Usually the night doctor sat there with her.

Often she would work herself into exhaustion and sleep late the following morning. He would come downstairs by himself and find the night doctor already waiting for him, standing in a corner or staring out the window.

It dragged on this way for months. One night Elaine woke him up in the middle of the night, her pale face hanging over him. He gently lay his hand on her wet face—she'd been crying. "I don't want to leave you by yourself," she whispered hoarsely.

He glanced past her, his eyes scanning the room, finding the tall quiet figure with the large eyes and the too-narrow face, the squirming bag. "You won't be," Sam replied.

DULL FIRE
Gary McMahon

We lay naked in the lamplight for a long time after making love, not saying anything, just looking at each other, taking it all in. I was resting on my side, with my chin perched bird-like in the cup of my hand and my elbow pressed against the hard mattress. She was reclining alongside me, staring without blinking into my eyes.

She reached out and touched my cheek, and then her steady finger traced a line down to the corner of my mouth, along the top of my lips, and back up again to my nose. She rubbed her fingertip up my nose and towards my forehead, following the crooked line.

"What happened?" she said, softly. "How did you do this? Was it a boxing injury?"

I shook my head, but didn't say anything.

"Did it happen when you were a kid?"

I nodded. "Yes."

"Tell me."

I closed my eyes and saw red behind the lids: the wavering glow of dull fire, like something ablaze in the distance. I'd been seeing it for a couple of weeks now. I wondered if it was some kind of prophetic vision or a sign that I had a brain tumour. When I opened my eyes again she was still there. She wasn't going anywhere, not this one. Every other woman I had known had left me for some reason or other—some of them genuine, others made up as an excuse. This woman, it seemed, was going to hang around.

"When I was eleven years old, my father punched me in the face and broke my nose."

She breathed in sharply, but she wasn't as shocked as I'd expected. "Why did he do that?" Her eyes shone in the dimness, eager to take in the details.

"My father was a violent man. He drank a lot. His dreams all died when I was born and he took it out on me. He was too weak to do anything else but blame a child for his failures."

Her hand was still resting against my cheek. The skin of her palm was warm and moist.

"I need to piss," I said, sliding off the bed.

"You're a real charmer," she said, smiling.

I went into the bathroom and closed the door. The ceiling light flickered a few times when I switched it on – this was a cheap room in a rundown hotel. The amenities were basic. It was clean but vaguely depressing, like the kind of place lonely suicides might come to end their miserable days.

I stared at my face in the mirror, but thankfully I didn't experience the cliché of my father staring back at me. I'd always looked more like my mother: fair hair, blue eyes, prominent cheekbones that she always said could slice through butter.

Turning away from the mirror, I stood over the toilet bowl and waited for nature to take its course. We'd been drinking a lot, Lisa and I, so I knew my bladder was full, but for some reason it was taking its time to come to terms with the fact.

"I hope you gave her one for me." My father was lying on his back in the small bathtub, his bare feet dangling over the end. "She's a looker, that one. I bet she goes like a bunny rabbit." His laughter was hollow and empty in the small room. He had his hands down the front of his trousers.

I tried to ignore him, just like always; and, as always, I failed. "Leave me alone," I said.

"I'd love to, but somehow, no matter how much I'd rather be elsewhere, I always end up back at your side. I think I must be cursed."

The piss crawled back along my urethra and inside me. I couldn't go; he had spoiled it, just like he did everything else in my life. I flushed the toilet anyway and turned around, deliberately keeping my gaze away from the bathtub.

"When you go back out there for round two, think of your old man when you get to the vinegar strokes."

I turned off the light and opened the door. Lisa was still in bed. She had put on her glasses and was reading a book. She always carried a book. It was one of the things I found interesting about her.

"You okay?" She looked up at me, her dark eyes filled with something I knew I could start to rely on if I wasn't too careful, her lips slightly apart, showing a glimpse of wet white teeth.

"Couldn't go," I said, easing back down on the bed beside her. "I thought I could, but it didn't happen." There was a weight to my words that I didn't intend; a dark double meaning I couldn't quite understand.

"You were telling me about your father."

I thought about the bathroom, and the old bastard slithering around in the tub masturbating. "There isn't much to tell, if I'm honest. It's a sad, boring old story."

"So tell me anyway." She put down her book and snuggled close, slipping off her reading glasses. I could feel the warmth of her body; the heat of our recent passion still clung stubbornly to her flesh.

"He beat me regularly until I was sixteen, when I got too big for him to push around. He backed off before I had the common sense to knock him out, and started to drink even more than before. Because he couldn't hit me anymore, he decided to hit the bottle instead."

Lisa stared at me, rapt, all of her attention focused on what I was telling her.

"He died when I was eighteen. It was from a sudden, but not entirely unexpected, heart attack. I didn't go to the funeral. There was no reason for me to attend. By that time my mother was already in a nursing home, so she wasn't there either. She had early onset dementia. I was an only child so I inherited everything: the house, the car, and the gambling debts he'd left behind. I had to sell it all and still I owed a couple of thousand. That's why I started to kickbox. Cage fighting paid more than bartending. It was also a way of controlling the violence he'd left me along with the debts."

"Jesus, what a prick…"

"Is that me, my father, or both of us?" I smiled to let her know I was teasing.

"Don't be silly." Her face was hard; she looked more serious than I'd ever seen her in the short time we'd been together. "He left more scars on you than just a broken nose."

"I know."

"So do I, babe. Believe me, I know." She sat up, resting her back against the scratched pine headboard. "My mother was the same. My dad died in a car accident when I was a baby and she never forgave me for surviving the crash. Ever since I can remember, she would nip me, prick me with pins, jam my fingers in the door... little accidents, or so it seemed. She was the clumsiest mother in the world. The doctors used to laugh at her like it was all a big joke."

My chest was tight; I was having trouble breathing.

"So I know... I know all about your scars, and how they never heal properly." She groped for my hand, held it, and squeezed it tight. "I have matching scars of my own."

"You *don't* know... nobody does. It isn't how you think." I was on the verge of telling her about the way my father would always come back into my life, hanging around like a dirty smell and creating misery. All I had to do was to drag her off the bed and lead her to the bathroom. If I opened the door, she would see him there, pulling on his dick and laughing like the psycho he had always been. But I couldn't. I was too afraid that she might not see him after all. I couldn't take the risk that I was insane, and instead of seeing his ghost all I really saw was a reflection of my own pain.

"I do know, babe. Believe me, I *do*." She leaned into me and I put my arms around her, searching for that warmth. But it was all gone now; she'd gone cold. Everybody went cold in the end.

❊

The next day we were on the road by nine am. She looked nice. She'd put on a new dress that showed a lot of leg, and her hair and make-up were perfect. My father was sitting on the back seat, staring at me in the rear-view mirror.

Lisa hadn't said a word.

Just as I'd feared, she couldn't see a thing. I was the only one who could see him. Last night we'd been like soldiers exchanging war stories, but today the world seemed slightly brighter, as if by talking about these things we had moved out of the shadows, at least for a little while.

I glanced at Lisa but she wasn't looking at me. She kept looking in the mirror or glancing over her shoulder, as if she were searching for something on the road behind us. Or maybe she could actually see my father and she was afraid to tell me in case I thought she was crazy. The latter thought held a deep irony for me, and I suppressed a smile.

"Where are we going?"

I watched the road ahead. It was empty of traffic. "I don't know. I thought we might just drift. We don't have to go back for a week. I don't have another fight for three months. Why bother making plans when we can just go wherever the wind blows us?"

"That's one of the things I… *like* most about you." She'd almost said love but changed it at the last minute. It was too early for that kind of talk, but I knew the words would come eventually. "You hate to make plans. You're spontaneous. That's cool by me."

I smiled. "I spend most of my life training for fights, so when I have some downtime a plan or a routine is the last thing I need."

The road unfurled beneath us, a long black ribbon leading to wherever we chose.

We drove in silence for a mile or two, enjoying the view: fields of flat brown grass stretched under a flat blue sky on each side of the road, dotted here and there with the abandoned carcasses of old stone buildings. In the distance, I could see a farm. A tractor moved slowly along a gravel drive, cows stood in a broad, colourless pasture, and a sheepdog ran around in circles in a field beside the burnt out shell of a pick-up truck.

"Where the hell is this, anyway?" Her voice was low, sombre. "I don't think I like it here."

"I have no idea. I stopped looking at the map a day ago. I'm just trying to keep off the main roads and motorways so we can see something a bit more picturesque than lorries, other cars, blacktop and service stations."

She laughed but didn't bother to explain why.

I glanced at the rear-view mirror. My father was no longer in the back of the car. I looked right, towards those dun, uninteresting fields, and saw him there, running alongside the car, losing ground as we sped along the narrow road. I knew from experience that he would catch up – he always did—but I allowed myself to enjoy the feeling that I was leaving him behind.

"I'm hungry," said Lisa, pouting like a child.

"I'll stop as soon as we see somewhere. A village, a pub, a shop… anything like that… Keep your eyes peeled."

"What's that?" She was pointing straight ahead, through the dusty windscreen.

I slowed the car and tried to make out what she had noticed. As we got closer I saw that it was one of those roadside snack joints, the kind that's just a trailer somebody drags to some quiet lay-by in the morning and then picks up again later in the day. I stopped the car a few yards away and switched off the engine.

"You want junk food for breakfast?"

She nodded. "Why the hell not? We're on holiday, aren't we?"

We got out of the car and walked slowly towards the trailer. I could smell hot grease. The trailer was small, grubby, and the front hatch was propped open with a child's plastic spade. The front end was resting on two small piles of bricks; the rear balanced precariously on a couple of tiny wheels. Whatever vehicle was used to tow this thing, I doubted it could go too far or move very fast.

Handwritten menus adorned the area around the hatch: hot dogs, burgers, bacon sandwiches, teas and coffees, warm cans of cola. The woman inside the trailer was sitting on a low stool and smoking a cigarette. "Hygienic," I whispered. Lisa giggled.

"Morning," said the woman. She had short curly hair the colour of road dirt. Her eyes were narrow; she had a permanent Clint Eastwood squint framing a thousand-yard stare. "What can I do for you?" She took the cigarette out of her mouth and flicked it into the dirt beside the trailer.

I turned to Lisa. "How does two bacon sandwiches sound?" She nodded in agreement.

"Two bacon coming right up," said the woman. The open grill began to sizzle when she threw on the rashers. Behind me, I heard a car door slam. I turned and looked but there were no other cars at the side of the road, only mine. I could just about make out the shape of a figure seated in the rear—my father, returned from his stupid, teasing run. Lisa hadn't noticed; she was watching the woman cook the bacon.

The sandwiches were surprisingly good, as they often are from those kinds of places. The bread was cheap, but the meat was of a decent quality, probably supplied by a local pig farmer. We finished eating and walked back to the car. As we got closer, I started to become more afraid. I didn't want to see him. I wished that I could chase him away but I didn't know how. No matter how many fights I had, or however tough I thought I was, this was one opponent I could never defeat.

"Don't get nervous," said Lisa, placing a hand on my arm so that I would stop.

"What do you mean?"

"When you see her. Don't get nervous. Everything will be okay. I promise."

It wasn't my father sitting in the back of the car. Instead, there was a middle-aged woman with black shoulder-length hair and the same dark eyes as her daughter.

"This is my mother." She took hold of my hand and gripped it as if she were trying to prevent me from running away. "I thought she might like to meet your father."

He was standing nearby, in the shade of a tree. He had on his favourite baseball cap and a pair of baggy jeans. His shirt was hanging out of the waistband of his jeans and the buttons were open to the middle of his hairless chest.

"I told you I understood." She squeezed my hand tighter; so damn tight that it began to hurt. "We have a lot in common, you and me."

I closed my eyes and stared into the familiar dull fire. This time the blaze drew closer, closer, and when it was right in front of me I could see that it was in fact a house on fire. The flames had almost consumed the place, and a woman was standing in a first floor window waving her hands. I couldn't make out her features because of the smoke, but she had dark hair down to her shoulders. Her mouth was open in a silent scream. I couldn't see her eyes.

Tentatively at first, but gaining in confidence as she got into her flow, Lisa started to speak: "She died in a fire when I was thirteen. I squirted lighter fuel on the bed while she was sleeping and got the flames going with a box of matches I'd shoplifted from the local shop. It went on for longer than I expected. In the movies, they always make it look so quick. When she finally stopped screaming I could still hear the sound ringing in my ears." She spoke in a monotone, as if the facts no longer touched her: an actress reciting her lines.

My father walked over from his spot under the tree. He winked at me, opened the rear door and climbed in. Lisa's mother shifted sideways to accommodate him. He nodded at her but they didn't speak. She held his gaze for a couple of seconds and then looked away. There was a bruise on her cheek. I didn't think it had been there before.

"Let's go," said Lisa. "Let's get moving."

I didn't know what else to do, so I got in the car and started the engine.

We were a few miles down the road before the man and the woman in the back of the car started hitting each other. They took it in turns to throw punches; it was all incredibly civilised. The sound of fists hitting flesh and bone was unbearable at first, but I've learned that it's possible to get used to anything if you're exposed to it for a sustained period of time.

Lisa rested her hand on my knee as I drove. She didn't say anything; she simply wanted me to know that she was there, that she would always be there, right on till the end of the road—wherever and whenever that might be. We were a family now. We were together.

I tried not to look into the rear-view mirror. The sounds were enough; I didn't need to see what was going on. The blows took on their own rhythm after a while, a brutal song played by a dark musician. It was the percussion of hurt, the awful drumbeat of abuse.

Before long, I stopped wincing at the sound of each blow and ceased wondering if they could feel any pain.

Continuous violence can have a numbing effect. A person becomes immune to it. If you're not careful, you can even start to like it.

❊

Whenever I close my eyes I can still see that dull fire. But every time I do so, it gets a little further away, diminishing, moving gradually towards some point where it will disappear altogether from view.

The endlessly burning house is nothing but somebody else's memory. Soon it will not even be there. I am certain of this. I know it to be true.

I often wonder what Lisa sees when she closes her eyes.

I wonder, but I'm too afraid to ask in case she ever gives me an answer.

There are some things we don't need to know, and everybody wears scars that should never be shown, even to those whom we claim to love the most.

THE BOOK AND THE RING
Reggie Oliver

The name Jeremiah Staveley (?1540-1595) is now becoming increasingly well known to lovers of early music as a composer of church motets in the Elizabethan period. I am not going to claim that he is up there with Tallis or Byrd, but he is a considerable figure and his remarkable forty part setting of *Per Flumina Babylonis* ("By the Waters of Babylon") bears comparison with Tallis' exquisite and justly famous *Spem in Alium*. Most visitors to Morchester Cathedral will remember seeing his rather bizarre tomb in the North Transept with its odd inscription.

Last year I was commissioned to write the sleeve notes for a CD devoted entirely to Staveley's choral music, so I visited the library of Morchester Cathedral to do some research on his life. Besides unearthing some hitherto undiscovered manuscripts of his—anthems mostly, and one or two madrigals— I managed to work out an outline of his life.

Having been a chorister at the Chapel Royal during the reign of Bloody Mary, he had reverted to Anglican Protestantism when Elizabeth came to the throne and taken holy orders. Most of his best compositions come from the years 1590-1595 when he was a canon of Morchester Cathedral and the choir master. In various documents I came across scraps of legend about his life and sudden death which are very picturesque but not easy to substantiate. It is true however that he was buried, rather bizarrely, standing upright in the wall of the North transept according to his own instructions and self-penned epitaph to be seen on his tomb:

BEHINDE THESE SACRED STONES IN DEATH STAND I
FOR THAT IN LIFE MOST BASELY DID I LIE
IN WORD AND SINNE FORSAKING GOD HIS LAWE

I DANCED MY SOULE IN SATANN'S VERIE MAWE
WHEREFORE IN PENANCE I THIS VIGILL KEEPE
ENTOMBÉD UPRIGHT THUS WHERE I SHOULDE SLEEPE
WHEN DEAD RISE UP I'LL READYE BE IN PLACE
TO MEET MY JUDGE AND MAKER FACE TO FACE
STRANGER, REST NOT MY CORSE UNTIL THAT DAYE
LEST I TORMENT THEE WITH MY SORE DISMAYE

That is strange enough, but stranger still is the manuscript that I discovered in a box full of deeds and documents from the Elizabethan period. The fact that it was jumbled up with them may account for the fact that it has been hitherto unnoticed. I did not use any of its material in my sleeve notes for reasons that will become obvious.

The opening page has on it the following verses by Staveley and nothing more.

I wandered in ten thousand wayes
Seeking the gates of Life and Death
Through manye a desert, manye a maze
I journeyed till I scarce had breath
And when all hope had bene forsook
I found deliv'rence in a booke

It open'd on a path that led
Unto two portals fasten'd well
Before which stood the countless dead
The gates of Paradise and Hell
And those who know whereon they look
Have found their answer in that booke

Both gates are heavy, rude and dark
My booke hath said by what device
I might both open, learne and mark
The gates of Hell, and Paradise

So I a fearfull path have took
By reading of that cursèd booke

Jeremiah Staveley anno 1595.

On the following and subsequent pages Staveley had written a kind of testament. It is penned in crabbed and tiny handwriting which I found very difficult to transcribe. I have preserved as much as I could the original spellings and have not tried to modernise any of its constructions apart from adding some modern punctuation. You may make of it what you will. Certainly it provides ample evidence of the weird psychology of the Elizabethan mind and that, to paraphrase L. P. Hartley, in the past they do things differently.

I, Jeremiah Staveley do here faithfully sette downe my testament and confessioun, knowing that my mortall body approaches with dreadfull and unfaltering pace its finall dissolution, and my immortall soul stands on the very threshold of the pitt of everlastynge fire. I here sett downe that you may knowe and praye for my soule, limed and ensnared as it is in the net of sin, awaiting in terror the ravishment of that Great Beaste which stands yet silent on the borders of my waking minde and roars even now in my dreams, yet distant, as the cry of the wolf is heard in a lonely forest at midnight, heralding the inevitable and frightfull feaste. Oh, Christe Jesu, woulde that I had knowne! Yet knowe I did after a fashioun, and in this manner as I shall tell without further ado.

In the yeare 1590 I was appointed Canon in Ordinary to the Cathedrall of St Anselme's in Morchester. Many thought my preferment long overdue for I was knowne for my skill and genius in Musick. Yet there were ever those who murmured against me and did utter all manner of wicked slander against my person, such as that my giftes were of the Devill and not of God, and suchlike foolishness and damned malice. Yet my merits, though they were conspicuous enough to overcome such calumnies, yet these mutterings ceased not. Notwithstanding, I applied myself most diligently and with much rigour, to improve the musickal capacity of the cathedrall choir such that men and women did stand amazed at my mastery of these arts.

Such being the way of the world, the more I excelled at my art, the more did certain folk of inferiour genius carp and cavill, and, seeking to bring me down from my exalted state above them, saw only that the most monstrous libels and slanders might effect it. Thus in deepe secrecy they did harbour dark designes against me, and I all unknowing stood in the light of innocence unsuspecting.

It was well known, for I made no secrett of it, that I was in the habit of wandering abroad in the countryside around Morchester, to visit the country folk and to extract from them memorialls of old tunes, songs and ditties that they, all unlearned in the higher arts, had taken from their rude forefathers before them. And many of these said tunes, roundes, catches and rhymes were reliques, as I suspect, of ancient rituals and superstitions that went back even to Pagann times before yet the light of the most true Gospel of Christ did shine upon our green hills and fair-flowered meadows.

On Midsummer's Eve Anno 1592 I hearde an olde blinde fiddler playe a fine melodious tune (though somewhat melancholique) in a field. They that stoode bye called it the *Dance of Damned Soules*, and certaine, I did see some white figures in robes like grave cerements at the end of the field who did writhe and turne to his playing, but when I did approache they all vanish'd away like smoke in the summer dusk. And I did thinke, though t'was but my fancy and not to be regarded, that they were the dead or damned on holidaye for a brief sojourne from their infernall home

I sought these things, not merely for my owne curiose learning, but as a refreshment to my musickall genius and invencion. But being greene in the ways of the world, I heeded not that some of these songs were or might be seen as incantacions, summonings of the spirits or demons, spells, or yet curses and maledictions emanating from that prince of Demons, Satann no less.

There was one goodwyfe or beldame, Mother Durden was her name, from whom I acquired many of these cantrips and fancies. She dwelt in a cabin in the woods below Cutberrow Hill, and many were the tales told of her. The countryfolk round about would have it that she was possessed of demons, that a hare was her familiar; others told me that she could turn herself to a fox by anointing her body with the fat from a hanged man's corse. But for all their pratings these dolts would go to her for a salve if they had warts, or to cure a sick beaste. In my prudence I would visit her in secret and had from her many ancient sayings and incantations, many wise saws and prophesies, so that I was many hours in her company. Yet, for all the benefit she did impart to me, I had to summon all my forbearance to stay in her company, for her person was most noisome and stinking and her ancient face like an old misshapen rock that has stood too long in the rain scored with deep lines of bitterness and hatred. Her cabin, moreover, was dark and dank, o'er run with rats and other vermin, and when she spat into her fire—which was a habit of hers—it was green bile that sang in the embers and gave off a choking and most vile smoke.

This notwithstanding, I persisted with the old crone, for she had yet one secret, which she did call 'the secret of her heart' that she would have me know, but forebore to tell me, indicating that such a secret would be of great profit and encompass all desires. At length, seeing me growe impatient, she did impart it to me. She told me that from her mother she was of the ancient family of Cutbirth, of great note hereabouts since before the Conqueror, yet of ill repute to some. This mother of hers, she says, was gently born, but most ill-favoured, so that no gentleman would have her to wife, for all her fortune, and she would be condemned to live and die a maid. But one day a common ploughboy spied and wooed her and they lay together in the grass on Cutberrow Hill at Midsummer's Eve, so that by Michaelmas she was seen to be big with child. Then the family of Cutbirth, which to this day remains over mindfull of the lustre of its ancient lineage, was incensed with her and cast her out. For a while she lived with her rustick swaine in a cabin in the woods—the same still occupied by Mother Durden—but, after the birth of their daughter, he wearied of her and deserted the unfortunate mother.

Mother Durden's parent, thus bereft, made strenuous effortes to reconcile herself with her family, but they would have none of it. They left her to rot in the utmost poverty. It was in these unhappy circumstances that her child (who bore the name Durden from her father) was brought up, schooled by her mother in many secret arts and in great bitterness against the family of Cutbirth. Her mother taught her many strange things about the family of Cutbirth, for they were a family long steeped in ancient lore.

One thing especially Mother Durden was told by her own mother and this concerned a certain booke. This volume has been called by many names, such as *Booke of Shadows*, *Mysterium Arcanum*, *Booke of Secret Keyes*, but it has been most vulgarly called the BOKE OF THE DIVILL. This booke, according to the most ancient tradition of the Cutbirth family, was taken or stolen from them by none other than Holy Anselme, founder of our Cathedrall and buried certaine fathoms deepe in the earthe where lay also her ancestor Cutbirth of Bartonstone.

It was Mother Durden's most earnest wish, and that of her mother also before her, to recover this said booke, for she felte it hers by right, as 'twere, of disinheritance. In recovering the booke, she would gaine power over her enemies, and especially over the family that had blighted her life.

She knew for certaine that this booke was buried in the cathedrall, somewhere in the crypte, and that she knew by what signes on the stone flags, one might finde the booke. But she herself might not enter the cathedrall, knowing her movements watched and suspect, and so it was only by some second party or Intermediary, she sayde, that she might discover that booke.

Then she made me a bargaine, and would to Christe I had not accepted it, yet I did never, as some may secretlie believe, sign aught; nor make a mark in my bloode upon a pact; nor kisse the Devill's arse as a token of my allegiance; nor any suchlike foolish whim-wham. It was meerly this: I consented that I should endeavour to recover this said booke for her, having access to the cathedrall, and that if I did so,

Mother Durden would grante me a share in the marvellous wisdome which, she assured me, it contained.

This I consented unto, yet for many dayes gave it no further thought. It seemed to me an idle plot, impossible of execution. Yet in my mind, the thought was never absent from me, for to tell truth, I received at that time many slights from my fellow clerks, and my great skills in musick were ever contemned by lesser minds. Some malicious worme of a Precentor reported me to the Dean for drunkennesse in a low ale-house which, when I came before him, I most vigorously denied, yet was I not believed and I was shamefully rebuked. My merits were despised, and my imagined vices bruited abroad by green-eyed jealousie. Such things festered in my hearte, so that I longed to strike down my unrighteous oppressors.

One evening, I had, to console myself, gone to a Maying at Great Bartonstone, to observe the dances, and take some note of the viol and hautboy tunes that were played. It was a fair evening, cloudless and still, as fine as any I have known, yet all was not well about my heart. There was dancing about the maypole and I saw some fine rumps of beef being roasted on spits. The laughter of children was all about me.

Then I saw one mother gather her two daughters into her skirts and hurry them indoors. I wondered what was to do until I saw at the edge of the village green a solitary figure in black looking upon the scene. It was Mother Durden. Some men who saw her were for taking up cudgels and driving her by force from the spot. But I restrained them, saying that I would see her on her way, and they, out of reverence for the clerical garb I had on, held back.

Mother Durden met my gaze as I advanced on her, but said nothing. Together and in silence we walked from the village and, as we did so, the villagers who had opened their doors to welcome in the evening sun, closed them as we passed by. At length when we were on the open cart track beyond the bounds of Great Bartonstone, Mother Durden spoke.

"Where is my booke?"

I tolde her of the many and various obstacles which stood in the way of my achieving the volume, that I would consider a strategy and bring it to her in good time, but that at present I saw no chance of its fulfillment. In suchlike manner I excused my tardiness, talking in a most politic manner and with great subtletie, but she would heare none of it. Straightway she led me to her cabin and, having no inke, penne, or paper to hand, she tooke an old dried calf's skin, and, cutting her arm with a paring knife she dipped one of her long finger nails in her blood and with it wrote upon the skin. In truth, her writing was very ill, for she was all but unlettered and her hands, withered and curled with age, looked with their great nails for all the world like the talons of some monstrous antique bird which, except she grasped one hand with the other to be steady, shook with the palsye.

Talking all the while, she drew upon the skin certain signes whereby the floor stones of the crypte were marked, and, in short, showed me where the booke had been laid to rest. Upon which I made many complaintes, videlicet: what if the booke were lost, or taken, or had rotted away in the damp of that ancient charnel house? But she would have none of it and told me to bring her the book by the next full moon.

Fool that I was, I now felt compelled to carry out her wishes: whether because of the vellum scratched with her blood, or the baleful glance of her eye, or by my own secret desire, I know not. Yet still I delayed like a coward, letting 'I dare not' o'erwhelm 'I would' like the cat in the old tale, till my dreams denied me rest. For in them I saw Mother Durden seated in a vast cave, yet like her cabin, dark and noisome, illumined only by the red embers of her fire, and surrounded by a vast concourse of foul things: demons, boggarts, sprites, chimaeras, headless men who spake through their bellies and other suchlike terrors. And all of them did crye with one voice: delay not! Hesitate and you are lost!

And so at last I did summon up my courage, if courage it may be called, and, one night, concealed my self in the organ loft after evening prayer with pick, spade and lantern. Then, the great doores of the cathedrall being locked, I tooke myself down into the crypte, using all carefullie, and there lit my lantern.

The crypte is at all times and in all seasons a most dismall place, and at night, lit only by a lanterne it is very dreadfull. Some blast, damp and noisome, blew through it from I knew not where. Now and then my eare caught a faint scuttering, as it might be of rats, but I sawe none. Then, taking Mother Durden's hide from my coat, I began to search among the tombs for the signs she had drawn in her blood. Many times I had to sweep away the dust to see what was scratched on the floore slabs, and it was long before I had satisfied myselfe that I had the very stone under which the booke was buryed.

It was a long stone of some whitish marble layed against the South wall in the far eastern corner of the crypte. I divined this to be the one, for it was carved very faintly with the head of a bearded man with hair all around him, like the image of the Sun God, Blad in Ancient Aquae Sulis, and this was also the blazon on the arms of Cutbirth to this day. And there were certain other carvings in ancient runic letters upon the stone by which, Mother Durden told me, I might know this was the stone to lift.

I had much to do, and yet I was assisted in that the mortar which bound the slab to its fellows was very old and had crumbled away in parts. At length I found my pick pierced through into a space beneath and, by dint of much leverage, I was able to lift out the stone slab and put my lamp in to see the space I had discovered.

There I found a pit, deeper than I had expected, about the height of a man, and at its bottom lay a man—or rather its skeleton—armed and richly bedight with gold and jewells, yet very strangely, not like the knights we see on tombs, but more resembling the Barbarians on Roman Monuments. His helmet was a mask of bronze, gilded, and the face of the mask was of a wild man, like the Green Man of the country folk. Through the gaps for its mouth and eyes I could see the eye sockets of the skull, dark as hell's night, and a set of teeth that grinned at his owne fallen pomp. The bone hands were clasped across the breast and they held in their grip a dark thing like a boxe or bag of black leather: and this was the booke.

89

Then my heart rose and I was seized with a wild delight. Taking my lanterne I leaped into the grave, yet in my falle I let go the lanterne so that it smashed and fell and in no way could I find it, nor could I discover tinder and flint to ignite once more a flame. Now all was black, blinde black, and no single thread of light. Yet I despaired not, and groping about with my hands I first put my fingers through the mouth of the dead man and felt his teeth. All at once I recoiled and felt down further until I came upon the skeleton hand that held fast that thing of leather. I grasped it to prize it away from the dead man thinking them too feeble to resist, yet something in the sinews held it fast, so that I must exert all my strength to take it. And when I did it was as if something gave a great sigh and all the tombe breathed.

But at length I had the booke in my hands, and still my trouble was not over for all was impenetrable night and I must climb out of the grave. And it seemed to me, doubtlesse in my terrour, that the walls of the grave were growne taller, higher than mine own heighte and that I was at the base of a deepe pitt and indeed in the very pitt of death itself. Then I knew mortall fear and despaire which was doubtlesse why I felt, or imagined that I felt, the dead and flesheless hands of that ancient warriour clawing at my feete in the grave, so that I began to trample underfoot his mouldering corse in my rage. Then, thinking at least to save the booke, I hurled it out of the pitt and heard it fall with a great commotion onto the floore of the crypte so that the whole vaulte echoed. Then I myself made a great leape and found my hands on the stone slab which then began to slip towards me and so crush me by its weight in that hideous sepulchre. Then by some grace my other hand grasped the edge of the grave, I let go the marble slab which fell with a mighty crack into the tomb, missing my person by a bare inch.

Thus did I finde myself on the floore of the lightless crypte. I felt for and founde the booke and with it made my way, crawling and not upright lest I fall againe, until I at length found the steps and the waye up into the dim cathedrall where through its vast windows the first streakes of a grey dawne were beginning to anointe its sacred walles with light.

Finding a candle I returned to the crypte where I took my pick and spade, and made all seem as though no man—or woman—had been there that night and that the ruin of the tombe was but the naturall decadence of age and decay. I hidde the booke with my spade and pick in the loft of the pipe organ, and I thanked God that the zealots of Protestant faith (some, surelie, enemies of mine) had not succeeded in removing this noble instrument from the Cathedrall, then, having a key to a side door of the cathedrall I made my way secretly out of that sacred house.

Never did blessed dawn come sweeter upon a troubled soule! I breathed free air, I had accomplished my purpose. Though I had known no sleepe that night I felt refreshed by the pure air. Rooks were stirring in their parliament among the elms. I bethought myself to take a cup of ale at an Inn, then perhaps to my bedd. I had left the Cathedrall close and was come into the towne when of a sudden I heard a noise as of a great concourse of people which I greatly wondered at, it being barely past six of the clock, albeit in a bright summer morning.

As yet I saw no-one in the bare streets of Morchester, and in my affrighted and exalted state, I thought that the Day of Judgement had come, and that the noise I heard was of all the dead rising from their graves to come before the Awfull Throne of punishment and rewarde. In the next moment my wild apprehensions were put at rest.

I saw a great throng of men and women come up the main street and in their midst was a cart which some were drawing along the road. Upon the cart sat a figure muffled and bounde, but yet I saw her face, and it was Mother Durden. On the instant I concealed myself so that she would not knowe me, but I had seen in her eyes the dreadfull knowledge of her own doome and death.

Placing myself in the crowde behind the cart I asked my fellowes what was to do. They told me that they were bringing Mother Durden to the house of the Justice of the Peace, Sir Digby Fell, and were to lay before him most grave charges of witchcraft. I asked them on what groundes of evidence this charge was brought and they told me that she had brought a murraine on the cattle of Sir Everard Cutbirth, and that when Mother Durden had begged a cup of water off Goodwife Tebbitt, she being refused had bitten her thumb at her, and that very night Goodwife Tebbitt was seized with paines in her belly and did shit in her bedd some small stones very like the balls of a muskett. I followed them to the house of Sir Digby Fell where she was arraigned before the said magistrate, and he still in his nightshirte and marvellously distempered that he should be roused from his slumbers. And when Mother Durden was unbounde and brought unto the magistrate she cried out with a loud voice that before God she was innocent of the charges brought.

I was standing at the back of Sir Digby's parlour and far removed from her, but yet she saw me, and called out for aid, but the crowd drowned out her speach with their shouting. Even so, some who stood by me had guessed that she had called out to me, so that they did question me, saying: "Did not Mother Durden call out to you for aid?" And I denied it. Then another came, saying: "Have I not seen you consort with that damned witch in the woods about Bartonstone?" And I told them I knew her not. And yet another, a most ill-favoured woman with but one eye and no teeth to her mouth said: "Yea, I have seen him, and he has been into her cabin in the woods to make the two-backed beaste in foule and most unholy congress with that limbe of Satann." And I said to her: "Be silent you toothless turde! Have you no regarde to my priestly gowne! I tell you, I never sawe her before this day. Begone, foule lump of carrion!" And if any cock crew at that moment—for I had denyed her thrice—I never hearde it, but Mother Durden was taken to a gaol where she was watched day and night and doubtless put to the question under torture, for three dayes later she did make a full confessioun and set her mark in blood to a document wherein it was written.

And therein she tolde how she met a man in black in the woods and did reverence to him as being the Lorde of this Worlde, and did kisse his excrements as a token thereof. And he in returne did give her five familiar spirits or imps, to wit: a boare-hounde with a calve's head named *Cutbushe*, a ram withoute any leggs at all called *Farte-of-my-*

Arse, and three very small pigges, the size of ratts, named *Hickitt, Hackitt* and *Hockitt*. But whether, even in the very extremity of her agonies, she mocked her tormentors, I dare not say.

And she said nothing of me, but the day she was to be brought before the assize she sent for me. And I did go, out of fear that if I did not she might betray me and say I had entered a pacte of Satann with her. I founde her in a most noisome cell, yet it was no fouler than her own cabin in the woods, and she was crouched like a stricken beaste on a pile of filthy straw in the corner. And her eyes burned in their dark sockets and she seemed much stricken with terror and rage against all the world.

Bidding the gaoler go, saying that I would hear her penitence in private, I then asked her why she had summoned me. She asked me if I had the booke and I told her that I had, yet I had not yet removed it from the organ loft where it lay concealed. She told me that I should take the booke to a secret place under the starres and there consult it, for she said, it must surelie containe her meanes of deliverence, but how she would not say, and I doubt that she knew. I told her that I was to do as she asked but on strict condition that she was to say not a worde of me or of our doings with the booke. To this she did consent most readily.

There is a tower at St Paul's church upon which on certain nights I and the Reverend Mr. Bowles, the Rector of that church would sometimes come to contemplate the stars. He was my only friend, the only man in Morchester to match my wit and know my genius, a man of rare understanding far above the common herd. Yet even he proved unworthy in the end.

One evening I stole out of the cathedrall with the booke under my gowne, makyng my way to St Paul's. There I told Mr. Bowles that I would have an hour of contemplation to myself, so taking a lantern and mounted the steps of the tower. The night was beauteous cleare and a full moon was out so that I could all but read the booke without the aid of a lampe. Below me lay the city like a foule midden that teamed with little life. Up from below came the paltry cries of small lives as of a cloud of mayflies in an evening haze, small follies, and the little sinnes of fooles. Then to the East stood the great monstrous sentinel of St Anselme's cathedrall looking down on us all below but blindly as doth the church.

Then did I open the booke which is called THE BOKE OF THE DIVILL and looked within it. At first I was much amazed for the first few pages seemed to be black, as black as night, and they were soft to the touch as if it were made from the hide of some beaste, like a mole, but vast for there were no sewings together of small peltes. And, as I looked, there were stirrings within the darknesse, but, not caring to see further I pressed on and found many pages on which were written strange devices, and some words which were in the Latin tongue, and some in Greek and Hebrew, and some in what I took to be the Moorish script of the Heathen Mahometans, and some in a language I knew not but took to be, from some indicacions, to be the Saxon tongue of those in Britain before the coming of the Norman Kings into our island.

I will not say further what I read, for it is forbidden, but this I will say: that should any man or woman look in this booke, let them beware, for they will see as 'twere in a glass, but darkly, the image of themselves, their desires and their fears, their longings and their hatreds. And I say this booke is forbidden, as the tree of the Knowledge of Good and Evil was to our first parents Adam and Eve, for to know Good and Evil is to know one's self truly, and no man nor woman will bear that much reality except he or she be pure of heart, and then, even then, at greate paine. But I was a man set aside from the Common Herd and I endured the blast of that booke. A man may finde great profit in this work, yet let him not wish too hard, for all that is wished for may be granted and therein lies immortall danger.

I believe that at the first much was saved me for I sought the means of deliverence not for myselfe but for Mother Durden, for I had pledged to bring about her rescue from the *profanum vulgus*, and I feared her retribution even from beyond the grave. And so I looked in these pages for some help to this end, and I came across this passage which was in Latin, or some other tongue of which I yet knew its meaning, and I read as here set downe:

To make SOLOMON'S RING by which ye may passe unseen through crowdes and make your way unharmed to any place. Take unto you two ounces of pure gold and an ounce of silver and make thee a seal ring, and on the bezel thereof let there be engraved this signe or sigil.

And thereopon that very signe was inscribed in the booke.

And on taking this ring, let the wearer speake the wordes: Abrax Abraxas, *and he shall pass safely on his way.*

Then I removed the booke from the tower and concealed it in the church of St Paul's without Mr Bowles's knowing, for I dare not put it in my lodging, knowing the mistress of my lodging house to be a prod-nose, a busy-legges and a most arrant prattler and teller of tales. In the morning I took me to a jeweller, Master Gotobed in the towne whom I knew to be most discreet and greedy withall, so that I might stop his mouth with gold. And I had him make the ring according to my instructions.

Now the time for the assizes when Mother Durden was to be tried approached whereopon she did send for me once more. And I went unto her very secretly passing money to the gaoler to let me in unseen. And she lay in her cell on the foul straw and groaned, for she greatly feared the paines that awaited her in this life, and, I doubt not, the next. And when she saw me she crawled to me and grasped my gowne and asked me when was the hour of her deliverence. I told her a little of what had passed and said it would be soon, but yet I did not tell her by what contrivance it might be done.

The next day she was brought before Sir Digby Fell in the assizes and I crepte into the assizes and saw her stricken face as she stood accused by that clamorous array of vermin that were her accusers. And ever and anon I saw her eyes, red with rage and distress, search among the crowd, doubtless for me her supposed deliverer. And I stole away so as not to be seene by her. So I went to Master Gotobed and he said he had made the ring and would know what it signified. I said that as I had paid him a fair price what was it to him what it signified? But he said that there was much talk abroad of the Devill being loose in the land and of Mother Durden and her cursed imps, and he would not be seduced to being a party to some act of damned witchcraft in making the said ring. Then I said, *what would you?* And he asked for further recompense for endangering his immortall soule. Then I cursed him for a damned canting hypocrite, a whited sepulchre and a pharisaicall turde. And I picked up a moulding iron from his array of instruments and struck him over the mazzard that he fell down dead. Then, though I was seized with great terrour at what I had done, yet I still kepte my witts. So I fastened his house and took his body privily to feed it in pieces to the furnace in his cellar of work. And this business did take most of the night, so that when all was done and his body consumed it was the dawne of another day and I must creepe forth. There were already several folk about and one that I knew, Goodwife Samson, the mother of one of my choir boyes, a fat-guts, a prating lard-barrel, yet not without cunning. I saw her look up in amaze at Master Gotobed's chimney which doubtless still belched most foule smoke, the dark and oily remnants of his unshriven body and soul.

Then I was once more afeared, so I did put on the ring and saying the words *Abrax Abraxas*, I went forth boldly, albeit from the back doore of Master Gotobed's shoppe. And when I came into the streete Goodwife Samson did for a moment look upon me but yet she did not call out nor seem to heed my presence and so I passed away safely. But when I came to the market square I was greatly amazed, for I did see a vast pile of faggots amassed in its middle and within that mountain of wood a single stake upright and alone. Then I asked one standing by what might this signify, but he paid no heed to me, as if I truly were not there. So I removed my ring and asked him againe. And he said to me: "Did not you know? Mother Durden was very swiftly condemned at the assize yester eve, and Sir Digby was most eager that this damned slave of Satann be burned out of this world and into perdition with all haste, lest she foul the air with her curses and her wickednesse pollute us further."

At that my heart seemed to fall within me and I knew I was as damned as she. Then began my descent to where I stand now, at the doorway of darkness, from which only the infinite Mercy of Christ may yet redeem me. At that moment I heard a murmuring sound and saw a great crowd begin to gather about the pyre. Then I saw Mother Durden being brought to the fire amid the howling of the common people and I saw in her eyes what I hope never to see either on this or on t'other side of the grave, a black despair, all hope abandoned. At that look everie mouth should have fallen silent but they roared and threw up their sweaty caps and rejoiced at their own cruel folly. And two strong men brought her to the post to bind her to it, but as they did so her eyes sought and found me and she began to struggle and cry out in a rage, so that the men, powerful as they were, had much ado to bind her.

I thought then that all the world would turn to look at me for I knew it was at me she stared, but they did not. The common folk gathered there only thought this was some devilry of the old woman and laughed and rejoiced the more to see her agony redoubled by rage. I cowered into obscurity behind a butcher and his boy, for I had no more to do and Mother Durden was beyond rescue. I saw the faggots lit and the smoke rise and Mother Durden's screams above the crowd whose hooting had now sunk to a low murmur. Now at last even these clods had been subdued by the prospect of a fellow human being in her death agony. I saw her skin turn black and erupt in blisters and pustules as in one last mute appeal she stretched her hand towards me over the flames. Then I could bear no more and left the scene. I went to the cathedrall to pray for Mother Durden's soul, but though words came from me, my thoughts remained below, as black as sin itself.

For some days my spirit remained prostrate within me while to the outward eye I continued to conduct myself as before. I did not neglect my duties with the choir and in making sacred musick. Then one night as I returned home to my lodgings I chanced to see two of my colleagues walking in the town. One of them, Canon Costard, an idle fellow, but stiff and precise, a religious caterpillar, and it was he who had told malicious tales of me to the Dean. He said he had seen me in a low ale-house. I saw him, then, but he and his companion had yet to see me. I shrank into a doorway and my hand felt in my purse for the ring which Master Gotobed had made for me at such cost, Solomon's ring. In the next instant I had it placed on the finger and uttered the words *Abrax Abraxas*. The two men passed me by as I stood in the doorway and though Canon Costard's companion, the Verger Master Cantwell, turned to look towards me, he did not seem to know my features, though I knew him.

When they had passed me I resolved to follow them and presently I saw them enter an ale house, such a one as that canting shit-breeches Costard had said I frequented. I did not follow them in but straightway went to my lodgings to secure me a stout cudgel that I kept among my effects. Returning to the ale house I assured myself they were still there and waited till they came out whereupon I struck them both down with my cudgel and ground their faces into the mud of the street, and left them for dead taking their purses with me.

The next day, I found that Masters Costard and Cantwell had lived but were sadly battered and disgraced for their pains. The Dean asked me if I knew aught of what had brought them to this pass but I made a great show of innocence, though restraining any indignation I might have felt at these disgraced topers. Indeed I was much commended for my forbearance towards these fooles.

For all the shock and shame of what had gone before I began to feel rising within me a new spirit, as befitting a man who had at his command the powers of earth and air. Once more I went in secret to St Paul's church where I had concealed my book behinde a panel in the belfry. There, avoiding the curiosity of my friend Mr Bowles, I removed it and lighting a candle began to read.

I must not say much of what I saw, but I must observe that the booke did not appeare to be the one which I had first looked at. The pages made of some dark, softe substance like the skin of a mole had increased in number but what most astonished me was the sighte of myself. It was a portrait in miniature, most exquisitely done in the manner of Master Hilliard, prince of limners, painted in an oval upon a sheet of vellum in the booke. It showed me in my clerke's gowne, head and shoulders, but standing against a sheet of burning flame as some lovers are now depicted by these limners. The eyes were marvellously executed and, though the picture was but some three inches wide, they stared out at me as if they were living and I were looking upon myself in a glasse. I wondered greatly at this and was filled with a fear which has not left me, and yet I cannot fully divine its root.

I turned the page and encountered these words.

TO FINDE A TREASURE HIDDE IN A FIELD

There then followed instructions which I may not repeat but which I took down with the greatest care, then, hiding my booke once more in the belfry I hurried down into the church. There I founde my friend the Rev'd Mr Bowles who looked upon me with much curiosity.

"Will you tarry with me and take a cup of sack?" said he. But I would not. "Whither away so fast?" said he, and I would not answer but straightway went out of the church and into the night.

The next morning I found myself in a field near Bartonstone on the margins of Sir Everard Cutbirth's land. At the very rising of the sunne, at the cold margins of the day I made certain conjurations and uttered certain words I dare not mention at which there rose out of the grounde like a black mist a very dark figure who in silence beckoned me forward.

I could not see if it were man or woman, for the thing had only thin legs, as 'twere of smoke and the clothes were ragged and vaporous. I could not see the face which was veiled and turned from me. The creature led me towards a certain ancient oak in the woods of Sir Everard's park, then with insisting gestures to the ground it bade me dig in a certain place beneathe the oak. I had brought with me my pick and spade and so I dug until I found a box of ox hide studded with brasse. This I broke open with ease and founde therein the bones of a little child wrapped in a white lace robe all stained with the amber colour of ancient bloud and beneath this a greate store of jewels and gold coins. Then I looked up from my amazement at this sight to see the figure that had led me to the treasure, and within the blackness and smoke I saw the face of Mother Durden as I had last seen her in the hour of her immolation. Her face was all black and pumpled with blisterings and burnings and the eyes burned with a hidden fire.

Yet had I no time to wonder in terrour at this sight, for down the field and towards the oak came riding a man with a deer hound gambolling at his side and he was shouting out loud when he saw me as if I were any common trespasser. Then the black figure that was Mother Durden's hellish spirit on a sudden made a rush towards the rider, so that his horse reared up and he himself fell to the ground. Then I, without looking further, took the box of treasure and ran from the scene.

I later discovered that this rider was no less than Sir Everard Cutbirth and that he had broken his neck in a fall from his horse and died thereof. But I now found myself a rich man, though I showed caution and stelthe in display and disbursement. I bought myself a fine house in the city and gowns trimmed with furre, and I also gave almes to the poore and a gift to the cathedrall where I yet kept to my post. But for all that I was modest, yet open handed towards lesser folk, yet still the murmurings against me would not cease. They said that my new founde wealth was from consorting with the Devill, though I told any who would listen that it was a legacy, but still I was dogged and found that the envy of my genius was compounded by envy at my wealth. So may a man never know content for if he sinks low he is despised and if he rises above, then is green-eyed jealousie ever at his heels.

I took to being alone, except when at the cathedrall in my work. If I went abroad it was at night, and then often wearing Solomon's ring to afford me protection from prying eyes. It seemed often as if I walked in a city of the dead when I did so and many a time I have glimpsed a shadow that looked like someone long dead, lurking in the grey streets of evening. My life became a half of what it was and my riches seemed to me but ashes, for the pleasures that they promised gave me no delight, neither wine, nor fine fabrics nor the purchased pleasures of the flesh.

And now I am grown sick so that I know death is near, and I must face myself and my deeds. Several nights ago, though weak, I took my walk abroad at night through dark and desert streets in Morchester. Though black and moonless yet methought I could see my way as through a thin grey mist, and all the town was soft and uncertain as if the very stones were made of dreams and smoke. The world was silent but for the faint sound of steps hurrying behind me. Once I turned and saw a creature like black smoke at the end of the street and it was the figure of Mother Durden who had guided me to the treasure and paved my way to Hell itself. The next night she was there also but nearer to me, so that now I dare not venture abroad even in daylight. I lie here in my chamber and write and look for some way to make myself right with my God before the hour of my judgement. Yet I have no hope of Paradise. Hell beckons and still I struggle. My candle gutters and I order fresh ones. Bring up the light, before the darkness comes to me. I am alone. Christ Jesu deliver me hence. Have mercy. Begone from my chamber, foule witch!

> *Seeke not to finde by what device*
> *Men climb from Hell to Paradise*
> *Nor understand why Satann Fell*
> *From starrie Paradise to Hell*
> *For thou art damn'd, if thou dost looke*
> *To find it in the Divill's Booke*

EASTMOUTH
Alison Moore

Sonia stands on the slabs of the promenade, looking out across the pebbly beach. It is like so many of the seaside resorts from her childhood. She remembers one whose tarred pebbles left their sticky blackness on her bare feet and legs and the seat of her swimsuit. She had to be scrubbed red raw in the bath at the B&B. Her hands are wrapped around the railings, whose old paint is flaking off. When she lets go, her palms will smell of rust.

The visibility is poor. She can't see land beyond Eastmouth.

"I've missed the sound of the gulls," says Peter, watching them circling overhead.

He says this, thinks Sonia, as if he has not heard them for years, but during the time they've been at university, he got the train home most weekends. Sonia does not think she would have missed the gulls. She is used to the Midlands and to city life.

She lets go of the railings and they walk on down the promenade. Sonia, in a thin, brightly coloured jacket, has dressed for warmer weather. Shivering, she huddles into herself. "Let's get you home," says Peter. For the last half hour of their journey, while the train was pulling in and all the way from the station he's been saying things like that: "We're almost home," and, "Won't it be nice to be home?" as if this were her home too. Their suitcases, pulled on wheels behind them, are noisy on the crooked slabs. "They'll know we're here," says Peter.

"Who will?" asks Sonia.

"Everyone," says Peter.

Sonia, looking around, sees a lone figure in the bay window of a retirement home, and a woman in a transparent mac sitting on a bench in a shelter. Peter nods at the woman as they pass.

"It's quiet," says Sonia.

"It's quiet most of the year," says Peter.

He points out a modernist, pre-war building just ahead of them. "I've always loved coming to see the shows," he says. "My all-time favourite act is Cannon and Ball." Reaching this seafront pavilion, they stop to look at the posters. "Look," says Peter, "Cannon and Ball." He is beaming, cheerful when he says, "Nothing changes."

✳

Peter lets them into the house with a key that he wears on a chain around his neck. His mother comes into the hallway with her arms wide open, saying to Sonia as much as to Peter, "You're home!" Taking Sonia's jacket, looking at its bright colours, she says to Sonia, "Blue and green should never be seen!" and then she puts the jacket away.

As they sit down to dinner, Peter's mother says, "Sonia, what were you planning to do with your summer?"

"I've applied for a job up north," says Sonia. "I had the interview yesterday, and I think it went well. I should hear tomorrow whether or not I've got it. I gave them this number—Peter said that was all right. If I get the job, I'll save up for a while and then I want to go to Las Vegas." She mentions pictures she's seen of the place, all the lights.

"If you like that sort of thing," says Peter's father, "you should take an evening stroll along our prom. You'll see it all lit up." He chews his food for a while before saying, "It's a lot hotter there, though. It wouldn't suit me. We stick to England, the south coast."

A gust rattles the window and Sonia turns to see the wind stripping the last of the leaves from a potted shrub in the backyard.

"Look," says Peter's father, "the sun's coming out for you," and he nods towards a patch of sunlight the colour of weak urine on a whitewashed, breeze-block wall.

Peter's mother opens the wine and says to Sonia, "You'll be needing this." Sonia supposes she is referring to their long train journey, or perhaps the cold weather; it isn't clear.

❊

"It's nice to have you home," says Peter's mother, later, when they are clearing the table.

"I think Peter's glad to be home," says Sonia.

"And what about you?"

"I don't live here," says Sonia. She is surprised that Peter's mother does not know this.

"You didn't grow up here," agrees Peter's mother. Opening the back door, she throws the scraps into the yard and the seagulls appear out of nowhere, descending instantly, filling the yard with their shrieks. "Our home is your home," she says, as she closes the door, "but I do remember what it's like to be young and independent. There are lots of empty flats around here and they always need people at the pavilion. The place is crying out for young blood."

"I wasn't planning on staying long," says Sonia.

Peter's mother nods. She looks around the kitchen and says, "Well, I think that will do. I'll go and change the sheets on your bed."

❊

Their bags are side by side in the corner of Peter's bedroom. Hers has a sticker on the side saying *I ♥ Las Vegas*, even though she has never been there. His has a label giving his name—Peter Webster—and his home address, his parents' address, so that it can't get lost.

They go to bed early but Sonia lies awake in the darkness, in between the cold wall and Peter, who is fast asleep. She finally drops off in the early hours before being woken at dawn by what she thinks is the sound of babies crying, but it is only the gulls. She finds the noise depressing.

❊

Sonia, in the bathroom, doing up the belt of her jeans, can hear Peter's mother talking on the phone at the bottom of the stairs. "No," she is saying, "I don't want it. I've changed my mind. Please don't call here again." Sonia checks her face in the mirror before coming out, finding Peter's mother on the landing now, outside the bathroom door. "All right, dear?" says Peter's mother. "Come down to breakfast. I've made pancakes with syrup, just like they have in America!"

Sonia stays in all day. At the end of the afternoon, at ten to five, she phones the company she had hoped would call to offer her a job. She speaks to a receptionist who says, "Please hold." Then she speaks to a secretary who tells her that the job has been offered to someone else. The secretary sounds impatient and terminates the conversation as soon as she can. Sonia redials—she has some questions to ask—but no one picks up; they've all gone home.

When Sonia goes up to bed that night, she finds that the sticker on her bag has been doctored with a permanent marker. 'Las' has been neatly changed to 'East' but 'Vegas' required a heavier hand, a thicker line. *I Eastmouth.*

✳

The following day is Saturday. After breakfast, Sonia watches the dead-eyed gulls gathering on the wall of the yard. They grab at the scraps Peter's mother puts out, and if the door is not kept closed they will come inside, wanting the cat food, taking more than they have been given.

"I think I'll go for a walk," says Sonia.

"I'll come with you," says Peter, beginning to get to his feet.

"I'd rather go on my own," says Sonia. Mr and Mrs Webster stop what they are doing and look at her. They watch her as she leaves the room.

She puts on her shoes and looks for her jacket but she can't find it. She asks Peter's mother if she's seen it and Peter's mother says, "I'm washing it. Wear mine." She takes down a heavy beige coat and helps Sonia into it. "Yours was too thin anyway," says Peter's mother. "You'll need something warmer now you're here."

Sonia walks a mile along the promenade before coming to a stop, leaning on the railings and looking out to sea, watching a yellow helicopter that is circling in the distance. As a child, she used to wave to rescue helicopters even though she knew they weren't really looking for her; it was just for fun or for practice. She raises her hands now and waves, scissoring her arms above her head, like semaphore, as if she were someone in a high-vis jacket on a runway, although she does not know semaphore; she does not know how to say 'stop'. The helicopter turns away and leaves.

"Sonia."

She turns around and finds Peter's parents standing behind her.

"We thought we'd walk with you," says Peter's mother. "What a good idea, a little leg stretch."

They walk along with her, nodding to the woman in the transparent mac as they pass the shelter.

When they reach the end of the promenade, Peter's father says, "We should turn back," and as they walk Sonia home again they tell her about the evening's entertainment: a show at the pavilion and dinner at the Grand.

"I've booked you a table," says Peter's father. "It's a fine place. It's where I proposed to Peter's mother. We go there every year for our anniversary."

"Have the seafood platter," says Peter's mother.

✳

Peter, wearing one of his father's ties, walks Sonia along the blustery promenade. The seafront is all lit up with light bulbs strung between the lampposts. "See?" says Peter. "Who needs Las Vegas?" At the pavilion, they see an Elvis. Sonia finds him disappointing. When the show is over, they go on to the Grand.

They are greeted as 'Mr and Mrs Webster' and Sonia opens her mouth to correct the misapprehension but they are already being led through the restaurant towards their table in the corner, and in the end she says nothing.

When the waiter comes to take their order, Sonia asks for a pasta dish.

"Are you not going to have the seafood platter?" asks Peter.

"I don't think so," says Sonia.

Peter looks concerned. He orders his own meal without looking at the menu.

Sonia, looking around at the decor, says to Peter, "I doubt they've changed a thing since your parents first came here."

Peter touches the flock wallpaper and says, "That's a nice thought."

The waiter returns to light their candle and pour the wine. They raise their glasses, touching the thin rims together. Sonia brings hers close to her mouth but barely wets her lips before putting it down again.

"All right?" says Peter.

Sonia nods. She has not yet told him about the test she did in his parents' bathroom, about the white plastic stick with the little window in the middle, the vertical line that proved the test was working, and the sky-blue, sea-blue flat line that made her think of a distant horizon seen through an aeroplane window. She has not told him that when she came out of the bathroom with the plastic stick still in her hand, Peter's mother was standing there, and that when, after breakfast, she looked for the stick, it had been moved.

The waiter returns with their meals. Peter, smiling down at the food on his plate, picking up his fork, begins to talk to Sonia about the possibility of a management position at the pavilion. His dad, he says, can pull a few strings.

The waiter is coming back already. He is going to ask them if everything is all right, and Sonia is going to say yes even though she has barely had a taste yet. Peter is holding his fork out across the table towards Sonia, offering her a piece of something whose fishy smell reminds her of the stony beach, the tarry pebbles, and the gulls that will wake her at dawn.

She sees, in the molten wax around the wick of the candle, an insect. Sonia picks up her fork, aiming the handle into this hot moat. She is an air-sea rescue unit arriving on the scene to lift the insect to safety.

Carefully, she places the insect on a serviette to recover, as if it has only been floating in a sticky drink.

"I think that one's had it," says Peter, and Sonia looks at it and thinks he might be right.

✳

Peter, who had the whole bottle of wine to himself, is still sleeping the next morning when Sonia gets up, puts on the beige coat and lets herself out of the house. She walks down the promenade again, away from Peter's parents' house, heading in the direction she and Peter came from when they arrived here. She goes as far as the end of the promenade, where she stops to watch the gulls, and then she goes further, climbing up above the town until she is standing a hundred metres above sea level in the wind. She is still in Eastmouth, though. She cannot see across to the next town. When she looks at her watch, she realises that she has been gone for a while now. As she makes her way down from the cliffs, she hears the tolling of a bell; it is coming from the church that stands on top of one of the hills that surround the otherwise flat town.

On the promenade, all the shelters are empty. All the bay windows of all the retirement homes are empty. She realises that it's Sunday and wonders if everyone's at church. Peter's parents might be there, and perhaps even Peter.

She veers slightly away from the promenade now. It is the start of the summer and ought to be warmer, but it is windy and cold and she is glad of Peter's mother's coat. She has her purse in the pocket. She heads down a side street that brings her out at the train station, which is overlooked by the church.

Alone on the platform, she stands in front of the train timetable. She looks at her watch, although pointlessly, as it turns out, because when she consults the timetable she finds that no trains run on Sundays. She wanders to the edge of the platform and looks along the tracks in the direction she would go to get home, and then in the opposite direction.

Is there really nothing at all on a Sunday, she wonders; does nothing even pass through?

She is still there when she notices that the woman in the transparent mac is now standing at one end of the platform. She is talking on a mobile phone but she is looking at Sonia and so Sonia nods at her. She doesn't know whether she has been recognised. The woman, putting away the phone, approaches. When she is within touching distance, she says, "You're the Websters' girl."

"No," says Sonia, preparing to introduce herself, whilst at the same time noticing the locals coming down the hill, coming from church. The service is over. It seems as if the whole town is heading towards them, like an army in beige and lilac.

"Yes," says the woman. "You are. You're the Websters' girl."

The crowd is nearing the foot of the hill; they are close now and one by one they look at the woman in the transparent mac and they nod.

CARRY WITHIN SOME SMALL SLIVER OF ME
Robert Shearman

Beverly McRoberts looked like both her parents, and that was quite a feat, considering that they in no way resembled one another. She had her father's nose, large and bulbous and with nostrils that had a propensity to flare—she also had his deep blue eyes and his cold thin lips and his hair. And she had her mother's skin with all of its strange milky pallor; Beverly sometimes imagined that her mother was a big sack of milk and that if she were cut open all the milk would come pouring out, and if that were true of her mother she supposed it was also true of her, and she'd pat at her stomach and listen to all the milk sloshing about inside – she also had her mother's little hands and her crooked teeth and her ears. Whenever she got lonely at school, and missed the parents who loved her, Beverly would go into the toilets and gaze into the half-length mirror by the washbasins. And there she'd see her parents gazing right back—Beverly would gaze at different body parts dependent on which one of her parents that day she'd decided to love the most.

And she'd asked if she could have her ears pierced, just like her mother's were, and her parents had always said no, no, she was too young—and then she'd turned eleven, and they'd changed their minds, because eleven meant she was very nearly a teenager, and a teenager meant she was very nearly grown up! And Beverly's mother had one ring in her left ear and two rings in her right, and that looked unusual but had apparently been quite the fashion once. That's what Beverly wanted, just the same style, please. Mother pierced Beverly's ears herself. She told Beverly to keep still and be brave. Beverly couldn't sit still but she wasn't frightened, she was excited, it was a completely different sort of not sitting still—Mother used some rubbing alcohol and a needle and made three little holes in Beverly's lobes, and she gave Beverly three little stud earrings, just like the ones she wore, and Beverly was proud.

And when her parents weren't watching Beverly might take out her father's pipe from the cabinet in the drawing room. She'd never seen her father smoke a pipe—he once told her, laughing, that he'd only smoked it when he was young and pretentious—but he'd kept the pipe anyway, didn't it make a nice ornament, it was wooden and looked so grand. And Beverly would put the stem of the pipe into her mouth, and imagine her father's lips had been there once, years ago, before she had even been born, before she'd even been dreamed of. She didn't like to suck at it, the stale taste made her tongue curl. She liked to blow down it as if it were a whistle, if she blew hard enough a sound might come out too high for human beings to hear.

But the best days were when they all went out together. Perhaps to the park—and they'd all hold hands, and Beverly would be in the middle, father to one side, mother at the other, they'd march to the big pond, and her parents would let her throw bread for the ducks, they'd let go of her hands just so she could do that, her aim was getting better, sometimes she'd hit those ducks right on the head! And if not the park then the supermarket, but they couldn't walk hand in hand there, it blocked the aisle. And even the worst days were like the best days—not to the park, not to the supermarket, just staying at home, watching television, eating dinner, sitting about not doing much at all—but they'd still be *together*, that was the main thing, they'd still be a family.

Beverly had friends at school, but not too many, and none very close. They thought she was a bit odd.

The letter for Beverly arrived on a school day. And so her parents could have easily intercepted it. They could have opened it, or destroyed it unread, and they didn't because they loved their daughter and they didn't believe she'd ever betray them. And so the envelope sat on the table for hours, unassuming, flat, waiting for Beverly to come home and find it.

Beverly didn't receive many letters, not unless it was her birthday, and it wouldn't be her birthday for ages. It was exciting. She took the letter upstairs, and lay down upon her bed, and opened it, and she hoped that the message inside would be terribly long and full of great incident and detail.

It wasn't very long at all. "You should know this," it said. "Your father has died."

That was it. Beverly turned over the letter, and then turned it over again. She looked down at the bed as if some other words might have slipped off the page without her realising. The handwriting was small and mean, the message at the top of the sheet and the rest of it left blank, it seemed oddly cruel so much of the paper had been wasted.

The handwriting on the envelope was just as mean, and Beverly shivered to see her name and address written there so coldly. On the back was a series of numbers, and Beverly thought it might be a telephone number, but when she counted it was a few digits short.

And then she was crying—*bawling*, so that it hurt her throat—and she didn't even know why, only that she felt grief, though she had no idea whom or what the grief was for.

Mother came in and sat on the bed next to Beverly, and held her hand, although she didn't hold it too tightly, as if that were no longer allowed. Father stood at the doorway, tall and upright and so serious. Father told Beverly that she was adopted. He told her that it didn't matter she was adopted, he and Mother loved Beverly very much, and surely that was what was important? In the scheme of things? He told her that they hadn't been able to have children of their own, but they'd been given the chance to make one very special girl the happiest and most beloved darling there ever was, she was lucky really, didn't she feel lucky, even a bit? "We were going to tell you when you were older," he added, and he looked away, and Beverly knew he was lying.

"They shouldn't have written," said the woman Beverly had thought was her mother. "It was supposed to be confidential!"

"We love you very much," said the father figure by the door.

"Did you know my real parents?" said Beverly.

"No," said Mother, and let go of Beverly's hand.

"No, kiddo," said Father, and tried to smile.

"Do you know where I can find them?"

"It was supposed to be confidential," said Mother again, and she seemed close to tears herself. "We have to move away!"

"Would you like that, kiddo?" said Father. "Shall we move away? Somewhere they'll never ever find us, so we can be left in peace?"

Beverly wasn't a spiteful girl, and she knew what they said was true, that their love was all that mattered. During dinner she tried to behave the same way she always had, she was nice, she smiled from time to time, she even laughed when Father made one of his terrible jokes. But it seemed to her that she was watching herself from a distance, and her laughter sounded so false, as false as everything else in the world, and the smile made her face hurt. The parents offered her extra pudding because she was being such a good girl, and she thanked them both politely, she asked to be excused, she wanted to go to bed.

She got into her pyjamas, brushed her teeth. The toothpaste tasted off. She looked at herself in the mirror, she looked really hard. She realised she didn't resemble either of the grown-ups downstairs at all.

She went to sleep.

And maybe she dreamed it, but in the night she thought she looked up and saw her mother standing over, watching her. Not her mother, of course, she'd have to correct that, she'd have to find something else to call her, but what, what? "Hey," said Mother softly. "Hey. I don't want to disturb you."

"It's all right," said Beverly.

Mother sat down on the bed, and began to stroke Beverly's hair.

"I love you so much," said Mother.

Beverly promptly said the same thing back.

"We lied earlier," said Mother. And she continued to stroke the hair.

113

And then, nothing else was said, not for a while, and Beverly thought that that was it, that she wouldn't have to hear what the lie was, maybe it was all a lie, every single scrap of it, and she closed her eyes tight and pretended she was still asleep.

Then Mother spoke on, so very softly, never raising her voice. "We *can* have children. We had a child once. A proper child of our own. I hated it, darling. I hated my own daughter, can you imagine? I could feel it, for months, growing inside my stomach. Eating the food I swallowed. Kicking me. Making me feel so sick, sick like you can't believe, sick that just wouldn't go away, and then giving me so much pain. I wanted to get rid of it. I didn't want it in me. I didn't want this monster." All the time, still, still stroking Beverly's hair.

"Mother," said Beverly. "I'm asleep."

"When it was born, I pushed and strained, I wanted it out of me. Parasite. And out it came, and how it screamed. What did it have to scream about? What did she? She wasn't the one who. She wasn't the one who had to. She had nothing, *nothing*, to scream about."

"I'm asleep now. Please. Please let me sleep."

"They said I would adjust, feel differently. Give it time. I gave it time, but I never did. I never did. We gave it away. We gave it up for adoption. But this is the truth," Mother said, and she loomed ever closer to Beverly, Beverly thought she would bite her ear she was so close, "I always wanted a daughter. Just not that one. Not her. I wanted to love someone who had never hurt me. Was that so wrong? Was it wrong to adopt you, my perfect little girl? To want all the good times, and not have the bad? I don't know. I don't see why. I don't know."

She kissed Beverly then, and got up off her bed, and left the bedroom, and closed the door behind her.

Beverly cried one last time, and she knew now what she was grieving, and it wasn't a father she had never met. And then she decided she was never going to cry again, not ever, not about anything. That was all over now. And so it was.

She waited until the house was still. And then she studied the row of digits on the envelope that was too short to be a phone number, and she went downstairs, and she dialled the number anyway.

It rang for several minutes, but Beverly was patient, it wasn't as if she had anything else to do. And by the time the woman on the other end picked up, Beverly knew exactly what she wanted to ask her.

✳

Beverly was strangely relieved that the woman lived so very far away. Had she been close, Beverly could have slipped out of the house to meet her and been back before her parents knew it. She might have had some thin hope that everything could be put back to normal, and that hope would have made her anxious, it would have been something to fight for. But the woman told her she was in a town Beverly had never heard of, and the name didn't seem real, it had too many syllables and too few vowels, and when Beverly found it on a map she could see that it would take her all day to get there, all day and part of the night, there was no way her mother and father wouldn't realise she'd abandoned them. So that was that.

She left home in the middle of the night. By the time she reached her destination it was the middle of the night again – the next night, probably, or maybe the one after. Beverly had had to catch so many trains, all of them so slow and winding, and she'd slept only fitfully on each of them, she couldn't tell how much time had passed.

The cafe was right where the woman said it would be, out of the railway station, turn right, then turn right again – but the town was so dark, all the houses were shut up and still, there wasn't even a single street lamp to throw any light. And Beverly thought the cafe wouldn't be open, it couldn't be open, not when the rest of the town was so dark and dead. But there it was – lights poured out abruptly from the windows and gave the pitch black outside it some little warmth. Beverly went up close, shivered in that warmth. There was chatter indoors. Something like laughter. Even music from an old jukebox.

A bell tinkled as Beverly pushed open the door, and she went into the cafe, and everybody looked up at her, just for a moment. The cafe was full, not a single table was free, and it seemed to Beverly that all manner of people were there—policemen, bikers, men in pinstripe suits. Women in ball-gowns who looked as if they'd just escaped from a dance, their hair up in beehives, and their faces heavy with make-up. Entire families with children and grandchildren and great-grandchildren besides. For that one moment they looked at her, and some of them smiled, and most of them looked tired, and one of the ball gowned women burst into tears.

And even now Beverly thought this must be a mistake, that she'd be told by some grown-up that she couldn't come in – she thought that with all these people inside, the one she'd come so far to meet wouldn't be there. But then, from the other side of the cafe, sitting in a pink plastic booth by the window, a woman gave her a single wave in greeting.

Beverly went to her. The woman looked her up and down appraisingly. Then shrugged. "Well, sit down then," she said. Beverly did.

"You wrote to me?" said Beverly. "About my father? We spoke on the phone?"

"Yes," said the woman, "and yes, and yes. And they changed your name to Beverly? Well. Why not? Why not indeed? It's as good a name as any other."

"I was called something else?"

"It doesn't matter now. May I pour you a coffee?"

"Mother says I'm not old enough to drink coffee," said Beverly, and then blushed bright red.

"If you can have your ears pierced, you can drink coffee. And if you can drink coffee, we can talk like adults." The woman pulled back her hair, showed Beverly there were rings dangling from her lobes. "See? We're both old enough." She poured the coffee, it came out thick and slow like treacle, she pushed the mug across the table to Beverly. The coffee smelled strong and bitter.

Beverly stared at the woman closely. Her skin wasn't milky, but dull like sackcloth. Her nose wasn't bulbous, the nostrils were well-behaved and refused to flare. "Are you my mother?"

The woman looked scandalised, and then barked out a laugh. "Good God, no! I have children. I have three fine sons, and I got them the normal way. I don't need *you*. Look. I have photographs. Look. Look." From a neat little purse she took three photographs, spread them out on the table. "That's Harry, he works in insurance. And that's Gary. And that's Larry, he works in insurance. You can keep the photographs if you like," the woman added helpfully. "Really. I have plenty."

Beverly thanked her. "Do you have a photograph of my mother?"

"No."

"Do you have a photograph of my father?"

"Before or after he died?"

"Um. Before."

"No. I thought you should be told he died." And she screwed her face into something that looked somewhat sympathetic. "I always think the children should be told."

"How did my father die?"

"Good God! It's not as if you even know how he lived! Ask how he lived first!"

"I'm sorry. How did my father live?"

The woman gave this some thought. "Clumsily. I always knew he'd die horribly one day."

"And did he die...?"

"Horribly? Yes. Suffocation. Believe me. It's not as painless as it looks!"

Somewhere on another table a small boy began to cry, and his mother comforted him. On another table a policeman started crying, and no one cared. Beverly looked for the ball-gowned woman, but she had gone, all the women in ball-gowns had paid up and left. "Can I see my mother?" she asked.

"Your mother doesn't want to see you."

Beverly felt tears prick at her own eyes, and she blinked them away, she wasn't ever going to do that again. "Why not?"

"She doesn't want to see any of the children. Not afterwards. Don't," and she touched Beverly's arm in a sudden act of tenderness, "take it too personally. Or, rather," she added, letting go of the arm, and sitting back, and shrugging, "*do* take it personally, if you like. It probably is personal."

"Oh."

"Was there anything else?" And the woman was making for her purse, closing it with a tight snap. Beverly felt a last chance slipping away from her.

"Please," said Beverly. "Do you know her? Are you her friend? Please. Tell me what she's like."

The woman gave this some thought. "You could say I'm a friend of your mother's," she said, at last. "I suppose, in a way, I am. I care for her. I do the best I can. She's not easy to care for. Your mother is a very demanding person. But special. We all think she's special." The woman frowned, as if assessing the accuracy of her response, then gave a single nod, and pulled herself up from the booth. "I'm sorry for your loss," she said. "Losses are irritating things. I've taken care of the bill. Don't try to follow me."

The woman left.

Beverly sipped at her coffee. Just for show, so the woman would think she wouldn't follow. It was too hot, but the taste was surprisingly sweet, Beverly wanted nothing more suddenly than to stay and finish it. It took effort to set it back down on the table. And as soon as she heard the bell on the door sound, and she knew the woman had left, she made to her feet. Her legs felt weak, she had to grasp on to the booth to steady herself, and the pink plastic was soft and yielding, her fingers sank in deep and it would have been the easiest thing in the world to let them sink further, to sit back down on to the comforting warmth of the padded seat, to drown in it.

With all the nonchalance she could muster she walked through the cafe, walked to the door. This time none of the customers looked up at her, they had their own lives to worry about, and that was just as well, Beverly didn't want anything to do with them, all she wanted was her mother—and even as she thought of that, of that word, 'mother', it seemed like such a precious lie, all her life she had never understood how precious, and if it were a lie, well, so, what of that? And so excited, and so nervous, almost walking on air, she stepped out into the dark. She'd forgotten how very black the dark was, and this time even the lights of the cafe couldn't penetrate it, and there was a moment of panic, she couldn't see which direction the woman had taken. But then— there—just a few metres away—she was leaning against the wall, she was fiddling with something, her purse, her hair, her shoelace, it didn't matter—she had delayed, and that was a stroke of luck.

And now the two of them were walking on into the night— Beverly trying to tread quietly so she wouldn't be heard, trying to keep her distance—the woman striding into the pitch black with such confidence, as if she knew every junction, every corner, every loose paving stone (and perhaps she did)—her heels tapping out on the ground a beat for Beverly to follow. Every so often Beverly thought she'd lost her, that the woman had got too far ahead, but the woman would always stop and deal with that meddlesome shoelace again, and Beverly would catch up. They walked on like this for an hour, maybe longer. Until at last the woman stopped, and turned to one of the houses lining the pavement, and it was only then that Beverly realised there were houses there at all, it had been so dark and the houses so bland; the woman took some keys from her purse, and marched up to the front door. She unlocked the door. She turned around. She looked back out, she seemed to stare right at Beverly. Beverly froze, tried to make herself invisible, or at least see-through, or at least as black as the night—and maybe it worked, because the woman turned around again, and entered the house, and closed the door behind her.

So this was the house where her mother lived—and Beverly felt a strange recognition, a *belonging* somehow; it was an anonymous house, it was no different in shape or size to the others either side, but it was so very special. She wanted to know what the address was, what this special house was called, but there were no street signs, and there was no number on the front door. She looked around for any landmarks, anything that might help her identify the house again in the daylight—nothing—really, nothing. And she thought that she'd just have to stay there, then—she'd stand on the pavement outside her mother's house all night, just to be sure she wouldn't lose it, she would *never* lose it now, she wouldn't even take her eyes off it in case it slipped away—and then, suddenly, there was light. So startling and dazzling that for a moment Beverly was blinded, and she thought the house might have vanished in the flash, that when her eyes adjusted to the glare the house would be gone and her mother would have gone with it, gone forever. The woman had pulled open the curtains to the front room, and Beverly could see inside so nice and bright, and the woman was smiling, it was as if she *wanted* her to see.

And there was her mother.

Her mother was pregnant again. Beverly realised she had expected her mother to be pregnant, this was no shock. All she knew of her mother was that she could pump out babies, it made some strange sense to find her like this. The shock was how pronounced was the pregnancy, that it made her mother so fat and swollen. And ugly too—because it wasn't the stomach that was swollen, Beverly thought she could have accepted that, no matter how gross and distended that stomach might have been. It was the head. It was the head. The head was swollen. Somehow balanced upon what was still a perfectly slender neck—and it was to this neck that Beverly kept lowering her eyes, the neck was the beginning of what was normal and the end of what was obscene—balanced upon that stick-thin neck was a head maybe four or five times the size it should have been. It looked like an enormous balloon, filled with air to the point of bursting—and yet, not like a balloon at all, because balloons are neat and round, and this head had grown into such a lumpen shape, bits of the skull rising sharply out of the skin like crude horns. The nose had been smoothed down to a point; one of the eyes had been stretched thin and wide across the face, the other seemed almost normal, though sunken rather, and a little dull, and a little teary, as if it knew it wasn't as impressive as the other. And the jaw looked crushed with the weight of it all.

When the first thrill of horror had passed, Beverly felt a surge of such pity. Her mother was in pain. Her mother was *trapped*—she was sitting upright on a hard wooden chair, and her ankles were tied to the chair legs. And a thick leather strap ran around her mother's forehead, fastening the back of the head against the wall—and she could see how tight the strap was, how the fat skin pooled and bulged white against it. The woman from the cafe—her captor?—was smiling still. Her mother couldn't smile back, she wouldn't have been able to frame that contorted mouth into any sort of reciprocal position—but she did raise a hand in greeting. Beverly wondered whether the strap was a restraint at all. She thought that maybe the strap was there to keep the head balanced. She thought that maybe, without that balance, the head would simply fall off.

And then there was, what? A ripple, yes, across her mother's face? Something passing close underneath the skin, something on the move. And the ripple passed over the flat eye, and it popped out big and wide and shining, it seemed to attempt an almost flirty wink.

The woman from the cafe was talking now. And then taking something out from a metal box on the table, it looked silver and so glamorous, like an old cigarette box. Chunks of meat—and they looked to Beverly red and raw, was it beef, was it something else? Talking again, and waving the beef at the mother playfully; Beverly could see her mother start to drool, a whole stream of it spilling out over the flab of the bottom lip, gushing now like a geyser. The woman went up to the mother, and with both hands grabbed hold of those fat lips. And then she began to prise them apart, to pull the mouth open— it was obviously quite a strain, and the woman put her all into the job, and the mother didn't have the strength to help her, she sat there looking down at the woman's efforts uselessly and apologetic—the woman set her own mouth hard with the effort, and her mouth was so puny and ridiculous in comparison—the woman heaved, she was up to the task, she had done this before, she was expert at opening Mother's mouth, Beverly could see that and could admire her for it— and was there some give?—was there some dark hole peeping out between those lips?—the mouth finally gave way, it swung open large and wide and wet. And quickly the woman produced a block of wood, she wedged it in to keep the mouth from slamming shut again. There weren't many teeth left, and they were small and fractured—they were pebbles bobbing to the surface on a sea of hard red gum.

Time to serve dinner. And the woman tossed the lump of raw steak into the gaping maw. The steak was lost from view—and then, just for an instant, Beverly could see it again—it was held aloft—it was held high and proud—it was gripped tight within the grasp of a tiny hand. A tiny hand sticking out from the mouth, and it looked so neat and so perfect, the little knuckles, the little fingernails.

And then—and then, the woman turned to the window. She looked straight out. She looked straight out at Beverly. She gave a smile. Maybe it was a smile of triumph. It wasn't a cruel smile.

And the mother at last looked towards the window too. She strained against the straps, her head slowly turned. She stared out at her daughter—at her own child, pretty and smart and wearing earrings like a grown-up. Beverly could see that in spite of everything, the mother did look like her. Somehow, there was a resemblance.

Mother raised a hand to her. In greeting? In need?

And the little baby that was growing inside her mother's mouth raised a hand in greeting too.

There seemed to be a sound in her head. It couldn't really be there—but maybe it was like a blast from a whistle too high-pitched for human beings to hear.

So warm in here, big sister. But soon I'll come out to play. And oh! What fun we shall have.

And that's when Beverly turned and ran.

❊

She dozed on the trains, she didn't know for how long. But whenever she opened her eyes it was always dark outside.

And at first she had nightmares, but they soon wore off, soon her dreams were sweet and peaceful. She slept soundly, even though she now knew what she was.

At one point she decided to open her mouth wide, as wide as possible. All those years and she'd never thought to see how far it could go, now it would be such fun to find out. She let her jaw droop, she stretched and stretched, she had to grit her teeth hard and concentrate, these were muscles that were weak and lazy, but Beverly had no patience with weakness any more. She heard something splinter, and she tasted blood, but there was no pain, or not much, at any rate—and soon she could fit her hand inside her mouth, the whole hand even with the fingers splayed, and then her whole arm, she could push in the arm right up to the elbow, she could push it in as deep as she liked.

At first she wasn't sure she would even recognise her old house. But there it was, she found it on the street side just where she'd left it, looking up at it seemed like such sweet nostalgia. Had she really made that her home for the past eleven years? It was dark. All was still. She found a key in her pocket, and she put it into the lock, and it fitted, and it turned, and the door was open, and so she went inside.

She could see her parents had been worried. There were leaflets about missing children, what to do in the event of... and how to cope with... thick pamphlets that made merry with words like 'grief' and 'trauma'. They were scattered all around the sitting room, and that was the main clue something was wrong, her old mother and father had been so neat and tidy. She felt a stab of guilt, she hadn't wanted them to suffer. She wondered how long she'd been away.

But when she went into her parents' bedroom, when she stood over their sleeping bodies, they looked so calm and carefree, they looked innocent as babes.

She stood over them for quite a while. She enjoyed the peace. She didn't want to disturb it.

Eventually, with a soft sigh of resignation, she went to her father's side, and she picked up his pillow, and his head went ker-thunk! down upon his mattress, and that was funny, and he didn't even think to wake up. And she pressed the pillow down hard on to his face, right over his mouth and that bulbous nose, and that's when he stirred from sleep, too little too late, he struggled so limply and then stopped struggling at all. She lifted off the pillow, and he just lay there, still, and he didn't look any different in death—suffocation agreed with him, if indeed it *were* suffocation, as she pressed down she had heard a little snap and had wondered vaguely whether she had broken his neck.

Her mother slept on. She walked round to her mother's side, she lifted her pillow, the head did the ker-thunk thing again but it wasn't so heavy and wasn't so funny. She considered. Her mother wasn't old, she was healthy. Beverly sniffed, and there was a faint coppery tang to the air, and she knew her mother was still fertile. The heart thrummed, Beverly could hear it, and it sounded confident and strong, it sounded strong enough to support two. Beverly put down the pillow. She sat down by her mother's side. She stroked her hair, she stroked her milky skin. Her mother gave a little whimper at that, and cuddled into Beverly closer, and Beverly felt happy.

When dawn broke Beverly stood up and left the bedroom. She took her father's pipe from the cabinet. She took his other things too— the whisky that only he ever drank, the collection of commemorative coins, all the photographs, every single one. She put them into a sack, and left them outside by the dustbins. And then Beverly came back inside, and made herself a coffee, good, strong and black, and sat at the kitchen table, and waited for the woman upstairs to wake up.

THE DEVIL'S INTERVAL
Conrad Williams

Each time he unzipped the padded case and withdrew the guitar Fleckney felt a sting of self-consciousness. It was a Fender Squier Stratocaster, so not the greatest axe in existence, but "no POS", as Pat, his guitar tutor, had confirmed to him. The guitar, made in Japan in 1989, had a cherry-red body with a black pick guard. A dark rosewood neck. It had cost him £90, a dent in his wallet back when he was eighteen, but not a huge amount for a secondhand Strat. It was probably worth much more nowadays, mainly because it was an unusual model: just one volume pot (no tone controls) and there was only one pickup, where normally there were three. That pickup was a double humbucker and it produced a savage sound that he really liked. No, any self-consciousness was more to do with Pat, who must have been twenty years younger than him. He wondered what Pat thought of this middle-aged, balding, overweight, bespectacled guy who turned up every Thursday evening without fail, but had trouble remembering his scales, or seldom managed to do anything interesting with them beyond slavishly running up and down the notes.

Fleckney had always wanted to be a guitarist but life (and laziness) had got in the way of his ambition. At sixth form college he'd cadged a handful of lessons from the mother of a friend who knew how to play chords. Once he'd learned a clutch of major and minor triads she could teach him no more, but put him in touch with a professional teacher who opened up the secrets of the minor pentatonic and barre chords. And then he took his 'A' levels and moved to Durham to study and suddenly he didn't have enough money to pay for lessons. Other students were forming bands with overblown names—Wendigo Amok, Knee Cheese and Bakelite Heart were some that stuck in his memory—but even though they were only playing with three chords (if that) he didn't feel confident enough in his own abilities to follow suit. So he stagnated, but he never felt tempted to sell his guitar, even during those grim days of student loans and swingeing overdrafts.

It wasn't until his fortieth birthday, when he found the original plectrum his first teacher had given him, that he felt a pang of nostalgia, and regret. He dug out his old guitar and took it to a luthier who cleaned it up and put on a fresh set of strings. He found himself in a rush to learn, keen to understand the theory behind the practicalities, but he felt the frustration of his need versus the amount of years he had left. He didn't want to suddenly crack the guitar's secrets only to find he was too arthritic to shape the chords.

Pat didn't seem to share his impatience. He was very laid back. More and more Fleckney believed Pat's insouciance was down to a lack of concern. It was in his interests for Fleckney to progress at a sloth-like pace. Ten pounds for half an hour didn't seem like much money until it hit home that he'd been coming for lessons once a week for just over two years. That was over a grand that he could have spent on an American Standard, one of the best Strats you could buy, before you headed into the realms of silly money for custom versions of old classics, or signature editions. Was it really so hard to teach yourself? But he knew very well the answer to that. He'd tried, but the sheer mass of information online, and his own lack of conviction when it came to proceeding in a practical, linear fashion, only served to confuse him. There was so much to take in: left-hand stuff like chords, scales, arpeggios, modes, but also the intricacies of right-hand work: finger-picking, legato, sweep picking, tremolo, sforzando, rasgueado... Christ, there was so much. Where did you start? Where did you stop? What was the most effective way to advance? He knew that whole careers had been built on three-chord riffs, but he wanted it all, he wanted to acquire the sophistry that he saw and heard in the work of his heroes: Hendrix, Page, Summers, Buckley.

He'd promised, once he'd become proficient, that he would treat himself to a brand new guitar, a real beauty. Maybe one of those American Standards. An Olympic white model with a maple neck. It didn't matter that there was nobody around to hear him play. Except

Pat with his smirk and his effortless ability and the faux enthusiastic encouragement he gave him. Playing guitar had always been just about him and his own limits. It had nothing to do with songwriting, or trying to attract women. It would be a way to express himself, he felt. A release valve, because there were no others.

He thought about the guitar when it wasn't actually in his hands. At work—he was an office manager for an architectural organisation based in the suburbs south of Manchester—he would go about his business diligently but was always trying to visualise where the different notes were on the neck of the guitar, or listening out for undemanding riffs being played on the radio in the kitchen that he might be able to replicate. He carried a finger grip around with him and tensed it whenever he was on the phone. There was always a plectrum or two in his pocket to fiddle with. Occasionally he would meet a resident who had played in a band back in the day and he would ask him how he learned, how long it had taken, what was the key to knowledge.

He wished he'd never admitted to his ambitions at work. Not a day went by without some joker—Jackson or Volant or Darnley—handing him an air guitar and asking him to play a few licks, or telling him his shredding technique needed improvement when he was getting rid of some documents, or reciting the same jokes with tedious frequency. Jackson: "Hey everyone, what's the difference between an onion and Flecko's guitar? Not much... they'll both have you in tears"; Volant: "Hey everyone, how can you tell Flecko's at the door? He knocks out of time and comes in too early"; Darnley: "Hey everyone, how do you make a chainsaw sound like Flecko's guitar playing? Add vibrato". Everyone laughed politely—Fleckney included—and he smiled courteously whenever Jackson perched on his desk and told him about the band he used to be in when he was a teenager, and the pedal board he'd constructed, and the girls he'd picked up on the strength of his solos.

"So why don't you play anymore?" Fleckney had asked him, too late realising the trap he'd built for himself.

"Playing guitar is a young man's sport, Flecko," he said. "I've got better things to do these days than trying to finger A minor."

✳

Now he was in his den tuning his Strat and gazing out of the back window at the kids playing football in the street. There was that scruffy looking boy, smaller than everyone else, with his hair in a permanent cowlick, his hand-me-down clothes always too small or too big for his body. Eddie, was that his name? He was sitting on the kerb by himself, staring at some unidentifiable thing in the gutter, his hands tucked under his chin. He saw the other boys getting closer. He saw fingers being pointed. Fleckney felt the pang of recognition; misery was moments away.

One of the bigger boys deliberately kicked the ball at Eddie. It slammed into the side of his head and caused him to pitch over. His knee barked the edge of the kerb. He righted himself, hand rubbing his face, and even at this distance Fleckney could see the stoicism in his features, the determination not to cry.

Now they were gathering around him, the football forgotten, the blood high in their veins, the dark thrill of bullying overcoming them. Fleckney opened the window. He plugged his guitar into the amp and turned the master volume all the way up. He stomped on his overdrive pedal and the speakers began growling, as if in anticipation. He placed his fingers on the neck of the guitar and crashed his plectrum into the strings: a G5 power chord. He felt the floor vibrate. The glass in the window frame shivered. And every face in the street turned to see what the noise was. For a second he felt like someone on a stage wielding incredible magic, the ability to draw focus. And then the boys were giving him the Vs, but at least they were moving away from Eddie, who was still sitting on the kerb, rubbing his face. He got to his feet and began shuffling away in the opposite direction. He turned and waved at Fleckney, as if remembering his manners.

Fleckney closed the window and turned down the volume of the amp. It was still burbling away. His heart was beating hard. He stared at the guitar as if seeing it for the first time. He wondered about the guitar's history, its providence before it had come to him: who might have picked it up and swung it like a weapon around a stage; where it might have travelled to or from. All those dozens of fingers—short and stubby like his own, or elegant and spiderish—that had caressed its neck. It was his instrument, but in so many ways it was not.

The noise had been amazing. He understood, he thought, in those few moments, a little of why performing live was such a drug for some musicians. And now he was going back to the subdued fumble, the sad twang of a note striven for but not quite reached. The long road between no good to less than mediocre. Excellence wasn't a bus stop on his route. He wondered if Jimi had ever been all thumbs, if Eric had sometimes stumbled trying to pinpoint the root of the harmonic minor in D sharp.

Come on then. Let's get it done.

He flicked through his folder of tabulated guitar parts and selected the opening riff from *Alive*, an old Pearl Jam track that he admired, but wasn't too demanding. His efforts never seemed to correspond with the recording, however. The strings buzzed as he mis-fretted. He had to resolve notes that were outside the scale he was trying to target. His wrist started seizing up. He remembered reading an interview with Dave Grohl, the former Nirvana drummer and Foo Fighters main man, who said that he didn't have time for people who learned scales and that they should just pick up a guitar and have fun, but how could you have fun with an instrument if you didn't know anything about how to use it? Surely Grohl had taken lessons, even if he was self-taught. You had to start somewhere. You had to have some kind of guidance. And for those who *were* self-taught, how did you know what order in which to learn things? Chords first? Or dive into the pentatonic? How did you know what you were doing was right?

His frustration was partly due to the knowledge he had always been a man inclined to structure and method. He followed rules. He was mistrustful of anything that was random, or wild: he hated jazz, for example. Maybe he was too tightly wired, too trapped by his own apparent eagerness to fail to be able to release the creative spirit he thought he saw in himself.

He put the guitar down and rubbed his aching wrist.

He ate dinner. He drank a glass of beer in front of a football match. He went to bed.

❄

A black wet mouth opening in the night, barred with saliva: strings across a sound hole. *Mi contra Fa diabolus est in musica*. The wet mouth closing. Dried blood bracketing it, adhering to the cracks like flecks of rust on a fissured drainpipe. His red guitar falling through shadows, redder than he remembered it; redder than he liked. A voice edged with sarcasm and age. *Your guitar... older than you think.*

❄

He jerked out of sleep and the sounds of dissonance came with him, or to him; he could not be sure. He listened in the dark and thought he heard the ghost of a chord recently strummed. It resonated in the air like electricity after a storm. He sat for hours in his bed, straining for silence.

❄

What are the notes on the B string? he thought to himself, on the bus ride into the office. *Open B. C. C sharp. D. D sharp. E. F. F sharp. G. G sharp. A. A sharp.* The B String. They'd called it the *Beast Ring* in music classes at school. Ha ha. Ho ho. The B string was different to all the others. It was an awkward bugger. When you reached the Beast Ring, you had to change what you did or things would go south.

He arranged meetings. He made coffee. He flexed his finger muscles and fiddled with his plectrum. The day faded like Gilmour's solo at the end of *Comfortably Numb*.

He watched one of his colleagues, Alice, yawn and stretch. She caught his eye and smiled guiltily. It was five o'clock. The evening spread out before him with all its attendant disappointments. He would eat an under-seasoned dinner alone with the radio, and then he'd slope off to his room and cause Jimi and Gary and Kurt to turn in their graves for an hour or two.

Alice got up from her desk and made her way to the ladies. Fleckney began packing away his things. By the time he had pulled on his jacket and switched off his computer monitor, Alice was back, dramatically transformed from a drab, grey, tired creature into a woman shimmering, Kohl-eyed. Her skin seemed to gleam. She caught him staring at her and smiled. "Amazing what a bit of lippy and the promise of a cocktail can do for the soul, isn't it?"

He falteringly asked Pat, at his lesson that evening, if he knew anything about the Devil's Interval. He expected Pat to scoff, but he seemed pleased to have been asked a question. Maybe it was because it meant he would be spared having to listen to Fleckney make the guitar sound like something newly stabbed in an abattoir.

"A little," Pat said, rubbing at the stubble on his chin. "Less theatrically, you're talking about something called a tritone, a musical interval – you remember what an interval is, right? – composed of three adjacent whole tones. It produces dissonance. If you omit the perfect fifth and highlight the diminished fifth – so play a C followed by an F sharp – you get a... forbidding sound. It was given this Devil's interval name because it sounds, I don't know, scary? Evil? It's no biggie. You'll hear it in Hendrix and Black Sabbath. But you'll also hear it in Liszt and Wagner." He laughed. "You'll find it in the theme tune to *The Simpsons*. Now, how have we been getting on with that minor arpeggio?"

On the journey back through the city to his home in the suburbs he thought about Alice and saw how he might perform his own transformation. The guitar could not change; basically it was a tool, a means to an end, and the notes were ineluctable, unless you started messing around with different tunings, which was something he was

131

not interested in. It was he, Fleckney, who had to change. Learn the notes, know the neck, and its mysteries would open up to him, he was sure. What was that saying? *Perfect practice makes perfect.*

When he arrived home, he went straight to his study and switched on the amp. The guitar gleamed, as Alice had done. It felt solid beneath his fingers. He felt the power surge softly through the body and neck. The strings made an ethereal hum as if they might sound out without any contact to aid them. Last night's dream seemed as disconnected from this beautiful instrument as he was from Jimmy Page's talent. *Perfect practice.* A new start. A routine. Five minutes of finger stretches. Five minutes on one scale. A new chord every day. And finish off by choosing a key to play in, and creating a little riff. Half an hour.

That thirty minutes disappeared in what seemed like seconds. His fingertips tingled where they had pressed against the strings. Five minutes of repetition had rewarded him with a new chord—Dsus4, picked at random from an online chord library—implanted in his muscle memory, and he felt confident with the shape of the natural minor scale that he had played in G. He made a note of his new chord on a notebook and set his goals for the following day. Usually his frustration would force squeals and groans from the Strat. But this time it had sounded all right because he had taken his time and worked diligently through the exercises he set himself. There was no rush, no exasperated pauses where he thrust the guitar away from him and stalked off to make a cup of tea. There had been tangible progress made. He was excited about the possibilities. A simple little bit of planning had given him fresh drive and direction.

He stretched and left the room, without the hot, regretful feelings he usually suffered. He drew a deep bath and relaxed in it with a glass of wine. He ate dinner and watched a recording of Jimi Hendrix playing at a concert on the Isle of White. There was no longer the mild jealousy he felt when he watched Jimi segue from his improvisation on the wah pedal into *Voodoo Chile*, nor the confusion over trying to demystify what was being played, and how. He went to bed and fell asleep immediately.

*

The dream crashed through him like a falling wall of plangent chords. He was in a stadium: Shea stadium, New York, the baseball ground where The Beatles had performed the first major outdoor concert in '65 and The Police played to 70,000 in '83. The stadium now, though, was apparently empty. Not a hint of any staff or security. Just him, alone on the stage, while a beam of cold blue light arced crazily around the stadium, uncontrolled, random. Fleckney shivered as if the ghosts of Harrison and Lennon had moved through him on the stage. He was trying to plug the lead from his guitar into the giant stack of amps behind him, but it was too dark to see, and anyway, there was something wrong with the cables; they felt wet in his fist. He thought maybe it was a good thing that he couldn't see to complete his task because he might only succeed in electrocuting himself. He thought of Keith Relf of The Yardbirds who had done just that. Maybe he should leave all this to the roadies and go home. But the grip of the dream would not allow it. Now he saw that what he held in his hands was cabling, but the kind of organic cabling that ought to be packed away inside a body. The blue light swerved across the great expanse of the baseball pitch and picked out a figure staring at him, its body opened like a great red flower. It stretched out its arms to him and the hands fell open like a clumsily packed roll of tools; the fingers seemed too long for the hands. Far too long… He looked back at the guitar in his fist and it was not his guitar, if it could even be called such a thing. This thing now, this *thing* fashioned from so much matted hair and bone and gut.

The chords seemed to follow him out of sleep. They sounded like the shrieks and growls of something deep in pain. He bolted upright. The noise did not dissipate; someone was playing on his guitar. A grinding, ragged sound, as if something metallic was being dragged along the strings. He felt the vibrations in his own fingers as if he was the architect. He was too scared to rise from his bed even though his mind was trying to overcome the fog of fear and provide a logical reason: he had forgotten to turn the amp off and the guitar had slipped over causing a riot of feedback. That must be it. That must be it.

Or despite the reality piling in on him, his dream had not finished. Maybe it was the stress of work, or his new regime. Maybe his brain was flushing itself of all the toxic build-up of the past months or years. This was a good thing, really then, this dream of chaotic sound. The belief he was still guarded by sleep gave him steel. He rose and felt the pile from the carpet spread under his toes. He padded along the hallway to his den. He switched on the light and the noise died; only the echo of those final, discordant notes remained. His guitar was where he had left it, in its stand. The power indicator light on the amp was dead. He went to his guitar and pressed his fingers hesitantly against the neck. It was warm; vibrations died under his touch. Dried flakes of blood fell from the strings. A wet smell of iron was everywhere.

Dawn was there in the threadbare weave of his curtains, soaking through them. The dream crumbled like a vampire in light. He dressed and went downstairs. He took a cup of coffee into the garden. He thought of Karen, the only woman he'd ever been really interested in and who had shown any kind of interest in him. He thought of how good it had been and how bad it had become. He thought about practice and whether it applied to relationships. Probably. There was another self-taught failure.

He saw the kid again, in a school tie with a comically large knot. He was walking briskly, head down, towards school. He was carrying a guitar case. Fleckney felt a twinge of jealousy. *If only I'd started that young*. He called him over to the fence when he drew level.

"Hi," he said. "Eddie isn't it? I didn't know you could play guitar."

"Just starting," he said. His skin was bruised under his eyes. His face was changing from that of an infant to a young boy. Fleckney hoped that sadness wouldn't be trapped within it. It could dog you your whole life.

"Great," Fleckney said. "What are you working on? Simple chords?"

"No," Eddie said. "We're learning how to read music. Minims and crotchets. We did E, B and G last week. We're learning A and C today.

Dad played guitar in a band in the eighties. He wants to pass on what he knows to me."

"And what about those boys? Are they giving you any more trouble?"

"A bit."

"Just walk away."

"They follow."

"Then tell someone," Fleckney urged.

"You?"

"What about your mum and dad?"

"I don't have a mum. Dad just tells me to fight back."

"Why do they pick on you?'

Eddie looked at him as if it was the most stupid question in history. Perhaps it was. But Eddie shrugged. "Dad says it's because I don't make an effort to join in with people. He says I'm a loner."

"Nothing wrong with that."

"Are you a loner?"

"How's the guitar coming along anyway? You enjoying it?"

Eddie nodded. "Except the strings hurt my fingers after a while."

"That will stop, soon enough," Fleckney said. "All the pain will be worth it in the end."

Eddie glanced at Fleckney's fingers. "Sometimes Dad says that I mustn't be related to him."

"Really? I'm sure he must only be joking."

"He says we're totally different notes. He says the distance between us is too great. He said he and mum were harmony but me and him are dissonance."

Fleckney didn't know what to say. He was shocked.

"I've got to go," he said.

"Good luck," Fleckney said.

He ignored his guitar while he readied himself for work. In the past he would have grabbed it before leaving and performed some half-arsed noodle, which more often than not left him feeling dissatisfied. He had defined his practice schedule now and would not deviate from it. At the weekend he would think about extending that programme, but only if he could guarantee that it would be a fulfilling session and not descend into random, pointless strumming.

He tore out a sheet from a pad of paper in the kitchen and spent the bus journey working out the notes of the major and minor chords he knew, given their respective formulae.

When he returned, he was feeling spiky, unsettled. He was also excited about the half hour of practice he was due. But it wasn't solely down to that. He'd given Jackson a mouthful in response to the latest jibe at the expense of his passion. They'd almost come to blows and both had received a carpeting from their boss, a normally ultra-placid guy called Wearing who brought his slippers into the office. Fleckney and Jackson had both apologised profusely to Wearing and each other. On the way out of the office, Jackson had said to Fleckney that he'd ram his guitar down his throat if he ever saw him with it. The rage had only just begun to subside; last night's lack of sleep and the dream entangled within it probably had something to do with it too.

He picked up the guitar with some amount of dread but after checking the strings—no blood, only the normal gunk of dead skin, sweat and oils—he switched on the amp and worked through his new routine. He was a few minutes from the end, unpicking the secrets of the introduction to *My Iron Lung*, when the phone rang. It was the office. It was Alice.

"You're working late," said Fleckney.

"Sorry to call you now," she said, and her voice was all wrong. "I've got some bad news."

Panic flooded him. I'm sacked? What did I do? The argument with Jackson? But we cleared the—

"Bob Jackson was found dead this evening at his flat."

His first insane impulse was to yell: "It wasn't me." But he pressed his lips tight against it. He didn't say anything.

"Trevor?"

"I'm here."

"He was murdered, Trevor. He was found on the floor of his

bathroom. Someone broke down his door and... well they're not saying exactly what happened, but I heard he was stabbed. Repeatedly. Slashed apart. Can you believe it?"

"No I can't," Trevor said.

"So Chris said we should come in tomorrow afternoon. Take the morning off. He said the police will be here and we'll need to make statements."

"Okay."

"I just thought I should give you the heads-up, you know... given what happened earlier."

"It was just a stupid row, Alice," Fleckney said. "He rowed with everyone, not just me."

"Well, yes," she said, "but today he only rowed with *you*."

Suddenly he wanted to get off the line. Nausea was filling him up. He gazed down at his left hand. It had remained on the neck of his guitar. His fingers had somehow accomplished a stretch between the first and the sixth frets. He'd never managed a reach anywhere near that before. Alice was saying something else now but he could no longer hear her. He concentrated on his little finger. He tried shifting it one more fret to the right. And then another. And another. When his little finger had stretched to the tenth fret – the distance between his fingers was now something like ten inches... impossible... impossible – he dropped the telephone and placed the guitar back in its stand. He put his plectrum in the drawer and closed his music book. He switched off the amp.

In the bedroom, in the dark, he watched until he saw Eddie's front door open, and the boy moved into the street. He was carrying his guitar case. He walked past the gang of older kids, trying to keep his gaze fixed on the floor in front of him. One of the boys tripped him over. He landed heavily, and—Fleckney could hear it—either he or his guitar made a long, lonely groan of pain. He got to his feet and stared back at the gang. He rubbed his raw palms. Then he picked up his guitar and walked away. His jaw was set: the same determined refusal to cry. Fleckney watched the boy who had stuck out a leg. From his den he could hear his Strat begin to rumble and wail, as if in response to the other instrument. *The first. The diminished fifth.* He didn't dare look down at his hands.

He waited. The doorbell rang. Fleckney sighed and went downstairs. He opened it and Eddie was there, staring up at him with his black, glossy eyes. He had unsheathed his guitar; now he held it out, like an offering.

"Teach me," he said.

STOLEN KISSES
Michael Marshall Smith

Well, yes, okay, if you want to call it "stealing" then I guess I did steal
him from her. But I didn't hear him complaining, okay? The man did
not fight. At any point. And stealing's a strange word anyhow when it
comes to emotions and relationships, don't you think? Stealing says
you took something that *belonged* to someone else—but a person is
not a thing and so I don't see how he or she can "belong" to anyone.
A person is not property. Okay, they were in fact married, yes, I know
that—God, don't I know it! I was one of the first she showed the big-
ass ring to, duh. I was at the fucking *wedding*, ringside seat. I bought
the bitch a huge set of premium bakeware to show just how fucking
cool I was with the whole thing, because if your best friend gets
married that's what you do even though you *know* she doesn't deserve
the guy and she's got him under some kind of frikkin' spell.

Okay, not an actual *spell*.

She was very pretty. Still is. I get that. And she was all "Let's have
a family, *right now*", and he was totally into that. But so was I, or I
was *going* to be, when the time came. We were *only twenty years old*,
for God's sake—it was *way* too early. Like, insane, right? Who gets
married at twenty these days? This is not the Middle fucking Ages.
I'd figured we'd all hang out together a few more years and he'd get
around to asking me out on a date when everyone's oats had been
duly sown and it was time to pick a lane and start cooking up the next
generation, so they could go out and make the mistakes we hadn't
even finished making yet ourselves.

I figured wrong.

And I figured wrong, I finally realised—drunk as a skunk at that
fucking wedding, watching their first dance and grinning and clapping
along like everyone else—because in fact, he hadn't been thinking of
me at all.

✳

I'd assumed too much. I'd read between lines it turned out had not even been there. But we'd hung out a *lot*. We talked all the time, we laughed, we really *got* each other. How could I not think that he'd realised I was more fun and a lot smarter than Lisa could ever be? I assumed he'd understood that there was a pure connection between him and me, something real and deep and strong, and it was only a matter of letting it mature.

In the meantime I'd played the field, sure. I had my times and some of them were good. But then boom—suddenly they're married, and it dawned on me, way too late, that all my good times had just been about *marking* time. It had always really been about him.

I know most women might think "Huh, well that's the end of that" at this point—but I am not most women. For a while I let it be, of course, and you know what? That was me being nice. I figured that if they'd done the thing, if he'd gone down on one knee and she'd said yes and they'd strutted down the aisle and declared "I do" in front of pretty much everyone in town, I had to let it ride. I owed it to him, my love. If it turned out he was blissfully happy... then I'd let it be. I am not someone who wants to bring sadness into the world unnecessarily.

Sure, I was pissed. I was *miserable*—I'd been in love with the guy since the eighth grade. I'd had him in mind all along, and I'd assumed, hoped, whatever—taken for granted, I guess—we'd been following signs leading us up the same road. I was bitterly fucking sad to find myself now walking that path by myself. I was not heartbroken, though, because I knew nothing's over until the fat lady sings.

And no overweight woman had yet sung.

✳

So we all stayed friends. Why wouldn't we? She'd been my BFF since forever, and had no idea I wanted her man. He didn't either, evidently. So we rubbed along. We hung out. For years I watched the two of them building a life together, step by step. They rented an apartment. Then they bought a house and furniture. The cars they drove got bigger and bigger. They graduated from thrift store and Ikea to Crate & Barrel and Restoration Hardware. Her clothes got fancier and upper arms heavier, unlike mine. They stopped having keg parties and started throwing dinner parties instead. They kept ticking boxes.

But there were no kids.

Lisa talked to me about it, a lot, the troubles they were having. The doctors said it was likely her fault, though they couldn't be sure. I thought the doctors were most likely right, though I kept the opinion to myself.

In the meantime I watched them get older, saw the lines that started to appear around his eyes. I thought about telling him that I could kiss them away, if he'd let me, with a hundred stolen kisses. But I did not.

I waited.

For the time being she still had a lock on his love, but I knew my time would come and that I would not hesitate when the moment arrived. And I did not.

So I stole my best friend's husband, yes.

I do not feel bad about it and I never will. I know she's hurting now but that's an unfortunate side effect of the situation, collateral damage—and I stand by saying there's no such thing as stealing when it comes to the heart. There *is* no God looking down on us like some bearded super-cop, watching to see if we break his laws. Those laws are not even *real*. They're only there in our heads, and even if there is a God then I truly believe that he wishes us to be happy above all else. If two people are going out or living together or whatever and one decides to be with someone else, *that's* not stealing, is it? So why should it be stealing just because they were married? 'Stolen' is nothing but a word, and if a man's happier being held by you than he ever was in her arms, then it's not the right word to use.

I look at him now and I know that's how it is. He tells me he loves me every day and every night. There is joy on his lips when we kiss. I know he's better with me, in every way, so much happier with me, that the years we lost were a mistake, and it was her fault for being too fast, and mine for being too slow.

I loved him first, after all. In fact, if you look at it one way, it was actually *her* who stole him from *me*. All I did was put it right. Maybe you disagree, but what's done is done. Yes, I took a man from another woman, and if you want to call that stealing, then okay – I stole. Fuck you. My bet is that she'll get over it in a year, but I don't really care.

The bottom line is she never deserved him, and the evidence was plain to see. He'd been in the ground three months before I brought him home, and the lazy bitch hadn't even gotten round to putting up a stone.

CURES FOR A SICKENED WORLD
Brian Hodge

Mr Sunshine woke up with a hangover as hard-earned as I'd ever seen. When you're a road manager for touring bands, hangovers are as much a part of the routine as sound checks and the bleary-eyed boredom of all-night drives. After twenty-three years of this, I'd witnessed people coming to and sweating out the effects of everything that could possibly come in a bottle or a small, unmarked packet. But someone who'd been out for the last thirty-plus hours and two thousand miles… this was new.

A scheduled cocktail of injectable benzodiazepines will do that, keep you asleep or in a stupor for the duration.

Mr Sunshine spent a few groggy minutes rubbing his head and blinking at the sky and the trees and the nearby slopes and snow-spattered peaks in the distance. He could see the barn from here, and maybe the cottage through the trees. He was getting the idea: he was rousing in the ass-end of nowhere.

He groped one hand across the ground for purchase, then tried to push himself upright, toppling back to the spring-lush meadow three times before he figured out the reason he couldn't stand was because his ankles were laced together with zip-tie cuffs.

Tomas tossed him a bottle of water. He had to be thirsty down there. Every pull at the bottle let him speak a little more clearly – though that didn't necessarily mean he had anything worth saying.

His given name was Derrick. Derrick Yardley. Mr Sunshine was the byline he wrote under, obviously meant to be ironic. Guys like him are all about the irony. All about the smirk.

"First off, nobody's going to believe you," Tomas told him. "Nobody. Second, that's enough out of you for now. There's only so many times you can say 'what the fuck' before it gets old."

He was focusing, finally, but it was obvious that he still had no idea who was talking to him, much less who I was. Apparently he only knew what Tomas looked like onstage, or in promo photos, the persona that Tomas Lundvall called Ghast. At the moment, in camo pants and a black sweatshirt, he looked like a particularly intense hunter. He was clean-shaven again, too, ridding himself of his beard because it was starting to grey early, and he no longer wanted to waste the time or mental energy dyeing it.

"Third," Tomas said. "Normally I have no use for stupid dichotomies about how there are two kinds of people in the world. But just this once I'm going to make an exception. There *are* two kinds. There are those who'll be missed. And there's you."

"Where am I?" Derrick Yardley croaked.

When you don't know, one range of mountains looks about the same as another. All he would know was that the Cascades of Oregon looked nothing like downtown Chicago. There was a lot of distance between him and the roofie that first put him under; the sycophant at the club who wasn't what he thought she was.

"Let's call it a hell of your own making," Tomas said.

And I didn't know what I was thinking, signing off on this. That's the thing with bands like Balrog, guys like Tomas. You spend enough time on the road with them, and the craziness starts to seem reasonable. My whole thing was organisation and logistics, making sure that people and gear got from Point A to Points B through Z on time and intact. By the end of a fifty-four-date North American tour, even a kidnapping victim stops seeming out of the ordinary. It's just a prank. He's just one more piece of cargo, who needs the right kind of van.

"Sorry about the bad review," Derrick tried, but even he looked aware of how empty that was.

"I've had bad reviews before," Tomas said. "Do I look like someone who's going to let a bad review leave a mark on my day?"

Onstage he looked like a charred nightmare. But even without his stage wear on—without the crusted old leather, without the war paint, or more accurately, corpse paint, without the blood—he was still an imposing figure. He stood tall and lanky, ropy muscle knotted over a towering framework of bone. His eyes and demeanour could project warmth when he was feeling it. He didn't appear to be feeling it now.

"But what you do, you can't call them reviews, can you? You don't seem to ever talk about what's there. You just react to the idea of its existence."

From one pocket, Tomas pulled out a couple of quartered pages, a printout from the online magazine that Derrick Yardley wrote for, a pop culture site called *The Pipeline*. Tomas dropped them into Derrick's lap.

"Go on," he said. "Read it. Out loud."

We waited for him to unfold the pages, and Derrick's face went the colour of cream cheese. Now, finally, he knew.

"Hey. It's just… it's not…"

"Go *on*." This time, Tomas punted a boot tip into Derrick's ribs for emphasis. "Read it like you mean it."

"Come on, it was supposed to be funny."

"Then make me laugh."

He was squirming now, getting a full sense of how isolated we were. "I'm not really a performer."

"Apparently I'm not much of one either, but that's never stopped me." Tomas gave him a harder kick that sent him scuttling back with a yelp.

Go on, just read the stupid thing, I willed him, and after a couple of shaky breaths, he smoothed the pages and got started:

> *Well, fuck me with a pentagram, points and all, but that's rich. If you're going to call your new album* Cures For A Sickened World, *maybe you might first want to make sure you haven't spent your previous nine albums establishing yourself as part of the disease.*

Derrick peeked over the top of the pages to see if any more pain was coming but Tomas only stood there as impassive as a granite carving, so he continued.

> *Listen, dipshits, I've got your cure right here. Kill yourselves! Do it onstage, film it as a how-to video for every other lame-ass band that would stoop to follow in your wake, and take as much of your poxy audience with you as you can, because if they're supporting you, then they're part of the disease too. Do that much, and the rest of us will all feel so much better in the morning. Because, if I haven't made myself clear enough, the prospect of performing acupuncture on my testicles with rusty needles is preferable to the idea of waking up tomorrow suffering the knowledge that this is still a world afflicted with a Balrog infestation.*

The entire band had taken exception to this broadside, but none more so than Tomas. Co-founder. Rhythm guitar. Lead vocals. Main songwriter. He wasn't a solo artist, but it was very much *his* band.

> *Balrog. See how their name has R−O−G in it? They're missing a huge opportunity here, but I'll get back to that. For now, just look at these asshats. I know it hurts, but look at them. Take a good, hard look and keep trying to remember these are grown men. Allegedly. Grown men painted up like fucking rodeo clowns that the ancient Greeks might've sent into the fucking Labyrinth to distract the fucking Minotaur, because even the Minotaur would have to possess enough of a sense of humor to fall down fucking laughing. We get it, you twats! You're evil! With a capital Eve! Or something.*

Interesting that he chose to deride them for being grown men. Because, just based on his approach to so-called journalism, I would've thought it was coming from some smarmy douchebag still in college, or not long out. But he'd obviously seen his thirtieth birthday, maybe even his thirty-fifth.

> *I don't even know where to begin. So why bother. Just this: if this pack of sheep in wolves' clothing proves anything, it's that pretend-evil can still be a lucrative career path as long as your amp knobs go to eleven and you're lucky enough to find four other hairy dudes with the same birth defect that gives them a super scary scowl. Didn't these short-bus regulars have mothers around to warn them that their faces were going to freeze like that? Sorry, my bad. They didn't have mothers! They were born of goats!*

Okay, so the guys had gotten a laugh out of that part.

> *Speaking of goats, that's how much I don't want to hear any more from these shit-mongers. I'd rather be staked out spread-eagle while Satan's most incontinent he-goat takes a steaming infernal dump on my face than listen to another minute of this. I can almost guarantee that the sound of it would be more musical. I would rather scarf up a rotting platter of serpent roadkill scraped off the Highway To Hell, tail-to-head, washed down with a bucket of demon jizz.*
>
> *Back to that R−O−G in their name: They've got it backwards. In the world of so-called extreme metal, you can't swing a ritually sacrificed cat without hitting some band with G−O−R in its name. I looked it up so you don't have to. Gorgoroth.*

Gorguts. Gorefest. Belphegor. Cirith Gorgor. Don't make me go on. So what I humbly suggest is that the brainiacs in Balrog change their name to Gorgonzola, so they can quit dicking around and lay claim, once and for all, to the title of Cheesiest Metal Band In The World.

And that was that. Mr Sunshine folded the papers again and, when Tomas made no move to take them back, set them on the grass, lightly, as if hoping they might vanish in a puff of fairy dust.

Tomas stood with folded arms. "You never even listened to the review copy, did you?"

Getting through the reading without another kick in the ribs seemed to have given him a little fire. "You're so fucking wise and all-seeing, what do *you* think?"

"I think it was a rhetorical question," Tomas said. "They're all like that, aren't they? Your 'reviews'. Every line trying to be more insulting than the line before. I got bored looking for anything different before I could find it."

"You'd be looking a long time."

"I'm curious," Tomas said. "Did you aspire to be a sham all along, or did that just happen? There's no other word for it. Sham. You occupy a position that implies objectivity, but your mind is made up about something before it even occurs to the creator to create it. Your hatred isn't just cowardly. It's lazy."

One corner of his mouth curled into a self-satisfied sneer. "It's consistent."

I'd already figured him for the kind that couldn't lose. The readers who lapped it up, thought his shtick was the funniest thing they'd ever seen, that was pure validation. But so were the ones who thought he was a plague, and took the time to say so. The more pique in their comments, the better. Attention was attention. He was the kind who'd find scorn just as nutritious as praise.

As long as no one was actually holding him accountable.

So when Tomas squatted next to him, Derrick began to squirm with unease again. Tomas could go a long time without blinking. Silence didn't bother him. Eye contact didn't bother him. He was a master of simmering hostility.

"The hatreds I have, I come by them honestly. They're considered," he said. "Let me tell you a few of them. I hate smug little hipsters in retro cardigans and thick black glasses. I hate disingenuousness. I hate people who say 'my bad.' I hate people who lack the courage to back up their professed convictions." He pushed his hair back out of his eyes so nothing got in the way of the glare. "All my hatreds, they're earned. I've put the time and effort into cultivating them. They're pure. But you… you dishonour that ethos."

Now, finally, Tomas took back the printout, although he didn't unfold it. What he needed was already in memory. "Do you get off when people quote your own words back to you? 'I'd rather be staked out spread-eagle while Satan's most incontinent he-goat takes a steaming infernal dump on my face than listen to another minute of this.' When I read that, I didn't see hyperbole. What I saw was you laying down a challenge for yourself."

Tomas stood again, as, moment by moment, Derrick started to put the pieces together.

"You may find this disappointing, but Satan is about as real to me as Saturday morning cartoons. You might've even picked up on that if you'd bothered to look into the album a little."

Still weakened by his hours of sedation, Derek was in no condition to put up a fight as Tomas dragged him by his bound ankles halfway across the meadow, where a quartet of iron stakes was already driven into the ground.

"But I do believe in goats," he said. "We'll start there."

There wasn't much of a struggle even when Tomas lashed him, limb by limb, to the stakes, although he had plenty to say to Tomas' back as he walked away.

It was when Tomas reappeared, leading the shaggy, horned thing from the barn, that Mr Sunshine really started to squeal.

✳

The band was based out of Seattle, but hardly anyone knew about this remote place that Tomas Lundvall owned high in the Cascades, across the border in Oregon. The rest of the band knew. I assumed there was a real estate agent who knew. Now I knew. And, naturally, so did Mr Sunshine—not exactly trustworthy inner circle material.

"When you told him that nobody's going to believe him," I said to Tomas later, inside the cottage's kitchen. "I need to know you mean that. I need to know there's not going to be blowback from this once we get him back home. This is the kind of thing that the term 'federal crime' was invented for."

Tomas looked amused. "Isn't it a little late to start looking for assurances now?"

"I trusted you on faith when that's all there was time for. I never said details wouldn't matter."

"No, you didn't," Tomas said. "He can talk all he wants, if he's not too afraid to do it, and it's only going to sound like so much delirium. He'll never know where he's been, exactly. You'll drop him off outside an emergency room, and with everything in his system, it's only going to look like he's been on a bender for a few days. While he's gone, there's somebody in Chicago still using his ATM card once or twice a day. And his phone. There are pictures on the phone from a couple nights ago at the club, and he's having a good time. There'll be a few more by the end, too blurry to make out. It's all time-stamped. He'll have it all with him again by the time he lands at the ER." Tomas see-sawed his upturned hands like a balance scale. "Which would you believe?"

A bit later, as the sun was starting to fade, Tomas went out to hose Derrick Yardley down and get him moved from the meadow into the barn for the night and take him a plate of food.

He was quiet now, had either screamed himself hoarse or given it up hours ago as pointless. There was no one coming, no one to hear. The nearest neighbour seemed to be at least a mile away, along winding roads, while the hills and valleys would contain almost any mortal sound.

This was land made to shield miseries from view, and keep them secret.

The place seemed as if it might have first sprung up as some long-ago settler's homestead. The barn may have even been original, minus repairs, although the cottage was clearly newer, a replacement built on the foundation of the original. Its rustic nature seemed more by design than scarcity, and it was solid through and through, built of heavy timber, with a lot of stonework, too, including a rock fireplace that would have fit right into a hunting lodge.

As a getaway home, it was an unusual choice. Retreats, for those who could afford them, usually meant luxury and ostentation, oceanside villas and penthouses thirty floors above the great unwashed. I didn't have to be Tomas Lundvall's accountant to know that, even after seventeen years of second-tier success in the music industry, he didn't have that kind of money... but then, he didn't have those kind of aspirations, either. He had no use for a place that others would look at and envy. Instead, I figured, he would need a place to exile himself from the stink of humanity.

He was back in the cottage after a few minutes.

"You're just going to leave him by himself all night?" I asked.

"If you're worried he's going to get away, you can join him and keep watch. As for myself, I have faith in the chain and the anvil."

I wasn't expecting that. "You've chained him to an anvil?"

"It's a very big anvil."

He looked at me then as if studying me. It was blatant. All these years of working for the band, and I'd never managed to decide if he did that with people because he was assessing what made them tick, or forever looking for something he was missing.

"End of the tour leg and all," he said. We had a month of precious downtime before heading to Europe for the summer festival circuit. "Are you sure you don't have someplace better you'd rather be?"

"Apparently I don't. But you know that already." I'd married late, and even then, because of all the time on the road, it hadn't lasted. I wouldn't try again until I was a stationary target, if there was someone out there who would even have me by then. "You did ask for my help with this, remember."

"It wasn't part of your job description. You could have said no."

"I figured you would've gone through with it anyway. I didn't want to hear about it going wrong because somebody else fucked it up for you."

He appeared pleased by this. Although even I wasn't sure if it came out of a warped sense of loyalty or just the challenge of it, to see if I could get away with this madness. Had I really become that bored with life? That desperate to avoid going home to an empty apartment before helming the next leg of the tour got me out again?

"Having second thoughts?" Tomas asked.

"It's just a lot of trouble to go to, and a lot of risk, to get back at some prick who said nasty things about you."

He looked at me as if I didn't understand anything. "It's not about revenge. Punishment is only a means to an end. He needs to be educated. He needs to be corrected. If I feed his own words straight back to him, then maybe he'll realise he should use them better in the future."

"And you don't think this is a little excessive?"

"The stove has to be hot if you're ever going to learn not to touch it."

"I've only ever heard that about kids," I said. "He's not a kid."

"Exactly the point," Tomas said. "He's not a child, but he's still no better than a baby who's just learned to stand up and reach a wall so he can smear it with whatever he's managed to scoop out of his diaper. There have always been people like that, but they were ignored by most people who recognised them for what they were. Now... now they set the parameters of conversation. They've found each other. They try to outdo each other in pointlessness, and their last allegiance is to the truth, or even accuracy, if that means it would take three more minutes of their time to check. They set the agenda. They have a voice that drowns out whatever remains of basic intelligence and actual thought. They're the human equivalent of a car alarm that won't shut off."

"And you're educating exactly one of them."

But Tomas seemed unconcerned by the math. "Even the longest symphony starts with a single note."

❉

Day two: *"I would rather scarf up a rotting platter of serpent roadkill scraped off the Highway To Hell, tail-to-head, washed down with a bucket of demon jizz."*

Tomas held him to it.

It wasn't anything I wanted to see, so I'm not sure what he had prepared, exactly. In contrast to yesterday's ordeal, this was something that required Derrick's active participation, rather than passively lying on the ground as it happened to him. Which explained the taser that Tomas took with him to the barn. Cooperation now meant coercion.

So no, I didn't want to see it. But I could hear it.

Mr Sunshine was in stronger voice this morning, and I could clearly make out what he was saying when he shouted that he would listen to the music, for fuck's sake, he would listen all day, it had just been figures of speech, exaggeration for laughs, just empty words, nothing that any sane person would take seriously.

He still hadn't grasped that it wasn't about that at all.

From the kitchen table in the cottage, still working on morning coffee, I found it a one-sided conversation. I couldn't hear anything Tomas said. I once heard him profess that he wanted whatever he had to say to be worth straining to hear, and so it must have been in the barn. Wrath, with him, was not coloured red. It was the blue of glacial ice.

All I could hear were the sounds of pain, and soon the sounds of sickness, of gagging and retching, broken up by wails of utter despair. It came and went in cycles, as if after a certain point Derrick Yardley was too stricken to go on, and Tomas allowed him time to recover before resuming the putrefied feast where he'd left off.

It went on all morning.

You could call such things a taint on what was otherwise a glorious late spring morning in an unspoiled paradise. But they only augmented and enhanced something that was already there.

I didn't like this place.

After twenty-three years of reducing world travel to a daily grind, I'd developed a sensitivity to places. I don't know how, it just accrued, an awareness of what certain places had absorbed and what they exuded. Clubs and concert halls radiate an energy from all the performances they've hosted. Hotel rooms are mostly soulless and anonymous, but now and then I've stepped into one that's toxic, and known that something very bad happened there.

Here, though, it wasn't the cottage so much as everything else.

I could step outside and come face-to-face with it, in any direction, until it drove me back inside for the illusion of refuge. It was in the hills, and the way they seemed to leer down in curiosity and contempt. It was in the trees, and the way so many of them grew twisted even though they were sheltered from the corkscrewing gales that would have done this to them. It was in the rocks and the way they weathered, as if some truer, crueller form were trying to break through. It was in the shadows, and the way they seemed to hide something, all but its piercing and inquisitive gaze. It was in the wind, and how it fell just short of an intelligible whisper that I feared I would learn to decipher if I stayed long enough. And when a torrential shower swept through that afternoon, it was in that, too, if only because, in conspiracy, it cloaked everything else and gave me room to doubt, wondering if it wasn't just my imagination. Three months of exhaustion, jitters, and road nerves catching up with me all at once.

"What made you buy this place?" I asked Tomas that evening, as the sun went down on another terrible day in Derrick Yardley's life, and we sat before the fireplace sharing wine.

"Don't you know anything about real estate?" he said. "Location, location, location."

"You know what I mean."

Tomas nodded, studying me again. "So you're cueing into it already. I wondered. I can't say what most people are like because hardly anyone has been here and I want to keep it that way."

"Somebody had to bring you up here the first time. What about them?"

"It was just another normal transaction for both of us. I sensed it was a good fit. I sensed that very strongly, but I couldn't have explained why. I try not to be arrogant enough to think whatever's in this place might have sprung up or settled here because of me, but it's hard. That huge rock star ego, you know." I caught a strong whiff of sarcasm. "Maybe some of both. We fed each other."

I imagined him here alone, doing the things you would expect anyone in his line of work to do: recharging, decompressing after spending months meeting the demands of other people, writing new songs. Exploring, too; there was a strong undercurrent of nature worship in Balrog's music.

But I could also envision him doing the sorts of things that you might *not* expect, not if you dismissed the band as nothing but creatures of hollow image.

They and I went back far enough that I took it for granted that their look, their sound, their lyrics, everything, was more than mere theatre. While theatre was important, it was still a reflection of something real. Ghast wasn't just Tomas Lundvall's stage name, a character he put on along with the leather and paint. It was a part of him.

"Balrog isn't a band that's about exorcising demons," I once overheard him say in a backstage interview. *"What we're about is communicating with them."*

Sure, that could only be more myth making. Yet I believed he meant it. I was just never sure exactly where the lines were with him.

So I had to ask: "Am I even going to be taking Yardley back to Chicago?"

Tomas didn't seem surprised by the question. "Why would you still be here if you weren't?"

"To give me time to get used to the idea," I said. "You couldn't have me just drop him off and turn around, because that would be admitting upfront that he wasn't going to be leaving here alive."

Tomas swirled his wine and held it up to the fire, mesmerised by its red glow. "Would it be a problem if he didn't?"

"I didn't sign on for that."

"I know. The question is, what would you do about it?"

Could I take Tomas, if it came to that—was this the bottom line question here? Almost certainly I could. Yes, he was imposing, and almost fifteen years younger, but I was the size of a movie Viking and still had the muscle from back when I started as a roadie, along with fifteen years more experience brawling. We could both put a hurt on each other.

"I don't know," I finally said. "Yet."

"Neither do I."

"You sure you're not just playing coy?" I almost jumped when, in the fireplace, a knot of wood went off like a rifle shot, in a shower of sparks. "I know what that review says. I know what's coming tomorrow. Go through with that, and you'd be sending him back with physical damage."

"And your point is…?"

"That makes it harder to square with him losing a week to a binge. He doesn't just have a wild story now. He's got real injuries, and, oh hey look, they're exactly what he wrote about in his review of *you*. You'd be stupid to send him back with actual evidence. You know that."

"You're right. So maybe I shouldn't."

When shit gets real—I'd heard this expression for years, but had never felt the full weight of it until now. Finally, I recognised the real reason why I'd gone along with Tomas' plan. I was in awe. Who would be crazy enough, committed enough, to do something like this? I could think of only two scenes. Some rappers, maybe. But it wouldn't be this elaborate. Just quick payback, all about the disrespect. And then there was the darkest fringe of extreme metal, where they thought the devil was real.

Except Tomas didn't believe in him either.

"Why don't we name it," I said. "Sacrifice? Is that what you're thinking about?"

"That's too simplistic a concept. But for the sake of discussion… okay."

"Weren't you just saying yesterday that the devil is as real to you as Saturday morning cartoons?"

"That's why I called it too simplistic a concept." He lingered a moment, as if he'd never had to explain himself before. "The way I see it, there are things infinitely older than any childish conceptions of god and some adversarial devil. There's only chaos, and the manifest forms that come out of it, and the fleeting intelligences that guide them. Magnitudes of order rise and fall, and all we are are the building blocks it uses to make things and then topple them over to start again."

He stared out at the dusk, and the only sound was the fire and, beyond the open window, the dripping of the newly ended rain from the eaves.

"I can't say for certain what's going on in this place," he told me. "If it's that the membrane between chaos and order is thin here. Or if it's because, right here, the process has already reached its height on one side of the fulcrum, and now it's started to drop the other way…

"I just know that, if you're willing to put in the work, you can play with the other blocks."

Later that evening I went out to the barn to see Derrick Yardley for myself. He was a disheveled figure huddled against a rough wall under the tepid light of a dangling sixty-watt bulb. Something else dangled from another crossbeam, low enough to hang tools on, but this one I had to stare at until I comprehended that it was the ragged, meat-stripped skeleton of a snake longer than my arm. The barn interior stank of bile and decay.

Across the dirt floor, in a pen, yesterday's goat munched happily on sweetgrass. No place smells bad to a goat.

Mr Sunshine was as degraded a human being as I'd ever seen. A thick leather cuff was snug around one ankle and a ten-foot chain anchored him to a huge, honest-to-god anvil that looked like it had been around since the formation of the earth. In a radius around him, and on nearly every square inch of him, was the evidence of violent and explosive sickness.

"Fuck you too," he croaked as I approached.

I offered him a plastic bottle with the clinical look of something that had come from behind a pharmacy counter.

He eyed it with suspicion. "What's that? Something else for me to puke up?"

"It's an antibiotic. Liquid ampicillin. He thought it would be a good idea." I looked at the chunks and splatters in the dirt. "Considering."

He grabbed it, uncapped and sniffed it, and took a sip.

"Not all at once. Just a swig or two every few hours."

"I know how antibiotics work. Jesus. Now, if I just had a clock to tell me when a few hours have gone by." He rolled his eyes. "Are we done here?"

I respected that he wasn't feigning gratitude, trying to win me over, beg. No Stockholm Syndrome for him. It was business as usual: all spite, all the time.

"You've got a style to what you do. No denying that. I'm just curious why. Why take that approach?"

He stared at me like I'd spoken gibberish. "*Why…?* I don't get the question."

He really didn't, did he? "What do you get out of it?"

Again, more incredulity. That little open-mouthed, side-to-side headshake when someone can't believe he's hearing such idiocy. "I get more hits than anyone else there. More page views, more sticky-time, more link follow-throughs. I win."

Okay, I thought. Just as calm and clearheaded as could be.

Fuck this guy.

Maybe 90% of everything really was crap. I don't know. But he'd made it his life's mission to punish people for even trying, regardless of the outcome.

"Yeah," I said. "We're done here."

Then, finally, I looked up into the hayloft, because I was starting to feel gutless for avoiding it, telling myself that whatever I'd heard shifting around up there was just a rat. Or a barn owl. Or a snake the size of a fire hose. Or any of the other manifest forms allowed by chaos. In that moment it looked like all of them, all at once, at least what I could make out from filling in the gaps between the shadows… until even the shadows unravelled, and perhaps there had been nothing to see after all.

So maybe Derrick should've paid attention to the music. He might have learned something: that in stirring up all that hate, he should've expected to someday summon up something worse than a simple ass-kicking.

✳

Day three: "*The prospect of performing acupuncture on my testicles with rusty needles is preferable to the idea of waking up tomorrow suffering the knowledge that this is still a world afflicted with a Balrog infestation.*"

When you're in, you might as well go all the way.

The day threw another downpour at us, and I was glad of it, the sonic insulation between my ears and what was going on inside the barn. The shrieking rose and fell, sometimes cutting through lulls in the rain. But for the most part it sounded far away, the kind of screams you're willing to dismiss as coming from a neighbour's TV.

At what point had I stopped seeing Derrick Yardley as human? At what point had this become irreversible? I had a long drive ahead to mull that over. My luggage was packed and ready to go, not that it took long. I'd been travelling light for twenty-three years... lighter than ever, now that I seemed to have left my conscience behind. Maybe I would find it at home. Maybe I'd lost it along some road I would never recognise if I travelled it again.

I stepped out the cottage's back door and stood beneath the awning, staring through the watery curtain at the mouth of the barn. There was no sound but the rain. I wished Mr Sunshine a quick death. A *meaningful* death, as one of the building blocks of chaos and order.

I didn't know what Tomas' specific intentions were, and he hadn't said, maybe because he didn't want the embarrassment of committing to something he couldn't deliver. Some kind of transfiguration, maybe. Some act of will that would send ripples through what he called the noosphere... the sphere of human thought. The world according to Ghast.

By now I was considering that I'd been wrong all along about what Tomas' stage persona meant to him. I could see it, finally. It wasn't so much that Ghast was a part of him but, rather, something he aspired to be.

And then he came out of the barn and walked up to me, standing there looking hesitant and soaked to the skin. His hair hung to his chest in sodden tendrils and he had to blink water from his eyes. Just another wet guy in the rain.

"Are you ready to take him back?" he asked.

"If that's what you want," I said. "What changed your mind?"

He started to say something, then shook his head. Nothing he wanted to articulate, to admit to. He just pushed past me, inside the cottage.

"I need to get the BZD, put him to sleep for the trip," was all he said.

A part of me was relieved—the better part, I hoped. But another part of me was deeply disappointed. Because I was curious. I'd felt the currents churning around us, in the fabric of earth and rock and trees and sky. I'd seen *something* in the hayloft, be it manifest form or fleeting intelligence. I was ready to believe that nothing might be true, that everything might be permitted. Tomas—or Ghast—had persuaded me of that much.

So I wondered what would've happened next, if his nerve had held out a little longer.

Syringe in hand, Tomas—just Tomas—pushed past me again and returned to the barn.

And the rain hammered down.

I knew him well enough to suspect that this surrender of plans was something he'd want to handle without an audience, so I waited a couple minutes. Then a couple more. How long did it take to sedate one guy, anyway?

At least it doesn't take any special powers to know when something's not right.

So now it was my turn to get soaked to the skin.

I found Tomas on the barn floor, beneath the anvil. The enormous anvil heavy enough to anchor a man in place for three days. His chest and ribcage were as caved in as the bones of a serpent run over on the highway. But it hadn't only hit him there. He'd taken a blow to the head, as well.

Put it this way: he no longer needed makeup to look like a nightmare.

And Derrick Yardley? He was as far away as ten feet of chain would allow, every last inch of it, wide-eyed and pressed against a support beam as if he wanted to merge with it. He was trying to talk. He just wasn't there yet.

I looked up at the hayloft.

By day, the barn's shadows retreated higher, and I followed them, drawn by movement that I sensed more than saw. But something was up there, and whether it scurried or flowed I couldn't say, this malformed collective of rat and owl and snake... and now goat. The pen was empty. I followed its path up the sloping underside of the roof, until it reached the peak and kept going through the angled juncture, as if squeezing through a crack in time.

With nothing more to see overhead, I looked at Tomas again, not merely killed, but demolished. If I had to ascribe motivation to something beyond understanding, I'd have to say it was disappointed in him.

"It said it didn't have much time," Derrick Yardley finally got out, in a halting voice. "It said I'm more their servant than he ever was. What did it mean?"

He looked at me, pleading yet cunning, as if I were supposed to have his answers.

"What did it mean?"

When I left, I closed the barn door behind me, and would've chained it shut, except the only chain I knew of was attached to Derrick Yardley already. I had a sense that it wouldn't matter for long, anyway.

As the rain let up, anyone could feel it in the air.

THE OCTOBER WIDOW
Angela Slatter

Mirabel Morgan suspected herself hunted, though she'd caught no trace of whoever pursued her.

She was careful when she left the house, keeping a weather eye on the rear-view mirror, but able to discern no particular vehicle standing out from those sharing the road with her. At night, she made sure to close the curtains well before darkness fell, when lights might pick her out as a target against the evening gloom. Yet no one appeared on the pavement or stoop, there were no raps at the door, no envelopes in the mailbox. No sign that she should flee. She watched the calendar tick over with inexorable certainty and, as the day paced closer, the grid of nerves inside her chest tightened like wires pulled by circus strongmen.

Tendrils of white had appeared at her temples regular as clockwork, and her face, though still handsome, had crow's feet radiating from the corners of her eyes, and lines formed parentheses from nose to mouth. The chin was less firm than it had been, but her cheekbones still soared high, kept her profile patrician. Her knuckles were swollen, like dough sewn with yeast and carelessly kneaded, furrows left embedded. They'd been aching since the temperatures had lowered, the same gnawing pain that afflicted her at this time. Made it harder to do things when she most needed to be agile if not sprightly. Every cycle she told herself that the next would be different, that she'd be better prepared. Yet each turning she did the bare minimum, ensuring the new abode was liveable, then went off to enjoy her annual youth while it lasted.

In the garden, the leaves changed colours, swapped out their green for amber and yellow, ochre and sepia. Those so inclined fell and were carried off on the biting breeze. The sky, perpetually iron-grey at this point, was occasionally lightened by white clouds, however more often darkened to thunderous black. The vegetables and flowers had died, turned dry and shrivelled. She didn't plant fruit trees any more for she moved so often, and hated to watch them wither prematurely as they inevitably synched with her eternal, truncated rhythm. The small town of Ashdown had served her well, and she in turn had served it, bringing all the boons attendant upon the October Widow's tenure. The secret tithes she took seemed, to her, rather insignificant. The tiny offerings that staved off the moment when a larger one had to be made.

✳

Henry did as he usually did and went straight around the back of the house, to the little shed where Mrs Morgan kept her hand-mower. He was late, but he knew the older woman wouldn't mind. "As long as it's done by nightfall on Friday, Henry, I don't care what part of Friday you do it!" she'd said. But he liked to be reliable. He liked her to know that she could count on him. This morning his pickup had a punctured tyre; it looked as though a knife had been stuck into the tread, but he couldn't for the life of him figure out who would want to do him an ill turn. He'd taken his brother's battered VW instead of wasting time changing the flat.

He began where he always did, out the front, with its tiny patches of grass broken up by flower beds filled with dead plants. The rose bushes looked especially sad, bare but for their thorns and the crinkled brown remains of red and pink blooms. The mower was stubborn, though he'd oiled it only last week, and took more than a few enthusiastic shoves before the blades loosened and did their job. He hated the thing, but enjoyed the workout it gave. If it were a bit warmer he'd have his hoodie and T-shirt off so the three teenage girls who lived next door could peek out and watch him sweat and glisten in the afternoon sun. But that time was done, the season passed. Too cold now for such exhibitionism; he had to keep his peacock preening to the public bar in the evenings until next summer.

He moved into the back, which was the easier spot, the vegetable beds running along the side fences, out of the way, leaving the rest a clear run right up to the edge of the property where lawn met woods in a hard line. The garden did not gradually grow wild and blend into a creeping foliage that led to full-blown forest. Just ended in a stern demarcation line between the tame and the uncultivated. A creak and a tumbling sound snapped his head up to see three crows flapping and finding new perches; their previous branch had broken and hit the ground just as he looked. Black eyes regarded him, curiously, somehow fondly. There must have been something dead in the undergrowth he decided, or dying. They were waiting until it was weak enough.

He reached the boundary and turned the recalcitrant machine. The curtains on the kitchen window twitched aside. Mrs Morgan stood at the sink, giving him a wide smile. She made the usual hand gestures: *Come inside when you're finished, I'll make you a hot drink*. And there'd be buns too, freshly baked, warm enough to melt the butter and run the thick raspberry jam thin. She'd put a little whiskey in his coffee: *Irish it up*, she'd say like she always did. And she'd smile and he'd smile back, watch her as she moved around the small kitchen, never still, but never hurried, always assured, seemingly always in the spot where she was meant to be. And he'd watch how her hips swayed, how her breath made the breasts covered by her lilac blouse shift up and down, how shapely her calves were beneath the hem of the black skirt. How her face was shaped just like a sweetheart, her lips full, her skin creamy, her eyes not quite blue and not quite green but caught somewhere between. How any wrinkles were shallow and made by laughter not loss. How graceful her hands, her wrists, her fingers were as they reached towards him to lead him upstairs so he might see to Mirabel Morgan's other needs.

Cecil Davis, despite his grief and rage, had not become sloppy in anything but his personal hygiene. If the woman had gotten wind of his presence, she'd have fled, he was certain, no matter how invested she was in remaining in Ashdown. He'd tracked her for so long and, having found her, rented a house two doors down and on the opposite side of the street. It gave him an uninterrupted view of her property. He kept the curtains closed, but affixed cameras under the eaves, trained them on the woman's cottage. The place had come furnished, which was convenient, but hadn't mattered one way or the other to him. He'd have happily brought along the sleeping bag and air mattress he'd once used for camping and then, later still, for surveillance after...

He'd even managed to plant a GPS tracking device on her car, something impossible to notice unless you were actively looking for it. He didn't have to leave his four walls, just stared at the monitors he had rigged up so he could keep an eye on her comings and goings while he still managed to run his software support business from a separate laptop. The business he'd hoped to pass on now had as its sole purpose keeping the money coming in to fund his mission.

She was going by *Mrs Morgan* now, though his researches showed she recycled her names as she went, different ones each time, no discernable pattern, but he'd learned them, if not all then many. Knowing what to look for meant he had found her at last, though it took him seven years. Seven years of hacking utilities records, bank records, seeing patterns, recognising names, catching the scent. As much as anything it was his willingness to believe in strange things when no one else would. It had taken all his determination, all the internal resources that had made him a successful businessman, to keep him focused. To keep him going after...

Of course, he could only watch the exterior of the house. He'd not gone into her home, couldn't bring himself to do that, though he'd never admit it was fear. It was caution, pure and simple. *Caution*, he'd have said if there'd been anyone to talk to about it; if the police in Ottery St Mary's had listened with anything but pity, or the parents in the other small villages he'd gone to after...

The young man who did the gardening was there again, in spite of the penknife Cecil had stuck in the back tyre of his vehicle, trying to put an obstacle in his way. Cecil had to admit it hadn't been a very effective obstacle. He was aware that if he approached the man, tried to tell him what he knew, he'd come across as a nutter; that the lad would back away, go straight to the woman and warn her. Though he'd let things like bathing and general grooming fall by the wayside, Cecil knew there were some illusions he needed to keep intact.

He'd do what he could to protect the lad, within reason. He was someone's son after all, and Cecil had no wish for another father, another mother, to go through what he had; to wake and find their boy gone forever, become no more than motes of dust on the wind. He blinked as thoughts of Gil, tall and strong, young and vital, made heated tears rise, made the tendons of his heart thrum deep and discordant.

Cecil looked away from the screens, to the corner of the sitting room, where his gear lay in a pile. He still wasn't sure what to take with him. He knew where she would be, where she'd been going these past weeks, the place she had been preparing. But he didn't know what to take, what would work, he didn't really know *what* she was.

He only knew that when he confronted her there would be no words, no recriminations, no time wasting that might give her a moment's chance to escape. He doubted she remembered Gil. He doubted she remembered any, certainly not by name. He suspected there had been so many she couldn't keep track of them all.

No. No words. Whatever he might say didn't matter. Wouldn't matter. It was only what he *did* tomorrow evening that mattered.

She lay back, listening to Henry's heavy footsteps retreating down the stairs, the rattling of the pipes as he ran a shower. The smell of him was strong in her nostrils, the sweat from manual labour ever an aphrodisiac. He'd been worried, when they first started this, that she'd become pregnant. She'd laughed so hard at the idea he'd been offended, thought she was impugning his fertility, his God-given right to get her up the duff. He'd required stroking, reassuring, promises that it wasn't him but *her*. In their months together he'd had no more cause for complaint; his time might be brief but she gave him the best of herself, helped him live full. He got what he wanted and she took pleasure in it too; taught him a few things that had made his eyes grow round. Taught him a few more things she didn't mind if he tried out on others, younger women. She was not jealous, did not need his singular adoration; considered her lessons a gift. *You're welcome*.

The mattress beneath her was soft and she gave it a fond pat. A fine thing that had done good service. She wasn't always so lucky when she rented a new house: fully furnished was essential for her lifestyle. Having to pick up and pack everything once a year was a burden she'd long ago dispensed with. Only ever own what you can't do without. Only ever have essential things that you can fit in a single small bag. Travel lightly, live deeply, serve faithfully.

And she had done that. Done it for so long she could barely remember when she hadn't been what she'd become. What she was. Could barely remember a time before that first fire, that first night, before she took the mantle from the one before her. She saw no time in front of her, either, when she might relinquish the position. It was her duty, her obligation, her keeping of faith. She would not let it go easily. Besides, where might she find someone to replace her?

Sometimes it was hard, she admitted, to maintain such single-minded devotion when the world around her changed quickly, quickly. Much more so than before. Difficult to be a fixed point in a whirling universe, holding to an idea, a certainty, an allegiance, a moral obligation. She took some comfort when the core of things stayed true: soul cakes had become candy, but the idea of *benefaction* was still there.

And the fires.

The fires were always lit.

The fires remained.

And the sacrifices could still be made, though the ideas underpinning them drew cries and condemnations in this soft society. Still they were needful things; if only people appreciated that something had to be given back in order for the wheel to spin, for the earth to bloom anew.

A child lost here, a pet taken there; the tiny sacrifices that kept the world going until the larger giving might happen.

She did not like to take small girls, little cauldrons of life that they were, so much potential lost when their flame guttered. An unhelpful sacrifice that almost lost more than it gained. But the wee boys... ah, the boys were like tadpoles, only good for Mischief Night pranks, and so many of them spawned... how could one or three be missed? How could they be seen as anything but small coin in return for the greatest gift?

But no one thought like her any more. Or no one worthwhile. Murderers, cultists, wasters, and nihilists, who neither knew nor cared what they did. Whose killings and leavings brought no benefit, just the brief satisfaction of destruction for the individual.

No, no one thought like her any more. That was why she'd had to prepare the glade on the wooded tor herself, prepare the fire alone; there were no acolytes nowadays, no pretty maids to do the grunt work; her only handmaidens were black and feathered, sharp-eyed and beaked. She grinned. Just her, lugging branches, oak and larch and yew, collecting the smaller tinder, and constructing it all into something that resembled a bed, a bier, a pyre. Threading it with mistletoe, mandrake, mugwort and rue. Doing what was required for when the doors between life and un-life opened and the dead danced through, to visit loved ones or to exact vengeance on rivals and enemies.

Downstairs the closing of the front door sounded. Henry was gone. Strangely, she felt bereft. She rolled onto her side, curled into a ball and closed her eyes, slowed her breathing, commanding her body to sleep deep and late. Soon the changes would come and she would need all her energy for the next night.

*

The day began deathly grey and did not improve. The afternoon light into which Henry stepped was so weak and ineffectual that he almost missed the crouched man. If he'd not been heading towards the pickup he'd spent part of the morning changing the tyre of, he'd not have seen the man at all. As he got closer Henry saw the dull gleam of a blade, not terribly big, but big enough to do damage. The man was about to puncture the tyre yet again.

A red veil covered Henry's eyes. His temper wasn't short, not by a long shot, but nor was he inclined to forgive this kind of spiteful vandalism. He didn't know who the bloke was or why he was targeting Henry, and at that point he didn't care. The youth took swift steps, got close enough for the other to hear him and begin to turn and rise.

Henry threw himself forward.

Henry stopped.

The rank body odour hit him first, then the man's fist punched him in the stomach. Henry caught a glimpse of a frightened weary face, rumpled as if someone had slept in it too long, mud-green eyes swimming in fear and guilt, and a mouth that kept saying something over and over. Henry's hearing had deserted him, the world fallen silent, and his belly flared both hot and cold.

He looked down.

The knife was protruding from his hard-earned six pack.

He didn't think the man had meant to do it; it was just the angle, Henry's momentum, the man's fright. He wanted to say *It's okay*, that he knew it hadn't been on purpose. Noise began to seep back to him, and he heard the man yelling *Help! Help!* as he caught at Henry and laid him down on the footpath. *Help! Help!* as he ran away so he wouldn't get caught. As if he had something better to do.

Chills rushed through him, up and down. Henry hoped someone would let Mrs Morgan know he wouldn't make it tonight. He hoped he wouldn't feel worse. He hoped someone would come soon.

❊

Cecil ran like he'd never done before. He wasn't a runner. He was a short, fat, middle-aged man burdened by grief and junk food. After

Gil had gone, after Cecil's wife had left him, no one cared for him, not even Cecil. He just kept going, knowing he needed nourishment and nothing more. He didn't eat for taste or enjoyment or health, just to exist. It meant he wasn't fussy with portions or calories; it meant things fried deeply and provided quickly formed a major part of his diet. He couldn't remember the last time he'd eaten a piece of fruit, or there'd been something in his fridge that was green because it was meant to be, rather than green because it was going off and Cecil's refrigerator was the place things went to die. He ran, though he knew he couldn't be as fast as he felt, as if things sped by in the grey dusk. As if he flew along the deserted streets as he fled the terrible mistake he'd made.

He'd stopped shouting soon after he'd let the boy down, pressing the lad's large hands to the wound. He'd pulled out the knife, knowing it would make the lad bleed all the worse, but Cecil couldn't leave it behind. There were his prints—a drunk driving conviction fifteen years ago meant he'd be on file—and he didn't want to let the thing go because it had been Gil's. He hoped someone had gone to the boy's aid, hoped it wasn't the sort of neighbourhood where shouting caused people to secure their doors and huddle inside until everything seemed quiet again. But he couldn't stay. He couldn't get caught. He was so close.

He stumbled over the threshold of his rented house and slammed the door, pressed his forehead against it, then turned, rested his back on the wood, waited until the breath shooting from his lungs didn't feel like fire, until the shaking of his limbs had calmed. And then he bent over and vomited hard on the tenant-resistant, slate-coloured carpet. He huddled, hands wrapped around his head, ragged nails biting through his thinning hair into the pale scalp beneath.

The pain brought him back to himself.

He had to focus.

He had to go on.

This was his chance.

He couldn't let it—her—slip away again.

He forced himself upwards. He had hours yet; he should clean the mess he'd made, watch the monitors. But somehow he knew he couldn't wait them out here. He should go. He should go before the streets began to hold traces of random trick-or-treaters. What if someone had seen? What if he'd left some trace, though he couldn't image what it might be? What if, what if what if? What if the police were already speeding towards this place?

That thought galvanised him. He picked through the gear in the sitting room, extracted the sleeping bag for warmth and the ghillie suit for camouflage. In the end he took only the Swiss Army Knife, wiping its blade as clean as he could, stuffing it in a trouser pocket.

He knew where she would go.

He knew where he would meet her.

The air was brisk, lacing her lungs as she breathed deeply, taking long strides up the incline. Once she'd have carried a burning brand to illuminate her track, to ignite the pyre, but that might have caught attention. So, it was a Maglite in her hand, providing a bright circle to follow, but giving off no warmth the way an old torch would. It was enough that the *form* of things be honoured in spirit, not slavish mimicry.

Around her foxes yipped and badgers snuffled; other things she couldn't identify made noise too, but Mirabel had no fear of the dark, no fear of the forest. She'd walked across the fields, then taken the path around the base of the tor, traversing rills and ditches, stiles and fallen trees, marking the way with light, the way that must lead ever upwards. When she passed under the canopy of trees that would take her to the glade, where Henry would be waiting, she sighed contentedly. In her long years she had never been let down by any of her chosen. All things had their time, their natural conclusion.

Everything she directed her existence towards was coming to fruition.

✳

Cecil almost gasped as she moved past him in the darkness. Her face was shadowed, but he knew it was her, knew her shape; he'd watched her enough from the first time they'd met. From when she'd moved in across the street from his family home in Otter St Mary and lived there for a year. The lovely, gracious woman who'd asked politely if their son, their only child, just turned nineteen, might be kind enough to do some gardening for her. Effortlessly attractive, effortlessly desirable.

The woman who'd come and gone like a storm, like a flood, stealing something so precious he'd not cared to see what she'd left behind, the benefits she'd given to a village that had been foundering, its crops poor and stunted, its children pale and sickly, its businesses and farms dying a slow death. A village that, after Gil had gone, began to breathe, to produce, to be *fertile* again, though that benevolence gladdened Cecil's heart not a jot.

She walked slowly, he noticed, slower than seemed normal. He wondered if she'd injured herself crossing dark fields, then reminded himself it didn't matter. He waited until she was well ahead, then rolled from the sleeping bag, left it and the ghillie suit behind, and began to follow.

✳

She reached the top of the slope, stepped into the clearing. The bulk of the woven bed was there, picked out by the beam of the Maglite. On top lay the torch she'd made, a branch of yew, one end wrapped around with dried henbane and belladonna and other lesser kindling. She lit it with the matches in her coat pocket and switched off the flashlight. The burning brand gave better light and she nodded with satisfaction, feeling her blood warmed by the leaping blue-orange flame. She held it high and looked around.

No sign of Henry.

She frowned.

Called his name and received no reply.

Looked at the cheap watch on her wrist, though she didn't need to; the tides in her veins kept track of the hours. Fifteen minutes. He still had fifteen minutes.

She threw the brand onto the pyre; that at least could be started. She felt the heat and smiled, welcoming it like an old friend to warm her ancient bones.

Once the blaze was settled, she turned her back to it as she always did, knowing the bright amber light made of her a silhouette so Henry, as he came up the bridal path, could not see the change in her. Could not see how, on Halloween Eve, age had rushed in upon her, how all the seasons' endings had converged where she stood, rendering her old, weakened, vulnerable.

Tension was beginning to take a hold on Mirabel when she at last saw the blurred shape appear at the mouth of the path; her eyes aged too, let her down. A man, yes. Henry, she thought and relaxed into a smile. He wouldn't see her face, not until the last moment and by then it wouldn't matter.

She raised her hands, stretched out her arms to welcome him, though it caused an ache in her hoary joints, a popping she feared was audible. Her smile would not be dimmed, however, as she felt the ebbing that was essential for a new beginning.

Henry came towards her, faster now, faster, and as he got closer she knew something was wrong.

❋

Her face was a blank, black oval to Cecil, his eyes burned by the glare of the bonfire behind her, but he saw in the way she shifted that she *knew*. She knew somehow.

That something was not right.

And Cecil was filled with an unreasoning terror that she would get away. That she would turn into a puff of smoke, sprout wings and fly, become airy in the extreme and sink into the earth's arms, away from his. He put on a burst of speed, the last he'd ever make, propelling his fat little self forward until his soft body met her bony one, and he heard bones break with the impact, heard her gasp turn into a shriek as they both plummeted back, against the pyre, then into its heart as flames reached up and around to envelop them.

And in that moment, that final moment, Cecil experienced with startling clarity a rare self-awareness. He knew, at last, that his question for the October Widow was not and had never been *Why my son?* but rather *Why not me?*

When she woke she sensed an earth changed and not for the better, and that she had changed, also not for the better. She ached, not as badly as on her last night, but still a dull throb of pain ran through her. Where was the spring in her step, the strength in her form that renewal had always promised and ever delivered?

The October Widow had slept for two solid days in the ashes and bones, the dirt and cinders, while the land and her body re-knitted themselves, made themselves anew, the debt called in with the blood of the young king.

She shook her head. Her memories were loose, scrambled, rattling around in her head as though her skull were too big for her brain. Lying back in her cold charcoal bed, Mirabel closed her eyes, breathed deep, trying to centre herself, to pull the core together.

No. Not the young king. Not her consort, *not* her sacrifice.

Someone else. A man, yes, but not Henry. A man, older, soft and lost, barely holding on to his life. A man weak and whimpering, clasping her as if she were a mother who'd failed to love him.

A man who didn't know what he'd done.

Slowly she raised her hands, examined them. Brown-spotted, dry, fingers twigs, nails broken and brittle, joints swollen. She put them to her face and felt the damage there: skin corrugated, furrowed like a field before planting. The eyebrows bushy, the dips beneath the eyes so soft they felt like decayed fruit, and the chin—oh, the chin! Raised lumps... not moles, nothing so benign, but *warts*. With stiff sharp hairs growing from them.

Slowly she rolled to one side, drew her legs towards her chest, then rolled onto hands and knees, as if to search for something in the cinders, as if to beg. When at last she found her feet, she dug them through the clinkers and soot, ignoring the sharp bits of broken, unconsumed bone, until she found the ground proper. Looked down at her naked body as she waited, saw firsthand the damage done by an inappropriate forfeit: stretch-marked skin, empty dugs for breasts, scrawny arms, a hollow pelvis, thighs destined never to meet, knees like knucklebones, calves no more than long ankles. The October Widow shuddered. She closed her eyes again, concentrated. Listened. Felt.

She'd always known where to travel next for the pulse of the world directed her. But now... now it was weak, so weak she could barely feel it beneath the soles of her feet. She had to kneel once more, press her ear and her palms to the dirt, heedless of the grey-black that coated her flesh, to try and find it. To hear its voice more clearly.

She straightened. There was a message, yes, but it wasn't a location, not yet. The world wasn't strong enough to know, for everywhere the slow decline that a lesser offering brought was beginning. That man, she thought, that stupid sad little man had dumped all his grieving, all his pain into the sacred fire, into her, into the earth. Left his mark behind and it would not be easily erased.

But it *could* be done.

She *would* do it.

In that renewal would be her own, the little man's stain washed away with a tide of young blood.

THE SLISTA
Stephen Laws

You must be gud, says Svival. You must be gud, or The Slista will come get you.

Svival has been a-telling us about The Slista long as we can member. It is the only thing what we are fright about. No thing other has us a-fright. Not the hair-things I done found called rats now, which can bite and go scratcsh but taste good. Not the all kinds Big Noyse that go past window of our under-the-ground place in the Big Howse. Not the sky thunders, not nothing else. But The Slista – this is the big scare thing.

Svival told us long tyme that we are all safe here in the under-ground place where no one go. No one no we here—the five of us. We are the famly—me, and my name is Critch (which now I can rite when I been looking at story-book brung down once by Svival). Then there is Kate, who is next down from me. Then Morris, he boy. Then Declin and True. One time there was six—but Kenny come out of Kate very little small and he not good with noyses. No noyse be made when peepuls come. That is why we be safe all tyme. So Svival, he come down from up the-stare-place very a-noyed and Kenny not make noyse no more and we not need rats for long tyme. Svival say—no noyse, or peepul here and tell The Slista. It come home and taken all us away to Bad Place away from under-ground place. So, shhhhhhh.

We all have the Big Love here in dark. We all brothers (that is word in book) and sisters (that is also word in book). We strong but all different. Kate has fingers gud for tear-up. Morris, he fast and move no hearing noyses. Declin, eyes that see thru and tell all. True, go on up-wall to (ceiling)—that word from book. True, teeth long and sharp for byting. Me, all kinds things. But me Big One and love and keep all.

Then one day, Svival come down say listen. We listen, and there are noyses coming up with his voyce. Wet noyses. His two eyes wet and

I say Svival, what is rong? He sit bump on wood stare and say You all must listen. We listen, and he say I am going sleep and no wake lyke Kenny. Morris make wet eyes, but Svival say no, no, no and no! I have been telling many tymes that all sleep long tyme but go Happy Place, isn't that right? Morris make eyes dry, and we say yes Svival we always reddy for long sleep and not being sad becoz you said. Svival nod and say yes, yes, you must let me go to Long Tyme Sleeping Place and you must all leave the Big Love in the Downstares Dark. Go out and find different Big Love in the Downstares Dark. There are lots of them. One will be waiting some-wheres for you. So you will find it.

Why asks True? Why Svival, if you go to Long Tyme Sleeping Place we no stay in the Big Love here? Becoz, says Svival—and you must not be feared—I must go to Long Tyme Sleeping Place very soon and The Slista will come.

Now we are a-fright, but Svival say No! Do not be a-fright! The Slista will come in the Big Car (You member Big Car what you seen thru little looking-place?) We say yes, Svival—we member Big Car. Well, say Svival—he come in Big Car and find me in Long Tyme Sleeping Place and he say Good, now I will eat Svival and take away Big Howse. But you will be gone-way to diffrint place and he will not be finding any of Svival's Lovelies.

How can The Slista be doing these things, we ask? Svival say The Slista come from Big Place called Offis or Offises, with Magic Papers that have Magic Words that can take happy places and happy peepuls lyke us away frever.

We all ask—What must we do, Svival? Be gone away, be gone away, says Svival. And member all things I been telling you since little tymes. Look after you and yous all. Pro-tect and keep the Big Love.

These are the Rules of Svival, he says.

And then he is gone to Long Tyme Sleeping Place there on the wood stare. And at same tyme, with no tyme for the wet eyes, True says listen there is noyse of the Big Car out-side. We go run little looking place and yes there is Big Car. Do not be a-fright I say when Man in

Black Cloth-rap stuff get out Big Car and come with skware bag. But I am a-fright insyde, becoz this is The Slista and skware bag will have Magic Papers and Magic Words. But also and but—I am Big One for love and keep all and I am now new Svival becoz old Svival is now gone to Long Tyme Sleeping Place. So I must be the Big Up.

Morris, I say, be fast and go to the up-the-stare place and be make no noyse. Declin, I say, go all-so and open the Ding-Dong Door when go Ding-Dong, then hide up on hi place. True, I say, you go other too – and up on up-wall (ceiling) for to wait. When Ding-Dong Door go Ding-Dong—I will be speeking with Svival voice and I will say: Cum in wy doanchoo? (Lyke we heer befor lots of tymes). My Svival voice better coz is rumbler than other Lovelies. Kate, I say, be reddy with fingers. True, I say, also to be reddy with the byting.

We go and we are been reddy.

Ding-Dong says the Ding-Dong Door.

So now we are been going away from the Old Big Love under-the-ground Old Place and—just lyke the old Svival sayed—we are finding the New Big Love under-the-ground New Place and we are reddy to come into it. When the peepuls who are in the up-the-stares don't see, me and the Lovelies will come into it and be new Happy.

They are wanting me to keep old name Critch, but I say oh no, oh no, I will be now the new Svival not the old Critch. Becoz that is the job of the oldest to do, and they say oh all-ryte, yes then are glad. But I am gud in-side because they love me as the Old Critch and will love me as the new Svival.

Svival was kind to us and I will be kind to them. This is the Laws of Svival, member?

I will be kind and we will be warm and happy and hirt ennyone what will want harm us. We will eat nyce things all tyme. Nycer and nycer things. And when Long Sleep will come for me then Kate will be new Svival after me—and we will be going on. I lyke thinking when I go Long Tyme Sleeping Place, they will be eet of me and I will be of them hear in bodees and of them in Long Tyme Sleeping Place also.

Happy lyke when we eet Old Svival.

But not Happy lyke when we eet The Slista.
He not tasting nyce.
Not nyce, at all.

OUTSIDE HEAVENLY
Rio Youers

The pillar of black smoke could be seen from Heavenly. The townsfolk looked from their windows and gathered on sidewalks. They knew it was the Roth place burning, and they prayed for the girls but not the man.

✻

Police Chief John Peck sat on the hood of his cruiser and watched the volunteer fire department hush the flames. It took all of the one thousand gallons carried in the engine and most of the two thousand carried in the tanker, but they got it down and when the smoke cleared the remains stood like an incomplete sketch. Ashes swirled and clung to the tall grass. Sassafras and oak at the edges of the lot creaked disagreeably. Some leaves were blackened. Beyond, the sky paled to iris-blue and a murmuration of starlings made a shape in the air and disappeared.

Calloway's voice crackled over the radio. Peck had posted Calloway on Dogwood Road to turn away the curious, and with the Roth place in flames they could be many. Calloway told him that a truckful of menfolk had turned up to help, but Peck knew what they really wanted was to witness, up close, Roth struck low.

"It's under control," Peck said. Through haze and dancing ash he saw the fire chief approaching. "You thank them boys and send them on their way."

He slid off the hood and met the fire chief in the climbing sunlight, away from the smoke and ash.

"She's out, but we'll keep a close eye." Joe Neath had headed Heavenly's fire department for seven years. In his other life, he was the foreman at Gator Steel and a father of five. "Out doesn't mean dead, 'specially in this heat."

"Any idea what started it?"

"No obvious point of origin, but Perry Horne will be out later and he can tell us more." Joe unzipped his jacket a little way and palmed sweat from his throat. "I don't need a fire marshal to tell you it wasn't an accident, though."

Peck sighed and stiffened his jaw. The fire chief nodded, started toward the ruin. Peck followed. They skirted the yard where dry grass ticked, then crossed to the house's eastern face, intact but damaged. The ground was soupy from the hoses' spray. Peck stepped around the deeper puddles where the sky was reflected dull. A child's soft toy stared at him with stitches for eyes.

"You might want to ready yourself," Joe said.

Heat drove off the building and kinked the air and Peck felt his shirt latch to his back. The smell was char and smoke but something else, too. A sharp scent that kicked like ammonia. Peck cupped a hand over his nose and mouth. Ashes brushed his cheeks. They neared a window black as a box of soot with the glass broken and faux wooden blinds part-melted to the frame. Within, the carbonised remains of the living room. Most everything was stripped to whatever wouldn't burn. Peck noted the steel frame of a bed that had collapsed from the room above and what remained of the armchair where Beau Roth no doubt watched TV and sank beer and contemplated wrongs. Peck would study the scene later, when it was safer, but for now he couldn't see much beyond the savagery.

The corpse hung by its arms from a support beam. It was headless and naked. The stomach was open from sternum to groin and the entrails strung around the room. They—like the rest of the body— were red and blistered but not burned through.

"Jesus Christ." Peck turned away and tried to breathe deeply but the air was too choked. He spluttered and spat in the dirt.

"No accident," Joe said.

"Well, Christ." Peck looked again and turned away quicker than before. His nostrils flared. "That Beau, you think?"

"I'd say." Joe wiped more sweat from his throat. "Torso's about the right size."

"Yeah." Peck nodded. "Why didn't he burn up?"

"Makes no sense."

"The girls?"

"No sign."

The two men looked at each other. They were the same age and height—forty-three, a little under six feet—and shared a similar build, once muscular but starting to soften. It was as if growing up in Heavenly had shaped them similarly, like two dunes sculpted by the same winds. They said nothing but much passed between them. Peck sleeved grey sweat from his brow and shook his head.

A small section of the back wall crumbled and fell. Embers lifted and died in the air. Peck's radio squawked and he grabbed it, thankful for the diversion. He started to speak but got a chestful of that bad air and coughed. He strode clear of the house and tried again.

"What you got, Ty?"

Tyler Bray was a part-time cop and most-time grease monkey at Go Auto, which made him useful when it came to maintaining the department's two vehicles. He was young and enthusiastic, but better with a wrench than he was with a badge. Peck had him skirting Roth's two acres for signs of anything untoward, mainly to keep him out of the way.

"I found Mary Roth, Chief."

"What's your twenty?"

"A short sprint northerly." Ty's voice was tight with nervous excitement; he wasn't rotating tires now. "A hundred yards, I'd say. There's an old pickup sitting on blocks, but I doubt you'll see it with the grass being–"

"Step on the roof a moment, Ty. Flap those long arms."

Peck looked north where the grass moved like a great hand was brushing over it, and after a moment Ty's head poked up and he waved his arms. Peck started briskly toward him, cutting a trail through grass that started at his knees, then climbed to his chest and beyond. Rat snakes whipped out of sight and some tightened as he stepped over them, tongues at the air. Peck kept the mast of dark smoke at his back and turned often to keep his bearing.

Mary Roth knelt head down, arms crossed over her face. Her dress was faded, dirty, and had rucked up to her pale stomach. Her thighs were smeared with soot and grime.

"She say anything?" Peck asked Ty, stepping abreast of him.

"Not a word, Chief."

"Mary? Mary… it's Chief Peck."

The sun had risen fast and seemed dedicated to this thin clearing behind the abandoned pickup. Peck felt sweat trickle to his beltline and the heat at the back of his neck was heavy as a metal bar. He blew over his upper lip and crouched beside the woman. He could smell the smoke in her hair.

"Mary?"

Peck had known her all her life—Beau's only child, and to look at her was to cry, imagining what she might have been under kinder circumstances. But Beau was a fiercely wicked man who crushed all that could be loved. Mary—like all—was born beautiful. Thirty-two now with ghosts on her shoulders, her spirit withered like some sweet fruit dried in the heat.

"Talk to me, Mary."

He crouched lower and saw her mouth through her crossed arms. Teeth clenched.

"Are you hurt?"

A beat, and then she shook her head and uncrossed her arms. She used the hem of her dress to mop wet eyes. Soot beneath her fingernails. Smudged across her brow. She breathed and her upper body trembled, as if the world's hard edges had been packed into her lungs.

"This all…" Mary gestured at the truck and the clearing, then wider: at the trees, sky, and everything. "This all seems lesser now, like something that can be opened and poured out."

Peck wiped his eyes and saw Beau Roth disemboweled and headless. Crows bristled suddenly from the grass and made south, calling.

"You need to tell me what happened, Mary."

She almost smiled. There was red in her eyes. "Nothing but the devil's doing." Her hands trembled, curled to fists. "That son of a bitch got what he deserved."

＊

Mary Roth weighed all of one hundred and twenty pounds and her fifteen-year-old daughter—Cindy: missing—was yet smaller. There was no way that, even working together, they could have strung up Beau's corpse. He was a truck of a man, loaded with old muscle. Peck knew he had some work to do.

The interview room was small and cool and—until about an hour ago—used mainly for storage. Interrogation was not one of Peck's regular duties. His days were spent on admin, general upkeep, and—when there was time—patrolling. Every now and then he'd be called to settle a dust-up, or would ticket speeders on the open stretch of blacktop between Heavenly and Gray Point. It was an unremarkable department, comprised of three full-time cops, one part-timer, and one volunteer. Enough for a two-stoplight town. Even so, Peck rarely worked fewer than sixty hours a week.

He and Ty cleared the interview room while Mary Roth got cleaned up and checked by paramedics. Calloway led her in just a little shy of noon. Her chestnut hair had been brushed and clasped back from her face, which was pale and sad, and her eyes had the look of cold water. She wore clothes salvaged from the town hall's lost and found. A Nike sweatshirt and a pair of basketball shorts almost as long on her as pants. She took a seat and placed her trembling hands flat on the table. Her fingernails had been scrubbed.

"Am I under arrest?"

"No, Mary."

"I may as well be; I got nowhere else to go."

She closed her eyes and a tear slipped fast onto her cheek. Peck nodded at Calloway and he left the room. For a moment the only sound was electricity in the walls and the sigh of the A/C. Peck set the audio recorder running. Tape spooled with a hiss.

"Tell me what happened, Mary. Leave nothing out."

She looked at him. "I tell you a lie and you'll think I'm guilty." She looked away. "I tell you the truth and you'll think I'm insane."

"Let's go with the truth."

"I already told you." Another tear, quick as the first. "It was the devil's doing."

Peck looked at the running tape and knew that the clock was ticking. County forensic units were already on the scene. If he didn't get answers soon, Pine County or state police investigators would take the reins. They'd be direct, insensitive. Peck didn't want them in his town.

"Your father's dead," he said. "Your daughter's missing. No doubt the devil played his part."

Mary wiped her eyes and they flickered and she stared for a long moment at the blank wall. There was a depth to her expression that made him turn away. He'd learned to study aspect and body language, where the truths were often clearer than anything spoken. The weight of her eyelids, the set of her mouth, her hands palm-down on the table, illustrated a single truth that unnerved him: Mary was haunted.

"I want to help you," Peck said.

"I'm beyond that."

"And I want to find Cindy."

"She's been gone a long time."

"Talk to me, Mary."

A mile out of town the Roth place—what remained—stood black and wet. The air still smelled of smoke and that other thing, sharp like ammonia. The vehicles plugging the yard belonged to the fire marshal and the county forensics unit, each working to assemble pieces that might make something like a picture. In Heavenly proper, tongues ran like a new fire and the devil was mentioned more than once, always in regard to Beau himself. In the interview room, the tape ran and the A/C purred. John Peck said little. Mary Roth blinked tears that flashed and unbridled her ghosts.

✳

"Momma died. Some brain thing, so they say. Thirty and dead, and I think God walked out on us the day we parked her box in the ground. Daddy got closer. First in a way that was affectionate, and then overly familiar. He raped me on my eleventh birthday. I felt afterward like a dress that had been left out in the wind and sun, all colourless and tattered. Something that could never be worn pretty. At fourteen I was pregnant with his child. You didn't know about that. The child was born—a boy—and at five months he fell off the bed and knocked his head good. He cried a lot and died in the night. Daddy buried him in the garden, like a dog with a bone. This all has nothing to do with the fire, except it does: when God is so missing from your life, the devil has more room to move."

Peck inhaled through his nose, his teeth locked and lightly grinding. He showed no emotion, but felt inside as though a match had been struck close to his heart.

"Daddy lost his job when Gator Steel cut loose a lot of manpower, and life moved from bad to worse in a hurry. I thought about running away. Even killing myself. I don't know if it's courage or stupidity that keeps a person from doing those things, but whatever it is, I got plenty of it. Daddy found work after a time. Nothing solid. Just here-and-there jobs. Cutting wood. Raking leaves. That kind of thing. I started waitressing at Captain Griddle. Daddy didn't like me leaving the house, but I brought in as much money as him and he found no room to argue. Anyway, that's where I met Gordy Lee. Short order cook. Some sweet, but not exactly busy between the ears."

Peck nodded. He remembered Gordy. Cleft lip and a stutter. Gordy got knocked around by his older brothers. Peck would often see him cooking eggs with bruises about his face and then one day he wasn't cooking eggs any more. Rumour was he'd made tracks to Canada, but nobody knew for sure.

"We fooled around," Mary said, "but it was nothing much. Then one night when we were alone, cleaning up, he lifted my skirt and pumped himself into me, and I didn't stop him. Boy came like a horse and we made more than eggs in that kitchen. I told him a couple months later and he ripped quick out of town. Guess he wasn't ready to be a daddy—or to deal with *my* daddy. Chicken-livered, harelipped ol' son of a whore, either way you cut it."

"And Gordy is Cindy's father?"

"Yes, sir. She got his brown eyes and that's all."

"You ever hear from him?"

"No, sir."

"You don't know where he is?"

"No, sir."

Peck let his mind run an unlikely track: Gordy Lee—nearly sixteen years tougher and uglier—shooting south to claim his little girl, and taking care of Beau Roth in the bargain. Again Peck saw Beau hanging by his wrists, headless, guts strung about the blackened room. He remembered the bruised, skinny kid cooking eggs at Captain Griddle and couldn't get the pieces to fit, no matter which way he turned them.

Still, he asked, "You think Gordy may have tried to get in touch with Cindy?"

"No, sir." Mary shook her head. "Boy was a coward. A stupid one, at that. He could cook eggs and fuck like a bug, but that's about it."

Peck nodded and made a gesture for her to continue.

"I'm telling you what happened, for better or worse. You don't need your police hat right now. You need your *believing* hat. This little slice of family history shows that I'm done hiding, and I got no interest in lies. You might want to bear that in mind as we move along."

Peck nodded again.

"I kept being pregnant from Daddy for as long as I could. But a woman will usually show sooner with her second child, and by four months not even the biggest of my dresses could hide the bump. Daddy didn't take it well. I never told him that Gordy was the father—never told nobody, until now—but he wanted blood, just the same. He got into a lot of fistfights around town, and I guess he spent a few nights in those cells you have downstairs. I tried to stay out of his way. There's a clearing in Brack Wood where the sun shines in and the flowers grow long and pretty, and I'd go there all the time—just sit and daydream with my hands curled around my belly. I wouldn't go home 'til after dark when I knew Daddy would be passed out drunk. But I couldn't avoid him all the time and he found ways to hurt me. One time he suffocated me with a pillow. Held it over my face until the whole world faded, then took it away at the last moment. Another time he pinned me to the kitchen floor and shouted hateful things at my belly—shouted until his throat split like old wood. I've never hated him more."

Mary took one hand from the table and stroked her stomach. A soothing, circular motion. She looked at Peck and then away. The tears came again. These bigger, slower. She let them run down her face and drop from her chin.

"Ain't life a string of woe?" she said.

"It can get better," Peck said.

She shook her head as if she didn't believe that, and Peck could hardly blame her. She could live until everything about her withered, but might always feel that contentment was like the clothes they'd appropriated from the lost and found: not hers by right, something she'd never grow in to.

"If the best God can do for me is a few tall flowers in the wood, I fear He may be outgunned." A stiff, bitter smile. Her yellow teeth gleamed. "The devil has cast a wider net, and left a deeper mark."

Peck bridged his fingers. He still smelled smoke when he inhaled.

"Heavenly is a small town and people talk. I could hear the whispers from my house. A sound like bugs in the grass. And the way you all looked at me. Part wonder. Part sympathy. The way you'd look at someone born with a deformity. It's no wonder I didn't come looking for help." She uttered a brittle laugh. "But for all the talk, you got no clue how bad it was. I spent my days in fear and always crying. Then Cindy came along and I feared for her, too. But abuse isn't like an uncomfortable pair of boots you can just kick off. It's like being the passenger in a car speeding the wrong way down the highway. You know there's hurt ahead, but you're too scared to jump out. All you can do is hope it slows down, or better still, that it stops completely. Maybe it's different for other victims, who have more family and friends, or who live in a bigger town. But I don't know of much beyond Heavenly and Daddy. This is all I got. This is my life."

Mary drew a long breath. Spittle glimmered on her lips and she wiped her face with baggy sleeves. A little time passed. Peck thought about his wife and boys, relieved to erase—if only for a moment— Beau Roth from his mind. He'd take the boys fishing this weekend, he decided. And tonight, instead of sitting on the porch with a beer or two, he'd hold Gracie. Hold her tight. Grateful that he could.

"Seeing Daddy with Cindy, the way he treated her—the way he *mis*treated her—was bad. Feeling that I couldn't protect her was worse. And knowing that *I* brought her into this…" She trailed off, wet eyes rolling to the ceiling. "She used to beg me to run away with her. She had it all planned out. We'd leave while Daddy was at work. Hitchhike to Carver, then catch a bus to New York City. We'd be dancers, she said. Pretty as flowers, she said. I recall a time when she took her makeup box and made us both up, and we sat for a long time looking at one another in the mirror. Painted like dolls. It was like looking through a window into what *could* be. Then we turned the radio on and danced until we were short of breath. I've never known such joy. Couple nights later, Daddy rolled in drunk and took to us both. He knocked me out cold and when I came to, I saw his ugly bull of a body atop Cindy, pounding into her while she cried and bled. Her eyes met mine and I remembered how we'd looked in the mirror, and I knew then that I had to do something. But Cindy beat me to it. She was gone two days later. Up and left—jumped out of that speeding car. I found a note in her makeup box and it read GONE DANCING with a little X for a kiss. Fourteen years old. I thought the world would tear her to pieces and my heart just broke for her. For *me*, too. I was alone with the monster again. I didn't think life could get any worse. But I was wrong about that."

Mary placed her damp hands on the table and they left prints that glimmered in the light. Her breath hitched twice in her chest like a cold engine starting. Tears, still, running from some deep reservoir.

"Cindy came home a few months later."

✻

Flowers with petals like lace, their stems withered, placed in a bunch on the ground. Peck thought: *He cried a lot and died in the night. Daddy buried him in the garden, like a dog with a bone.* Had a feeling that if he dug down just a little way, he'd find a tiny human skeleton. He shook his head and made a note to get on that. Give the boy a decent burial, stone and all, even if he had to pay for it himself.

A pale morning after a night of stripped sleep and Peck was at the Roth place early. Beau's body had been removed and now all that remained was the burned shell surrounded by yellow tape. It rippled with a sound almost lonesome. There was more at the head of the driveway, tied between trees, where officers had been posted in shifts to keep away prying townsfolk. Peck received the call last night that state police were taking over the investigation, which meant that he could go back to pushing his pen around and attending fundraisers. He turned from the little grave marked only with dry flowers and approached the blackened house. That ammonia smell still touched the air. He looked through the charred window where he had seen Beau's body hanging. Reddened and blistered but not burned through. *Makes no sense,* Joe Neath had said. Peck looked at his watch. Five of eight. State police would roll in at noon, suited and clean. Until then, this was his.

Perry Horne, the county fire marshal, had called him last night, too. His investigation was hindered by anomalies, cause of the blaze chief among them. "This'll take some time," he said. "I've known you twenty-some years, Peck, friend and colleague, and I don't mind telling you I'm at a loss. There's no obvious origin point, direction of melt is not consistent, and the char patterns—normally clear as footprints—have got me in circles. There's no evidence of an electrical fault or accelerants, and every room is evenly damaged. If I didn't know better, I'd say the entire house spontaneously ripped into flames."

"Can that happen?"

"Well shit, no." Perry had made an exasperated sound. "Every fire has cause and origin, Peck. But not this one. Not that I can see."

Peck had asked about Beau's corpse.

"I've got no answer for that, either," Perry replied. "Second-degree burns are not consistent with the damage to the house. Temperature in there would have been over a thousand degrees Fahrenheit. He should have been barbecue."

"That's what I thought."

"The way I see it, the house was deep in flames—the fire department likely rolling into the yard—before Beau was strung up."

"That's impossible."

"Yeah, it is." And Perry had barked a short, humourless laugh. "This whole thing is one big question mark."

"There has to be an explanation."

"When you find it, you let me know."

Peck walked away from the house and the hard thoughts associated with it, but couldn't get distance from the latter. They followed him like hungry children. The sun lifted from behind a shelf of cloud on the horizon and his shadow sprang ahead of him. He skirted the infant's grave and made through the high grass toward a cluster of trees—Brack Wood—with leaves catching the morning light. A vague trail linked the edge of Beau's lot to the trees, marking Mary's frequent passage. Peck followed it. The woods smelled of pine and turned earth and the light was a cool, watery green. After a time he came to the clearing Mary spoke of and the flowers were tall. Snakeroot and bellwort and Carolina lily. They nodded their bright, pretty heads. The only sounds were birdsong and the branches whickering.

This was where Mary—and perhaps Cindy, too—had come to escape the monster. A shallow scoop of serenity within their troubled lives. And the earth was fuller, the needles greener, for having absorbed so many daydreams. Peck sat with his back propped against a yellow pine and gathered his knees to his chest. Eyes closed, he sought patience and open-mindedness. Guidance, too. He inhaled the forest smells and they were kind. After a long moment, he opened his eyes and tears spilled onto his cheeks. It occurred to him—and not for the first time—that he could have helped those girls a long time ago. *Should* have.

Peck linked his hands and brought his knuckles to his forehead.

"God hear me..."

He'd tried praying last night. He'd prayed with his wife, their hands joined, but he hadn't sensed God and it was the same now.

The sun rode higher as he walked back to the house. The day's heat was already hard. Peck rounded the field and approached from a different direction, more northeasterly. Here the ground was patchy, long grass in places but mostly bare earth cracked and polished by the sun. Peck kept an eye out for carelessly discarded evidence—anything Tyler may have missed. They still hadn't found Beau's severed head. The thinking was that—unlike the rest of Beau—it had burned up in the blaze, and that Perry Horne would find his blackened teeth, or the tough knots of his skull, while sifting through the ashes.

Closer to the house, Peck discovered several black tracks in the dry grass. He squatted to his haunches to examine them in more detail. They were each about ten inches long, as wide as his hand and arched on the inside. Eleven in total, tracking away from the Roth place. Peck measured them against his own stride. He touched the scorched grass and smelled his fingers.

Yes, they were burn marks, but they were also footprints.

*

She wore the same clothes as the day before and the same haunted expression. Her hair wasn't clasped but looped onto her shoulders. It looked a shade lighter.

Peck's finger paused over the red button on the audio recorder.

"Listen, Mary, the state police will be here this afternoon and they'll want to question you. They don't know Heavenly, and they have little patience for small town ways. They'll be stiff-necked and businesslike.

That's the way they work. The more you tell me now—the more we get on tape—the less you'll have to tell them. Do you understand?"

Her eyes were heavy and dark. Peck thought she might be the only person in all of Heavenly who'd had less sleep than him.

"You don't live with Daddy for thirty-two years," she began with a dry smile, "only to be intimidated by a couple of suit-and-tie cops from the city. They can ask their damn questions, and they can be as businesslike as they please. I'll tell them everything I know, just like I'm telling you. This investigation won't depend on my cooperation, but on how quickly you can explain the unexplainable."

Peck recalled Perry Horne declaring this whole thing one big question mark. He felt something like a knot in his chest.

"Just thought you should know," he said.

She nodded.

Peck pushed the red button. The tape rolled.

"Do you know how your father died, Mary?"

Her hands were clasped in her lap and she looked at them and when she looked up her eyes fixed on Peck and did not waver. She shook her head once and then, realising this wouldn't come across on tape, said, "No. I was in the yard at the time."

"Do you know who killed him?"

"The devil," she said, still looking at him straight.

"You get a good look at him?" Peck asked. "The devil?"

"*Her.*"

"I'm sorry?"

"Devil's a she," Mary said. Another dry smile. "And yeah, I got a good look. She slept under the same roof as me. Baked bread with me. I cooked her meals and washed her clothes."

"You're talking about Cindy?"

"I'm talking about the devil," Mary said. "She just *looked* like Cindy. Same hair, same eyes, same skin. But inside... not my little girl. No, sir."

Peck took a calming breath. Any other time he would have applied a little pressure—let Mary know that neighbourly indulgence only carried so far. This was not a game, and he was not going to be played with. The mystery of this all stood before him, though, and he could not as yet see around it. He remembered the clearing with its tall flowers, and how he'd prayed for open-mindedness.

"Help me out, Mary," he said.

Mary sat back in her seat. She still looked at Peck but didn't really see him. Her expression glazed as her mind drifted elsewhere. Peck sat back in his own seat and it creaked and he waited. Mary shook her head. The tears came again and she didn't try to wipe them away. It looked like she had her face turned up to the rain. Just her face. She started to speak, but then stopped and broke down. "Not my little girl," she managed between sobs, and didn't say anything else for a long time.

Peck fetched her Kleenex and hot coffee in a paper cup and gave her a moment. The clock inched toward noon.

She said once her eyes were damp but not dry, "Cindy came home, but she wasn't the same. Something had happened to her out there. Wherever she went. She'd moved from being a young girl to a young woman, but it was more than that. A mother knows."

Peck felt like saying that years of abuse will wilt even the prettiest flower, but he bit his lip. He encouraged Mary with warm eyes and she kept talking.

"There was an edge to her. She was always fine with me, but with Daddy, the way she looked at him sometimes… she could drive nails with a stare like that. And Daddy felt it, too, because he didn't take to her the way he used to. Oh, he was still heavy-handed, and plenty so, but he kindly backed away afterward. I'd never seen him like that. Not scared but… *uncertain*. And that scared *me*."

Another long silence and she looked away again, remembering. Peck counted time in his head. Only his chest moved as he breathed.

"But it wasn't only this edge," she continued. "No, sir, there was an outright wrongness about her. She was still some sweet but it felt like thin ice—like something that could crack at any time. I thought it was depression. I made an appointment to see Doctor Everett but

Daddy stopped us from going. He said Cindy would snap out of it—that Everett would only go poking where he had no business, and no good would come of that."

Peck felt the anger and guilt tick inside him again.

"You surprised she was acting that way?" he asked. "Given everything that went on in that house?"

"It wasn't depression."

"She needed help, Mary."

"Don't we all?" Mary fixed him with the same unwavering glare and colour rose from inside her collar, touched her jaw. "Judge me all you like, Chief, for something I did or didn't do, but save a few stones for yourself, for this whole shitheel town. And remember this: casting judgment on someone who's seen hell is just about the same as whipping the dead."

She and Peck took long breaths and something in the air realigned itself.

"Okay, Mary." He nodded. "Continue."

"Cindy said that the only reason she came home was to get me. Said she'd found a place where I'd be made stronger, and where I'd never be hurt again. She begged me to go back with her but I didn't, for all the reasons I said before. I told her to go alone, to be happy and strong, but she said she wasn't leaving without me. I guess that's when all the strange things started happening."

"Strange?"

"Growling in the walls. The trees moving closer to the house. Two moons appearing in the sky, one as red as a drop of blood. Crows crowding the roof and windows. Rats and snakes pouring from the well." Mary counted off on her fingers but now she spread her hands wide. "Lots of things. Strange."

Peck nodded. He'd seen his share of strange just lately, but still believed he'd find the truth. Nothing real was truly unexplainable.

"One night—Daddy was mean-drunk and had just taken to me with his belt—I looked out the windows, front and back, and saw at least a hundred coyotes sitting in a circle around the house. They didn't howl or fuss. They just sat there, like they were waiting for something. Cindy asked me again to leave with her. I told her no. Then she stepped onto the porch, spoke some language I didn't understand, and those coyotes turned tail and slipped into the dark. Let me tell you, Chief, I've never been so scared. Not even when Daddy was at his worst."

Peck opened his mouth but found he had nothing to say.

"Clocks running backward. Windows and doors blowing open. Rain falling hard on the house and not a cloud in the sky. Flies everywhere, inside the house and out—so many damn flies. And don't get me started on the smell."

"Like ammonia?" Peck shifted in his seat.

"I guess," Mary said. "Sharp and bitter. Back of the throat."

Peck knew the smell, and this at least rang true, but he let everything else sit for now. Very little about this whole mess was normal, but a picture had started to form in his mind. He saw Cindy leaving home, getting in with some vigilante group—strong boys and arsonists among them—who decided to take the law into their own hands. It didn't come close to explaining everything, but Peck felt he was on the right track.

"This place," he said, studying Mary's dark-ringed eyes. "Where Cindy went. Where she wanted to take you. She ever tell you where it is?"

"No, sir."

"You don't know anything about it?"

"I tried asking, but she wouldn't say much. Got all tight-lipped and sullen."

"Tell me whatever you remember, Mary."

She thought a while, sitting back in her chair with her brow knitted, picking at her fingernails. Peck, for his part, worked to push away the unexplainable, and concentrate on solid facts. He figured everything else would slide into place once he had a strong foundation.

"Outside Heavenly," Mary said. She frowned a little deeper, then nodded. "She went on foot. That I know. Must've gone east because she said she passed the old water tower—said its shadow was like a big ol' spider. All them legs, you know?"

Peck nodded.

"She walked, but I don't know how far. All she said about the place was that the raptors circle clockwise there, except for one—him bigger—going aboutways."

Peck pulled a notebook from his pocket and wrote this down. "Anything else? Landmarks? Or distinct sounds—you know, like a river, or a train? Anything?"

"No, sir."

"How about the people she was with? She give you any names? Descriptions?"

Mary stopped picking her fingernails and linked her hands much as Peck had in the clearing. "For what it's worth." And here the frown was replaced with a cold little smile. "She called them the boys with the black feet."

✳

Peck pulled over at the side of Cotton Road. Sun on the windshield like a branding iron. To his left, beyond a rusted chain link fence, Ring Field and the old water tower which had stood dry for more than ten years. Faded letters across the tank once read HEAVENLY. In a certain light you could see the ghosts of those letters, but not now. Peck stepped out of the cruiser and Tyler Bray followed. They scaled the fence like children. Ty tore his pants and swore.

East the way was flat and hard. Rocky ground and dust devils with the sun always like a hammer thrashing. A mile beyond, Forney Creek marked the town limits. They stopped to douse their hats in water, to fill their hands and drink. They crossed where it was shallowest but still got wet to the thighs, even Ty with his crane fly legs. Here Peck had no jurisdiction. Here he turned from a lawmaker to a citizen with a gun.

"How far we walking, Chief?"

"Until I say."

"This ain't even Heavenly."

Across the cracked grassland to the southwest of Gray Point, through a sparse forest where the boughs rattled dryly, skirting marshland where bullfrogs croaked and a fetid mist rose from between the reeds. Beyond this the flies grew fat and many. The men slapped at them with their hats. Peck looked at the sky but it was bare and blue. They walked another twenty minutes then rested a while. Peck checked the time but his watch had stopped.

"Got the time there, Ty?"

Ty checked. "I got two twenty."

"Well, shit. That can't be right."

"That's what I got."

They carried on but with languor, following no course other than Peck's instinct. Across barren fields and through a narrow valley of mostly shale, where the sun was reflected in bullets and horned lizards blinked at them sleepily. They emerged into a field where grass swayed chest-high. The flies grew in number but were slower, fatter. Ty wheezed and wanted to rest but Peck spurred him on. He was tired too, and the heat had placed a fierce ache across the inside of his skull. Whenever he felt like stopping, he remembered Mary Roth in her borrowed, too-big clothes. So many tears, like a face in the rain.

Tell me about the night of the fire, Mary.

She'd be with the state police now. They'd lean hard on her. Cross-examine her. They'd listen to the tape and believe not a word.

Daddy saw all the strange happenings, too. He was stupid and angry, but not blind. It all got too much for him. He felt threatened, I guess. So he took me aside and told me that Cindy had been chained by the devil, and that it was our duty to set her free. I'd had the same thoughts – had even contemplated calling Reverend Mathis. I told Daddy this, but he wouldn't let me bring an outsider into the house. Not even a man of the cloth. He said he had his own way of handling it, and just as Christian.

Their hats dried in the heat and felt stiff on their heads, and Ty peeled his off and fanned his face with it. His shirt was black with sweat.

"You notice anything strange?" he gasped.

Peck searched the sky and the long grass and it *all* felt strange. *Thin*, almost, like a bleached and moistureless backdrop with something darker behind. He thought Ty was referring to the smell, though. It rose from the earth here. Caustic and foul. Back of the throat, Mary had said.

"That smell," Peck said, nodding. "Same as at the Roth place. Maybe we're getting close."

"Smell's bad, but that ain't it." Ty knuckled sweat from his eyes. Foamy spittle nestled at the corners of his mouth. "We're walking east, right?"

"More or less."

"Then why is the sun setting ahead of us?" Ty pointed at the fried bullet hole in the sky, and even *it* appeared to be sweating. "Should be behind us, this time of day."

Peck pulled up and frowned and turned a loose circle. He took off his hat and scratched his head. "Must've got turned around somehow."

"We walked a straight line and you know it."

"Just keep going." Peck put on his hat and sniffed the air, following his nose now. "East or west, don't matter. We're close."

Ty used his hat to shade the sun. "And don't it look like a drop of blood?"

It was the early hours. I was sleeping. Not deeply. I'm always aware of the sounds around me. It's like sleeping with one eye open, I guess. I heard a commotion and stirred, but then the screaming started and I jumped out of bed like there was a rattler between the sheets. I ran downstairs and saw Daddy stepping outside, Cindy slung over one shoulder like a sack of firewood. He'd tied her wrists and ankles with rope. I screamed and followed, and he shouted back at me to stay in the house, that I didn't need to see any of this. Normally I do what Daddy says, but not this time. No, sir. I staggered outside and saw Daddy drop Cindy next to the woodpile. He grabbed her hair and dragged her head down across the chopping block. Then he took up his axe.

They kept walking and Peck felt blisters growing inside his boots and it wasn't long after that he noticed the sleek shapes in the grass. They flowed alongside and the grass rippled. Peck tried to get a sense of their number. He knew what they were long before Ty drew his sidearm.

"Coyotes," Ty said.

"They won't hurt you." But Peck wasn't sure about that. He placed a hand on the grip of his own Glock and walked wary.

"This is crazy, Chief."

"Keep walking."

"We shouldn't be doing this." Ty stopped suddenly and the shapes in the grass stopped too. "We got no business out here."

"We got every business."

"You're chasing shadows." Ty holstered his weapon. Flies crawled across his face. Some were so big they dragged. "This is a state police matter. Let *them* trek through hell and back." He flapped at the flies but only some buzzed away.

"You listen to me, Ty Bray, and you listen good. We—that's you, me, the whole damn town—we spent too many years ignoring what was happening at the Roth place. Hid inside our comfortable little lives and didn't do a goddamn thing to help those girls. It's time to put that right. There's a truth out here somewhere and we're going to find it."

Ty wiped his eyes. "Let the state cops find it."

"They won't believe a word Mary tells them." Peck's face was a shade of red and his headache almost blinding. "They'll think she's hiding something and tear her to pieces. She may wind up confessing to something she didn't do, and I can't let that happen. She's been through enough."

Daddy raised his axe and I ran at him – bounced off him, more than anything. I clawed at his legs and he kicked me away. I would have gone at him again, of course, but then Cindy started talking in that weird language, same as when she spoke to the coyotes. I saw a glow beneath her skin, deep and orange, and the ropes binding her turned to ash. She got to her feet as Daddy was raising the axe again, and he just about fell over backward. Her eyes… they were like burning coals, pouring smoke. The axe toppled from his hands and she pushed him. It was like she was pushing a door open – that easy – and he flew halfway across the yard like a leaf in the wind. He got to his feet and reeled into the house. Cindy picked up the axe and followed.

Ty now fifteen feet behind and staggering. Teeth clamped, shaking his head. He'd given up on swatting away the flies and they droned around him and settled and drank the sweat from his open pink pores. Peck flapped his own hat and saw ahead a scratch of forest. He sniffed at the bitter air and walked that way.

Cooler beneath the canopy, but darker. Here the coyotes were shadows and some howled in the gloom. Something else ticked among the branches. Peck waited for Ty, resting his hand on a gnarled trunk that twisted beneath him and when he looked he saw no trunk, no tree. Evening light spilled through the canopy, like wine through a cracked glass.

"Let's stop awhile," Ty panted.

"I don't want to stop here."

They trudged on with Peck barely looking, his dread tamped down by determination. The thunder in his head was his heartbeat – a reckless, spirited thing. They made it through the forest and the light now was burned purple. Across a wide, dry riverbed and into a field marked by the outlines of trees and rocks. The grass here was knee-high and the coyotes' backs showed like otters in water.

"There's a hill ahead," Peck said, pointing to where the ground rose. "We can maybe get a bearing from there."

Ty nodded but he looked close to tears, no doubt wishing he was changing oil at Go Auto or hanging out with his girl. They struggled up the hill, which wasn't steep, but both men fairly crawled. At the summit, Peck looked around but saw nothing he recognised. The sky had grown pale. He'd swear it was getting light again. They caught their breaths and pushed on. Midway down the hill, Peck noticed—not a mile away—a small settlement. Glass and aluminum winked in the sunlight. It was definitely getting lighter. Hotter, too.

"This is some kind of nightmare," Ty said.

Peck's gaze drifted upward, and he saw several birds in the sky above the settlement. Red-tailed hawks, he thought, judging from the size. They circled clockwise, all but one—a raptor Peck had no name for, with a broader, crooked span—looping the other way.

He moved on. His stride was long.

"We're here," he said.

I can't tell you what happened in the house because I stayed in the yard. And I wasn't alone. The coyotes were back, sitting in the long grass with their ears high and their eyes shining. Seemed the devil was all ways and if there was any heaven to be found, I didn't know where. So I stayed put. And how I screamed, but not as loud as Daddy, and not for as long. Then the house went up. You know when you set fire to a book of matches and it flares in your hand all at once? It was like that. I thought for sure they were both dead, then Cindy stepped out of the flames. She was on fire, but she wasn't burning. I know how that sounds, but I swear it's true. It's like she controlled those flames; like the coyotes, they did whatever she told them to, and ain't that the devil's way? I watched her walk across the grass and away, all those coyotes by her side, and for a while I followed her flame and then she was gone. Then I took to my heels. I wanted to find my clearing but got lost in the dark. I wound up by that old truck in the field, and there I hid, and there you found me.

Peck thought 'settlement' too grand a word for what amounted to a few tumble-down shacks and trailers. Some were painted faded colours, their windows either blacked-out or boarded over. There were no satellite dishes or barbecues. No washing strung to dry. Peck would think it abandoned but for the feeling they were being watched – and not only by the coyotes, mostly gathered in the grass around the site. Others sat on the tall rocks with their backs straight.

"What is this place?" Ty asked. He was a step or two behind Peck.

"I'm not sure."

Cogongrass sprung from the baked earth, strewn with trash. A dusty flag Peck didn't recognise rippled softly. They advanced cautiously and came across four listless hogs tied to a stake in the earth. The smell in the air was that same bitter ammonia, hard to breathe. The sun rode directly overhead and the heat was thick as tar.

"*Anybody home?*" Ty screamed. He brushed at the flies on his face. "*Anybody? I figured hell would be busier.*"

"Hush." Peck placed a hand on Ty's chest and he knocked it away. "Don't touch me."

Sound of a door opening, closing with a snap. They turned and saw a boy walking toward them, bare-chested, eating something from a bowl. Five years old, Peck figured, having a boy of his own that age.

"Keep it together," Peck whispered to Ty. "Remember, we got no jurisdiction here, but these people don't know that. Keep your weapon holstered. Pull that trigger and you'll have a lot of questions to answer."

The boy wore faded blue jeans turned up at the ankles. His feet were soot-black. The bowl was filled with dry corn. It rattled between his teeth when he spoke.

"You probably shouldn't be here."

"We're looking for somebody," Peck said. He turned on his friendly police officer smile, perhaps to make up for his shapeless hat and the flies on his throat. "Maybe you can help me. Girl. Fifteen years old. Brown hair. Goes by the name of Cindy."

"She's with us now," the little boy said. He took a mouthful of corn that rattled. "And she ain't Cindy no more."

Even in the heat, these words sent a chill motoring up Peck's spine. They mirrored what Mary had said. Not that he needed more convincing. As a lawman he'd always favoured a logical line, but after everything he'd seen and heard, that line wasn't nearly as solid.

"Where is she?" Ty asked.

The boy softened corn in his mouth. He spat yellow in the dirt, then turned around and walked away.

"Hey!"

"Rubin's trailer." He flicked a finger to his left.

The men—bone-weary but still upright—moved in that direction, beyond a screen of raggedy shrubs and toward a trailer the colour of an old dime. It sat on its underbelly, wheels and jack long gone. Dry weed snaked through holes in the panelling and the windows were marked with red Xs. There were two coyotes perched on the roof, coats clotted with dirt and teeth showing. Somebody had buried an axe in the trunk of a nearby tree. A tin bucket hung from a branch by a length of twine.

Peck looked over his shoulder and saw the little boy watching and grinning. In the heat it looked like his black feet were smoking.

"We find her and go," Peck said. "We'll send the big boys back here to ask questions."

"Amen," Ty said.

Peck turned back toward the trailer and in so doing walked clumsily into the tin bucket hanging from the branch. A drove of flies were disturbed but didn't go far. The bucket swung and the branch creaked. Peck looked inside and saw Beau Roth's head, parched and blistered. One eye was filled with flies.

"Christ and Jesus." He staggered backward and drew his gun and Ty drew his too. Peck flapped a hand at him that didn't make any sense and Ty hunkered, confused, and the barrel of his weapon moved unsurely. The flies settled again on the bucket. The coyotes on the roof howled. Peck looked the way they had come and saw the little boy laughing. He imagined the corn rattling between his teeth and had an urge to run a bullet through his narrow chest, then a door squeaked open and he turned to see Cindy Roth standing outside the trailer. Not the same girl who sat quietly at the back of the class while Peck gave one of his school talks, or the girl he often saw walking the mile from Sunshine Shopper to her house, weighed down with groceries, and who wouldn't accept a ride when he offered it. Cindy Roth now was fierce-eyed, closer to a woman, and with a charge about her—some deep thing desperate to break out. She smiled and stepped toward Peck. Her feet were black.

"Hello, Chief," she said.

❊

All Peck wanted was a shred of solid evidence, something to lend credence to Mary Roth's story, enough for the state police to investigate further. He'd brought Ty along because he didn't want to be alone, but also because Ty—unlike Calloway—was green enough to follow, even when they went beyond the town limits.

He hoped he'd live to regret his decisions.

It all happened quickly.

There came a whirl of heat and dust and suddenly they were surrounded by black-footed boys, including two atop Rubin's trailer – thin and naked both—in place of the coyotes. Peck backed away and raised his gun in warning. Ty showed no such restraint. He fired two shots at the boys on the trailer and missed them both. Peck screamed at him to cease fire but he didn't listen. He turned and shot the little boy dead. Blew him backward, black feet smoking. His bowl of corn spilled everywhere.

Peck recalled Mary gesturing at the sky—at everything—and saying that it all seemed lesser, like something that could be opened and poured out, and now he knew exactly what she meant. He did then the one thing he thought would save his hide: turned his gun on Ty and shot him in the throat. Ty went down, dead as stone before he hit the ground.

Still the fire came.

The crooked raptor landed in a flurry of thick black feathers, squawking as flames ripped suddenly, viciously, around the site. Peck shielded his eyes and when he looked again, the bird was gone. A man strode toward him—black-footed, like the boys—over eight feet tall and narrow-faced. Smoke rippled from his eyes and he spat coal and bones. Peck was lifted into the air without being touched, fully ten feet above the ground, and then dropped. The boys howled and Peck tried to reel away but was lifted again. He saw the site burning and the fields beyond. He saw Cindy Roth twisting in the flames and laughing. Embers burst from her mouth and spiralled around her. Again Peck was dropped and he landed hard, breaking both legs. Still he tried to crawl.

Fire surrounded him. It sucked the oxygen from the air and he wheezed and reached for help that would never come. His skin bubbled in the heat but did not blacken.

The man stood over him. Flames crackled from the tips of his fingers.

Peck lifted his gun and pulled the trigger desperately. The first and second shots hit the tall man square in the chest. Fire and feathers flew. The third hit Cindy Roth and threw her thin, fifteen-year-old body back through the door of the trailer. Eleven rounds left in the mag and Peck spent them all. Some of those shots went astray but most found a home. Bodies and fire all around.

Peck tried to scream but there wasn't the air. He wished he'd kept a bullet for himself. He crawled a little way and then fell chest down in the dirt. The cogongrass crackled as it burned and he heard the hogs squealing.

The last thing he saw before passing out was the little boy Ty had shot, back on his feet and scooping corn—popped now—off the ground and into his mouth. His smile was almost beautiful.

He came around with the fires still burning and the skin on his face and hands blistered. All the shacks and trailers were gone. The boys with the black feet were gone. Not a body in the dirt, nor a drop of blood. Not even Ty's.

Just him and that bucket twisting in the heat.

Peck dragged his broken legs and screamed. The fire raged around him, branding a shape on the land he felt but could not see: a five-pointed star enclosed in a perfect circle, burning hungrily and—from point to point—many miles wide.

THE LIFE INSPECTOR
John Llewellyn Probert

The front doorbell rang at nine a.m. precisely.

Franklin knew it was nine because that was the time Eleanor had told him he needed to take the laundry out of the washing machine. She had put in a load just before leaving an hour earlier, herding Jocasta (eight) and Tobias (seven) in front of her down the garden path and into the shiny silver 4 x 4 she insisted they leave parked outside the house. There was a perfectly serviceable garage tucked away behind the laurel bushes and apple trees that bordered their gravel drive, but, she had explained to Franklin, what was the point of buying a brand new Audi if you were going to keep it hidden away where the neighbours couldn't see it?

Franklin had merely shrugged and returned his attention to the stock market prices. It was something he was very good at, which was why they lived where they did (a very nice part of Bristol, thank you very much), sent the children to the school they attended (expensive and exclusive and full of other children that might grow up to be useful business contacts in the future, not to mention prospective marriage partners), and why Eleanor was able to squander so much time and money at designer clothes shops. Franklin never questioned her spending habits, and in return she never questioned any of his bedroom predilections. For those reasons, more than any others, it was a relationship that worked very well indeed.

The bell rang again.

Franklin pushed a stray sock back into the shiny confines of the aluminium drum and wiped his hands. The sooner they could get another decent housekeeper the better, he thought, as he made his way to the door, preparing to decline politely the advances of the Jehovah's Witness waiting there (the most likely possibility); explain that he had no money on him if it was a charity collector (there were more and more of them these days—you couldn't trip up without some support group being formed to help you and people like you, and of course they all wanted your money); or to use rather more terse terms to let the salesperson know that this was a No Doorstep Selling Neighbourhood, before drawing the hapless individual's attention to the bright yellow sticker in the front window that signified (and explained in no uncertain terms) that his house was a member of said scheme.

The caller was none of the above.

Franklin was able to take note of the narrow spectacles rimmed in cheap black plastic, the toothbrush moustache that was the same shade of charcoal as the neatly trimmed hair (and the three quarter length raincoat), before the man standing on the doorstep spoke.

"Mr Chalmers?"

Franklin allowed the man a wary nod.

"Mr Franklin Chalmers?"

"Yes."

That seemed to please the man no end. He smiled without showing his teeth and used a Bic biro to place a heavy tick at the top of the black clipboard he was holding.

"Excellent," he said. "May I come in?"

No you bloody well may not, Franklin thought. However he came out with "That really rather depends on why you're here," to maintain a semblance of politeness until he was able to determine whether this was some kind of impromptu tax inspection, or whether the fellow had just been sent round to check the drains.

The response was another tick scratched on the form. Franklin could see a little bit of it now that the man was leaning slightly to the left. It was pink and looked very complicated, with more boxes than the lottery tickets Eleanor insisted they buy despite their affluence.

The man noticed Franklin looking and tilted the clipboard away.

"My apologies, Mr Chalmers, for not introducing myself properly." He reached into the pocket of his raincoat and produced a small piece of white pasteboard. "My card."

The design sported the characteristic lack of imagination of government departments, right down to the soulless font that announced the following:

Mr M Norton
HM Life Inspection Department

"It's time for yours," said Mr Norton, attempting to step inside Franklin's house.

Franklin stopped him.

"My what?"

Mr Norton raised rat-coloured eyebrows. "Your inspection, of course. Does the card not make it clear? A great deal of work was put into making it understandable to the general public. It went through three committees, seven versions, and ended up receiving a commendation in the 2013 Plain English Awards." He sniffed. "We were quite proud of that."

"I'm very pleased for you," said Franklin, still keeping his temper in case the man really did work for the government. "But I have to confess I have never heard of any department with such a name, nor am I aware of my requiring any kind of 'assessment'."

Mr Norton sighed. "We're far too busy with the actual job of assessing to give our department much publicity."

"Nevertheless, I don't know anyone who has been through what you're suggesting," said Franklin, "and I know a lot of people."

"Ah," said Mr Norton, as if that explained everything. "That's because of the Oath of Secrecy."

Franklin's eyes narrowed. "The what?"

"The Oath of Secrecy." Mr Norton tucked the clipboard under his right arm. "Once your Life Assessment has been completed, you will be required to sign a document confirming that you swear not to reveal either the contents of the interview, or the fact that you have indeed been interviewed, to anyone." He scratched the side of his nose with the Bic. "It prevents people from swotting up beforehand."

"Swotting up?" Franklin snorted. "I've never heard of anything so ridiculous in my life. Now, if you would be so kind as to move onto whomever else you would like to bother with your crack-brained ideas, I have work to do."

He tried to close the door but the toe of a highly polished black Oxford prevented him from doing so.

"I'm sorry to have to do this," said Mr Norton, reaching into his raincoat pocket once more. "But you leave me no choice."

Franklin felt a pang of panic as he waited for this obvious lunatic to draw either a gun or a knife. When he saw it was a mobile phone he relaxed. Mr Norton tapped the screen twice to bring up a video feed, and then held it so Franklin could see.

On the screen Franklin's wife Eleanor and his two children, Jocasta (eight) and Tobias (seven) were tied to chairs in the darkened confines of what looked like someone's garage. Their faces were tear-stained, but as far as he could tell, they were unharmed.

"A brief glimpse into HM Department of Corrections," said Mr Norton. "If you are happy to continue with your assessment, then hopefully I won't have to show you any more of their work."

Franklin wasn't listening. He was still staring at the screen, and so Mr Norton switched it off and put it away.

"I'm sorry I had to do that," he said, "but we've found it the best way to encourage uncooperative individuals to see sense." He tapped the clipboard. "Now, I have a quota that must be satisfied by the end of the morning, so can we get on?"

Still in a state of shock, Franklin nodded dumbly and held the door open.

Mr Norton made another mark on his sheet and stepped inside with a curt, "Thank you."

The hallway was given a quick once over, with a glance to the staircase on the left before Mr Norton's eye was caught by the framed certificate on the opposite wall. He peered at it and wrote something on the form.

"It's Jocasta's piano exam," Franklin explained.

"Yes."

"Grade One."

"I see."

"We were very proud of her for getting a distinction."

"How interesting." The man ticked another box.

"Really?"

"No, not really." Mr Norton looked around. "Is there somewhere we can sit down?"

Franklin gestured to the lounge.

Mr Norton shook his head. "I'd prefer somewhere with a table."

"How do you know there isn't one in there?"

The man in grey shook his head in a way that suggested Franklin should have known better. "Of course I know," he said. "Shall we go in to the kitchen?"

Franklin didn't need to lead the way, which merely served to disconcert him further.

"Very nice," said Mr Norton as he beheld the bright and airy space into which every conceivable (and, at Eleanor's insistence, very fashionable) modern convenience had been unobtrusively fitted.

Franklin pulled out a chair from the matching pine table that dominated the floor space. "I would have imagined you already knew what it looked like," he said.

"I do." Mr Norton sat opposite him, crossed his legs, and rested the clipboard on his upraised knee. "I was just being polite."

"How very kind of you."

The response this time was a thin, pitying smile that made Franklin more annoyed. Then he remembered the image on the phone and did his best to curb his fury. He tried to keep calm but couldn't help digging his fingernails into the overpriced wood. The action did not go unnoticed. Mr Norton wrote something on the form and then sat there quietly, regarding Franklin with calm detachment.

Franklin stared back.

It wasn't long before the silence became unbearable. The silence and the waiting and that awful image of Eleanor and the kids that he couldn't stop thinking about. What did this man want? Surely he couldn't really be the person the card claimed? A Life Inspector? It had to be a ruse, a scam, some new and horrible way of getting money out of decent hardworking people like himself.

Money.

That was it.

And almost before he realised he was doing it, Franklin found himself blurting:

"Ten thousand pounds!"

Mr Norton raised an eyebrow at the broken stillness. "I beg your pardon?"

Franklin clasped his hands to stop them shaking. It helped a little bit.

"I don't know who you really are," he said, "but we both know this is going to come down to money sooner or later. So how about I write you a cheque now, or you accompany me to the bank while I make a money transfer, or however else you want it, but can we please stop this?"

Mr Norton frowned—not in anger, but in confusion. In fact, he made the kind of face someone at the post office counter might make if you asked for a new tax disc for your car but had forgotten the MOT certificate.

"We can't 'stop it', Mr Chalmers," he said. "That's not how it works."

Franklin's knuckles were white.

"How does it work then?"

Mr Norton looked pleased now that Franklin seemed to be cooperating. "It's quite simple, Mr Chalmers. I ask you questions and you answer them."

Franklin didn't know what to say. Was this really how he was meant to save the lives of his family?

"There's no other way?"

Mr Norton shook his head. "No other way."

"At all?"

"Not at all. If there were alternatives I'd be suggesting them. But there aren't. Which is why I'm not."

Not for the first time that morning Franklin was subject to the sensation of his stomach trying to invert itself. He made an attempt to stop his voice from shaking.

"Let's get started then, shall we?"

Mr Norton removed the tissue-thin sheet from his clipboard and turned it over. "Oh, we've already done that, Mr Chalmers," he said as he secured it back in place. "We're on to Section B now."

Franklin could feel his small intestine trying to go one better than his stomach by tying itself into a sequence of granny knots.

"But you haven't asked me anything yet!"

Mr Norton wrote more on the form. "I have," he said as he underlined something twice. "You just haven't been paying attention."

The knots tightened.

"Well, can we start again then?" he spluttered. "I wasn't ready."

"No we can't." Mr Norton looked ever so slightly annoyed. "That's the point. I told you that earlier."

Another tick on the form.

"Tell me, Mr Chalmers, do you read a daily newspaper?"

"You mean to tell me you actually don't know something?" The words were out before Franklin could stop them. "I'm sorry, I didn't mean that."

But it was no good. "Oh I think you did, and for your information, yes, we do know, but it's your response to the question that's important."

"In that case, we—"

"What are you doing?"

"Telling you what newspaper we take."

Mr Norton put the pen down. "You do seem to have trouble understanding, don't you? I just explained that it's your response to the question that's important. You've already given me your answer to that one, so now we move on."

"But I haven't told you anything!"

"You have."

What was the point of arguing?

"Would it help if I told you we take the *Daily Mail*?" Franklin gave Mr Norton what he hoped was an imploring look.

"No."

"Or," Franklin said, furiously trying to backpedal, "that it's only my wife who reads it? I can't stand it myself."

"You can say what you like, Mr Chalmers. I've already filled in the box for that question, so it doesn't really matter. Do you think it does?"

Franklin frowned. "Does what?"

"Matter."

This was getting ridiculous. "Of course it matters! You should give your interviewees some time to think—not just accept the first thing that comes into their heads. That's not fair at all!"

Mr Norton wrote something on the form.

"Was that my next question?" Franklin groaned.

"It might have been," said Mr Norton. "Of course, I might just have been making an addendum."

"You can do those, then?" Franklin saw a straw of finest gossamer being offered to him, one he knew he had to clutch ever so gently or his desperate grasp would tear it. "Okay, how about ten thousand pounds to rip that form up and start all over again? I promise I won't tell a soul."

"I didn't say I *could* make an addendum," Mr Norton replied. "I said I *might* be doing that." He uncrossed his legs. "And, on an unrelated note, do I strike you as the kind of man who would agree to a bribe of such proportions?"

Franklin was about to blurt a desperate yes, but immediately thought better of it. Instead he gave the man a strangled reply in the negative.

For the first time since he had invaded Franklin's home Mr Norton gave him the hint of a smile.

"A sensible answer for once," he said.

"Will that count in my favour?"

"We don't like to use words like 'favour', Mr Chalmers. That's not really the point of the inspection."

"And what exactly is the point?"

"You'll find out in just a minute." Mr Norton turned the sheet over, added a few more ticks and then scribbled something at the bottom. "We're pretty much finished."

Finished? That was absurd! "How can we be finished?" Franklin resisted the urge to tear the forms from Mr Norton's clipboard. "You've hardly asked me anything!"

"I've gathered all the information I need, Mr Chalmers." Mr Norton signed the form with a flourish. "We decide what's important and what isn't about an individual."

Franklin was incensed. "This is nonsense," he said. "There is no way you have just carried out an accurate inspection of my life."

"Oh, but I have." Mr Norton scanned the two sheets of pink paper, poking his tongue out in concentration as he added the marks up with his biro. He wrote a number at the bottom of the final page and then gave Franklin a very solemn look.

"Mr Chalmers, I am very sorry to have to inform you that by the process approved by Her Majesty's Department of Life Inspection you have failed."

"Failed?" Franklin said with a snorting laugh.

Mr Norton regarded him without any emotion whatsoever.

"It's no laughing matter, Mr Chalmers. I know this sort of thing doesn't happen very often, but when it does, we believe the occasion should be treated with rather more seriousness than you seem to be giving it."

Franklin got to his feet.

"I'm not treating this seriously because it's bloody stupid," he said, grabbing the cordless phone from the mottled granite of the kitchen work surface. "Now get out of here before I call the police."

Franklin punched 999 and put the handset to his ear.

The phone was dead.

Franklin tried again.

Silence.

"Bloody thing."

Franklin rammed the phone back into its cradle and took his mobile from his back pocket.

No signal.

Mr Norton didn't move, but he did assume a slightly more sympathetic expression.

"You can't telephone anyone, Mr Chalmers." His voice was softer now, his manner appropriate for dealing with someone who has suffered a recent loss.

"Rubbish!" Franklin made his way into the hall where there was another telephone.

That was dead too.

"There must be a problem with the lines," he said as he replaced the receiver.

"There's no problem with the telephone," said Mr Norton, who had followed him with silent steps. "The problem is with you."

"No," Franklin pointed a shaking finger at the little grey man. "The problem is with you, my friend, and you have just gone one step too far."

Franklin turned and opened the front door.

To be confronted with the black, yawning gulf of absolute nothingness.

He slammed the door shut and looked out of the window.

Through the patterned glass Franklin could see a normal street. His street. The street where he and his family had lived for the last three years. The sun was shining. The old lady from number 37 was taking her terrier for a walk. The damn thing was shitting where it always did.

He yanked open the door to shout at her, like he always did.

Black nothingness lay beyond the gaping doorway.

Mr Norton allowed Franklin to repeat the door opening and closing ritual another three times before he spoke again.

"You can't leave the house," he explained, "because you don't exist."

"I don't..."

"...exist. Therefore you cannot interact with the real world. You failed your life inspection. Therefore you no longer have a life. Believe me, I don't enjoy failing people and I'm very sorry, but that's just the way it is."

Franklin looked out through the glass once more. The old lady and her dog had gone now, but he could hear the animal yapping. At the postman, probably.

The postman!

Sure enough there he was, and God bless him he had a handful of stuff to shove through the letterbox. Lovely circulars, wonderful bills—anything as long as they gave him the chance to communicate with another person.

As soon as the letterbox began to open Franklin screamed. It was a long, drawn out plea for assistance that began with the force of a bear but quickly tailed off into a sorrowful whine.

The second time Franklin tried all he got was the sorrowful whine.

The third time he got nothing.

"I'd save my breath if I were you," said Mr Norton. "You don't need a voice anymore, so it's not going to last much longer."

Franklin looked down at the envelopes that had fallen through the slot.

The envelopes that showed that someone else now resided at this address.

"Why?" he croaked.

The word was little more than a whisper, a dying breath stretched out across forty-five years of existence, of successes and disappointments, all to be rendered invalid because somehow, in some way, he had failed the most important test of all.

"I wish I could tell you, but I'm not allowed to, and it's not as if it's going to make any difference. Besides, it would take me longer than you have left."

"What about my... my..."

"If you don't exist then your family can hardly exist either, can they?

Your children have already gone and your wife has been reassigned. You'd be surprised how easy it is to adjust the world so that the removal of those who fail makes no difference whatsoever."

Mr Norton squeezed past the fading, wraith-like figure that had until recently been Franklin Chalmers. He had his hand on the front door handle when he stopped.

"Goodness me, I almost forgot," he said, tearing a perforated strip from the bottom of the form and handing it to the nebulous transparent shape, which, despite having already lost most of its higher thought processes, still possessed the instinct to take it.

"Wouldn't want you becoming a ghost now, would we?" Even though it would not be able to register it, Mr Norton gave the fragmenting shape a smile before stepping out into the street.

Once outside, the Life Inspector took a deep breath of the fresh mid-morning air, allowed himself a moment to appreciate the clear blue sky, and then consulted his clipboard once more. After all, he had a quota to fill by the end of the morning.

"Right," he said to himself. "Who's next?"

SOMETHING SINISTER IN SUNLIGHT
Lisa Tuttle

Another sunny day in L.A. It was getting him down—the weather, along with everything else. There was something sinister in sunlight. Not so much in England, when the weak, gentle sun made a special appearance, but day after day, unrelieved by clouds or rain, it struck Anson as unnatural. He found it just as perversely oppressive as the regulation smiles and bonhomie of store clerks and waiters. "Have a nice day, now!" It made him homesick, nostalgic for sullen youths with bad teeth, too proud to pretend they *enjoyed* being your server, while he missed the soft grey skies and sodden ground.

He'd created a whole little *schtick* about it—made Harry laugh when he'd skyped him—but it had fallen flat when he'd tried it out at a poolside party yesterday. Americans: they didn't take offense; they just didn't *get* it. The English sense of humour. British comedy was supposed to be big in the States just now, so maybe it was *him*. He wanted to prove his versatility, show another side to his character, and it didn't work. Producers, directors, audiences wanted just one thing from him, the same performance again and again. Maybe it was the best he could do. Who was he to say they were wrong?

He thought of his last conversation with his agent.

"So you're saying I should be grateful for *whatever* I'm offered?"

"Of course not, Anson. But those last two—they weren't bad parts—and not inconsiderable."

"They were the *same* part. Serial killer. Sinister, high-functioning sociopathic murderer."

"Well, you're *very good* at that. And you bring something to—"

"To an underwritten, clichéd part? I should bloody well hope so. Jay, it's depressing. Why can't I do something else?"

Jay had been silent for a worryingly long time. Afraid his agent was trying to come up with a new, more palatable formulation of the bitter truth, he had jumped in first.

"Look. I'm not saying I have to be the *lead*. I don't mind being the villain. I just want to do something different—something that is not just another replay of Cassius Fucking Crittenden."

It had been his first role in a major Hollywood motion picture—years ago. It was maybe a little strange to cast an English actor as a serial killer from the backwoods of Kentucky, but everybody knew the Brits were good at playing evil, and Anson thought he did a passable, if eccentric, job with his hillbilly accent. How much his performance contributed to the decision to transport the character of Cassius Crittenden into a new TV series, who could say, but Anson was offered the role. At the time, it had seemed like his big breakthrough, but in recent years he had come to feel it had been not just the high point, but also the end of his career.

Originally, the villain was slated to die at the end of the first season. But his character was too popular; so, in the second season it was revealed that the serial killer had survived his apparent immolation in a burning car, and he returned to taunt the detective hero.

In retrospect, Anson felt he should have walked away after the first season. As a character, Cassius had always been fond of masks and disguises, and the circumstances of his 'death' meant it would have been easy enough to use burns, scarring and plastic surgery as an explanation for the appearance of a different actor. But to walk away from a sure thing, from regular work—extremely well-paid—to return to the insecurity of the acting life was not in his character. And so, even though he'd never liked Los Angeles, he had stayed—for six years.

Six years on the series, and then it ended. It had been a relief to get back home, wonderful to have the freedom to do whatever he wanted. For a little while there had been plenty of offers; he could take his pick. He didn't have to go back to L.A. There were films, a role in a David Hare play, a TV series set in the 1960s, in which he played a hard-bitten yet soft-hearted journalist, and a string of smaller parts, which grew smaller and less frequent as the years went by.

Somehow, nothing else he did ever attracted the same attention. They were like a succession of wrong turns, each one leading him down a one-way street in a further wrong direction. Until finally it seemed he had never done anything noteworthy or memorable except play the continuing role of a psychotic killer on a popular American TV series. The roles he was offered became depressingly similar.

This trip to California, urged by his agent, now seemed to him the worst wrong turn of all, the final nail in the coffin of his career. If he was remembered at all, it was as Cassius Crittenden, and that memory fatally coloured the perception of every casting director, every producer, every show-runner... they could not imagine him, Anson Barker, successfully filling any other role. Didn't these people understand about *acting?* Or... was he kidding himself? Maybe he just wasn't any good.

Self-doubt, self-pity, all the personal fears came out when he was alone at night, like roaches through the floorboards and invisible cracks in the walls of the borrowed apartment.

He wished he was home, where he didn't have to cope with the eight-hour time difference before he could talk to Harry—where he could be in Harry's arms, not just looking at him on a screen—where he could call up some of his mates to meet for a drink, or just drop in to a pub or a cafe, one of the places where he was known—and *not* as the actor who used to be Cassius Crittenden.

He wished he had never come. But now that he was here, he had to see it through. A few more days, one last meeting, and then he'd put it all behind him, go back to London, find something else to do.

Making an effort to shake off his depression, he went out for a late breakfast at the Blu Jam Cafe. It had become a comforting habit—just a ten-minute drive, and French toast to die for.

It was crowded—closer to lunchtime than breakfast, he realised—and the waiter had just told him there'd be a half-hour wait, then paused and said, "Unless you're joining... her?"

Anson had not noticed the woman giving him a wave from her corner table, and once his attention had been drawn to her, he did not recognise her. But it was instantly more appealing than either going away or hanging around on the sidewalk for half an hour, so he agreed.

She was mid-thirties, he guessed, with sharp, not unattractive features, bright blue eyes, glossy, wavy auburn hair. She wore a bright blue blazer over a white shirt—something about the ensemble said 'estate agent' to him, although insurance or low-level finance seemed equally possible. She was vaguely familiar, but he still couldn't place her.

"You don't remember me, do you, Anson?"

"Sadly, no—but I shan't forget you again, I promise."

She stretched out her hand. "Elissa Condé. We met at Jack and Aura's party?"

"Of course. You're an architect."

She smiled so tightly it seemed more a grimace. "Good to know I'm not *utterly* forgettable."

He remembered her profession because *Harry* was an architect—and because he hadn't quite believed her. The other thing he remembered about her—now, and too late—was that she'd given off a crafty, vaguely stalkerish vibe; pretending to have no idea who he was, and asking none of the questions people normally asked when you said you were an actor. But she knew who he was, all right, he had seen it in her eyes, and she hadn't wanted him to know she knew. She wanted him to think their meeting was purely accidental—*like this one*—when in fact she had engineered it for her own purposes.

He felt a prickle of excitement. This woman might be dangerous... but he wasn't afraid. What could she do to him? She wanted something, and she thought he didn't know, whereas in fact he had the edge—he didn't *know,* but neither was he fooled. And it might be interesting to find out what she was up to.

He ordered the crunchy French toast and coffee; she asked for organic granola with soya milk, and a pot of green tea.

When the waiter had gone, Anson treated Elissa to a kindly,

avuncular gaze. "I'm sorry I had to abandon you so abruptly at the party. It must have seemed very rude. But I wasn't there to enjoy myself—it was all business. But now, here we are! We can make up for our missed opportunity. What would you like to talk about?"

She seemed a bit taken aback by this approach. "Oh, I don't know... what do you think of L.A.?"

"The traffic is even worse than it was when I lived here. *Not* my favourite place, I have to say. I'm looking forward to going home next week."

She looked worried. "Where's home?"

"London." He drummed his fingers on the table. "What about you? Native Angelino?"

"Pretty much, yeah."

"And you like it."

"Sure. It's OK. I mean, I don't really know, because I've never lived anywhere else."

"Travel much?"

"Some. But I hate flying."

"Sing it, sister! But what can you do? If you want to go anywhere..."

"I drive. It takes longer, but not always, when you consider the time you save hanging around in airports."

"That wouldn't work for me."

She looked at him blankly. "Why not?"

"London, remember? Can't drive across the sea."

"Oh, right. I wasn't thinking..."

"You've never been abroad?"

"I've been to Mexico."

"Okay. Did you like it?"

"Cozumel was pretty nice, but really, I wouldn't go again. It was my boyfriend's idea—my boyfriend at the time. I'm not with anybody now. But I mean... why go to Mexico, when you can get the same stuff here? The restaurants here are better. And for scenery—I'd rather go to Taos, or Monterrey."

He was baffled by her. Conversation was hard work, and she seemed strangely incurious about him—about everything, really. Or else she was keeping a really tight grip on her emotions, fearful of giving away her secret. What *was* her secret? That she was obsessed by him, in love with him, imagined they were soul-mates... or, more drearily, she'd written a script, had an idea for a series, thought he could get her an acting job? Well, she'd have to tell him eventually. To his own surprise, he was actually curious. Instead of being bored, he found himself touched by a deep, unexpressed sadness in her. The dreariness of her imagination somehow put his own worries into perspective.

Finally, television entered the conversation. Elissa became more natural, and openly enthusiastic, as she talked about her favourite shows, one of which, it came as no surprise, was the one Anson and Harry had taken to calling 'That Which Shall Not Be Named.' Yet still she said nothing that could be taken as an admission that she knew Anson had played the part of Cassius Crittenden—not even when she invited him to her house for dinner.

"You *have* to. Come on, don't try to wriggle out of it. You've already said you're not doing anything on Friday, and you're fed-up with take-outs. Blu Jam is closed in the evenings, and even if it wasn't, man cannot live by French toast alone."

That startled a laugh out of him; she was nothing like as dull as she'd seemed at first. Yet the prospect of spending an entire evening alone in her company made him uneasy.

"You said you liked Italian food. Well, let me tell you, I make The. Best. Lasagne. *Ever.* And there's somebody I want you to meet. Somebody you *have* to meet. You'll thank me for it."

"Really? Who is this paragon?"

"You have to come and find out."

He wagged a reproving finger. "You had better not be trying to match-make. I'm a happily married man."

She went pale, and he realised he had genuinely shocked her. "You're *not!*"

"Well, no, not really." He gave her a somewhat puzzled smile. "You're right. Same-sex marriage isn't legal *quite* yet, and I must admit Harry and I didn't sign up to a civil partnership, but we're quite the devoted couple, even so. Been together three years and six months. I'm not looking for anyone else."

"You *can't* be gay."

He put his napkin on the table, too cross and weary with her stupidity to respond.

"*Cassius* isn't gay!" It was a cry from the heart.

He had to laugh, although he wasn't amused. "No, no, *Cassius* isn't gay—nor is he English—nor *real*. It is called *acting*."

She began nodding her head rapidly, like a tic. "Of course. I hadn't thought..."

"Clearly not."

She gave him an anguished look. "I'm sorry. I didn't mean anything—I wasn't trying to—I'm sorry if I offended you. I was just so surprised, because, well... Cassius! He's so real to me, I forgot. It's just hard for me to remember, talking to *you*... that... even though you *look* like him, you're not... not the same."

"I know," he said, trying to be kind. But he didn't know how *anyone*—except the very youngest, most ignorant, mentally-challenged and obsessive fan—could confuse the player with the part. And especially when it was a case of an educated, urbane Englishman who had played the part of a crafty, hillbilly monster years ago. And if she really thought he was *anything* like Cassius, what on earth was she thinking, to invite him to dinner?

"It's very flattering, truly, to think I created a character that seems so real and matters so much to you, but..." Light flashed, searingly, off the blade of a butter knife; he blinked and rubbed his temples, feeling the faint, insidious throbbing of an incipient migraine. "But... I have often thought fans, rather than seeking out actors they *think* they admire, should take advice from the Wizard of Oz—what were his words? 'Pay no attention to the man behind the curtain!'"

"Oh, no! I don't agree *at all*. It was such a thrill to meet you! Such a *privilege*! I hope I haven't offended you. I could just *shoot* myself, honestly, what an idiot, so stupid. I don't have anything against gays—

I'm not *like* that—it was just such a shock, to think of *Cassius* as... as... I mean, you agree, don't you, that Cassius is *not* homosexual?"

It seemed to Anson that the fictional serial killer was driven by a lust for killing, not for what a normal person would categorise as sex, and that defining them by the gender of their victims was hardly significant, but he had no desire to argue the case with Elissa.

"You can claim him for heterosexuality— it doesn't make him normal."

"Oh, Anson!" She gazed at him reproachfully. "I'm not saying gay sex is abnormal! But Cassius is attracted to women. He doesn't have sex with men, only women."

"Before he *kills* them."

She smiled. "But he didn't kill *every* woman he slept with." A major plot point had Cassius falling in love with a woman called Melinda Valentine, and then, after one night of passion, having to renounce her, as he struggled against his conflicting urges, to kill her, or to keep her safe. In the end, that love proved to be his weakness, as he was finally captured—his death was seen by fans as self-willed, a deliberate sacrifice to save the only woman he had ever truly loved. It was all a load of tosh; pernicious tosh, Anson sometimes thought, for it made no sense at all, morally or psychologically, and it had allowed the villain, a degraded, psychopathic monster, to become a romantic anti-hero in the eyes of many.

"Of course. Melinda Valentine. Amazing what the *right woman* can do." Anson spoke automatically, his thoughts preoccupied by the tension building in his head, and the spot like an after-image in his visual field (he called it 'the solar flare'). He wondered if he could get home in time to ward off the worst of the migraine with a couple of tablets and two hours lying perfectly still in the dark. "I'm sorry about this, but I'm afraid I have to run."

"That's all right—as long as you've forgiven my stupidity, and you're still coming on Friday? Great! Seven o'clock? Here, my address and phone number. Give me a call if you need directions."

✻

The rental car had sat-nav, so Anson easily found Elissa's house, although it was much farther away than he'd expected, more than an hour's drive. Since he'd met her in a local cafe, he'd thought she lived in the neighbourhood.

But even at a quarter to eight, he was the first to arrive. He felt a flare of suspicion, as Elissa, bare-legged in a dark blue slip-dress under a grey cashmere cardigan, led him into her candle-lit living room, Tom Waits' gravelly voice from the speakers, the air redolent of a herby tomato sauce and melted cheese, but empty except for the two of them. He felt better when he saw the glass-topped table had been set with three places.

"I was about to apologise for being late, but I see your other friend isn't here yet."

She shrugged, smiling. "Never mind. He'll be welcome whenever he turns up."

She took away the bottle of wine he'd brought, and returned from the kitchen bearing two large glasses of red.

"Cheers."

They clinked glasses. He took a sip. It was not as good as the bottle he'd brought, but it was nice. Thinking of the long drive back, he resolved to be abstemious. Just the one.

Elissa sat down on the couch and patted the cushion beside her. When he sat down she moved, shifting her legs so that her short skirt rode up, revealing her thighs, and his mouth dried at what he saw there. Inked in shades of grey was a portrait of Anson's face as he'd looked portraying Cassius Crittenden.

That was the moment when he should have leapt up and run screaming from the room.

Without the benefit of hindsight, he took a big gulp of wine, repressed his natural horror, and said, "I hope that's not permanent."

"Why?"

"For *your* sake, dear. Hasn't it occurred to you what a *turn-off* it would be for anyone... anyone you cared to take to bed?"

She wet her lips, staring into his eyes. "Anyone... except Cassius."

"*Especially* Cassius. Unless you think he's an absolute monster of narcissism."

Her eyes widened in alarm. "No, of course not. I thought it would be like... well, I didn't think. It's not a real tattoo." She scrambled to her feet and hurried out of the room.

He heard another door open and shut, and then the sound of running water. And that was his second chance—as he thought later—to make his escape, while that crazy woman was busy scrubbing Cassius' visage from her inner thigh. But he wasn't afraid, and he was hungry, the smells from the kitchen making his mouth water, and the wine she had poured for him tasting more delicious with every sip.

When Elissa emerged from the bathroom she was flushed and slightly bedraggled looking, her left thigh red and moist from its scrubbing. She'd taken off the cardigan, and the slight, sleeveless dress, dampened with splashed water and her exertions, clung to her body. She didn't seem to be wearing anything else, and it looked more than ever like an undergarment, not meant for public view.

Anson jumped up, remembering his last film, set in the thirties, when gentlemen rose when a lady entered the room. He didn't want her to snuggle up close, or reveal any other hidden secrets. Now that her arms were bared he saw she had a tattoo, maybe a heart, red and black, just below her shoulder on her right arm.

"Perhaps you should give your friend a ring," he said. "Find out what's keeping him. I hate to think of your delicious lasagne drying to dust while we wait."

She stared for a moment as if not understanding, and then said flatly, "You're right, we may as well eat now."

"But your friend?"

"He'll come when he comes."

She brought out the lasagne and a bowl of green salad, and refilled his glass before he could stop her.

"I wonder... could I possibly trouble you for a glass of water?"

She giggled.

"I'm sorry?"

"I'm sorry. I shouldn't laugh, but... you sound so *different*."

He guessed he'd been exaggeratedly, hyper-English – some Americans brought it out in him, especially when he'd been drinking. He looked again at his glass, to see how much he'd had, but of course he couldn't tell, since she'd refilled it. Unnervingly, despite his resolve not to touch it, it looked not as full as a moment ago.

She brought him a glass of sparkling water, and he gulped down half of it immediately.

"Is the lasagne too salty?"

"No, it's delicious. Quite possibly, as you claimed, The. Best. Lasagne. *Ever.*"

Light flashed off the rim of a glass, like a solar flare. He shut his eyes.

"Are you all right?"

"Yes. No. I get these headaches. I'll be fine. It's just the light."

But he wasn't all right; he could barely stand. He didn't understand how it could have come on so suddenly; it was never like this. Was he about to pass out? Surely he hadn't had that much to drink.

He didn't want to go into her bedroom, but that's where she led him, into the blessed darkness, and he collapsed onto the bed with a groan.

"Please, leave me."

"Can't I do something?"

"Just leave."

✳

When he woke up, or came to, sun was shining through a gap in the curtains and he could hear birds cheeping monotonously outside. He had a dull, throbbing headache, but it was not a migraine. He was naked and alone in an unmade bed that reeked of sweat and sex—unmistakable.

The last time he'd had sex with a woman—more than ten years

ago—drugs had been involved, but *that* had been consensual, and he could remember it still today. Not like the events of last night.

She must have put something in his wine.

He groaned and shut his eyes, thinking of her reaction to *his* reaction to the painted face on her thigh, remembering how she had emerged from the bathroom, moist and pink, scrubbed clean... for him.

Why? Was it a fan's scalp-hunting... or something more sinister? Did she want his baby? *Christ!*

Ignoring the pounding in his head, he rolled out of bed, stumbled to the bathroom, vomited, then showered, attacking himself energetically with a flannel and shower gel until every last snail-trail of her touch had been eradicated.

Afterwards he prowled quickly and edgily through the house. It was obvious that she'd cleared out, knowing how angry he would be, but she might have left him a note. The dishes from last night's dinner were still on the table, the food congealing on two plates, the third place setting pristine. Of course, there never had been a second guest invited.

He felt a lust for revenge, considered doing something destructive while he had the chance: smashing the glassware, breaking the TV, cutting up her clothes, pissing on the carpet... but he could imagine too well how that could backfire. She might accuse *him* of rape; might even get him convicted of *her* crime. Nobody would believe what had *really* happened; he could hardly imagine it himself.

At last he left, stopping along the way in a neighbourhood he didn't know for breakfast at a fast-food outlet. He would never return to Blu Jam; he would change his habits for the few remaining days he'd be in this city. Although he had to go back to the apartment for his things, he decided to move into a hotel. At the thought that she might have discovered his address, might be waiting for him there, he went hot and cold, fury and horror combining in a toxic brew.

But there was no one in the apartment, which appeared unchanged from when he had left it the previous evening. Nevertheless, he began to pack as soon as he had changed his clothes, and it was then, as he checked the pockets of his jacket before putting it away, that he found Elissa's note.

My darling
You're reading this, so things did not work out as I wished. I knew the risk and chose to take it. I did it for you. I like to think that if we'd had more time together you would have come to love me as I love you. But since that didn't happen, take it as my gift. No regrets. I set you free. Now go and live your life as it was meant. Think of me kindly, if you can. The next woman

He began to shake and tears of sheer rage blurred his vision before he could read to the end. He crumpled the note in his fist and tried to control his breathing. The bitch, the crazy, reactionary, intolerant, ignorant, vicious, mad bitch— how *dare* she? Dope him and force him to have sex with her, stupidly convinced it would set him free. And yet, although he couldn't remember it, *something* had gone wrong; it wasn't the happy experience she'd imagined, and she could only try to salvage her fantasy by running away, leaving this silly, deluded note.

He tore it to shreds. He would have burned them, but for the lack of matches.

It was nearly three o'clock in L.A. which meant it was 23:00 hours—eleven o'clock at night—in London; time for his regularly scheduled Skype with Harry. He washed his face and composed himself. Much as he longed for the comfort of his lover's understanding, it was too strange and complicated a story to share now, when the distance of half a world still separated them. Better to wait until they were together, when he'd come to terms with what had happened, and knew how to tell the story.

Harry, sitting at the breakfast bar with his laptop open, his mug with the London skyline close at hand, the unkillable spider plant visible over his left shoulder, the print of wild horses on the wall behind him—the cosy familiarity of it all, softened by lamplight, might have made him cry, if only Harry's beloved face had not worn such a grim, unwelcoming expression.

"All right, let's hear it; make it good."

"What?"

"Your explanation. Your *apology*, Anson, for that fuckwitted, demented phone call this morning."

"This morning?"

"You're going to pretend you don't remember? I *thought* you were drunk, but really, that takes the biscuit. Time for the twelve steps if you're having *blackouts* now..."

Pain lanced through his temples; he put his hands on top of his head to keep it from splitting open. "Somebody drugged me. Put something in my drink. I can't remember calling—when did I call you? What did I say?"

Alarm warred with anger in his lover's face. "Seriously? Christ! Are you all right?"

"I'll tell you all about it—after I'm home. When did I call?"

"About nine—well after midnight your time—I was on my way out the door. You were doing a kind of Woody Harrelson *shtick*—it didn't make a lot of sense, to be honest. I don't really remember what you said, but I thought it was a shitty way of breaking up with me, if—"

"No!"

"Well, you seemed set on staying in California. Expressed your love for the golden state. I thought—reading between the lines—you'd been offered a part, open-ended, starting immediately, and you were too nervous to tell me honestly that you weren't coming back, so you'd got drunk and let this backwoodsman break it to me."

"Nobody's offered me anything. I've got a meeting on Monday, but even if he promises me the lead in *Die Hard: The Musical* I'm flying out of here the next day. I can't wait to get home. I miss you."

"You look like shit."

"I love you too."

"Migraine?"

Anson realised he was kneading his temples and squinting against a non-existent light. "Yeah. Quite a lot, recently. It's the sun, I think."

"Well, stay out of it. Go lie down. Take care of yourself, all right?"

❊

Anson didn't lie down after talking to Harry, even though his head was pounding. He took his tablets with a glass of water, and finished packing, eager to get away to the anonymity of a hotel room. Maybe he'd try the airport, where he could feel he was already on his way home.

The sun was low but still lancing painful beams of light off every reflective surface; each car in the small parking lot became an aggressor, and he all but closed his eyes as he shuffled towards his rental.

Opening the lid of the trunk immediately cut off those painfully distracting shafts and blades of light, and he opened his eyes wide, shocked by what he saw inside.

The woman's body had been carefully placed, lying curled on one side. She wore only the dark blue slip of a dress, arms and legs bare. There was no blood visible, and the distortions and discolouration of her dead face was hidden by the same sweep of hair that covered the damage done to her neck. It was the way Cassius Crittenden always dealt with his victims; after sex, while they lay relaxed and unsuspecting beside him, he strangled the woman with a tie or a belt, then he washed and dressed her before laying her down, curled up so she looked at first glance as if she'd merely fallen asleep.

His eyes were drawn to the tattoo on her upper arm; the tattoo he had glimpsed on Elissa's bare arm the previous evening. It was a dark red love-heart, with lacy scalloped edges, and the initials M.V. in the centre. He had seen it before, but not on this woman. He'd known it previously as a fake tattoo, created to adorn the arm of the actress who played Melinda Valentine to his Cassius Crittenden.

He heard the voice of Cassius as if it came from outside himself; knew it was impossible, but the drawling voice of an imaginary

American psychopath was the last thing he heard in his final moments of knowing himself to be an English actor called Anson Barker.

"Who did she think she was? Who did she think *I* was? Sorry, darlin', but you didn't know *what* you were messin' with, and now you've paid the price."

THIS VIDEO DOES NOT EXIST

Nicholas Royle

I wake up two minutes before the alarm is due to go off. I cancel the alarm and lie still for a few moments, trying to remember my dreams, with limited success. All I can sense is a vague feeling of loss or nostalgia. In a moment my wife will stir and I will climb out of bed and open the curtains.

"The Manchester skies are grey," I say as I look outside. How many times have I said these words upon opening the curtains? When does a running joke become an annoying habit? I suspect I will not find out until one day, when, instead of sleepily murmuring some benign response, my wife will retort, "We made the decision *together* to leave London. You know that as well as I do," or "It's been three years now. Can you not leave it alone?"

I forestall the possibility of this happening today by asking her, "Would you like some tea?"

"Yes please," says a voice from under the duvet.

I leave the bedroom. I enter the bathroom and open the window blind. The Manchester skies are grey at the rear of the house as well. I wonder what the weather is like in London. I imagine a version of myself opening curtains and blinds in London right now and reporting to a version of my wife that the London skies are blue. I feel certain that if I check the weather online it will be two degrees cooler in Manchester than in London.

I use the toilet, then move to the sink. I lean on the edge of the washbasin, staring at the spotless white porcelain beneath my hands.

How many mornings have I done what I'm about to do? How many mornings have I raised my head to see the same reflection looking back at me? How many mornings have I thought that I am looking old, that I may be closer to the end of my life than its beginning?

This morning, however, is different.

This morning I do not look older, but I do look as if the end of my life is upon me.

The man in the mirror is wearing the same crumpled T-shirt that I am wearing, although the writing across the chest is back to front, as you would expect. The arms are the same—lightly tanned, freckled. The neck is the same slightly scrawny neck that makes me look my age in photographs. But above the neck—nothing. No tired eyes, lined forehead, stubbly cheeks. No vertical frown line above the bridge of the nose. Nothing.

I look at my neck, but I can't see the end of it. There is no stump. Neither a flat, cartoonish disc like the end of a ham, nor the scraggy, gory mess of a victim in a splatter movie. Instead, it is like a tall building, its top lost in the clouds. I just can't see it.

I raise my hands—I see them rise in the mirror—but there is nothing for them to alight on. No puffy skin beneath my eyes, no incipient jowls. I cannot feel the stubble on the top of my head, which I shaved only two days ago. The top of my head is not there. My head is not there.

The man in the mirror has no head.

I turn from the washbasin and look out of the window. The sky remains grey. I look back in the mirror. I still have no head. I step away, turn around, walk towards the door, then come back to the washbasin and look in the mirror again. No change. With my fingers I try to feel where my neck ends, but I can't seem to gain purchase. Any sensation in my fingertips is weak. I don't know where or how my neck ends, but I know that it ends and that there is nothing above it.

I pause in the bathroom doorway. My wife is waiting for her tea. She will not wake fully until I bring it to her. I step out on to the carpeted landing. I can walk normally. I can see, even though I have no eyes to see with. I can hear birds singing in the trees at the front of the house. A slightly sour smell of bedding rises from my T-shirt as I head towards the stairs. I walk downstairs, my sense of balance unaffected. I enter the kitchen, fill the kettle and switch it on.

Every morning I start emptying the dishwasher while the kettle is boiling and complete the job while the tea is brewing. As I bend down to remove the cutlery basket, I ask myself if bending down feels any different. Sometimes I bend down too quickly and once I have straightened up again I feel light headed. This time, that doesn't happen.

I carry two cups of tea upstairs. I stand in front of the bedroom door as I remember approaching a road junction on my bike a day or two ago and not seeing a car that was coming towards me, because I was so intent on looking left and right. I saw it in time, but I had, for a few moments, been blind to it. I wonder if what I am experiencing now is a form of hysterical or selective blindness. I ask myself if I should place the cups of tea down on top of the bookcase on the landing and return to the mirror in the bathroom and have another look. But as I think this, I hear my wife getting out of bed and suddenly the bedroom door is open and she is standing in front of me.

"Oh," she says, giving a little jump. "You frightened me."

"Really?" I say.

"Yes, I didn't know you were there. Thank you," she says, taking one of the cups and moving past me to go to the bathroom. Did she actually look at me? I can't be sure.

I enter the bedroom and check in the full-length mirror my wife uses when she is getting dressed. There is no change. If I were more detached from the situation I would find it interesting. It would thrill me on a number of levels—aesthetic, visceral, intellectual. But it's hard to be detached.

My wife re-enters the bedroom and starts to get things out of her chest of drawers. She glances at me standing in front of the mirror and makes a humorous remark.

I ignore it and ask her, "Do I look tired to you?"

"Did you go to bed late?"

"Just look at me! Do I look tired to you?"

She turns and looks at me for a moment.

"There's no need to snap," she says. "You look neither tired nor not tired."

"Thanks," I say. "That's very helpful."

"Are you going to drink that?" she asks, lowering her eyes to the cup of tea I am still holding in my hand.

"Yes," I say. "No... I don't know."

I leave the bedroom with the cup of tea and pour it away down the sink in the bathroom.

"I'm going to have a shower," I shout.

"I'll be gone when you're done," my wife shouts back. "So I'll see you later."

"Okay. See you later."

I lock the bathroom door and look at myself in the mirror. No change.

I run the shower and wait until I hear the front door before switching it off. I return to the bedroom and start getting dressed, leaving my top half until last. I open my wardrobe and consider the separate piles of neatly folded T-shirts sorted by colour. I pick out a black one.

Downstairs I pull on my fluorescent jacket and zip it up. I open the cupboard where the rest of my cycling paraphernalia is kept and look at my helmet. I reach out and touch the cool plastic with a fingertip, but then withdraw my hand and close the cupboard door.

Cycling down our road I feel the wind on my face like pain in a phantom limb. I cut through the park, where dog-walkers take hold of their animals' collars at my approach and joggers carry water bottles shaped like bagels. Everything as normal, in other words. Exiting the park, I notice a woman waiting to cross the road; I nod to indicate she can go and she does, raising a hand in thanks.

I reach the university and find that someone has saved me the trouble of opening the door to the bike shelter. A colleague whose name I can never remember is struggling to get his bike past those nearest the door.

One of us comments on the inadequacy of the bike shelter's design and the other agrees. We lock up our bikes and leave and so enter the building at the same time. He presses the button for the lift and when it arrives and the doors slide open he gestures for me to go first. In the mirrored walls of the elevator I see an endless series of reflections of a headless man in a fluorescent jacket.

"Departmental meeting in half an hour," says my colleague.

"Yeah," I say. "I'm counting the minutes."

In the meeting, I sit next to Andy. Like me, Andy teaches film. I can see us reflected in the windows across the room.

"Andy," I say, "you'd tell me if I had, like, egg on my chin or something, right?"

Andy turns to look at me, leaning back as he does so. "What are you trying to say?"

"Do I look normal to you?"

"Define normal."

"Right," I say.

"I hope this doesn't go on for four hours like last time," he says. "I'm going to that London tomorrow and I've got a ton of marking to get done before then."

"Tell me about it. What you going to that London for?"

"Externals meeting at Birkbeck."

"Lucky you."

"Birkbeck?"

"London," I say. "I mean, Birkbeck as well, but, you know, just London."

The meeting proceeds along the usual lines. Every time we seem to have reached, if not a decision, then at least the end of the latest pointless discussion on a particular topic, one person, always the same person, will raise her hand and make a point that invariably starts with the words "I'm sorry, but…" and prompts further inconclusive debate, meaning that the end of the meeting is delayed by another ten or fifteen minutes. We are on the last item on the agenda – safety and environment – and a heated discussion about evacuation procedures for wheelchair users has just reached a sort of conclusion when a colleague – the same colleague – sticks her hand up and starts, "I'm sorry, but…", and I turn to Andy, who is already turning to me and drawing the blade of his right hand across his throat. The gesture makes me widen my eyes, but, if Andy notices, he fails to react.

After the meeting I sit in my office with a pile of dissertations on the desk in front of me. I open the top one and turn to the first page, read the opening paragraph and see that the writer has failed to make correct use of the semi-colon. I close the dissertation. There's a knock on the door. I look around, sit up straight in my chair, aware of a slight increase in my heart rate.

"Come in," I hear myself say.

The door opens to reveal a third-year undergraduate, Rebecca, whose dissertation I remember supervising.

"Hiya," she says. "I wanted to see you to talk about doing an MA."

"Come in," I say. "Sit down." I move the dissertations to one side of my desk. "I imagine yours is in this lot somewhere," I tell her.

She smiles.

"So you want to do an MA? That's great news."

"In London," she says.

"Oh."

"At Goldsmiths' or UCL or somewhere. I wanted to see if you thought that would be a good idea."

I look at her. She is one of those students my wife thought I would be tempted to have an affair with, or tempted to try to have an affair with: bright, attractive, a good critic, potentially susceptible to flattery from a widely published academic. She raises her eyebrows; the corners of her mouth turn up.

"No, I think it's a terrible idea," I say, watching her face fall, then leave it a couple of moments before adding: "I think you should do it here."

She laughs. "I really want to live in London," she says.

I look away at a line of DVDs standing between bookends on my desk. *Apocalypse Now*, *The Tenant*, *Eraserhead*, *Se7en*.

"Actually, I think it's a great idea," I say, turning back towards

Rebecca. "I'll write you a reference. I did the same thing myself twenty-five years ago." As I say it I realise the figure is actually closer to thirty. "It was when I saw all these for the first time," I add, indicating the films on my desk. "Well, apart from *Se7en*."

"That's great. Thanks," she says, looking straight into my eyes.

"You're welcome."

There is a pause. I often fill such pauses, feeling it is unfair to expect students to do so, but on this occasion I say nothing.

"So," she says, finally, "do you think I'll get on?"

"To one of those courses? Oh yes. You can punctuate a sentence."

She laughs uncertainly, pauses and then says, "Is that it? I can punctuate a sentence?"

"You'd be surprised how unusual that makes you these days," I say. "But luckily that's not all. You're one of the good ones. You're one of the ones I come in for. One of the ones I get up in the morning for."

"Thank you," she says, "I think."

"Rebecca?" I say.

"Yes?"

"Do I look any different to you today?"

"Er."

"It's all right. You don't have to answer that." I lift my hand, instinct or habit making me want to run it over my shaved head. Instead, it hovers in mid-air.

Rebecca gets up. "Thanks again," she says.

"You're welcome. Good luck. Put me down for those references," I say as she opens the door and leaves my office.

I watch the corridor through the doorway, since she has left the door open. A couple of first-year students pass by. I turn again to the pile of dissertations on my desk and look through them for Rebecca's. I pull it out, turn to the first page and read the opening paragraph, then close it and write on the marksheet: 80%.

I get my stuff together, thread my arms into my fluorescent jacket and pause with my hand on the door handle. I look back. I return to my desk and go through the dissertations until I find the first one I'd been looking at, the one with the faulty punctuation. I write on the marksheet: 50%.

I cycle home, where I go straight upstairs and stand in front of the bathroom mirror. I try to focus on my neck. I want to examine the extremity. But every time I get close to doing so, I find my mind drifting from the specific task in hand to my more general preoccupation with the overall problem—or absence. I get a hand mirror and hold it behind me, picturing as I do so a well-known Magritte painting of a man viewed from behind looking into a mirror, not at the reflection of his face, but at the back of his own head. This is what I should see in the reflected hand mirror, the back of my head, but I don't. If anything, this confirmation that my head is missing when viewed from behind – as well as from in front – is even more dismaying than the original sight in the mirror that morning, perhaps because I am mimicking the view that others have of me from behind, without my knowledge, without my ability to be aware, without any self-consciousness. But, instead, I wonder if it should encourage me that other people—my wife, strangers in the street, my colleagues and students—see nothing wrong.

Or nothing different from normal.

I have wandered out of the bathroom and now find myself in the bedroom, standing at the window looking down into the street. A neighbour from a few doors down walks past with her dogs and looks up and waves. I wave back. She sees nothing amiss. Can she not see? Is it that she is not looking at me properly?

I realise that I ought to be reminded of a different Magritte painting, in which a dead woman lies on a red couch, her head and neck at an unnatural angle to her body, a white scarf obscuring the conjunction of neck and torso.

I take my phone out of my pocket and open the address book. I find the number for the local GP surgery and my finger hovers over the call button for a moment. I look out of the window, see my neighbour turning the corner at the end of the street with her dogs. I press the button. A couple of rings and then the recorded voice of the practice manager. I know the spiel: I press the appropriate key to get through to make an appointment.

The receptionist offers me an appointment in a week's time. I tell her I don't necessarily have to see my own doctor. I'll see one of the others. She says I can see one of the other doctors in three days' time. I tell her I need to see someone today. She asks if it is an urgent matter. I pause for a moment, then tell her, yes, it is. She asks if I can explain what the problem is. I remain silent for a few seconds, thinking. She says my name, asks if I am still there. I tell her I can't tell her what the problem is. It's personal. She says she understands and that I should come down to the surgery and they will fit me in as soon as they can.

I walk down the road and enter the surgery. I see the receptionist and then sit in the waiting room and watch a procession of people with heads on their shoulders getting called to see the doctor before I do. Finally, I hear my name. I get up and leave the waiting room. As I turn into the corridor that leads to the consulting rooms I catch sight of my reflection in a pane of reinforced glass in the door that leads to the stairs. There's the same empty space where my head should be and, I presume, used to be. Is it possible I never had a head, but only hallucinated it? What kind of question is that to be asking yourself as you knock on your GP's door and hear her invite you to enter?

"Good morning, doctor," I say. "How are you?"

"Very well, thank you," she says, meeting my gaze. "How are you?"

I think carefully about my response. "I'm not sure," I say finally. "I suppose I want you to tell me."

"Well," she says, "you requested an emergency appointment."

"Yes," I say.

The doctor looks at me. Her face betrays neither surprise nor dismay, nor the slightly indecent excitement a doctor might feel when presented with an unusual case.

"I feel," I say, "like something is missing."

The doctor smiles and frowns at the same time.

"From your... life?"

"Something is missing and I feel as if I can't carry on without it, and yet it's very hard to say what it is… what it is that's missing. Do you see?"

"Have you been feeling depressed?" she asks.

"More alarmed than depressed," I say.

"Have you been feeling anxious?"

I look at her, unsure how to respond.

"Panic attacks, uncontrollable distress?"

I look away from her towards the frosted glass of the window.

"Do you feel as if you are losing your grip?" she asks.

"I think I need to go," I say.

The smile has disappeared and now there is only a concerned frown.

"If you'd like to see someone… a referral?"

"I'm okay," I say, getting to my feet. "I'll be okay."

"Are you sure?"

"I'm fine."

"Make an appointment to see me in a week or two."

I thank her and leave. I walk back home without delay.

I stand in the hall. The house is silent. I'm thinking. I go into the kitchen and open the drawer where we keep the larger saucepans and the rice cooker. Then I close it again. I try the tall cupboards. I open all the eye-level cupboards and look quickly inside each one before closing them again. I open the fridge. Milk, wine, butter, cheese, salad stuff, yoghurts, a bowl containing leftover chilli that will inevitably be thrown away.

In the cellar I open the doors to all the cupboards. I look in the old plastic dustbin I store firewood in. The shelves – nothing shouldn't be there, just jam jars containing screws and curtain hooks and Allen keys and brass hooks bought to go on the backs of doors that have never been fitted.

I climb the steps back to the hall. There are cupboards in the lounge containing LPs that have not been played in twenty years. The cushions on the settee conceal only biscuit crumbs, loose change and the TV remote control that has been missing for two days.

Upstairs I check the wardrobes and the airing cupboard. I pull down

245

piles of bedding and towels and leave them in a heap on the bathroom floor. I rummage behind the hot water tank. I look around the landing. The linen basket contains nothing but a few pairs of socks and some underwear. I take the stairs to the top floor and my study. The drawers of my filing cabinet are filled with hanging files overstuffed with papers and manuscripts and press cuttings. I look at the bookshelves. Books, DVDs, VHS tapes, copies of *Sight & Sound* going back fifteen years. There are no gaps on the shelves. There is nothing under my desk except my printer and a box I use as a footrest and lots of fluff and dust-furred wires and cables.

I go back down to the first floor. There's an empty wardrobe in the spare bedroom, but that's exactly what it is – empty. I carry a stool in from the bedroom and stand on it so I can see on top of the empty wardrobe, but all I see is empty space.

Slowly I walk downstairs. I open the front door and step outside. I approach the bins. The brown one, emptied recently, contains a couple of wine bottles and several tin cans; the blue bin is two-thirds filled with paper and cardboard; the green one is less than half-filled with grass cuttings and compostable bags of food waste; and the grey bin conceals a single bag of non-recyclable rubbish collected from various bins and baskets around the house. It has a drawstring neck and the plastic tape used to secure it has been tied in a knot.

I look up from the bin. The windows of the house across the street return a blank stare.

I reach into the grey bin and pull out the bag. I dump it on the drive and bend down to pick at the knot. It won't come, so I press my finger nails into the plastic at the top of the bag and tear it open. The bag is almost full. I plunge my hands into a mass of stained cotton wool balls, disintegrating toilet roll holders and spaghetti in tomato sauce that should have gone in the green bin. There are damp tissues and an empty blister pack of heavy-duty pain killers and a rolled-up ball of my wife's hair. Well, it's certainly not mine. I picture her standing at the sink, viewed through the half-open door, pulling the hair out of her brush and rolling it into a ball between her palms, looking up and seeing me watching her and then looking away to direct her right foot at the pedal bin.

I pick the bag up by its bottom corners and upend it over the drive. Its contents hit the asphalt in a large pile into which I delve, coming up empty handed.

As I'm shovelling the worst of the mess back into the bag, one of my neighbours walks past the end of the drive. She gives me a look similar to the one the doctor gave me.

❋

My wife comes home.

"What's all that mess on the drive?" she asks.

"I was looking for something," I say. "I'll clean it up."

I pour her a glass of wine, which she takes through into the lounge, while I locate the dustpan and brush in the cupboard under the sink. I hear the television go on and a newsreader's voice saying something about the situation in Syria. Violence in Damascus. Calls to arm the rebels. I take the dustpan and brush outside and start clearing up the mess. When I come back in, I can hear a reporter on the news doing a piece to camera. I stow the dustpan and brush and go upstairs to put the towels away and anything else I've left lying around in my hunt through various cupboards and drawers.

As I come back downstairs and enter the lounge, I hear another news reporter saying, "The head was removed by police, who are conducting further enquiries."

"*What's that*?" I say, aware of the sharpness in my voice.

"Severed head found in a plastic bag in London," my wife says, before draining her wine glass. "Was that an especially small glass you gave me?" she asks.

"What?"

"It didn't last long."

"*What*?"

"That glass of wine."

"What about the head, the severed head on the news?"

"I don't know," she says. "I wasn't really paying attention. Someone found a severed head in a Sainsbury's bag."

"Where?"

"I don't know. London, somewhere."

"Did you see it?"

"The head?"

"Yes."

"Of course I didn't see it. They're not going to put a severed head on the six o'clock news, are they?"

"Where in London was it? They must have said."

"I daresay they did. I wasn't really listening. What difference does it make? A severed head is a severed head wherever it's found."

I grab the remote and press rewind. The details are that a man's severed head was discovered by a woman out walking her dog at ten past eight that morning on the Parkland Walk between Highgate and Finsbury Park. It was, as my wife had said, inside a supermarket carrier bag.

"I wonder if it was a bag-for-life?" my wife says.

On to the screen comes a still image of an empty, regular Sainsbury's plastic carrier bag, orange and lightweight.

"Apparently not," she says. "You'd think they'd have used something a bit sturdier, wouldn't you? I mean, those things are no good at all. One medium-sized chicken and you're lucky if you can get it from the shopping trolley into the boot of the car without the bag going."

"Is this the last item on the news?" I ask her.

"What do you mean?"

"Is this the last item? The joke item. The light relief. You think it's funny?"

"I suppose you're right," she says. "I don't imagine the owner is laughing. Where was the remote anyway?"

I leave the room and climb the stairs two at a time. I open my laptop and go online, logging on to Network Rail. I book a ticket—a single— for the morning. It's expensive, but that's too bad.

"I'm going to London tomorrow," I tell my wife later in bed.

"Are you going to look for that severed head?" she murmurs, half-asleep.

"How did you guess?" I say, but her breathing has already slowed to a regular pace.

I lie there thinking about getting up early and catching the train. I think about taking the Northern line to Highgate and finding my way on to the Parkland Walk, heading south towards Finsbury Park under the tree canopy, eventually coming across a thicket of blue and white police tape, a uniform standing guard, fielding questions, perhaps, from a female reporter. She'll be in her late twenties, working for a local paper, thinking it may not be civil war in Syria, but it's a big story nevertheless. Her big break. I'll listen in, follow her when she leaves, introduce myself. She'll be suspicious, bound to be. I'll explain that I know something, I have information. She'll be dubious. I'll tell her I can help with identification. I just need to see a picture of the head. She must have seen one, or be able to find one. A headshot. Video removed from YouTube, grainy frame grab. She'll know all about it, she'll have access. Maybe we'll end up in a pub. Two halves of lager, one left untouched. I'll sense the possibility of the beginning of something-

It's no good. I can't sleep. I slip out of bed, reach for my dressing gown and leave the bedroom. Upstairs in my study I open the laptop. While it powers up, I turn to my right and crane my neck to look out of the window. The only reflection I see is of the bookshelves behind me. I turn back and lean forward over my desk, a middle-aged man roaming the internet in the middle of the night while his wife lies asleep, dreaming perhaps of new rooms discovered in old houses, of a more caring, less distracted husband.

I find nothing in the obvious places. A million distractions fail to distract me. I refine my search terms.

The first two links lead only to black oblongs, dead screens. Across the middle of each one runs a line: *This video does not exist*. The third link takes me to a page of text, no video. I read the report, which says nothing of interest. I go back to an earlier search term and modify it slightly. I scroll down the page of links, navigate to the second page, click on the third link down, one I have yet to try. The name of the web site is not familiar to me. In both the headline and the standfirst I am warned that the video contains 'graphic images'. I reflect on how the meaning of this word, 'graphic', has changed over a relatively short period of time. I read a paragraph that explains the context, then scroll down and click on the arrow on the video, which starts to play. I click on the full-screen symbol.

Beneath a forget-me-not blue sky with scattered puffs of white cloud, three men kneel, heads down, on a grassy hillside, hands tied behind their backs. A man wearing an Afghan-style soft cap and carrying an automatic weapon over his shoulder addresses a crowd of men and boys who wait in patient ranks like paparazzi at a première. The man in the cap, speaking in Arabic, talks about the men kneeling on the ground, indicating them in turn. In the background another man waits, a thickset Rasputin with his long dark straggly hair and long beard and black long-skirted costume. On a sign or a word from the man in the cap, the man with the long hair and the long beard pushes the first of the three condemned men face first on to the ground. The crowd becomes excited as everyone jostles for the best positions not only to see what is happening but to film it on their cameraphones. At the same time, the crowd finds its voice. *Allahu akbar, Allahu akbar, Allahu akbar.* I turn the volume down, briefly aware of my increased heart rate. The camera on which the video is being shot momentarily cuts out and when the picture is restored the man with the long hair is straddling the first of the condemned men and sawing at his neck with a ten-inch knife. The man with the long hair keeps having to stop and start, looking for a better angle. This is no easy task. He saws and he saws at the man's neck while other necks are craning for a better view and the camera lurches to one side. A shoulder moves into shot and, by the time it is possible to see clearly once more, the job is done and another man lifts the severed head to show it to the crowd before placing it, upright, facing forwards, on the dead man's back. It no longer looks real, but nor does it resemble a prop; it exists somewhere between reality and illusion. It no longer belongs to its former owner, but is part of something else now, something more abstract. *Allahu akbar, Allahu akbar*.

Attention turns to the second of the condemned men. He is wearing a blue suit. His blindfold is removed. Immediately to his left lies the first man's corpse. The condemned man does not turn to look, but continues to stare at the ground. The man with the long hair now pushes him forwards and then on to his side. He pulls the condemned man's head back and draws the blade across his throat back and forth, back and forth, like a child with a cello. The knife is not really suitable. A man I haven't noticed before hands him another knife and he drops the first knife on the grass, which is no longer green. This is a job for a serrated knife, but these knives do not appear to be serrated and the blood will make maintaining a steady grip on the slippery handle almost impossible. But still he cuts, still he works away at the crimson gash, pulling the head back by the chin, aided by hands from the crowd that pull on the man's arm. Finally, the head is detached and the man with the long hair places it on the dead man's back just in front of his still-bound hands. Another man picks it up to show it to the crowd and then he replaces it on the dead man's back. A boy of eleven or twelve in a yellow T-shirt and blue jeans and a green sweatshirt tied around his waist approaches for a closer look. *Allahu akbar, Allahu akbar, Allahu akbar*.

The video finishes before the execution of the third man is carried out.

I click in the top left-hand corner of the window and then close the laptop. My heart is beating fast and I realise I have a headache. I stand up too quickly and have to lean on the back of the chair for support. I look around my study. Everything in it – the books, the DVDs, the magazines; my chair, the desk, my laptop – looks the same and yet different. I leave the room and stand on the upper landing gazing up at the skylight in the sloping ceiling, my arms wrapped tightly around my body. I sit down on the top step and stare into the darkness of the stairwell for an indeterminate length of time. It could be minutes; it could be an hour.

I re-enter the bedroom and walk around the end of the bed to the window. I open the curtain and stand looking out at the street in the night, focusing and unfocusing my vision. I am still standing there when it begins to get light and my reflection gradually fades. Soon I can no longer see my face, the look in my eyes.

My wife stirs. "I thought you were going to London," she says.

"No," I say. "Not anymore."

NEWSPAPER HEART
Stephen Volk

A rocket whooshed and pop-popped somewhere in the night. Iris Gadney's heart jumped. She hated this time of year. It always crept up on her, and her biology reacted before her brain did. It was funny like that. She should know by now, but she never did. It was always unexpected, the knotting in her stomach that came with the smell of sulphur in the air. What was in fireworks anyway? Gunpowder, she imagined. She didn't really know. She could ask her husband. He taught chemistry after all. He'd know. But she didn't want to. She didn't care. She just wanted November the fifth to come and go and everything to return to normal. That's all she ever wanted — normality.

Des hadn't so much as twitched at the noise. In fact hadn't moved from behind the *Daily Express* for at least twenty minutes, but she knew better than to try to winkle him out of his shell into conversation. When he came home from work he was like one of those deep sea divers who have to go into a decompression chamber. He was never himself — whatever 'himself' was — until he'd gone through the sports results, always reading the paper backwards, as if world events like the Vietnam War and the famine in Biafra, the latest pronouncement by Prime Minister Ted Heath ('Ted *Teeth*' as Des called him) or the army firing rubber bullets in Northern Ireland, were of far less importance than men kicking a ball around — which, to him, they probably were.

She went into the tiny scullery at the back of the house, and was halfway through making tea, buttering sliced bread for some corned beef and Branston sandwiches, when she heard the familiar ding-dong (*Avon calling!*) of the doorbell.

"Who's that?"

"I don't know, do I?" Iris lowered her voice to a sarcastic murmur as she wiped her hands on a tea towel and strode past the expanse of newspaper. "I expect it's for me. I expect it's Blue Boy from *The High Chaparral*…"

By the time she got to the front door Kelvin had already opened it and her mood instantly lightened because he was facing another eight-year-old, Gareth Powell (she knew his mum Gloria, only by sight, mind). It hadn't happened much before—a friend coming to call. It hadn't happened *ever* before.

"Mum!" Her son looked over his shoulder at her with eager eyes under the scissor-line of his fringe. "Gareth wants me to go out to play. He says a whole pile of boys are up the quarry making a bonfire!"

"Well you can forget that for a start," Des said from the sitting room before she could answer. "There's probably a load of yobs from the Sec Mod up there, and I'm damned if I'm running you to hospital because some head case does something bloody daft."

"They're only collecting wood," Kelvin bleated.

"You're telling me they're not going to be messing round with sparklers? And matches? And *bangers*? 'Course they are—and little nippers like you are the ones that get picked on. When I was in school a lad called Truscott got a jackie jumper put in the hood of his duffel coat. We never saw him again after that."

"Gareth, love. Why don't you come in and play?" Iris offered, ever the peacemaker. "You can go in the middle room."

Kelvin frowned hard. "He *wants* to go up the *quarry*!"

"Yes, well, *you're* not—and that's final," his father called, shirtsleeves rolled up, tie still on. "If he wants to go, he can go on his own."

Kelvin swivelled his head back to his friend, who was already looking sheepish and backing away as if frightened. Perhaps his dad didn't talk to him the way Kelvin's dad talked to Kelvin.

"Gareth?" Iris said.

The boy didn't meet Kelvin's eyes and his cheeks reddened as he faded into the shadows beyond the glow of the porch light.

"I—I'll see you in school tomorr-"

The word was broken by a crackling rasp in the sky and splutter of magenta, the explosion above spilling arrows of sodium yellow. Iris' heart sank and he was gone.

"Hey. Children's hour is on." She pressed the door shut. Kelvin was already climbing the stairs, head downcast. "Tea's ready in a minute."

"I'm not *hungry*."

"Don't be ridiculous. You got to eat. Get down here. *Now*." The slight lift in his dad's voice was more than enough to get Kelvin to do as he was told. "I'm not in the mood for it, all right?"

✳

The corned beef and pickle sandwiches were eaten in silence. Kelvin had a face that looked like it was chewing cardboard, and that annoyed his father, who glowered. "Having a meal together is important. He can see his friends in school."

"Lots of things are important, Des," Iris said quietly. "Lots of things."

"Please may I leave the table?"

Kelvin's mother told him of course he could. His father told him not to slam the door. Both adults listened to his small footsteps on the stairs.

"He needs to watch that. The face on him." Des drank the last of his tea and replaced the cup in its saucer.

"He's only a kid. God help him, whatever he does he can't please you."

"Maybe he can't." Des said. "I never pleased *my* dad."

"That's no reason to take it out on him."

"Let's just pack it in there, can we? Christ…" Des ran his fingers through his flat Brylcreem-slick of hair.

"If it's work, don't take it out on him. That's all I'm saying. It's not his fault you don't get on with the new Head. It's not his fault you're taking on extra duties to try to impress her, things you—"

"It's not work," Des cut in.

And she knew it wasn't. She also knew he wouldn't talk about what it was. How the hell could he talk about it when he couldn't even look her in the eyes? In the beginning she'd wanted to say something, and sometimes she tried, but all she got was a stone wall, and no tears. Never any tears. The tears were all hers. And if he'd let go—just once—she might have thought they were sharing something. But he never did. Never could. And it made her feel like a cow, bringing this badness into his life every time she opened her mouth and every time she walked through the door. Sometimes she wanted to ask him if he wanted her gone. And she *would* go, except deep down she knew he needed her to cling to, like a drowning man needed driftwood. Not a particularly nice or wonderful piece of driftwood, just something that was better than nothing to keep him afloat.

He caught her wrist as she gathered the plates. "Hey. I love you."

"Well, love him too, occasionally."

"I can't help it."

"Yes, you can," Iris said firmly, managing to avoid her voice cracking. "If I can, you can."

❊

Kelvin was monosyllabic over his cornflakes, and Des seemed to want to match him for sullenness, as if two could play at that game. Iris, as ever, was piggy in the middle, relieved to have the house to herself as Des drove off up to Porth in time for assembly and Kelvin left to trudge his weary way down to the Primary School in Tyfica Road. By himself, of course. Always by himself. A lonely little figure—but perhaps he wasn't lonely at all. Still, it gave her a little stab in the heart every morning as she waved him goodbye. She always told herself he'd probably meet some mates on the way and chat and have a lark around, as boys do. But *what* mates? He never talked about any. Or he'd talk about one, and the next week they wouldn't be friends any more. She remembered the awful perils of her own playground life: finding a best friend one minute who turned into a horrible enemy the next. A bit like marriage. God, did she really think that?

At dinnertime Des stayed in Porth and got something from the school canteen—silly driving all the way home to barely have time to bolt his food—but Kelvin came back, and this was a time she looked forward to. They could talk about stupid things. Different things. But today Kelvin didn't seem to want to talk at all.

She asked him what was wrong. At first he didn't want to say. She asked if it was about his dad. He said no. What was it, then? "Come on. Tell me. I'm your mum."

"I don't know. I just saw these boys on the way home, and they had a toboggan, just a box with wheels on, but it had this guy in it and it had a—one of those—waistcoat things and a sheriff's badge pinned on it, and a face with a beard stuck on, and a floppy hat—and it looked *brilliant*."

She shrugged. "Well, we can make one of those."

"Can we?" His eyes looked like they'd pop out.

"'Course we can. Don't be daft. It's easy."

"Dad won't like it though."

"'Course he will. He did it himself when he was your age. Everyone did. Come on. He's staying in school to do some marking tonight, so we'll start it now and do the rest before he gets home." Before she'd finished the sentence her son was out of his chair, baked beans on toast abandoned. She smiled. For some reason she felt almost as excited as he did.

They chose the clothes together. Iris suggested that old, baggy pair of trousers Des wore when he was decorating. They'd seen better days and were only fit for the dustbin. Then there was that red polo-neck jumper that *had* been put out with the rubbish, shrunk in the wash and too tight for her husband's burgeoning pot belly—she salvaged that from amongst the potato peel and tin cans. It smelled of tomato soup and earth, but Kelvin said it was great, and he was the boss. He snatched it off her and she couldn't admonish him. It was fabulous to see him enthusiastic about something, lost as if in a quest for treasure as they raided bedroom drawers for a pair of old grey football socks and some woollen gloves that were a Christmas present from an auntie in Aberdare: white, with green holly leaves on the back.

They laid out all the items on the carpet in the sitting room. Even the rough shape of the trousers, socks, gloves and sweater had the immediate semblance of a person, although an extremely flat one—this was shortly about to change. Iris switched on the transistor radio. They sang along to the recent number one, *In the Summertime* by Mungo Jerry. Kelvin was grinning from ear to ear. Iris dumped a mound of old newspapers, which had been gathering beside the fireplace, and both of them started scrunching up the pages of newsprint into balls, stuffing them deep into trouser legs Iris had knotted at the ankles with string. In no time the lower limbs began to thicken lumpily, rolled-up paper filling in the hips, groin and pelvis.

"Don't do any more till I get home," Kelvin said breathlessly as he left for school, but Iris couldn't resist finishing the task she'd begun. Sewing box open beside her, she stitched the bottom of the poloneck to the waistline of the trousers, after which she bit off the loose thread with her teeth. Alone in the house now, looking down at the semi-deflated body draped across her lap, she felt ridiculously like a surgeon repairing some wound. Repairing a life. Not building, but resurrecting. Silly...

She abandoned it for the ironing, not even looking into the room for the rest of the afternoon. She didn't know why. But when Kelvin burst in his feet didn't touch the ground. He skidded on his knees onto the sitting room carpet and he was instantly shoving more screwed-up pages of the classified ads from the *Western Mail*—births, marriages, deaths— into the cavity of the pullover. She chuckled as he stuffed it into the open neck, watching the torso fill as if with bone and tissue. The arms were tied at the wrists and soon sported white woolly gloves with flappy, insubstantial fingers like the teats of uninflated balloons. They worked to *Tears of a Clown* by Smokey Robinson and the Miracles, *Back Home* by the England World Cup Squad, and *The Wonder of You* by Elvis Presley—a song Kelvin said was for old people but his mum said she liked it because it was romantic. She knelt on the floor with him and sewed the football socks, now bulked out with paper like the rest, onto the knotted stumps of the ankles.

"I know!" An idea galvanised Kelvin and he vanished upstairs, reappearing with a shiny, frog-green anorak that hung in his wardrobe even though he'd grown out of it a long time ago. Together they dressed the guy in it, sliding one arm then the other into the sleeves. It lolled between them, feeling as though it should be heavy but light as a feather. Kelvin stood back, admiring his handiwork. "He looks good doesn't he? I think he looks the *best*."

His mum smiled. "Needs a head though, don't you think?" The hood gaped like a feeble mouth. "What are we going to use?"

"We'll find something."

"Hang on. Where are you going?" He'd already hoisted the guy in his arms and was shuffling to the door en route to his bedroom. "Don't you want to show your father?"

Kelvin whispered, "Not yet." He put his finger to his lips as he heard the back door open and close. And when, over tea, Des detected the whiff of secrecy between them and asked what the two of them had been up to, both of them said, almost in unison: "Nothing."

❋

Friday was the day Iris got her meat and veg from Ponty market and, as often as not, if her timing coincided, went to Tyfica Road to collect her son from school at home time. Children were already drifting out of the school gates in twos and threes, chatting and playing boisterously or blowing pink spheres of bubble gum, yet her heart ached a little bit to see her own son walking alone, idly scuffing his feet along the pavement, the strap of his school bag pulling his jumper half-off his shoulder.

"Look!" He suddenly piped up as he saw her, running up, thrusting a punctured Adidas football in her face – the black and white patterned type they'd used that year for the World Cup in Mexico. Seeing her perplexed expression he swiftly added, almost too excited to get the words out: "For his *head!*"

❋

Des remarked that the boy had lost his appetite and found a horse's. Kelvin scoffed his fish fingers in record time, asked if he could leave the table and was gone in a flash.

"He's got ants in his pants."

"That's boys for you."

"What does he do up there?"

"I think he's got a hobby." Iris didn't like lying and knew she wasn't good at it. She watched her husband get up from the table, turn over the cushions on the settee, delve through the magazine rack. "What are you after?"

"Last week's *Echo*."

"I chucked it out, I expect."

"Thanks. I hadn't read that."

"Sorry. How was I to know?"

"Bloody hell. I better move quick round here or *I'll* get thrown out."

"That's true." She kissed him on the cheek, sat down and turned up the telly. Gordon Honeycombe was reading the ITV news and she pretended to watch, but she was thinking about the guy upstairs, with his Adidas football head, which she'd sewed into place on the throat of its scarlet polo-neck, sitting cross-legged on her son's bed, Kelvin watching her raptly, chin on his fists, before her husband got home.

❊

As she made the bed she stepped on a human hand and jumped back with a shrill yelp. Quietening her heart with the flat of her hand she looked down at the white Christmas glove at the end of a misshapen arm sheathed in anorak green.

Hell!

Annoyed, she poked it with her toe, but each time it fell back into place so she bent down to shove it back under the bed where the rest of the effigy was hidden. Now on her knees, she couldn't avoid seeing its bulbous chest packed with paper sinews sandwiched between the carpet and the bedsprings. In the dark it looked like a body wedged in a coffin. She didn't look at it for long, and stood up. It was Saturday so Des had gone to Cardiff with his cronies to see a match. Cardiff City were playing Hull F.C. at Ninian Park and they always went to a pub first to get the 'atmosphere' with other supporters over cheap pies and Brains bitter. Kelvin had nipped out to spend his pocket money, but when she heard the front door slam—that making her jump too—she knew he'd returned.

"What's that?" she said, meeting him on the landing. He was carrying a brown paper bag. He walked straight past her.

"Come and see."

By the time she'd entered the bedroom again he was hauling the guy out from its hiding place, and slung it, football-head nodding and jerking, onto the bed.

"I bought it from Gould's," Kelvin said, meaning the newsagent's round the corner from the Army Recruitment Office, opposite the Muni. It was where he bought his *Beezer*, *Dandy*, *Spider-Man* comics and Marvel Classics like *20,000 Leagues under the Sea*. But this wasn't any of those. This was a plastic mask with an elastic loop at the back. A shiny, pink mask of the face of a baby, with a ginger curl in the centre of its forehead and holes for pupils.

"Why that one?" Her thought came out in a breath. She heard it like it was said by somebody else, trying to blink but fixated on watching him place it over the blank football-head. "Why not Guy Fawkes, love? I mean—the traditional one, with a pointed beard?"

"I don't know." Kelvin shrugged, his back to her. "I just saw it and I thought it would suit him. Come on. I want to show you something else." He jumped up, taking her by the hand, the guy trailing under his other arm. "I got it from the dump."

At the bottom of the stairs was a pushchair, filthy and scuffed, but otherwise fairly intact.

"His car. His chariot," Kelvin said, hoisting the guy and plonking it into the seat. The baby face tilted to one side and he adjusted it, punching it gently into position, tucking in one stray, poking-out arm.

"Does he like it?" she found herself saying, just to say something.

Just to fill the air.

"He doesn't *like* it—he *loves* it!"

And—silly—she didn't remember much else except the squeak and squeal of the wobbly wheels as he manipulated the pushchair towards the open door. She didn't remember—silly thing—what he said, just that he was going out and she was still standing on the stairs and she remembered telling him, hand splayed on the wallpaper, not to be long and that she was going to have a (breath) lie down... Just a (breath) little lie down for five minutes...

❈

The door banged and she woke in fear. Her first thought was that Kelvin had just left, but why was she lying on the settee, and why was the room in darkness? Why wasn't the light on? Why was it dark outside and why weren't the curtains drawn? She looked at her watch and saw to her shock it was half past seven. She shot to her feet, but the blood drained from her head instantly and she had to steady herself on the back of a dining chair.

"What the bloody hell's going on?" Des filled the room, flicking the light on, blinding her. When she could see again she saw him marching in Kelvin like some condemned prisoner, the kid clutching the guy to him in a tight and resilient embrace with his father's meaty hands clamped on his shoulders.

"I don't know. I fell asleep. I told him not to be out long. Where was he?"

"Where *was* he? I'll tell you where he was. Down the bloody precinct! Out begging!" Her husband's eyes were ablaze. She'd never seen him so angry. Never so close to being out of control, and that frightened her, but instinct to protect her son overwhelmed it.

"Des. It's a *game*, for God's sake—they all do it."

"Yes, the layabouts! Those boys with no hope. The *poor* kids. Boozing and smoking fags because they've got nothing better to do. From Berw Road and up the Common. Educationally subnormal, the lot of them!" He tossed a sheet of cardboard emblazoned in black block capitals with the words PENNY FOR THE GUY onto the settee where she'd been curled up asleep moments before. He gestured at it, gasping for words, as if its very existence were a massive personal insult. "Is *that* what I'm working for, all the hours God sends, and your mother's slaving away at home for? Is it? For you to go out there and show us up? Well, *is it?*" Kelvin was staring at his shoes, his shoulders hunched, and Iris felt sorry for him, in fact she wanted to hug him, but dared not. "You know who was in the car with me? Elwyn, Dick, Ike Jones—my *friends*. The people I work with. What do you imagine they were thinking, eh?" Kelvin didn't have an answer, or didn't feel inclined to give one. "I'll tell you what they were thinking. That I can't look after my own son, and there he is out on the street like a bloody ragamuffin asking people for money because he doesn't get given enough at home! Like his parents are bloody *depriving*–"

"Des–"

"It's not *begging*," Kelvin muttered, showing a scowl now. "*Everybody* does it."

"Yes, well *you*'re not everybody!" Des heard his son mumble something. "What was that?"

"Nothing."

"Nothing. Good job it's nothing. It *better* be nothing, I tell you!" Des turned away, exasperated beyond his power of expression, walking back and forth in the miniscule sitting room like a bear in a cage. "I'm... I'm ashamed of you!" He snatched up the cardboard sign and threw it onto the open fire.

"Oh for God's sake!" Iris cried out, crouching quickly and retrieving it before it fully caught light. "I tell you what you should be ashamed of. The fact your son was afraid to tell you about this because he knew you'd blow a flamin' gasket!" She thrust the flimsy sign, only slightly charred, towards Kelvin, a gritty whiff of coal smoke stinging her nostrils. The boy held it tightly to his chest and backed away. Pulling out the sheet of cardboard made the glowing embers of the coal fire re-ignite with crackling vigour. But this was as nothing compared to the inferno Iris saw in her husband's dry and unblinking eyes as the realisation sank in.

"You *knew* about this?" His voice thinned like his lips in disbelief.

"Yes. Of course I did. I helped him, if you must know. What's wrong with that? All the kid wants to do is go out and enjoy himself with his friends."

Des laughed. "What 'friends'? He hasn't got any friends."

"Well we all know whose fault that is, don't we? You're like a bloody big kid yourself."

"And you're not? Making a doll for him? What's that supposed to do for him, eh? A big bloody doll. That's what it is, isn't it? Why don't you buy him a Barbie while you're at it?"

"Oh, go and boil your head. I'm sick of this. I'm sick of you and your…"

Iris stopped as she saw past Des that the ribbed glass door to the hallway was ajar, and beyond it the pushchair from the dump was parked, but there was no sign of the guy and no sign of Kelvin. She hurried past Des, shoving him out of her way, and stood at the foot of the stairs in time for them both to hear the slamming of Kelvin's bedroom door.

"Now look what you've done."

"Me?"

"Yes you." Iris returned to the room, shook an Embassy from her packet and lit it with trembling hands. "All he was doing was going out playing because you don't let him. What the hell is he supposed to do?"

Des pinched the bridge of his nose with his fingertips. "I don't care. I really don't."

"No, you care more about John Toshack than you care about that boy up there. Well you'd better. And bloody fast, too, I'm telling you. Or do you want him to grow up hating you?" He looked daggers at her for that. "Or does what your beloved cronies down the club think count for more than what I think?"

"Christ, I can't do anything for doing wrong, can I?"

"No. Poor you." Iris was too angry to back down. She wasn't having it. She'd had enough. And it was ridiculous. She took a long drag on the cigarette and blew smoke. The rat-a-tat of a firework stuttered a few streets away, followed by the distinctive skree of a rocket. "Go and talk to him."

"Let him stay up there. A clip round the ear, he wants. He needs to be taught a—"

"Go and talk to him. *Now*."

Bap bap bap! something went in the sky before fluttering and sparkling earthwards.

He could see she was upset, and more because of that than that he was in the wrong (he *wasn't* in the wrong – *bloody hell*...) he went upstairs, unbuttoning his mac and draping it over the banister before ascending. Iris watched his hand, rendered pink by the cold night air, gliding up the wooden rail until his creaking footsteps reached the landing.

Her hair felt brittle and she tore through it with her hairbrush. The skin on her face felt tight, her throat felt constricted as if half strangled, her skull blocked and salty, all the usual symptoms after she'd been weeping or felt it was imminent. She still didn't feel fully awake and hoped that the scene that had just happened was a dream, but it wasn't, and she wanted to wish it away, and she couldn't. Wishes didn't work. She of all people knew that.

Brushing her hair didn't do the trick. She needed to give herself a wash and headed upstairs to the bathroom, squeezing past the semi-rusted pushchair, the PENNY FOR THE GUY sign dumped in its seat at a skewed angle, and went up and give her cheeks a cold swill at the sink.

As she passed Kelvin's bedroom on her way back down, she couldn't help listening at the door. The man's voice was soft and sympathetic. Loving, even. It didn't sound like her husband at all. It sounded almost like the person he used to be. Almost.

"See, I say these things because I care about you, that's all. I get angry because I just want you to be safe and sound. I do it for your own good, see. What you got to remember is, not all people are dangerous, but some are, and when you're out on your own you don't know who's who, do you?"

She wished with all her heart she could see Kelvin's little face and know how he was reacting, whether he was nodding or just listening, snuggled down in his bed under the eiderdown, but she couldn't. After a moment of silence, Des spoke again:

"Hey. You done a good job. You and your mam."

"Me, mostly."

Iris smiled. Swallowed the lump in her throat.

"Don't!" Kelvin gasped suddenly, bursting into panic. "Don't move him!"

"Okay, okay, okay... Cool head... Here you are..."

"He wants to stay here and sleep next to me."

"Orright, orright... Let me tuck you in then, nibblo..." Her husband's voice grew faint as she padded downstairs, not wanting to reveal she was standing outside, earwigging the conversation. "You're a funny 'apeth." Fading away, her son replied that he wasn't. He wasn't any kind of 'apeth.

She switched on the TV. When it had warmed up it showed Mary Hopkins as a guest on *The Rolf Harris Show* on BBC1. Her trilling, virginal style of folk singing grated with Iris, in spite of her being Welsh and a discovery of Tom Jones – Ponty boy himself, bit of a boyo by all accounts, and without doubt the town's only claim to fame. She wasn't a big fan of the bearded Aussie either with his fair dinkum, down-under cheeriness. It always seemed entertainers were desperate to create happiness, but when the programme was switched off, where was the happiness then?

Presently Des came in, Schools Rugby tie loosened, easing the glass door shut after him, and sat in the armchair that was vacant—not the settee, which was always where she sat. Peculiar the habits you got set in. He sat in the glow of the screen. By the time she was crushing out a new cigarette in the ashtray she knew she had to speak, because she could hold it in no longer.

"Did you see the mask he bought?"

Des nodded, or flinched, she wasn't sure which. "Grotesque bloody thing."

"Why couldn't he get a Guy Fawkes mask like all the other kids?"

"Who knows what goes through that lad's mind. Honest to God. I give up. He can do what he likes."

"You don't mean that."

"I don't know what I mean." Des rose from the chair as if the act was a gigantic effort. His pallor was grey. He looked exhausted. Emotionally drained. Even to talk, talk normally—to her—was clearly too much for him to bear. "I'm going to bed."

Touch me. Touch me, she thought. *Kiss me.*

But he couldn't. How could he?

Do I smell of blood? she thought, in the empty room, eyes fixed blindly on the television programme. *Is that it? Do I, still?*

On Sunday morning when Iris opened his bedroom door she found Kelvin with a snakes and ladders board laid out between himself and the guy, moving one of the counters up a ladder. When she asked if he wanted to come down the park for a walk, he shot a look at the guy— for all the world, she'd swear, as if deferring for an answer. None being forthcoming, he scuttled over and whispered via a cupped hand to the side of its earless head.

"He doesn't want to stay in on a nice day like this, does he?" Iris said, persuasively, realising that her attempt to get her son to abandon the thing for a few hours was misguided.

Kelvin sat back on his heels. "Is Dad coming?"

"Not today. He's got some DIY to do." She didn't elaborate on what they'd actually said to each other: her trying to persuade Des that getting out the putty to re-glaze a window in the scullery was not exactly a priority, Des insisting it was a job he'd put off for months, and that was what Sundays were for. *If you say so*, being her final, curt reply as she got her coat.

She helped the boy put on his shoes at the bottom of the stairs, the guy with its plastic smile perched a few steps behind him, as if sitting pillion. Observing through its holes for eyes. Observing her as she double-knotted the laces.

Kelvin rearranged the guy's scarf, plumping the pillow in the pushchair behind its spineless back, evidently wanting the thing to be seen at its best.

"He likes sunshine."

"Good."

At the bottom of Mill Street they crossed the bridge over the Taff into Ynysangharad Park, the black water of the river below stark testimony to the industry of the Rhondda Valleys. As they passed the tennis courts—deserted at this time of year—she watched Kelvin run ahead with the pushchair at speed, with the intent of creating a thrill either for himself or, strangely, its immobile occupant, a figure that never looked straight or comfortable in its 'chariot' but awkward, ill-fitting, with an aspect of frozen entrapment reminiscent of a physically impaired child. It struck her horribly that, from a distance, a passer-by might take them for a family—especially the way Kelvin would regularly pause to tuck in a blanket around the thing's bulbous, paper-filled legs, and whisper to it in a way that—no, it didn't disturb her at all. Why should it? It was just play, and it was healthy for children to play, and use their imaginations. She just wanted to switch off her own.

The sticks of dead rockets lay on the tarmac, having fallen from the sky the night before. Their cardboard carcasses lay semi-charred and redundant—the spark of excitement they'd delivered now just a memory.

Iris buttoned her coat against the wind and stuck to their customary route past the cricket pavilion and band stand, inside which a small vortex of yellow leaves did a pirouette, and Iris paused to sit on a bench near the playground next to the mini-golf where Kelvin usually played on the slide and swings. She indulged in her last Embassy in the packet and opened the *Woman's Weekly* from her bag, but after a few minutes the words, "Penny for the guy… Penny for the guy…" made her look up.

To her dismay she saw that, far from playing with the other children, Kelvin was standing with the pushchair at the gates to the playground, delivering his repetitive litany to every adult who entered. He didn't seem unduly bothered by their disinterest and his mantra continued undiminished. This upset Iris more and more, as she saw the perplexed and then bemused looks on peoples' faces quickly turning into expressions of unease and pity as they hurried their own children in the opposite direction.

"Penny for the guy… Penny for the guy…"

Iris hurried over and took Kelvin's hand. "Come on. Let's go home, love. It's getting a bit cold and I need to get a cooked dinner on for your father…"

Heading towards the bus stop they passed Woolworths, its window resplendent with a vast display of Brock's fireworks boxes, gaudy and brash, and a cardboard cut-out Guy Fawkes in an Elizabethan ruff and tall hat, holding a sparkler like a magic wand. Kelvin gazed at the arrangement with what she first thought was wonder, but then saw was more of a worried puzzlement, and from being chatty all afternoon the boy became suddenly silent.

On the bus she tried to lighten the mood—*her* mood, if nothing else—by unwrapping a tube of fruit pastilles and offering him one.

"I don't like black ones," Kelvin said. "But he does. He *loves* them." He took a sweet between his thumb and forefinger and pressed it into the mask's mouth, then turned to his mother and popped an orange one into his own, grinning broadly.

Iris was looking at the little boy and his guy, side by side next to her in the back seat of the bus when the stout, greasy-haired conductor arrived, ticket machine thrusting from his midriff.

"One adult and two halves, please," she said.

Kelvin's grin spread into a laugh, and Iris smiled too, before she saw an elderly woman with the face of a boxer dog who'd been kicked up the bum by Sonny Liston was giving them a look like they were insane, or beneath contempt, or both.

"What are you staring at?" Iris said, and the old woman turned her considerable chin—or rather, chins—in the other direction.

Kelvin was still chuckling at this as the bus changed to a lower gear halfway up the hill, taking the wide, hair-pin curve from Graigwen Place into Pencerrig Street. But Iris was glad he didn't see what she saw, and what made her own smile fade very quickly. From the side window and then the back window, she got a passing glimpse up the rocky path leading to the quarry, where a large wigwam-like structure was taking form out of assorted planks of wood, fallen branches, sawn-down tree trunks, and pieces of discarded furniture. Even now a man dumped more wood on it from the boot of his car, and was dwarfed by the structure. It must've been fifteen foot high already, if not twenty. And to Iris—she didn't know why, or rather she *did* know why—resembled nothing so much as a funeral pyre.

❋

Still in his pyjamas, Kelvin brought down the guy and sat it on the settee while they all had breakfast. Des and Iris looked at each other but neither said a word. Kelvin was humming happily, his bare feet dangling under the table as he spread Marmite on his toast. Finishing first, Des picked up his car keys for the Anglia and said he was off. Iris didn't expect him to kiss her, and he didn't.

"You'd better run up and get dressed if you're not going to be late," she told her son. "Hang on. Aren't you going to take him back to your room?"

"No." Kelvin shot a glance at the guy. "He wants to stay down here today. He wants to keep you company."

Iris stared at the plate in front of her, not wanting to look at the dummy in case the dummy was looking at her, and rubbed her bare arms before faking a smile through clenched teeth. "That's nice." Then calling, "Don't forget to brush your teeth!" Then, in the silence, tried to address the remains of her toast but wasn't hungry and pushed it away. It was scorched. Black. She hated that. Bread tasting like coal, because coal tasted like death. Her grandfather had worked down the mine all his life and that's what he smelt like, however much carbolic he used to wash it off him.

Ten minutes later, when Kelvin came back down in his smart school clothes—corduroy trousers, V-neck, parka—she was sick of looking everywhere but at the thing half-sitting, half-lying on the settee. With a freshly-lit cigarette in her hand, she said:

"I'm not sure this is a good idea, love."

"Why?"

"I don't know what to do with him, that's all."

"Just make him feel at home. Just give him anything he wants."

"What does he want, though?"

"He might want the radio on."

Iris hid a laugh in a sigh. "Oh, I see. Okay. What kind of music does he like?"

"Any kind."

The front door banged and the house was hers. Whether she liked it or not. She looked for the Senior Service ashtray— relic of The Collier's—found it.

She switched on the transistor and it played *Yellow River* by Tony Christie and, by the time she'd finished the washing up, *All Kinds of Everything* by Dana. Drying the last teacup, she looked round the corner of the kitchen into the sitting room to see the settee side-on, and the guy hadn't moved. Of course it hadn't. How could it *move*?

She spent half an hour in the kitchen, tidying what needed to be tidied and wiping down the fablon surfaces and the hob of the oven, when she realised abruptly she was lingering there because she didn't want to go back into the sitting room, which was pathetic and silly. As an act of defiance, to her own nonsensical fear if nothing else, she strode back through, not even looking at the horrible object—though one of its socks brushed against her calf—and went into the hall to get the Hoover out from under the stairs. She shut the door behind her, but couldn't help seeing the vague, rippled shape of the occupant of the settee through the semi-opaque glass. As she moved her head from side to side it almost gave the illusion it was...

She carried the vacuum cleaner up to the landing and gave all three bedrooms a good going over. She didn't enjoy housework, but she was house proud—got that from her mother, never a speck of dust on anything—and she was a good worker, and soon lost herself in the mindlessness of the task. By the time she came back downstairs an hour later she'd forgotten the guy and when she saw it gave a start.

Bugger!

Left tilted at an angle, the gnomish creation had now slumped on its side and gave every appearance of snoozing, impossibly, behind its plastic grin.

Annoyed at her over-reaction, Iris grabbed it and dropped it unceremoniously on the carpet, leaving it a discarded and distorted sack while she vacuumed the upholstery, after which she sat it back in position, puffing the scatter cushions around it.

The machine droned and sucked. Afterwards she stood breathless with the spout of the appliance in her hand. The mask was looking at her like she was stupid. Like it knew something she didn't.

Sod you, she thought.

She desperately wanted a smoke. She poked the 'off' button with her toe and went to get the packet of Embassy from the mantelpiece, but it wasn't there. It wasn't on the stool next to her armchair either, which was always where she put it. It wasn't in the kitchen and it wasn't on the small table next to the telephone. She scanned the room, turning in a circle twice, but her eyes only fell on the inscrutable guy with its listless neck and hollow fingers in its freshly puffed-up throne.

"What have you done with my cigarettes?"

She didn't mean it literally, of course. She was just voicing her frustration at not finding them. But she found herself saying it again, out loud:

"What have you done with my cigarettes?"

It was mute. It had no lips. It had no voice.

She knew it didn't.

But when she made herself a mid-morning cup of coffee she didn't have it in the sitting room, she took it in the front room, the posh room, and drank it in the quiet away from the radio there, without opening the curtains.

❋

When Kelvin came home he burst past her as if she didn't exist, went straight into the sitting room and emerged almost immediately with the guy, his arm hooked round its midriff, trailing it with him as he hurried upstairs, its baggy limbs flailing. The bedroom door slammed. It would have been nice for him to say hello or to tell her about his day in school, but that was fine if that was the way he wanted it. She went back to her ironing.

At five to five she gave him a shout to tell him *Blue Peter* had started. There was no reply. She called again, louder, from the foot of the stairs but heard nothing but a solemn and disinterested, "Okay."

Twenty-odd minutes later the show finished with the usual chirpy goodbyes from Val Singleton, John Noakes and Peter Purves and its distinctive hornpipe theme music — but Kelvin still hadn't come down. Iris went upstairs to see what was so important to keep him from one of his favourite programmes.

As she approached the bedroom door, hand raised aloft to rap it with her knuckles, she frowned and froze. Could she hear not one but *two* voices coming from inside? Two children. Two boys in conversation, laughing and joking. One of them her son, yes... and the *other*?

She lowered her hand and twisted the door handle.

The scene that confronted her was an unremarkable one, yet not one that gave her any sense of relief — Kelvin sitting cross-legged on the bed with a comic open on his lap, the guy next to him, shoulder pressed against the wallpaper, mask askew on its round football head, arm twisted in a rubbery, inhuman curve. Kelvin looked at her as if interrupted mid-sentence.

"Sorry," Iris said, feeling foolish. The TV was on downstairs and the other voice must've come from that. Mustn't it? "I… I thought you had a mate in here."

"I do." Kelvin smiled.

It took her a moment to realise what he meant. When he grasped the guy's hollow Christmas-gloved hand in his, a damp chill dispersed in the bowl of her pelvis.

"Come downstairs." She stiffened, trying not to let the feeling intensify. "I don't like you spending all this time in your room."

"I do."

"Well I don't. Do as you're told." She found a firmness in her voice that didn't come naturally. "And put your friend out in the shed, please. He doesn't belong indoors."

"Who says?"

"*I'm* saying, and I'm your mam."

"I don't have to do what you say."

"Oh, don't you?"

"No. And neither does he."

"I'm not arguing, Kelvin. You can either do it now or you can talk to your father when he gets home. I'm not kidding." She said nothing more, ignored the fact he threw the comic onto the floor, and went back downstairs to let him stew.

She sat and watched the BBC news with Kenneth Kendall as her son put the back door on the snib and hauled the guy out into the yard to the garden shed in the corner with the peg holding closed the latch. Feeling sorry for him now, she went to the kitchen, made him a glass of orange squash, brought it in and put it on the table with a couple of chocolate digestives, but when she turned she saw him standing, still clutching the guy to his side.

"He doesn't like it in there. It's too dark and smelly. It smells of paint. It's horrible."

"I don't care," Iris said. "He'll like it in there when he gets used to it. He wants a home of his own."

"No he doesn't. He *said* he doesn't. It's too cold. He likes it in here. In *our* home."

"Kelvin, I said no." She was utterly powerless as he dragged the guy past her and back upstairs. "I said *No!*" But she knew he wasn't listening, wasn't even hearing. She didn't go up and, for the rest of the evening, he didn't come down.

Later, while Des was doing his marking in the middle room, she watched *Steptoe & Son* and couldn't concentrate at all. Albert had broken Harold's prize Ming vase and the audience on the laughter track was finding it hilarious, but it was all Iris could do to stop bursting into floods of tears.

It was Tuesday morning and she had some thinking to do, not something she was ever told she was good at. She didn't have a degree like her husband. The most she'd learned in school was how to sit up straight, and couldn't wait to leave that place, even if it meant working behind the bar in her father's pub, The Collier's, till her brother rolled in with a silly sod he'd met on National Service who pulled faces and acted the goat when she played *The Blue Danube* at the piano. Didn't think she'd go on and marry him. Not in a million years. Neither did his mother, who didn't approve and thought he could do better than a publican's daughter, and made that plain on more than one occasion. She wished she could speak to him now, about her fears, her daft ideas he'd probably call them, but how could she do that when she couldn't even talk to him about the chemistry of fireworks?

Instead she made herself a pot of tea and gradually let it warm her insides and the mug warm her hands. She wondered what a doctor might say about Kelvin and his new obsession with the object he had created? That there was no harm in it? That it was just like his collecting Mexico '70 coins? That it was just a phase he was going through? But what *sort* of phase, and why? She remembered, herself, as a ten-year-old having a sudden hankering to play with the teddy bear she'd adored when she was two or three, really wanting it back in her life, and asking her mother to find it in one of the tea chests in the attic. Had she wanted it to replace something missing? She couldn't remember. Did she just want it because it was somebody she loved, and she imagined loved her back?

She knew Des thought she wrapped the boy in cotton wool, that she was too much of a blinking softie half the time. Maybe men in general think a child should be told what's what. Do this, don't do that. Maybe it's about rules for them. *Their* rules, that is. But what about happiness? Did happiness ever come into it? She just wanted her son to be happy, and he wasn't. He couldn't be. Not when his best friend was a…

Then it struck her, what should've been blindingly obvious all along.

That if Kelvin had a real, proper friend there was a possibility he wouldn't need his make-believe one any more.

"Kelvin," she said at lunch time as he ate his sausages and beans. "Why don't you ask your friend Gareth to come over for tea tonight?" Kelvin stopped chewing. "I'll phone his mother and make sure it's all right with her, but I'm sure it will be. You can show off your guy. I'm sure he'll be impressed." She didn't get an immediate answer, and Kelvin buried himself back in his dinner.

"And *he*'ll enjoy it too," he said, looking over at the pile of clothes stitched into a human shape. "*He* hasn't got any friends either, see. Just me."

"Exactly," she said, wiping the drip of tomato sauce off his chin with her finger.

She phoned Gloria Powell while he ate his thin brick of Walls ice cream, then accompanied him to school, stopping off on the way back at Graigwen Stores to stock up with what she needed for tea. Jaffa cakes seemed a necessity, and she got a tin of salmon for sandwiches (it was a special occasion after all; *she* felt it was); oh, and some individually wrapped Cadbury's Swiss rolls, as well as bottles of white pop, Tizer and dandelion and burdock, just in case. It was a hike back home, but she found she had a spring in her step and didn't stop to catch her breath till she reached Jeff Beech's sweet shop, lightheaded, round the corner from her house in Highfield Terrace.

As it happened, Gareth said he'd like a cup of tea, please—he always had tea at tea time: didn't they? Iris said they didn't, not always. Or rather, she and Kelvin's dad had tea, but Kelvin didn't, he preferred squash. It already seemed a difficult conversation and she wondered why she was getting so flustered, given she was talking to an eight-year-old. The way he sniffed suspiciously at the salmon sandwich also didn't greatly enamour him to her. She said they could go upstairs and play with Kelvin's Scalextric if they liked, or Monopoly. Gareth said he always beat his sister at Monopoly. Kelvin said he didn't like Monopoly anyway, he liked draughts best. Gareth sniggered, repeating the word derisively and said his father was teaching him chess. He asked Kelvin what his dad was teaching him.

"Anyway, Gareth," Iris said. "What are you doing on November the fifth? Going up the quarry to the big bonfire?"

Gareth shook his head. "My dad gets a box of fireworks and lights them in the backyard. I'm allowed to hand him them, but he lights them."

"Quite right too. Light the blue touchpaper and stand well back!" Iris laughed, hoping the boys might laugh too, but they didn't see what was so funny. "I hope you keep your cats and dogs indoors."

"My mam and my sisters have to watch through the window. They always put their fingers in their ears. Dad says this year I can light a rocket."

Kelvin had left the table and now plonked himself down next to the guy on the settee. Frowning hard, he entwined its arm round his. "*He* wants to watch TV."

"What do you want to do, Gareth?"

Gareth shrugged.

"Well, you go and sit down and watch TV with Kelvin, and I'll get some cake and biscuits. How's that?"

Out in the kitchen she folded paper serviettes and arranged the mini-rolls on two small plates. A sense of satisfaction sank in as she heard nothing from the other room but the twinkly 'gallery' music from *Vision On*, played when they showed the drawings and paintings sent in by its child viewers. The boys were quiet. They were getting on, thank goodness, she thought. She'd been right. It was *working…* Then the spell was broken, the apparent calm torn asunder by a lilting, innocuous rhyme.

"Remember, remember, the—"

"*No!*—"

"Fifth of—"

"*Shut up!*"

"—vember. Gunpowder, treason and—"

"*Don't! Don't do that!*"

"—reason why gunpowder treason should *ever* be for—"

"*Don't! DON'T HURT HIM!*" This turning into a shriek. From her son.

Iris couldn't get into the sitting room quick enough. "What the heck is going on in—?"

Three small figures sprawled, entangled on the cushions of the settee, limbs for a moment indistinguishable. Kelvin was wrestling the guy away from Gareth who in turn seemed to be making pincer-like gestures at the effigy's polo-neck with crab-like hands. Kelvin tugged the guy's head towards him protectively and flung a foot out at the other boy, aimed at his face. Luckily this was countered by a swing of the arm, while Gareth's other arm swiped the guy with a karate chop in the middle of the chest, caving in the torso with a massive dent and bending it double. Kelvin emitted an even more ear-piercing shriek.

Iris caught his free hand, "Now! Stop it! Both of you!"

"He was pinching him!"

"I don't care what he was doing. You don't kick someone. Is that clear?"

"But he was—"

"I don't *care*! Is that *clear*?"

Kelvin scowled at his mother, eyebrows lowered, eyes black as coal. She was frightened by what she saw there—perhaps because she saw herself, her hatred of herself, or her husband's— but just as quickly the moment was snapped in half.

"*Owww-ah!*" This time the cry came from Gareth Powell, who was rolling around, knees in the air, one hand pressed into his armpit, then shot to his feet, tears springing to his eyes as he hopped up and down. "He bit me! The pigging thing *bit* me!" The boy held out his finger and the scratch across it welled with a ruby pearl of blood. Acting automatically, Iris held it in her hand and the boy continued sobbing pitifully—it made her think of the little baby he once must've been rather than the superior little prig he was now. She hastily took out her handkerchief and started dabbing, but it kept on bleeding. Damn, it wasn't just a scratch, it was a cut. A bloody deep one. How the *hell* had…?

She wrapped his finger in her hankie as she looked over at Kelvin, whose arms were wrapped round the guy, hugging it, rocking it slightly as if to comfort it after the unprovoked attack it had suffered at the hands of a stranger. Iris instantly saw that the safety pin that held the anorak in place over the guy's chest was undone.

"It's all right, love. It's just a nick. Just a flesh wound, like they say in the pictures, eh? Nothing serious. It was just the safety pin caught you, that's all, look…"

"It wasn't!" Gareth bleated, snot dribbling from his nose, his eyes reddening slits. "I didn't *touch* the safety pin! Wasn't anywhere *near* it! Didn't do *anything*!"

"All right, get upstairs you." Iris pointed Kelvin to the stairs and he shambled away with hunched shoulders, the wobbly-legged torso trailing after him by one inelegant sausage arm, one flaccid glove.

Gareth said he wanted to go home, and kept saying it throughout the process of Iris putting an Elastoplast on his wound—which wasn't that shocking, certainly not shocking enough for the hysteria it engendered. She then realised that Gareth wanted to go home not because he was hurting or in pain, but because he was terrified. He was terrified of staying there any longer, and the thing he was terrified of was upstairs.

✳

Des walked in and asked what was going on. Iris said she was taking Gareth home, she'd explain when she got back, and she did.

"Hell," he said, swilling a Scotch behind his teeth. He never drank spirits. Never drank at all, really. The bottles only came out at Christmas, and she'd never seen him tight. "This—this, whatever it is—attachment he's got, don't you think it's embarrassing enough without advertising it? Seriously?"

"I just wanted…" She rubbed the back of her neck.

"Well, great. Well done. Tomorrow it'll be all over the school. You know what children are like. He'll be a laughing stock. None of the other kids will touch him with a barge pole."

"It's a phase," she said, trying to convince herself.

"What if it isn't, Iris? What if it doesn't go away or get put right? What then?" He wanted his wife to answer but she didn't. Couldn't. "What do we do? Do we take him to a doctor?"

"No. I don't know." She held her head in her hands. "We just have to act like it's normal."

"It's *not* normal though, is it, eh?" A distant fire engine whined. Bangs and splutters adorned the air, more plentiful now than even the night before. "*Is* it?"

✳

At breakfast they sat in thorny silence over their plates as Kelvin chattered about how much blood was in the average human body, that the heart pumped it round and round, that's why we had redness in our cheeks, and other organs did other things, like the kidneys that got rid of things the body didn't need, but sometimes the things the body didn't need stayed in the body and got worse.

"How did you find out that?" Iris asked wearily. "From school?"

"No," said Kelvin with a mouthful of Frosties (*They're Grrrrrreat!*). "*He* told me."

The guy occupied one of the straight-backed dining chairs at the table, semi-deflated and lolling, its mask tilted, giving the illusion it was staring at the bowl of Coco Pops in front of it. Kelvin reached over and lifted a spoonful to its smiling slit of a mouth.

"For God's sake…" Her husband left his seat.

"Quiet," Iris said. "He's only playing."

"And I'm only on my way to work." Des struggled into the arms of his gabardine mac. She followed him to the kitchen, stopped him opening the back door. "This has gone beyond a joke," he whispered, fear and desperation as well as rage in his eyes. "That kid needs to see a bloody psychiatrist." She let the door open wide for him to go.

The bowl of Coco Pops was empty when she returned.

"Don't get upset," Kelvin was saying to the guy, tugging its sleeve. "You're one of the family. He loves you really. He just doesn't know how to show it."

The boy looked round at his mother. His lips twitched, but failed to resolve into a smile.

On the way back from shopping that day, Iris chose not to walk her usual route past the police bungalows and up the hill. Instead she decided to go the other way, up Graigwen Place, the way the bus went, then took the shortcut by foot round by the quarry. The bonfire had grown, and she wondered how, since nobody was in evidence. What made a person build a thing like this for enjoyment? Was it just children? Obviously not. Part of a fence had been added, as well as a broken ladder, and even a couple of doors—*doors!*—and a good number of large branches, of uneven lengths and thicknesses, some as hefty as telegraph poles, propped and criss-crossed, tepee fashion. She stood looking at it when a banger landed near her feet. It cracked, making her jump, then banged again two or three times, flitting around her before phutting out. She called out bitterly, telling someone they were stupid. Nobody replied, and she could hear only an aeroplane crossing the sky. She walked away rapidly. Whatever fool had done it was hiding, or was gone.

"God, what's wrong, love?"

Kelvin stumbled past her, flailing arms, red cheeks wet. His school bag hit the floor. He started to climb the staircase on all fours, then collapsed with his face buried in crossed arms.

"What's happened?" Iris went and placed the flat of her hand on his back, rubbing it in circles, feeling his tiny chest rising and falling in awful shudders—it almost made her well into tears herself. "Love? Tell me. Please. Tell your mam. She'll make it better."

He turned on her, viciously. "*How*? How will you make it *better*? You *can't*!"

"Well tell me what it is, love, please. I can't do anything if I don't know, can I? Come downstairs and I'll get you a nice glass of–"

"I don't want a glass of *anything!*" His voice cracked, throat already raw and swollen. "I just want…" The sentence disintegrated into sobs, and Iris could do nothing but tear off her apron, lie there on the stairs on top of him and wrap her arms around him, tight, whether he wished her to or not, whether he struggled or not, and let him wail until he could speak. His little body shook in the embrace of her. She felt the warmth of him, the salt-streaming helplessness of him and tried to absorb him and rid him of it, but she could not. And the cruelty was he didn't even want her, and pushed her off him, and clung to the banister rods instead, too much the man, not letting his mother see him cry, poor baby. Not wanting her. But *she* wanted. She wanted so much.

"They… they said it's *tomorrow…*"

"What's tomorrow, love?"

"Bonfire Night! November the fifth!" He was incensed at her

ignorance. "The boys in school said I'll have to burn him. I won't have to burn him, will I?"

"What boys?"

"Gareth. Everybody!"

"You don't want to listen to Gareth Powell…"

"It's *true* though, isn't it? The teacher said. We had a whole lesson about it. That's when they started laughing at me!"

"Oh, sweetheart…" She ruffled his hair and kissed him through his pullover. "It's November the fifth. It's okay. It's what everybody does. It's a celebration…"

"Why?"

"Guy Fawkes was a man who stored up barrels of gunpowder in the cellars under Parliament and was waiting there to light the fuse, but he got caught."

"But why do we have to *burn* him?"

"I don't know. I suppose we have bonfires and fireworks to give thanks he didn't succeed. Our politicians weren't blown sky high—so we burn our own poor old Guy Fawkes instead."

"Yes, but we don't *have* to, do we? Why does he have to *die*? It's not fair!"

"It doesn't matter. It's only a silly old bunch of clothes, love. He's not a human being. He's not alive."

Kelvin turned and began screaming into her face. "*You*'re not alive! *He* is! I *know* he is—but you're not! You don't care about him! You don't *love* him! But *I* do!"

With that he ran up to his bedroom, where she found him, face down in the pillow, next to the guy, which was lying on its back staring up at the ceiling, still bouncing very slightly from the weight that had just landed on the bed. To Iris it looked almost as if its head was moving from side to side. She sat on the bed next to her son and touched his body again. Couldn't bear not doing.

"Kelvin. Kelvin, love…"

He turned his head the other way, facing the guy and not her.

"We don't have to go to a bonfire," she said. "We don't have to go to a big firework display. Your dad can just light a few—"

"Stop it! Don't *talk* about it!"

"What? Firework night?"

"Shut up! Don't say those words! You're upsetting him!" Kelvin threw one arm across the guy's chest, tugging it closer to him and lowering his voice to a hush. "It's all right. Don't worry. I'm here. I know you're scared but nobody's going to hurt you. I won't let them."

"Kelvin, it's November the fifth and..."

"*Don't*! Don't mention it again!" He glared at her. "How would you like it? To be stuck on a pile of sticks and set *fire* to? It's horrible!" His head spun to the guy. "Nobody's going to burn you, I promise."

"Kelv, you have to burn him, lovely..."

"*Why*? Why should I? I don't want to. I'm not going to! There's no law against it. He's mine! I'm going to keep him, just like he is. You can't make me!"

A voice said, "Nobody's going to make you do anything, son."

Iris turned and saw her husband standing at the bedroom door.

❊

She struck a match and lit up, grateful to have the house to herself again. *Almost* to herself. Herself except for... *it*.

Des had told Kelvin to get his football togs on, sharpish; they were going to be late for the match if he didn't get his skates on. His voice had been uncharacteristically mellow, soft—not even rising to accuse his son of having forgotten the extra-curricular game. Iris' first instinct had been to think something was wrong. She expected Kelvin to resist, say he didn't want to go, but he didn't. He sat up, rubbing his eyes with the heels of his hands, probably not wanting his father to see the state he was in. *Come on. Shake a leg, buttie. You don't want to let the rest of the team down. They're waiting for you.* Kelvin had stripped to his underpants. She'd left the room, feeling redundant as Des helped him lace up his heavy, studded boots. *Atta boy...* Then she'd called out, wishing him good luck, then heard *'Bye, mam!* Though it was not

Kelvin who'd called back but her husband. A second later Kelvin's face appeared round the sitting room door, but he had no need to voice his anxiety. She'd already anticipated it:

"I'll look after him. You go and enjoy yourself."

She'd have liked a kiss on the cheek but that hadn't been forthcoming. She was a bad person now, in his eyes. She couldn't help that. Just hoped he'd return in a better mood, and that they could have a *cwtch* watching telly like they used to. Wished that more than anything.

Now, smoking as she bent to poke a lacklustre fire into life, then pulling a guard in front of it, she wondered how much of the conversation upstairs Des had heard. She'd known what he was doing—he was clever, with his degree and everything, after all— distracting the boy with something physical to get his mind away from the damned guy for five minutes. That much was obvious. But what did he think of *her*? Did he think she was being panicky? Shrill? A bit mad? Had she said the right things? Hell, why was she frightened of what he thought? *She* wasn't the problem after all, was she? And when her husband had opened and closed the front door he must've let the night air in, because she got that smell of sulphur again, rank and noxious in her throat.

From her chair Iris looked at the ceiling above her, picturing beyond the swirls of Artex her son's bedroom and its twisted, cuckoo occupant.

I'll look after him.

She wouldn't. She wouldn't go up there. Bugger that. She didn't want to, and didn't have to. She'd sit here and read her magazine by the fire and watch *Nationwide* and whatever else was on until they got home, and then it would be over with. They'd be a family again and she'd make supper on trays, or maybe Dad would get fish and chips from up the Graig, and that would be that.

Which was fine until she needed to go for a wee, and for once she wished she could go outside to the back toilet, but Des had converted it into an extension of the kitchen for the washing machine and tumble drier.

She literally crossed her legs. Then she thought: *This is damn silly.*

I'm not afraid of it. What the bloody hell is it I've got to be afraid of? It's not even made of anything. It's nothing.

With determination she shot out of her armchair and went upstairs, switching the landing light on and for some reason making her footfalls heavy, as if somebody might be listening, and wanting them to be aware she was coming.

She stiffly walked past her son's bedroom door to the bathroom at the end of the landing, once inside locking the door after her, even though she was the only one in the house. Sheer habit, she told herself, that was all.

She sat on the toilet seat but nothing came. Her bladder was empty. She felt desperately weary again, drained from seeing Kelvin so upset earlier, she supposed. As his mother she couldn't stop herself being affected by what affected him. It was part of what being a mother was. A kind of symbiosis you were never free of. If they suffered, you suffered. There was no getting away from it.

She stood up and pulled the chain even though she hadn't gone, staring at the swirling water and remembering the terrible day she'd seen blood staining the white of the pan.

She heard footsteps on the stairs. Light. Far too light for a grown man. More like a pet, but they had no pets. And not walking so much as scuttling.

"Kelvin?"

She zipped up her slacks and opened the bathroom door.

The landing was empty. Kelvin's bedroom door shut. Of course it was.

She was being stupid. It was probably the kids next door. The terrible twins. They were always running up and down stairs, causing a riot. That was it. Yes. Definitely. What else?

She went back, washed her hands at the sink with the brick of Imperial Leather, dried them with the towel, then tugged the ring-pull to switch off the bathroom light.

Downstairs she walked into the sitting room and saw the guy slumped on the settee in the glow of the TV set, for all the world as if watching it, stunted legs sticking out with socks dangling at the end of them, fat arms hanging limp at its sides, gloves bunched up, non-fingers at inconceivable angles.

Iris's hand clamped over her mouth.

Her first thought was that she had mis-remembered earlier, that was it, that must be it, and that Kelvin must've brought down the guy before he'd left for the match with his father—but she'd been sitting in the room only minutes earlier *and it wasn't there*! Surely that was true—wasn't it?

She laughed. She didn't decide to, she just did. It just began to happen. And she didn't even know what she was laughing at, but she couldn't stop.

Minutes later she ran out of breath, and went to the front room and raided the drinks on the hostess trolley and poured herself a gin and tonic, and when she'd drank it, poured a second one.

The guy was still there when she returned. It hadn't moved. That was one thing, at least—*it hadn't moved*. She wondered if she sat there long enough it would, while she was looking straight at it. But no, of course not—it was too clever for that. Cleverer than her, anyway. She knew where it got that from, its brains…

She switched the TV off, because she hadn't switched it on. She was positive she hadn't. And she sat cross-legged on the floor with her back to the screen, because that's where the guy's face was pointing.

"You're treating this like your house," she said to it bluntly, pleased that she was managing to disguise her emotions. "Well it isn't. It never was and it never will be." She sipped her drink and tried to discern what, in its cheap plastic smile, it was thinking. Or was it just mocking her? Mocking all of them? "What do you want with us?" Her eyes narrowed. "What do you want with *him*?"

Even as she said it, she knew the guy, in his cunning, would not reply.

✸

When the wanderers returned she was in her bedroom, curled up but not asleep, as far away from the guy as possible. Coming down when she heard the door slam, she asked how the team had done, whether he'd scored, but nobody told her. She crossed Kelvin on the stairs, his white shorts muddied and his knees scuffed. Down in the sitting room she found Des lifting the guy by one shoulder. "I better take this upstairs. Or he'll go nuts." Iris tightened the belt of her dressing gown as he—*they*—passed.

By the time Kelvin had had his bath, *Tom and Jerry* had finished and *Star Trek* was on, but the boy didn't come down to watch it, though he never missed an episode. He loved it. But tonight he wanted to be with the guy, Des reported. Because the thing had *missed him*, Des said.

"Didn't you tell him he had to?"

"You're forgetting who the boss is in this house."

"Who?"

"Well it's not bloody me."

At nine o'clock, just as *Special Branch* starring that actor with the thick lips started, Des took up a hot water bottle and put Kelvin to bed because Iris said she was still in the doghouse for some unknown reason. When he returned back down he was carrying the guy like a sack from its scrawny neck.

"I know. I know. You go and talk to him if you want to. He said it wants to sit with us and get to know us, apparently, so we'll 'grow to love' it."

"I don't *want* to love it," Iris said through gritted teeth. She didn't even want to look at it, either.

"That's his… logic, I don't know. I didn't know what to bloody say."

"You could've said 'Go to sleep.' And don't put it on my nice clean… Christ, put it over *there*." She pointed to one of the dining chairs over by the closed curtains, between the phone table and the TV set. Blowing air unhappily, he dumped it there, where it hung, boneless, baby mask snug in the receptacle of its hood.

Sniffing at his sleeves with repugnance, Des sank into the armchair at an angle to his wife's, also facing *Special Branch*. "I can smell it on my clothes…" Soon it was clear to both of them that neither were paying a great deal of attention to what the programme was about, though their eyes were fixed on it.

"Today… I was in the bathroom…" Iris shuddered, faltering. "Des?"

"What? I'm listening."

She shook her head, deciding she didn't want to go into details. "I… I just don't like having it in the house. I hate it."

Des grunted. "And I don't?"

"But to him it's like… I don't know…"

"Probably full of maggots from that pushchair, for a start… Goodness knows what diseases… Spreading its germs…" He plucked the *Express* from the foot stool and opened it wide, arms stretched.

"Some sort of a… friend… a…" Again, she floundered.

"Stinking out the house…"

"Des, I can't bear it…"

"You don't have to bear it," he said, eyes scanning the sports results. "Not for much longer. Roll on tomorrow and we'll be shot of the thing."

"Don't say that." Iris was aghast. "Don't even *think* that, for God's sake! We can't. He *loves* it. We can't be that cruel."

"We have to. For his own good. We have no choice."

"You said nobody was going to make him do anything. You said that to him a couple of hours ago."

"I know. I lied."

"He won't let you. You know that. He won't let him go."

"He'll have to," Des said. "He's got to grow up."

"Why?"

"Because we all have to."

Iris started to cry, and perhaps she wanted him to come over and put his arms round her and hold her tight, or perhaps she wanted him to fall to his knees and cup her hands in his, or wipe her tears away with his thumbs in a gentle and caring gesture. But what happened was, he sighed and folded up his newspaper, dropped it into his lap and turned to her with tight lips, dry eyes and an expression of intense irritation.

"What can I do? What do you want me to do? Tell me." When she didn't, he said, "Breathe. You know what the doctor said. Breathe." And she wished and prayed that his eyes weren't so dry and his lips weren't so tight and he would just tell her everything would be all right, but she knew he couldn't. He got up and turned down the volume on the telly, but that only made the chemistry of fireworks louder. "Tell me what you're thinking."

"You know…" she began. "You know how, when he was younger, Kelvin would have a nosebleed every so often, and it was weird – he didn't know it, but we did. It would always be at my time of the month. Like clockwork. I'd start to bleed, and the next thing, he'd be saying…"

"Iris…"

"No, like he was in tune with me. Like he was part of me, still. And if he's part of me, does he know what…"

"Stop."

"It was my body. I mean, did he feel…"

"*Stop it!*"

Now Des was on his knees in front of her, but not kissing her and not holding her, but gripping her wrists. She feared he would shake her. Strike her, even. But his grip became feeble, impotence turning to sudden alarm in his eyes.

"Why the hell are we *whispering*?" But they both knew the reason.

The reason was behind him, slumped half-on, half-off the dining chair like the imitation of a husk of a corpse at a wake, long arm dangling, chin sunk into the crater of its chest.

Remember, remember… Dread wasn't a word she thought about very often but dread was the only word that would do. As soon as she woke she couldn't wait for the day to be over. *The fifth of November…* The old feelings flooded back. She couldn't stop them. She didn't dress, and asked Des to make the boy his breakfast, please. *Gunpowder, treason and plot…* Alone in the double bed, she turned over into the pillow but was unable to drift back to sleep. She had a splitting headache pounding against her skull, a real humdinger. Not even a shower and two aspirins from the medicine cabinet did anything to shift it. *I see no reason why gunpowder treason…*

Hearing Des leave in the car, she shambled downstairs in her dressing gown and slippers to make a cup of tea. Maybe that would do the trick. Kelvin sat on the settee looking pale. She looked at her watch. She'd expected him to be halfway to school by now. He gave a few unconvincing little coughs into his fist.

"I don't feel well."

"You're going to school. I don't care what day it is." She tugged open the curtains, tied them back with the cords. The sky was like dirty dishwater.

"I've got a temperature."

"You think I don't know what you're playing at, young man? That's enough of that malarkey." She held out his school bag to him.

"I have to stay here with him. I have to protect him."

"Please, love. Not now. You're being silly." She rubbed her forehead. It was as sore and agonising as if she'd prodded a wound.

"I'm *not* being silly! People want to hurt him. People want to *burn* him!"

"Nobody's going to do anything. Nobody's going to get in here, are they? *I'm* here."

"But I don't want to leave him all alone—because he's scared, really scared!" Now her son's voice was going through her and she couldn't stand it. She certainly wasn't up to a full-volume row with a forceful and stubborn eight-year-old.

She crouched down, took his hand in hers and kissed it. "Sweetheart, I know he's been a really good friend, but…"

"But he's *not* a friend. He's not *just* a friend. You *know* that!"

Her heart flipped. Her throat tightened. What did he mean? *You know that?*

"All right." She let go of his soft flesh and stood up quickly. "Just this once, all right? You haven't got me round your little finger. Don't think that for one minute. I'll phone the school and say you're feeling poorly." No sooner were the words out than he got up and threw his arms round her hips, pressing his cheek to her tummy. She held in her breath, arms aloft, until he let go.

Moments later she could hear his voice as he reached his bedroom: "She said you can stay! She said you can stay forever and ever!" She saw herself shudder in the mirror over the mantelpiece.

Blap-ap-ap!

Rockets were going up early. She couldn't tell where, probably over Maes-y-Coed. She was protected by the windows from the occasional and unpredictable bursts—going off like some small-scale civil war— as she rang the secretary in the primary school office, saying her son had a cold and wouldn't be in today. When the secretary sounded sympathetic and said she hoped Kelvin felt better soon, Iris felt guilty and hung up abruptly, then regretted it. Goodness knows what impression it gave, but she felt under a lot of strain and she didn't want long conversations with people. Not today, of all days. Even that simple task had been an enormous strain—okay, it shouldn't have been, but it was.

Not long afterwards, Des rang, which he never did. Between lessons.

"How did he get off?"

Iris thought of lying, but didn't have the strength. "He wouldn't go." Des didn't sound as if this was totally unexpected, but it's hard to tell on the telephone exactly what somebody is thinking. Perhaps he was thinking it was her fault—being soft again. "It's only one day," she said. "What does it matter?"

"I'll see you at five-ish," he said. "I'll come straight home."

"You don't need to."

"I do."

Mid-morning she wanted to get a tin of Heinz cream of tomato soup for Kelvin's dinner. But the truth was she wanted to get out of the house. She was rattling in it and it was jangling her nerves. As she walked downhill to the shop in the burnt, already pungent, nitrogenous air, she wondered how the bonfire up the quarry was doing, whether it had enlarged, swelled, whether it was gathering bulk even now for the festivities that would kick off come nightfall when grown-ups and their offspring alike gathered to celebrate. Celebrate what? Celebrate death. She wished the air was clean and fresh and reviving but it wasn't.

"Penny for the guy?"

Two munchkin sentinels stood outside the Spar. One wore a mask of Frankenstein's monster in lurid green and the other, a girl in pigtails, the more traditional Guy Fawkes. Their construction, which sported a 'Dai' cap and cricket pullover, wasn't nearly as impressive as her son's—its face merely a child's crayon drawing wrapped onto a cardboard box with Sellotape.

Iris ignored their biscuit tin of coins as she went inside, and ignored them again as she came out.

"Penny for the guy? Penny for the guy, please, missus?"

The words screamed round the inside of her head with the repetitiveness of a stunt motorcyclist on the Wall of Death. Halfway up the hill she saw a four-year-old child in a pink duffel coat and woolly hat sitting on a wall. The little girl made shapes in the air with a lit sparkler, mesmerised by its intensity. The man and woman in charge of it smiled and Iris smiled back, but didn't pause. Kept her head down. She didn't know them, and didn't want to.

Before she reached her door and took out her key from her purse, she was rubbing drips of water from her cheeks brought on by the cold air, the blighted air, thinking:

He would have been four years old by now.

Four years old, to the day.

*

She couldn't hear anything from upstairs and she didn't want to go upstairs so she called Kelvin down, and he took his soup up on a tray with some sliced bread. The Grand Canyon of the afternoon widened ahead of her, as did the silence. She switched on the wireless. It was playing *Love Grows* by Edison Lighthouse. She made a cup of coffee and thought of the children with snotty faces and shoddy clothes—who should've been in school, not out playing truant—and the lumpen figures with twisted limbs at their feet.

Penny for the guy? Penny for the guy?

The coffee made her more jittery still. One hand on the newel post, she called upstairs.

"How is he?"

"Fine. I'm trying to keep his mind off it."

"Can I get you anything?"

"No, thanks. Oh, wait a minute. I'll ask him." Pause. "He says no, thanks very much."

Iris closed the door of the sitting room after her. She looked at the clock above the fireplace and wondered how she could fill the next couple of hours. She tried to read, but a flashing fizz in the sky would make her head jerk upright, or the sound of little padding footsteps across the bedroom floor above.

Penny for...

Penny for them...

Her mouth felt parchment-dry and she fetched herself a glass of water from the kitchen tap. She hated water. Never liked the taste of it – people always laughed when she said that – but she drank it nonetheless.

I see no reason...

No reason...

Des arrived ten minutes later than he'd predicted, holding up a large box of fireworks, the bright colours carnivalesque in the dull room. Horrified, Iris jumped up, snatched it off him and hid it in the sideboard, out of sight, slamming the drawer as if it were some illicit and disgusting contraband.

"I thought…"

"Really? You could've fooled me." She rubbed the goosebumps on her bare arms. "Don't you realise anything?"

"I thought he could watch from his bedroom window…"

Iris shook her head, eyes squeezed into squints of irritation. She bent forward and hooked her fingers into her hair.

Des looked down at the packet of sparklers in his hand, discarding it onto the table with a sigh. Then sat with his knees apart and his elbows on them, wiping the anguish from his face.

To her, the air in the room felt acrid, bitter, sour—perhaps she'd brought it in with her, but those were its ingredients. The stuff that contributed to the burning she felt inside. The chemistry that was her.

"My dad used to hammer a nail to the door of the shed for a Catherine Wheel, every year without fail." Her husband spoke, but she didn't even know if the words were for her. "I can see him lighting it, taking charge, standing back, all of us willing the little glow of light to burst into life. But it always just fizzled into nothing, spun round once or twice and went out. We all expected something so great and it never bloody worked."

She stared at the blank television screen. She could say nothing. Her throat felt scorched.

"I talked to the Head today. I told her the problem." *You didn't talk to me*, Iris thought, listening. *You didn't talk to me.* "She was very understanding, as a matter of fact. She wasn't the cow I thought she'd be, looking down her nose at me. She said we could get in a child psychologist." Iris didn't hear *child*, she just heard *psychologist*. She heard *get a psychologist*, just like she heard it four years ago, when the problem was her. "They know what they're doing, she said. She was very sympathetic, actually. I was pleasantly surprised."

"Bully for you," Iris said, without looking at him.

The silence hurt. He went into the middle room to smoke one of his Hamlet cigars and listen to the news. When he came back twenty minutes later he said:

"I'll call him for his tea."

"Leave him," she said. "He'll shout if he wants anything. If you want something, make it. There's ham and there's sliced bread." She didn't move as he walked past her, other than lift the cigarette to her lips.

Shall never be forgot...

Be forgot...

Des returned to the middle room while she watched *Top of the Pops*, the sexually provocative but, to her, faintly ridiculous Pan's People gyrating to the hardly ribald White Plains song *My Baby Loves Lovin'*. A sparkly green glow saturated the room and, peering between the curtains, she could make out the fronds of a Silver Fountain in the yard next door. Something red corkscrewed across the black sky, blooming into machine-gun arcs of lavender and puce. With another boom, copper blue and orange rain mushroomed and fell.

The blasting gust of a Roman Candle accompanied her pouring Kelvin's hot water bottle. The music had turned to Jethro Tull's *Living in the Past* as she went upstairs.

The guy was in his arms. Her son was fast asleep. Iris tugged it slightly but he woke immediately, whining and hugging it back to him.

"I'm only putting it to one side, love. He'll be here when you wake up. You don't want it in bed with you, do you?"

"Yes. I do. I *have* to."

His head sank back into the pillow. His lids were heavy. He had trouble keeping his eyes open, poor mite.

"Don't worry. It'll all be over tomorrow."

"Did you hear that?" he said to the baby mask, the football-head secreted in the sheath of its green anorak hood. "Tomorrow you'll be safe. She wouldn't lie to you." He struggled to keep his eyes open, drifting between sleep and wakefulness. Grasped one empty glove with urgency. "She knows you're special. She made you, silly. She doesn't want you to die. She wants you to live."

That feeling, that old feeling, that stab of acid in the churning ice bucket of her stomach, came again and she thought she might faint. Her hand pressed against it.

"Go to sleep, love."

"Don't let anything happen to him, mam, will you?"

"I know."

"Promise?"

"I promise." Iris switched off the bedside light, put last year's *Doctor Who* annual with Patrick Troughton and Jamie and a Cyberman on the cover back on the shelf. She leant over and kissed him, as she always did. His cheek was blisteringly warm, almost pulsating.

"You have to kiss him goodnight too."

She wanted to say no, but she knew he would insist. Her stomach loosened. She felt hollow. She felt outside herself, looking in. Not part of herself at all. She bent down, already feeling the tension in her back rebelling against it, and pressed her mouth to the inert plastic.

✻

Before entering the sitting room she wiped her mouth as if she had tasted something abhorrent. She'd pinched her lips together with her fingers as soon as she'd shut the bedroom door, but still her stomach jerked, wanting to void itself of something revolting, some intrusion, some infestation. She took several deep breaths, telling herself to pull herself together. That was all behind her now, the pain, the worthlessness, the drifting, disembodied *other*-ness that had possessed her for too long. She remembered being organised, being meticulous. Knowing something was wrong and going to her GP with a well-thought-out list:

Can't sleep (but always feeling tired)

No appetite

Aches and pains

Feeling of heaviness

Headaches

Anger

Don't want to go out / see people

Can't be bothered to do things I used to enjoy

Sex (difficulties)
Grief

The doctor looked down the list and showed her what was written at the bottom—the word *Grief*. He said, there's your answer right there. That was the cause of all the other things. And she mustn't put a time limit on it. Everybody's different. Not everyone has the same reaction or behaves the same, or gets over things the same way. There was no way of predicting it, but the one thing she shouldn't do is punish herself about it. Time is a great healer, he said. But sometimes it isn't. It just isn't.

✳

She sat with Des watching *Play for Today*. It was called *Angels Are So Few* and it was by somebody called Dennis Potter, who Des knew of but she didn't (she didn't pay attention to things like that), but it had that actor in it she liked, Tom Bell, from that film *The L-Shaped Room* – one of those ones who had a surly sort of charisma and was strong and handsome but didn't feel the need to smile a lot to make you like him. Hypnotised slightly by his face swimming in and out of shot, she realised she hadn't been following the story at all. It could have been *Sooty and Sweep* for all she was concerned.

"Do it," she said halfway through.

Des looked at her.

"Do it," she repeated. Elaboration was unnecessary.

He went into the hall and took his mac from the hook. Pulled his leather gloves from the pockets.

Iris listened not to Tom Bell in his television play, but the sound from the landing as Des crept into her son's bedroom, easing open the door.

She was alternately holding her breath and sucking at her cigarette, a combination that quickly made her feel light-headed. The picture on the TV screen became blurred and wishy-washy, the words gobbledegook.

Seconds later she heard his footfall on the stairs again.

She got up and stood by the door into the hall, one hand on the jamb, cigarette smoke rising, holding back behind an imaginary line as if present at an accident where her inexperience in what was needed might be a hindrance.

Des descended the stairs—the guy's fat, misshapen sleeves and green hood dangling down his back. The thing was slung over his right shoulder in a fireman's lift. His right hand held it in place where Iris had stitched the polo-neck to his old, paint-stained decorating trousers. His left hand reached to open the front door—and she knew her task was to close the Chubb quietly after him so the sound wouldn't rouse the boy. The sound from the TV set was garbled: its shimmer a nebulous flicker back-lighting her.

He left carrying his unnatural cargo without turning. As she closed the front door she saw them dissolve into the night as he walked to the garden gate and the path to Llwynmadoc Street...

And *after* she closed the door, now standing with her back pressed to it—did she see a slight *wiggling* of those arms, or was it caused by the natural sway of her husband's motion? Did she see what was—no, silly, ridiculous—empty white Christmas gloves *beating* on his back in tiny fists? Little malformed hands *clawing* at the material of his mac? A manic dwarf *struggling* in the flashing-then-dead strobe light of an exploding rocket?

How many fires were burning? How many children cheering in wonder, wrapped against the cold of night? She buried what she saw—*imagined* she saw?—in other thoughts, any thoughts. Turned up the TV, but the cacophony outdoors only seemed to cut through even more violently.

Remember, remember...

But she *did* remember. There was no need to demand it. She remembered that November four years ago when they had another child. One that died. She remember the fuzzy, crackling Tom Bell voice of the consultant, telling her of the abnormality they'd detected. She remembered him telling them that it wouldn't live after it was born. That they'd have to induce labour. She remembered asking him not to use that word. Please. Please don't...

Never be forgot...
Never. Never. Never.

❊

Des returned as the Big Ben chimes of *News at Ten* tolled their sonorous knell. Alastair Burnet and Reginald Bosanquet talked as he lowered himself into his armchair, brown leather-gloved hands resting on the white arm covers. He sat staring at the screen with blank eyes.

"Did you see it burn?"

"Yes."

"*Did* you?"

"*Yes.* Iris. I watched it *burn.* What more do you want me to say?" He made it sound as though he'd been made to do something unwillingly, and despicable. Then he softened, realising that had upset her and it wasn't fair. "There were others," he told her, "other guys already on fire. I threw our one in. High as I could, into the middle where the flames were biggest. A shout went up. I don't know who was doing the shouting. It buckled, went up. The mask started melting. Football head caved in. Gloves evaporated into ash. Something gave way behind and it fell into the centre, alight all over. Then some bangers went off. Kids were running round waving sparklers like they were Zorro. Mostyn Edwards and his boys were there. They said hello. They asked where Kelvin was. They asked where you were. I walked away. I didn't say hello back." He rubbed his eyes. They must have been stinging from the smoke. They were red-rimmed. "Yes, I watched it burn."

Iris stood up and switched the television off. In the silence she took his gloved hands in hers and kissed them. But in the silence also they could now discern Kelvin's gentle sobbing from upstairs.

Des moved to get up. "Oh, no..." If he'd woken, then he knew.

"I'll go," said Iris. She didn't relish the prospect, but somehow felt it was a responsibility that fell on her own shoulders. She would know how to break it to him. She would find the words. And she would be there for him to hold, to hug, or to hate, as she would always be.

She was halfway up the stairs when the doorbell unexpectedly rang. (*Ding-dong—Avon calling!*) She turned round but could see only darkness beyond the glass panels.

Des was already on his way. "I'll get it." He flipped the light switch for her, illuminating the stair carpet. "It's probably Elwyn."

"Offer him a cup of tea."

As she reached the landing, the door opened below and let the night in. She felt the cold on her back and the rancid tang of sulphur ushered in the memories as if it were yesterday, but of course it wasn't yesterday—it was today, November the fifth, when the nurses told them her and Des should hold their dead baby. That they'd regret it if they didn't see how *beautiful* he was. And he *was* beautiful. So *very* beautiful in her arms—and in his father's. Such a pretty face, a gorgeous, perfect face—but no head... no *head* at all...

She heard voices downstairs but not what they said. If it was Elwyn it was bound to be about rugby, so she wasn't that interested.

As she entered Kelvin's bedroom the opening door cast a wedge of light. Her son's crying clawed at her deep inside, as it always did. That's why she had to be the one to make it better.

The landing light was on, but she didn't want to startle him by switching on the bedroom light too. Consequently, while the side of the room behind her was lit, the bed itself was slathered in gloom. She could just about make out the staring eyes of Jon Pertwee in a magician-like pose as the new *Doctor Who* on an old *Radio Times* cover Sellotaped above the bedhead.

Her foot touched something not the texture of the carpet.

She looked down.

The latest issue of *TV21* was pinned down under her slipper.

She picked it up and placed it aside, next to the Airfix Lancaster bomber he and his dad had made together in meticulous wonder.

To her relief she could see that the guy was gone. Its absence finally confirmed, only the slightest indentation remaining in the blanket where it had lain. Kelvin lay flat on his back under the sheets, head sunk in the pillow, wearing the baby mask with the orange curl on the forehead.

She gasped. Then laughed.

"Oh, Kelvin, you monkey! That's a horrible trick to play on your mam, that is. You gave me a heart attack!"

But wait a minute—wasn't the *guy* wearing the mask? Didn't she see it when it was hanging over her husband's shoulder? No, because it was hanging face down. That was it. The mask must've fallen off as Des...

No sooner had she dismissed that worry than something perturbed her far more. Why wasn't her son answering, now that his prank had had the desired effect? Why was he still *sobbing*? In fact, why was he sobbing *at all*?

She moved towards the bed.

No, ta—we won't sit down, sir, all the same... The voices downstairs, though real, sounded as disembodied as those on the TV. *It's about your son, sir...* The man had more of a Welsh accent than her husband's, and was older. She pictured him with grey, bristly hair. *I'm afraid there's been a tragic accident...* She thought he must be talking about something else, not her, not her family, not them. *Doctor there with his family—too late to do anything... Children climb inside bonfires, see—do it for dares or whatnot... Must have got trapped... Fire was roaring, no-one could stop it... Members of the public started screaming, saw his face, his arms waving—trouble was, the more he waved, the more he fanned the flames.* Her pulse was leaping, belting through her body, thudding in her chest. *Mr Edwards—I believe you know Mr Edwards?—tried to call you back, but you were walking away... He said you probably couldn't hear because of all the fireworks going off...*

"Kelvin?"

Iris reached the bed. The smell filled her nostrils – earth, ash, rot, blood, sulphur, decay...

"Kelvin?"

She stood staring down at the child with the mask on, no longer able to tell whether the sobbing was coming from behind it or from the grown man downstairs. The lost, last sky rocked with rockets, thunderous in her head, spiked and buckled by the wounds of gunpowder.

She reached down to take away the mask, because what was a mask if not a face with no head? And she did so not only with dread but with incalculable longing. The two things fought in her violently in that moment as her fingertips touched plastic. And when she saw what was behind, something made of bone and fire closed around her heart, crushing it as if it were no more than a ball of paper.

CONTRIBUTORS

The *Oxford Companion to English Literature* describes **RAMSEY CAMPBELL** as "Britain's most respected living horror writer". He has been given more awards than any other writer in the field, including the Grand Master Award of the World Horror Convention, the Lifetime Achievement Award of the Horror Writers Association and the Living Legend Award of the International Horror Guild. Among his novels are *The Face That Must Die*, *Incarnate*, *Midnight Sun*, *The Count of Eleven*, *Silent Children*, *The Darkest Part of the Woods*, *The Overnight*, *Secret Story*, *The Grin of the Dark*, *Thieving Fear*, *Creatures of the Pool*, *The Seven Days of Cain*, *Ghosts Know* and *The Kind Folk*. Forthcoming are *Think Yourself Lucky* and *Thirteen Days at Sunset Beach*, and he is working on a trilogy, *The Three Births of Daoloth*. *Needing Ghosts*, *The Last Revelation of Gla'aki* and *The Pretence* are novellas. His collections include *Waking Nightmares*, *Alone with the Horrors*, *Ghosts and Grisly Things*, *Told by the Dead*, *Just Behind You* and *Holes for Faces*, and his non-fiction is collected as *Ramsey Campbell, Probably*. His novels *The Nameless* and *Pact of the Fathers* have been filmed in Spain. His regular columns appear in *Dead Reckonings* and *Video Watchdog*. He is the President of the Society of Fantastic Films. Ramsey Campbell lives on Merseyside with his wife Jenny. His pleasures include classical music, good food and wine, and whatever's in that pipe. His web site is at www.ramseycampbell.com

ALISON LITTLEWOOD is the author of *A Cold Season*, published by Jo Fletcher Books, an imprint of Quercus. The novel was selected for the Richard and Judy Book Club, where it was described as "perfect reading for a dark winter's night." Her second novel, *Path of Needles*, is a dark blend of fairy tales and crime fiction, and her third, *The Unquiet House*, is a ghost story set in the Yorkshire countryside. Alison's short stories have been picked for

The Best Horror of the Year and *The Mammoth Book of Best New Horror* anthologies, as well as *The Best British Fantasy 2013* and *The Mammoth Book of Best British Crime 10*. Other publication credits include the anthologies *Terror Tales of the Cotswolds*, *Where Are We Going?* and *Never Again*. Alison lives in Yorkshire with her partner Fergus. Visit her at www.alisonlittlewood.co.uk

HELEN MARSHALL is an award-winning Canadian author, editor, and doctor of medieval studies. Her debut collection of short stories, *Hair Side, Flesh Side* (ChiZine Publications 2012), was named one of the top ten books of 2012 by *January Magazine*. It won the 2013 British Fantasy Award for Best Newcomer and was shortlisted for a 2013 Aurora Award by the Canadian Society of Science Fiction and Fantasy. Her second collection, *Gifts for the One Who Comes After*, will be released in the autumn of 2014. She lives in Oxford, England where she spends most of her time staring at old books.

TOM FLETCHER was born in 1984. He is the author of numerous short stories and three novels—*The Leaping* (Quercus 2010), *The Thing on the Shore* (Quercus 2011), and *The Ravenglass Eye* (Jo Fletcher Books 2012). His first fantasy novel, *Gleam*, will be published by Jo Fletcher Books in September 2014. *The Times* said of him: "Fletcher... convinces me that there may be some truth at last in those rumours about a renaissance in British supernatural fiction." His website is www.endistic.wordpress.com, and he can be found on Twitter as @t_a_fletcher. He lives in Cumbria.

STEVE RASNIC TEM's latest novel *Blood Kin* (Solaris March 2014), alternating between the 1930s and the present day, is a Southern Gothic/ Horror blend of snake handling, ghosts, granny women, kudzu, and Melungeons. His previous novels are *Deadfall Hotel* (Solaris 2012), *The Man On The Ceiling* (Wizards of the Coast Discoveries 2008—written with Melanie Tem, an expansion of their novella), *The Book of Days* (Subterranean,2002), *Daughters* (Grand

Central 2001—also written with Melanie Tem), and *Excavation* (Avon 1987). Steve has also published over 400 short stories. His latest collection is this year's *Here With The Shadows*, a collection of traditionally inspired ghostly fiction from Ireland's Swan River Press. Other recent collections include *Ugly Behavior* (New Pulp 2012-noir fiction), *Onion Songs* (Chomu 2013), *Celestial Inventories* (ChiZine 2013), and *Twember* (NewCon 2013-science fiction.) In 2015 PS Publishing will bring out his novella *In the Lovecraft Museum*. You can visit the Tem home on the web at www.m-s-tem.com

GARY McMAHON is the acclaimed author of nine novels and several short story collections. His latest releases are a collection titled *Where You Live* and the novels *Beyond Here Lies Nothing, The Bones Of You* and *The End*. His short fiction has been reprinted in various *Year's Best* volumes. Gary lives with his family in Yorkshire, where he trains in Shotokan karate and likes running in the rain. His website can be found at: www.garymcmahon.com

REGGIE OLIVER has been a professional playwright, actor, and theatre director since 1975. Besides plays, his publications include the authorised biography of Stella Gibbons, *Out of the Woodshed*, published by Bloomsbury in 1998, and six collections of stories of supernatural terror, of which the fifth, *Mrs Midnight* (Tartarus 2011) won the *Children of the Night Award* for 'Best Work of Supernatural Fiction in 2011' and was nominated for two other awards. Tartarus has also reissued his first and second collections *The Dreams of Cardinal Vittorini* and *The Complete Symphonies of Adolf Hitler* in new editions with new illustrations by the author, as well as his latest collection *Flowers of the Sea*. A seventh collection *Holidays From Hell* is due out from Tartarus in 2015, as is a children's book *The Hauntings at Tankerton Park* with his own illustrations. His novel *The Dracula Papers I—The Scholar's Tale* (Chomu 2011) is the first of a projected four. Another novel *Virtue in Danger* was published in 2013 by Zagava Books. An omnibus edition of his stories entitled *Dramas from the Depths* is published by Centipede as part of its *Masters of the Weird Tale* series. His stories have appeared in over fifty anthologies.

ALISON MOORE's short fiction has been published in *Best British Short Stories* anthologies and broadcast on BBC Radio 4 Extra. The title story of her debut collection, *The Pre-War House and Other Stories*, won a *New Writer* novella prize. Her first novel, *The Lighthouse*, was shortlisted for the Man Booker Prize 2012 and the National Book Awards 2012 (New Writer of the Year), winning the McKitterick Prize 2013. Her second novel, *He Wants*, was published in August. Born in Manchester in 1971, she lives in a village on the Leicestershire-Nottinghamshire border. She is an honorary lecturer in the School of English at Nottingham University. www.alison-moore.com

ROBERT SHEARMAN has written four short story collections (*Tiny Deaths*, *Love Songs for the Shy and Cynical*, *Everyone's Just So So Special* and *Remember Why You Fear Me*), which between them have won the World Fantasy Award, the Shirley Jackson Award, the Edge Hill Readers Prize and three British Fantasy Awards. His background is in the theatre—he was resident dramatist at the Northcott Theatre in Exeter and a regular writer for Alan Ayckbourn at the Stephen Joseph Theatre in Scarborough—and his plays have won the Sunday Times Playwriting Award, the Sophie Winter Memorial Trust Award, the World Drama Trust Award, and the Guinness Award in association with the Royal National Theatre. He regularly writes plays and short stories for BBC Radio, and has won two Sony Awards for his interactive radio series *The Chain Gang*. However he is probably best known for reintroducing the Daleks to the BAFTA winning first season of the revived *Doctor Who*, in an episode that was a finalist for the Hugo Award. His forthcoming collection of stories, *They Do The Same Things Different There*, is to be released this summer.

CONRAD WILLIAMS is the author of seven novels: *Head Injuries*, *London Revenant*, *The Unblemished*, *One*, *Decay Inevitable*, *Loss of Separation* and *Blonde on a Stick*. He has also written four novellas and over 100 short stories, some of which are collected in *Use Once Then Destroy* and *Born With Teeth*. He is currently working on a sequel to *Blonde on a Stick*. In addition to his International Horror Guild Award for his novel *The Unblemished*, he is a triple recipient of the British Fantasy Award, including Best Novel for *One*. His debut anthology *Gutshot* was shortlisted at both the British Fantasy and World Fantasy Awards. He has also been a finalist for the Shirley Jackson Award on three occasions. He lives in Manchester with his wife, three sons and a big Maine Coon.

MICHAEL MARSHALL SMITH is a novelist and screenwriter. Under this name he has published eighty short stories, and three novels—*Only Forward, Spares* and *One of Us*—winning the Philip K. Dick, International Horror Guild, and August Derleth awards, along with the Prix Bob Morane in France. He has also won the British Fantasy Award for Best Short Fiction four times, more than any other author. Writing as **MICHAEL MARSHALL**, he has published seven internationally-bestselling thrillers including *The Straw Men*, *The Intruders*—soon to be a miniseries with BBC America starring John Simm and Mira Sorvino— and *Killer Move*. His most recent novel is *We Are Here*. He lives in Santa Cruz, California, with his wife, son, and two cats. His website can be found at www.michaelmarshallsmith.com

BRIAN HODGE is the award-winning author of eleven novels spanning horror, crime, and historical. He's also written over 110 short stories, novelettes, and novellas, and five full-length collections. His first collection *The Convulsion Factory* was ranked by critic Stanley Wiater among the 113 best books of modern horror. Recent or forthcoming books include *Whom the Gods Would Destroy* and *The Weight of the Dead*, both standalone novellas; *No*

Law Left Unbroken, a collection of crime fiction; an updated hardcover edition of *Dark Advent*, his early post-apocalyptic epic; *Worlds of Hurt*, an omnibus edition of the first four works of his Misbegotten mythos; and his latest novel, *Leaves of Sherwood*. Hodge lives in Colorado, where more of everything is in the works. He also dabbles in music, sound design, and photography; loves everything about organic gardening except the thieving squirrels; and trains in Krav Maga, grappling, and kickboxing, which are of no use at all against the squirrels. Connect with Brian through his web site at www.brianhodge.net or on Facebook at www.facebook.com/brianhodgewriter.

Specialising in dark fantasy and horror, **ANGELA SLATTER** is the author of the Aurealis Award-winning *The Girl with No Hands and Other Tales*, the World Fantasy Award finalist *Sourdough and Other Stories*, and the Aurealis finalist *Midnight and Moonshine* (with Lisa L. Hannett). Angela's short stories have appeared in such writerly venues as *The Mammoth Book of New Horror #22* and *#25*, *Fantasy*, *Nightmare* and *Lightspeed* Magazines, *Lady Churchill's Rosebud Wristlet*, *Fearie Tales*, *A Book of Horrors*, *Steampunk II: Steampunk Reloaded*, and Australian and US *Best Of* anthologies. In 2014 she will publish three new collections: *Black-Winged Angels* (Ticonderoga Publications), *The Bitterwood Bible and Other Recountings* (Tartarus Press), and *The Female Factory* (with Lisa L. Hannett) (Twelfth Planet Press). She is the first Australian to win a British Fantasy Award (for "The Coffin-Maker's Daughter" in *A Book of Horrors*, Stephen Jones, ed.). In 2013 she was awarded one of the inaugural Queensland Writers Fellowships. She has an MA and a PhD in Creative Writing, and is a graduate of Clarion South 2009 and the Tin House Summer Writers Workshop 2006. She blogs at www.angelaslatter.com about shiny things that catch her eye.

STEPHEN LAWS is an award winning British horror novelist whose work has been published all over the world. His novels include

Ghost Train, Spectre, The Frighteners, Darkfall, Gideon, Macabre, Daemonic, Somewhere South of Midnight, Chasm and *Ferocity*. His short fiction has appeared in *Year's Best* collections and *The Century's Best Horror Fiction* and can be found in his collection *The Midnight Man*. One of those stories, *The Secret*, was adapted as a short horror movie (in which he appears) and won the New York Macabre Faire Film Festival Award and AOL's Best Short Feature award.

RIO YOUERS is the British Fantasy Award–nominated author of *End Times* and *Old Man Scratch*. His short fiction has been published by, among others, St. Martin's Griffin, HarperCollins, and IDW Publishing. His latest novel *Westlake Soul* was recently nominated for Canada's prestigious Sunburst Award, and has been optioned for film by Hollywood producer Stephen Susco. Rio lives in southwestern Ontario with his wife Emily and their children Lily and Charlie.

JOHN LLEWELLYN PROBERT won the 2013 British Fantasy Award for his novella *The Nine Deaths of Dr Valentine* and 2014 will see the publication of its sequel *The Hammer of Dr Valentine* (both from Spectral Press). He is the author of over a hundred published short stories, six novellas and a novel, *The House That Death Built* (Atomic Fez). His first short story collection *The Faculty of Terror* won the 2006 Children of the Night award for best work of Gothic Fiction. His latest stories can be found in *Best British Horror 2014* (Salt Publishing), *Psycho Mania* (Constable Robinson), *La Femme* (NewCon Press) and *Terror Tales of Wales* (Gray Friar). Endeavour Press has published *Ward 19*, *Bloody Angels* and *The Pact*—three crime books featuring his pathologist heroine Parva Corcoran. He is currently trying to review every cult movie in existence at his House of Mortal Cinema (www.johnlprobert.blogspot.co.uk) and everything he is up to writing-wise can be found at www.johnlprobert.com. Future projects include a new short story collection, a lot more non-fiction writing and a couple of novels. He never sleeps.

LISA TUTTLE has been writing strange, weird stories nearly all her life, making her first professional sale in 1971. *Stranger in the House,* the first volume of her "Collected Short Supernatural Fiction" was published by Ash-Tree Press in 2010. She is a past winner of the John W. Campbell Award, the British Science Fiction Award, and the International Horror Guild Award. Her first novel, written in collaboration with George R.R. Martin, *Windhaven,* originally published in 1981, is still in print, and has been translated into many languages. Her other novels include *Lost Futures, The Mysteries* and, most recently, *The Silver Bough* (Jo Fletcher Books, 2013). A native of Texas, she has lived in the highlands of Scotland for more than twenty years.

NICHOLAS ROYLE is the author of *First Novel,* as well as six earlier novels including *Counterparts, The Director's Cut* and *Antwerp,* and a short story collection, *Mortality.* He has edited eighteen anthologies including *Darklands* and *Darklands 2* as well as four volumes of *The Best British Short Stories* (2011—2014). A senior lecturer in creative writing at Manchester Metropolitan University, he also runs Nightjar Press and works as an editor for Salt Publishing, where he has been responsible for Alison Moore's Man Booker-shortlisted *The Lighthouse,* Alice Thompson's *Burnt Island* and Stephen McGeagh's *Habit* among other titles.

STEPHEN VOLK is best known for inventing "Pipes" the poltergeist in the infamous BBC TV "Hallowe'en hoax" *Ghostwatch,* and as writer/creator of the award-winning paranormal ITV drama series *Afterlife.* Other screenplays include the recent big screen ghost story *The Awakening* starring Rebecca Hall and Dominic West, Ken Russell's hallucinogenic biopic *Gothic,* predatory nanny flick *The Guardian* (co-written and directed by William (*The Exorcist*) Friedkin), and *Octane* starring Madeleine Stowe and Norman Reedus. He also won a BAFTA for *The Deadness of Dad* starring Rhys Ifans and his play *The Chapel of Unrest* was presented exclusively for one night only at London's Bush Theatre starring Jim Broadbent and Reece Shearsmith. His short stories have earned selection in *Year's Best Fantasy and Horror*, *Mammoth Book of Best New Horror*, *Best British Mysteries*, and *Best British Horror 2014*, and he has been a Bram Stoker, British Fantasy and Shirley Jackson Award finalist. 2013 saw the publication of his highly acclaimed novella *Whitstable*, featuring the horror star Peter Cushing (Spectral Press), and his new collection *Monsters in the Heart* (Gray Friar Press) which have both been nominated for British Fantasy Awards in 2014, for 'Best Novella' and 'Best Collection' respectively. www.stephenvolk.net

Lightning Source UK Ltd.
Milton Keynes UK
UKOW06f1046310715

256163UK00015B/231/P